Other Avon Books by
Charlotte Hughes

AND AFTER THAT, THE DARK

*This book is dedicated, with all my love,
to my oldest son, Patrick Hughes*

Acknowledgments

I would like to thank Carrie Feron, for her encouragement and support. To Micki Nuding, a special word of appreciation, for her patience and wonderful sense of humor. And to Richard Curtis, for always being there.

To my husband, Ken, and my son, Eric, thanks for all you did to make my life easier when the pressure was on.

To Bob Hudson, good friend and computer doctor, thank you, thank you, thank you, for chasing all the demons from my computer. And to my pal, Bettie, for loaning me her husband during this difficult time, and for being such a special friend to me.

Much appreciation to Kari Hudson, research assistant, proofreader extraordinaire, therapist, and good buddy. Your humor kept me going when I forgot my flu shot and ended up too sick to die. And to Brenda Rollins, who proofed the sixth draft of this book (or was it the seventh?) and kept me laughing with her corny jokes.

Finally, a big hug to the kind folks at Bay Street Trading—Chris, Steve, Will, and Anne. Thanks for all your help and support. I only wish I got to see you guys more often!

Research

The research for *Valley of the Shadow* was extensive. Much thanks to the following people: Ms. Lois Walker, Research Librarian, Winthrop College Library, Rock Hill, South Carolina; Mr. Dennis Adams, Research Librarian, Beaufort, South Carolina; snake handler and expert, Mr. David Peden, Jr., Gray Court, South Carolina; Ms. Ginger Lyons, Tourism Director, Chamber of Commerce, Elizabethton, Tennessee; author Peg Sutherland; and reporter Debbie Radford, *Beaufort Gazette*, Beaufort, South Carolina.

Ned Irwin, Public Service Archivist, East Tennessee State University; the Audio-Visual Collections, Archives and Special Collection (Burton Snakehandling Trilogy); and the Center for Appalachian Studies and Services at East Tennessee State University, for their informative magazine, *Now and Then*.

Forensic anthropologist Dr. Murray Marks of the University of Tennessee, Knoxville; Dr. Earl Barton, pathologist, Atlanta, Georgia.

Frank Kane, OSHA.

Master Quilter Nan Tournier.

Books

Good News Bible, Today's English Version, published by Thomas Nelson, Inc., 1976; *The Holy Bible*, King James Version, Crusade Bible Publishers, Inc., Nashville, Tennessee.

The Foxfire Books, Doubleday, Anchor Books imprint; *Yesterday's People*, Jack E. Weller, University Press of Kentucky, 1993; *Modernizing the Mountaineer*, David E. Whisnant, The University of Tennessee Press, 1994; *Appalachian Portraits*, Shelby Lee Adams, Narrative, Lee Smith, University Press of Mississippi, 1993; *Latchpins of the Lost Cove*, Professor Malone Young, East Tennessee State University, 1986; *Pioneer Comforts and Kitchen Remedies*, Ferne Shelton, Hutcraft, 1965; *Aunt Sally's Tried and True Household Hints*, Outlet Books Company, Inc., Random House, 1993; *Trees, Shrubs, and Woody Vines of Great Smoky Mountains National Park*, Arthur Stupka, The University of Tennessee Press, 1964; *Taking Up Serpents*, David L. Kimbrough, The University of North Carolina Press, 1995; *Serpent-

Handling Believers, Thomas Burton, The University of Tennessee Press, 1993; *The Bone Detectives*, Donna M. Jackson, Little, Brown, 1996; *Police Procedural*, Russell Bintliff, Writer's Digest, 1993; *Cause of Death*, Keith D. Wilson, Writers Digest, 1992; *Forensic Detection*, Colin Evans, John Wiley & Sons, Inc., 1996; and *Childhood Asthma*, Drs. Neil Buchanan and Peter Cooper, Tricycle Press, 1991.

Valley of the Shadow is a work of fiction. Although I've tried to make it as accurate as possible, any mistakes or discrepancies are the sole fault of this author.

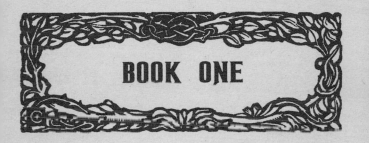

BOOK ONE

Prologue

A narrow, twisting mountain road at midnight.
Dark as a sinner's heart; treacherous as his deeds.
A slivered moon, a broken headlight, a vintage pickup
    truck
Make slow work of the journey.
From the bush along the road
Eyes glitter.
The driver suddenly brakes
And shudders
As his grim cargo rolls across the bed of the pickup truck.
A deer darts into the road;
Freezes, caught in the glare of headlights.
Eyes, fearful and trapped.
The man sees another pair of eyes
Horrified and bulging
As he'd closed his hands around her lovely throat
And silenced her forever.
Eyes that seem to watch him even now
Through the layers of the quilt he'd wrapped her in.
Her burial shroud.
He struggles with the urge to look over his shoulder.
Will he find those eyes watching him?
Will he see them every time he tries to sleep?
Only one answer.
Bury her deep.

I n my name shall they cast out devils; they shall
speak with new tongues; They shall take up serpents;
and if they drink any deadly thing, it shall not hurt them;
they shall lay hands on the sick, and they shall recover.

Mark 16: 17, 18

One

GOD, SHE had gone and lost her poor mind. Or what
was left of it, after these six months. Meg supposed
everybody had a breaking point, and she'd obviously
reached hers that morning outside of Mama's Used Cars.
That's the only excuse she could give for trading the eq-
uity in her gorgeous 1997 Ford Explorer, with its genuine
leather seats and custom cellular phone, for this aged avocado green camper with harvest gold shag carpeting and
dark paneling. That, and the fact that Mama's eldest boy,
Tank, was a slick-talking car salesman.

Now, as Meg Gentry stood beside her roommate outside their Atlanta apartment complex, she tried to sound
enthusiastic over the deal, but her voice was as flat and
leaden as the late October sky. Libby Simms stared at the
battered vehicle much the same way the Munchkins had
stared at Dorothy's house when it'd dropped from the sky
and landed in Munchkinland. She circled the camper,
peering at it through clumsy-looking glasses that had a

tendency to slide down the bridge of her nose so that she was forever pushing them back in place.

Meg shoved her hands into the pockets of her jeans and rocked back and forth on the heels of her high-top sneakers as she tried to gauge her friend's reaction. Libby was hard to read at times, probably a trait she'd developed throughout her years as a high school guidance counselor. Never let the other side know what you're thinking. Also, they were vastly different. At forty, Libby's dark hair was liberally streaked with gray, but it would never have occurred to her to color it. Meg, who was ten years younger, had her own light brown hair frosted blond every six months to sort of camouflage the gray when it appeared. One less thing to worry about, as far as she was concerned.

"Well?" Meg prodded curiously. When she had first moved in with Libby six months ago, her friend's approval had mattered a great deal. Of course, Meg's self-esteem had been lower than a mole hole at the time, thanks to her SOB husband, who'd left a crater in her heart the size of Kansas.

Libby looked at her. "I think it's finally gotten to you, kiddo. It's pushed you over the edge."

Meg knew she was referring to her divorce, which had become final the previous week. Three years down the toilet. In her mind, she still saw Roy the way he'd looked the first time they'd met, working a drive-by shooting in a neighborhood rife with crack houses and prostitution. Roy had been the detective in charge, and she was assigned to cover the story for the paper.

Police didn't like the media; they often accused them of getting in the way. But Meg had been on her best behavior the night she'd met Roy Gentry, her attention focused on the handsome, blond detective instead of the bulging body bags. Afterward, they'd driven to the Huddle House and gotten better acquainted over coffee and pecan pie. Meg knew the divorce rate was high among policemen because of job stress, but she'd filed that information in the back of her mind next to all she knew about lung cancer, though she smoked regardless.

Libby craned her neck, giving Meg a suspicious look. "Were you sober when you bought it?"

Meg shot her a dark look. "Please don't worry about offending me, Libby," she said. "Tell me what you *really* think."

"You should demand your money back."

Meg fumbled through her purse for her cigarettes. In the months since her separation, she'd become a bona fide chain-smoker, not an easy task considering it was illegal to smoke almost everywhere these days. She also drank more than she should, and had added a few more four-letter words to her repertoire of vile language. Libby claimed what she really needed was a good healthy cry, but Meg would've swallowed broken glass first.

"I *can't* get my money back," she said, lighting a cigarette and inhaling deeply. "It's a done deal. I've already got the title and everything."

"Oh, my—"

"You're not looking at it from a practical standpoint, Libby. I couldn't afford to keep up the payments on the Explorer. This way, I owe zero money, and not only do I have transportation, I have a place to sleep." Tank had made it sound so wise and sensible. And Meg had believed him, because she didn't think any man who still wore leisure suits and white loafers could outsmart her.

"You're not exactly broke, you know," Libby replied. "You still have half the money from the sale of your house."

Meg didn't want to think about the century-old fixer-upper she and Roy had bought shortly after their marriage. They had put so much hard work into the place. Later, she'd realized all that effort had been nothing more than a diversionary tactic, aimed at keeping her focus off their troubled relationship.

"I need to save that money. Now that I'm unemployed," she mumbled.

"So maybe you shouldn't have quit your job. I told you not to make any life-altering decisions until you'd had time to heal."

Meg couldn't believe Libby still had advice left, after all she'd already given. Quitting her job without giving notice hadn't been the best decision she'd ever made, but it had been a relief. In the three years she'd worked the crime beat, she'd been chased through a junkyard by a pit bull, taken hostage by a lunatic who'd mistaken her for an undercover cop, and found herself caught in the cross fire between a couple of drug dealers and the DEA—she'd had to crawl beneath a garbage truck to keep from being shot. And all this had happened while she was working. It didn't include the mugging outside Clancy's Sandwich Shop near her apartment, or the Peeping Tom problem that'd gone on for months before the creep had been apprehended.

She'd signed up for one of those self-defense courses where they taught you how to ward off purse snatchers and would-be rapists. She'd purchased a canister of Mace and learned to talk tough while covering crime scenes in Atlanta's seedier neighborhoods, where prissy-sounding women often became victims. She'd become known as "that smart-ass reporter from the *Journal*," the one with the attitude. That title had served her well over the years.

Roy had bought her a handgun as a wedding present, romantic fool that he was, and she'd given it right back. Statistics proved most gunshot victims died by their own weapons, either by accident or suicide. Meg had thought of those days just before her period when she felt bloated and life appeared so bleak, and she figured she and the rest of the world would be a safer place if she remained unarmed. Of course, she still had the hunting knife her father had insisted she keep beneath the seat of her car, in case she happened upon a crazed psychopath while stranded on an isolated stretch of road. Meg doubted she would ever be able to use it on another human being— except for Roy—but she kept the knife anyway. If she *did* get stranded, she figured she could always hunt for her own food.

Nevertheless, she was tired of big-city life. She was sick to death of writing about violence—drug deals gone wrong, grisly homicides that kept her awake nights, battered women who, more often than not, returned to their abusers as soon as they left the hospital. She had paid her dues; she deserved to be assigned the cushier jobs now and then. Her boss hadn't seen it that way. He assigned the good stories to his pet reporter, a Maria Shriver look-alike who wore panty hose on a regular basis.

Meg finished her cigarette, dropped it on the asphalt, and rubbed it out with the toe of her sneaker. "I've got to get out of this place. I've been thinking maybe I'll go home."

Libby offered her a blank look. "Home? You mean to Tennessee?"

Meg nodded. "I got a letter from my mother yesterday, and she said the leaves have started to turn. People travel from all over this time of year to see them. It's the most beautiful place in the world."

"You sound like you've already made up your mind."

Meg grinned. "Why do you think I bought this ugly-ass camper?"

Libby cocked her head to the side, as if looking at it from a new angle might make a difference. "You could always have it painted."

Meg wasn't listening. "I should drop by the Atlanta PD tomorrow and invite Roy and his new lover out to lunch. Park right out front, let everybody get a look at my new wheels."

Libby crossed her arms and gave Meg a stern look. "Do the words *restraining order* mean anything to you?"

"Yeah. It means Roy's a pussy." Meg was delighted to be able to use one of her new words in connection with her ex-husband. "I mean, seriously. What kind of man serves a woman with a restraining order? What could I possibly do to him?"

* * *

Roy Gentry stretched his long legs out before him and took another sip of the black coffee that had kept him and a dozen other detectives going for almost sixteen hours now. As they sat around the conference table, waiting for the captain to arrive, he could feel the tension building. The case wasn't going anywhere. The hand of blame pointed to him.

The fact that he was in charge didn't look good for him. He'd wanted to be chief detective more than anything. Hell, he'd even married for it, a last-ditch effort to appear more stable when it looked like someone else was going to get the position instead. After two and a half years on the job, he'd developed an ulcer and high blood pressure.

The stress was killing him.

Captain Bernard Maxwell pushed the door open and entered with the grace of a bulldozer. He was a squatty, hairless man whose bulldog face wore a perpetual frown. "Okay, now that I've canceled my goddamn fishing trip, I want some answers, and they better he good or somebody's head's gonna roll."

Roy braced himself. "It's like I said over the phone, sir. The call came in at twenty-two hundred hours. Albert Thurston's son heard a noise coming from his father's bedroom, and when he checked on him, the elder Thurston was nowhere to be found. The family suspects kidnapping."

"Have they received any ransom demands?"

"No sir."

"Then it's a bit premature to call it a kidnapping, don't you think?"

"Well, considering his vast wealth—"

"Did you put out an APB?"

"Yes sir. And I've spoken to the FBI."

"You contacted the goddamn FBI, and you don't even know if it's a kidnapping?"

"I thought under the circumstances—"

"What circumstances? You ain't got shit, Detective."
The captain was angry. He sputtered obscenities, spittle
forming at the corners of his mouth. "Thurston could've
run off with the town floozy for all you know, and I probably canceled my fishing trip for nothing. Do you have
any idea when I took my last vacation? Hell no, you don't
remember. You were still in diapers."

Someone knocked on the door. "Detective Gentry?"
A fresh-faced rookie stepped inside, holding a box. "This
just came for you, sir. Some guy said a woman paid him
fifty bucks to deliver it."

"That could be from the kidnappers," Maxwell said.
"Maybe they've discovered the family is nothing but a
bunch of dickheads, and they'd rather deal with us."

Roy wondered at the captain's sudden change of heart.
It wasn't likely any kidnapper would prefer dealing with
the police, but the box indeed looked suspicious. The
mailing address consisted of letters cut from a newspaper,
the fonts and sizes different. No return address. Just what
you'd expect to see in a ransom letter.

"Did you get the guy's name?" Roy asked the rookie.

"Naw. He just handed it to me and split."

"And you didn't even try to find out who the hell he
was?" Maxwell demanded. "Jesus Christ, what is this,
ballet class? Give me the damn box and get your scrawny
ass out looking for him!" Maxwell motioned to a couple
of detectives. "Go with him so he doesn't get lost." He
pulled a pocketknife from his trousers and cut the string
binding the box.

"You might want to have that x-rayed first, Captain,"
Roy said, not at all offended by his boss opening a package meant for him. He had too many enemies on the
street, druggies and pimps who felt they'd been given a
raw deal. He suddenly wished Maxwell weren't standing
so close. He'd heard stories of police officers losing their
hands and faces while opening unidentified packages.

Ignoring him, Maxwell pulled off the lid and stared into
the box for a moment. "Well, now. Looks like a bunch

of women's underwear to me, although I can't for the life of me figure what it has to do with Thurston.'' He rifled through nylon and satin, searching for clues.

The blood drained from Roy's face as recognition dawned. Panicked, he made to get up and leave the room, but his legs wouldn't move. Sweat beaded his brow; he felt sick.

Maxwell pulled out a large manila envelope and ripped it open. In his haste, he ignored the photos that fell and scattered across the conference table. ''Here we go.'' He pulled out a note and read from it.

''It says, 'Dear Roy. I'm sending you all my lingerie, even though that wasn't part of our divorce settlement. You always looked better in it than I did. And to show there's no hard feelings, I'm enclosing photos my private investigator took some months back. You and Tom make such a cute couple. Fondly, Meg.' ''

Maxwell suddenly snapped his head up as though just realizing what he'd read. His face turned an angry red. ''Is this some kind of joke, Gentry?'' he said, tossing the letter aside like it was yesterday's trash.

Roy tried to smile, but the muscles in his face were numb. ''My ex-wife has a strange sense of humor, sir. Tom Raford and I were on a case when those photos were taken. Under cover,'' he added.

The captain glared at him. ''Jesus Christ!'' He slammed out of the room.

Roy sat there while several uniformed and plainclothes officers sifted through the pictures. One or two snickered; they didn't believe the undercover story any more than the captain did. He looked at the box and almost wished it had contained a bomb.

In some ways, it had.

TWO

MEG WAS halfway to Blalock, Tennessee, before panic set in: What the hell was she going to tell her family? Her concentration faltered for a second, and the camper veered sharply to the right. She almost preferred running off the road to facing her mother with the truth.

Perhaps she shouldn't have painted such a rosy picture of her life in Atlanta. She should have mentioned she and Roy were having problems, and that she wasn't particularly crazy about her job. What would they say when they discovered she was divorced, unemployed, and homeless? She glanced at her camper. Well, not *completely* homeless.

Definitely, she should have told them about Roy.

Her mother had expected her to marry Idle Skinner's boy, Clay, whom Meg had dated during her junior and senior year of high school. Most mountain girls married in their late teens and started a family right away, and Meg could do worse than marrying a Skinner, Alma had reminded her more than once. Idle owned Blalock Plaza, which consisted of a convenience store, a Laundromat, and a barber shop. He'd later added a gas station and a drive-through car wash. Fill up your tank and you drove away in a clean car. But, despite strong feelings for Clay, Meg'd had her heart set on college, specifically UNC's journalism program.

Clay had not taken the news well. He hadn't even both-

ered to show up at the bus station the day she'd left for
Chapel Hill, North Carolina. She'd graduated with a 3.8
average, and a whole slew of student loans to pay back.
The high GPA had landed her a job at the *Journal*; her
job there enabled her to pay off what she'd borrowed.
After three years of performing grunt work, she'd found
herself working the crime beat, barfing up an occasional
breakfast and struggling with impossible deadlines.

Her next job was going to be less stressful, gar-run-
teed.

Eight hours after leaving Atlanta, Meg turned off the
interstate where a sign informed her that Blalock was just
ten miles away. She had not made great time; her little
house on wheels tended to vibrate like a washing machine
stuffed full of tennis shoes if the speedometer sneaked
past fifty miles an hour. The A-1 Truck Stop, complete
with restaurant, gas station, and hot showers, looked like
just the place to fill her stomach and her gas tank, and
give her the caffeine fix she needed. She pulled in and
parked beside a row of gas pumps.

The chilly mountain air greeted her as she climbed from
the cab, leaving her door open so she could grab her purse
once she'd gassed up. One thing ol' Tank had failed to
mention when she'd bought the camper was the fact that
it drank fuel like a Learjet. She unscrewed the gas cap
and reached for the nozzle, mentally calculating how
many miles she was getting to the gallon. She'd just about
decided it would be cheaper driving an eighteen wheeler,
when a battered blue pickup truck pulled up on the other
side of the pumps and parked. She fixed her gaze on the
whirring digits and thought of the fresh hot coffee that
waited inside.

The sound of boisterous male laughter made Meg
glance up as a beer-bellied man in a flannel shirt and
nylon vest shoved his door open and all but fell out of
the truck.

"Shee-it!" Beer sloshed from the Coors can he held,
and his baseball cap slipped off, exposing medium brown

hair that was in dire need of washing. A younger man climbed out of the passenger side and rounded the truck.

Meg thought they looked like *Hee Haw* rejects. Then it hit her—she knew them. Bert and Harley Attaway. White trash, her mother would've called them and been right. They'd terrorized the entire student body at Blalock High until they'd finally been expelled permanently.

"Damn, Harley, you're wastin' good beer," Bert said, pointing to the spill.

"Hey, wouldja look at that!" one of them said.

At first, Meg thought they were eyeballing her camper. Where they came from, they probably thought it was a Best Western on wheels. If they ever found out about the inside toilet, she'd never see it again.

"Hey, darlin'," Harley said. "You from around these parts?"

Meg didn't so much as look their way. She'd met her share of drunks and druggies while working the streets in Atlanta, and she had no patience for either. These men were simply a countrified version of what she was used to.

"I'm *talking* to you, blondie," Harley said, raising his voice.

"Maybe she don't want to talk to you," Bert replied, chuckling. "Or maybe she's waitin' for you to offer to pump her gas for her. Some women don't like pumpin' their own gas 'cause it leaves a nasty smell on their hands."

"I'll be glad to assist you, little lady," Harley said, crushing his beer can and tossing it into the back of his truck.

Little lady? Meg resisted the urge to laugh, but the desire was suddenly quenched when she felt the skin along the back of her neck prickle. She turned and found the man mere inches away, smelling of beer, fish, and a serious case of body odor.

Now, as she met Harley's bloodshot gaze, she was thankful for what she'd learned over the years. It was knowledge, not physical strength, that made people less afraid. "I don't want your help," she said stiffly. "Thanks just the same."

Not more than six feet away, Bert laughed and spit a wad of chewing tobacco on the ground. "Hear that, Harley? She don't want your help. Probably 'cause you ain't had a bath in three days. Yer stinkin' up the whole place."

"Shut up, asshole," he said, then flashed Meg a big smile as he reached for the nozzle. "Pretty thing like you ought not to have to pump her own gas."

Meg refused to let go of the nozzle, even as he tried to wrestle it from her. "I said I don't want your help. What's it take to get through to you?" Though Meg tried to hang on to it, Harley reached around and grabbed the nozzle from the other side, grasping it with both hands. Meg found herself trapped within his arms, his body pressed intimately against hers. He was hard. She scanned the parking lot. Not a soul around. Where were all those damned truckers needing gas and hot showers?

Harley rubbed his erection against her hip, humping her like a male dog with no manners while Bert guffawed in the background. Her anger flared.

"Let me go," she demanded between gritted teeth.

"Come on now, honey," he said, releasing the nozzle and tightening his grip on her. She twisted around in his arms and tried to shove her knee against his crotch, but he blocked it, and the look on his face turned mean. He slammed her against the camper, and her head hit the metal wall with such force her eyes watered.

He shot her a menacing look. "What s'matter with you, bitch? I'm just tryin' to be neighborly," he said, his foul breath hot and moist on her cheek. "Maybe you'd like to invite me and my brother inside that little camper of yours. We might be willing to put up a couple of six packs for a little poontang. Know what I mean?"

Meg's brain sent a sudden adrenaline rush through her body. With her camper standing between them and the building, it was unlikely anyone inside could see what was going on and come to her aid. If Harley was as ruthless as she remembered, he wouldn't think twice about dragging her into his truck and taking her to a patch of deserted woods. Bert certainly wouldn't stop him; he'd want a piece of the action.

Meg struggled against him, but Harley laughed as though he were having the time of his life. He'd obviously done this sort of thing before.

Knowing she was no match for him physically, Meg clamped her teeth on his arm and bit down as hard as she could. He cussed loudly and loosened his grip. She twisted free and scrambled toward the cab of her camper, thankful that she'd left the door open. Harley grabbed her shirt, and several buttons popped off as she strained to reach the hunting knife beneath her seat.

Giving a loud, angry snarl, Meg whipped around and pressed the point of the blade against Harley's crotch. "Okay, Attaway, let's play ball!"

He froze, and his smile suddenly drooped like a dying lily. Meg hoped the knife was having the same effect on his erection. His eyes flickered with apprehension. "What the hell do you think you're doing?" His voice wavered. He let her go and held up both hands as though surrendering, but his eyes remained fixed on the knife.

With a precision that surprised even her, Meg pressed the tip of the blade a fraction closer and knew the moment she'd hit tender flesh when he howled. "Hey, bitch, you just stuck me! Cut it out—I was just having a little fun with you."

Meg could hear the urgency in his voice, the pleading. His brother was silent. She shot him a look that dared him to move. "You ever seen what they do to male hogs to fatten them up, Harley?" she asked, her green eyes flashing with contempt. She saw him pale; he suddenly had the pasty look of someone who spent too much time indoors.

"You're crazy."

"Crazy enough to cut your nuts out and hang them

from my rearview mirror,'' she said with conviction. She gave him a nasty smile. "Or maybe I'll just feed 'em to you.''

He swallowed, and his Adam's apple bobbed erratically along the spine of his throat. "Look, I got a family.''

"The way I see it, I'll be doing them a big favor.''

Beads of sweat had popped out on his forehead and upper lip. "You don't understand. Me and my brother here . . . we been drinkin' for three days straight. I wuzn't thinkin'.''

"Okay, Harley,'' she said. "I'm only going to say this once, so you'd better listen closely. And since you're so stupid, I'll talk slow so you can keep up. You've got exactly thirty seconds to climb back into that truck and get out of my sight, or I swear to God I'll bury this knife in you so deep they won't ever find it.''

He met her gaze. Although he looked scared, he was obviously humiliated as well. It hadn't helped that his brother had witnessed the whole thing and would probably spill his guts once they got home. He seemed to be weighing his next move.

"I've got nothing to lose, Harley.''

He backed away, slowly at first, as though afraid she might change her mind and stick him anyway. He tripped on a gas hose, righted himself, and turned for his truck. "Come on, Bert,'' he said, shooting a malevolent look in her direction. "Let's get the hell outta here before the broad goes apeshit.''

Meg watched them climb into the pickup. They peeled out of the parking lot a moment later, spitting gravel and kicking up a cloud of dust. She waited until they were a safe distance away before returning the knife to its hiding place. Then, she grasped the gas nozzle once more and went back to filling her tank, her hands shaking.

She was still trembling when she went inside the store to pay. As she'd suspected, the clerk, who had her nose buried in a paperback, hadn't seen the trouble outside. She glanced up long enough to take Meg's money, then went back to reading.

The smell of food coming from the restaurant suddenly made Meg nauseous, and she made a beeline for the ladies' room, where she suffered through a bad case of dry heaves. Finally the spasms subsided, and she washed her face. She lit a cigarette and mopped her face with a wet paper towel.

She had just flushed the cigarette butt down the toilet when a red-haired woman in a pink waitress uniform peeked inside. "That your green camper out front, hon?"

Meg was almost ashamed to admit it. "Yes."

"Then I reckon you might be interested in knowing two guys just pulled up in a blue pickup truck and sprayed something on the back of it. Paint, I think."

Meg hurried from the bathroom and out the front door of the building just as Bert and Harley's pickup truck spun around in the parking lot and made for the highway. The bastards had come back. She hurried toward her camper and skidded to a halt as she spied the word BITCH painted in large black letters across the back. But that was tame compared to the crude silhouette of an enormous serpent with fangs that seemed to hiss at her. Even without knowing the reason behind the drawing, the image produced a specter of fear in her heart.

Three

THE MOUNTAIN View Lodge advertised cable TV, a complimentary breakfast, and the cleanest rooms in town, starting at thirty eight dollars for single occupancy. Meg decided a good night's sleep would go a long way toward improving her sour mood, brought on by the fine artwork that now graced the back of her camper. Fellow motorists were not only staring as they passed, they were locking their doors as well.

The room was by no means fancy, but it was clean, and Meg had managed to secure a late checkout so she could sleep in and drive over to her parents' place after church. She took a hot bath, smoked several cigarettes in front of the news on TV, and climbed beneath the covers.

The sheets were thin and worn and smelled of bleach and pine, and the mattress was a bit on the lumpy side, but none of that mattered. Meg fell asleep almost immediately. She awoke at ten the next morning, lit a cigarette, and looked out the window as she wondered what she was going to do with the rest of her life.

Mountains surrounded the town of Blalock like a fortress; she'd forgotten just how beautiful they were. Suddenly her problems didn't seem as enormous as they had before, and she felt a lift of hope that her decision to return home had been a good one.

It was almost noon by the time Meg checked out and climbed into her camper. She drove and smoked with one hand and sipped coffee from a large foam cup she held in the other. Traffic crawled, due to the number of leaf peepers, and she noticed how the town had grown in her absence. In fact, it seemed to have doubled in size. Meg passed various souvenir and T-shirt shops, as well as a pottery and wicker discount store that took up close to an entire block. There was a new Winn-Dixie and a Wal-Mart, and Blalock Plaza had added a video store.

She turned off the main road and took the narrow, two-lane highway that wound around the mountain and eventually ended at its summit. Her parents lived near the foothills, and their property, which amounted to some ten acres, was flat enough for farming. They subsidized what they made at their grocery store by growing their own vegetables and raising hogs and chickens. Meg remembered a time when customers could buy a dozen eggs at Holcombe Grocery for twenty-five cents.

The road was in sad shape, littered with potholes and bumpy as an old washboard. Warning signs with pictures of deer cautioned motorists to be on the lookout. Nobody from the Highway Department seemed concerned about the raccoons who roamed the roads at night; they were considered a nuisance. In the higher elevations, where poverty was at its highest and large families shared three-room shacks, folks were known to eat raccoon, opossum, squirrel, and anything else they could trap or shoot. The mountain children never missed a day of school; the free breakfast and lunch they received there kept them alive. That was a different world from the one Meg had grown up in, where there'd been plenty to eat.

As Meg continued to ease the camper up the mountain, she could see the town of Blalock spread out below her. Across the valley the trees were a flaming red, gold, and orange. In two weeks they'd be gone, leaving everything except the pines bare and dun colored. The tourists would go right along with them.

The Holcombe place looked the same, save for the hunter green shutters at the windows that dressed it up.

Azalea bushes and rhododendrons flanked the house, and mountain laurel grew wild on the property as it did on the rest of the mountain. Come summer, clusters of honeycomb-shaped flowers would burst forth, dotting the hillsides in pink and white.

Her father's pickup truck was in the driveway; beside it stood the station wagon her mother had driven for as long as Meg could remember. Parked along the road was a late model Jeep Cherokee that Meg knew belonged to her brother-in-law, Travis Lytle—whom she referred to as "whore-dog" behind his back, because he cheated on her sister. Travis was the operations manager for the local textile mill, and Meg suspected he made decent money because he went to such lengths to flaunt it. Her mother had written that Beryl seemed unhappy in her marriage— and here Meg had thought the woman had no insight— yet seemed to be more concerned with the fact her older daughter was letting herself go at thirty-five. How typical of her mother to worry about Beryl's thickening waistline, instead of the problems causing it.

Meg parked behind the Jeep and made her way up the front walk, sucking in the brisk mountain air with appreciation. The old metal glider on the porch had been painted to match the shutters. She and Clay Skinner had necked there in the dark on numerous occasions; he'd even managed to get his hands inside her jeans once or twice, scoundrel that he was. He was now married with a young daughter, but Meg suspected she would never be able to think of him without remembering her first orgasm.

As she climbed the porch steps, her father appeared at the storm door. His face lit up, and he pushed the door open. "Meg, honey, is that really you?"

He looked slightly different. His hair, completely gray now, was thinner, and he'd put on a few pounds. Still, he looked wonderful. She remembered a time when she thought he was the most handsome man in the world.

"Hi, Daddy."

"Well, my goodness, girl, I thought you forgot where we lived."

He opened his arms, and she rushed into them, eyes tearing at the familiar smells of his Old Spice and Brylcreem. Finally, she pulled away so she could get a better look at him. The skin beneath his eyes was looser, and the lines more deeply etched into his face. But he was still tall and sturdy, giving the impression that no problem was too big for him.

"Henry, who's at the door?" her mother's voice called from the kitchen. It was followed by the slap-slap of bedroom slippers against the wood floor. Her mother would have changed out of her heels the minute she arrived home. "I can't abide sore feet," she always said. Meg knew the reason her feet hurt was because she insisted on stuffing a size seven foot into a size six shoe.

Alma Holcombe appeared in the doorway and came to an abrupt halt at the sight of her younger daughter. "Oh, my!" she exclaimed. She stepped closer. "Margaret, is that you?"

Meg blinked several times at her mother. When had she decided to become a redhead? "It's me, Mama," she said, closing the distance between them. They hugged, Alma offered her cheek, and Meg bestowed the perfunctory kiss.

"My, you're so thin. You're not on some new weirdo diet, are you?" She leaned closer. "Wait'll you see Beryl." Meg's father cleared his throat, and Alma immediately changed the subject. "Why didn't you tell us you were coming?" she demanded, reaching up to adjust her hair. "And where's Roy?"

Meg suddenly realized her mother was wearing a wig. "Uh, Roy couldn't make it this time."

"What do you mean *this time*? We've never laid eyes on the boy. I can't believe my daughter's been married three years, and we don't know the first thing about her husband."

"Meg, is that you?"

Meg looked up to find Beryl standing in the doorway with Travis right behind, and the sisters embraced. They'd never been close, due to a five-year age difference and the fact that Meg had been a tomboy growing up and Beryl a bit of a priss. But her sister looked genuinely happy to see her.

"You're looking good, Beryl," Meg said, suspecting she didn't get many compliments these days.

Her sister blushed. "I guess you can tell I've put on a few pounds."

"I always thought you were too thin before."

"Hey, don't you have a hug for your favorite brother-in-law?" Travis asked.

Meg groaned inwardly. She had no desire to get close to her brother-in-law, but she didn't want to hurt Beryl's feelings. She suffered through a brief hug. "You haven't changed a bit, Travis," she said.

"I work out everyday," he said, obviously taking it as a compliment. "Same size as I was in high school." He patted his gut. "Hard as a rock. Go ahead, hit me."

She would have considered it had she been holding a steel pipe. "I'd rather not."

"It's okay, I won't feel a thing."

"I've had all these self-defense courses, Travis. My hands are registered, and I'm not allowed to use them unless I'm in serious danger. You'll just have to play with somebody less threatening." Meg smiled as she said it, and everybody chuckled except Travis. But Meg didn't waste any time worrying about it. Her niece and nephew had stepped into the room, and she made a big fuss over them.

"We were just about to have dinner," Alma said. "I hope you haven't eaten."

"Just coffee and Danish back at the motel."

"You stayed in a motel?" Her mother looked wounded. "Why on earth would you do that when you have a perfectly fine bedroom here?"

"I got in late last night and didn't want to wake you."

"Well, I never thought I'd see the day when one of my children came to visit and stayed in a motel," her mother said, using the same voice she'd used when Meg had called to say she and Roy had eloped. It was vintage Alma, meant to elicit a feeling of guilt, and it worked.

"Which motel, honey?" her father asked.

"The Mountain View Lodge."

"Oh, good heavens!" Alma clutched her chest as though afraid her heart would fly right out of it.

"Is something wrong with the Mountain View?" Meg asked, wondering if terrorists had gone in and killed a bunch of vacationing Southern Baptists or something.

"Last year the choir director at church got caught sneaking into one of the rooms with a woman from town," her father said, his tone giving it as much significance he would give choosing the color of his trash liners.

Alma sniffed as though the topic left a bad odor in the air. "Meg, dear, why don't you go freshen up while Beryl and I put the food on the table. Travis can bring in your luggage."

"I won't be staying here," Meg told her. "I have a camper. I can stay in that."

They all stared at her. Finally, her mother walked to the big picture window and drew back the curtain. She gasped aloud, and the others hurried over. Travis chuckled and Beryl shot him a dirty look.

"You came here in *that*?" Alma said, one hand flying to her chest again. "Oh, Margaret, you can't possibly stay in that thing. Henry, tell her she can't stay in that thing."

"Why don't we discuss it after dinner," her father said.

Much to her displeasure, Meg found herself sitting next to Travis at the dinner table. He handed her a platter of fried chicken. "So, are you on vacation?" he asked, giving her a look that made her skin crawl. An intimate look. Like he knew which kind of feminine protection she preferred.

"I needed to get away for a while," she said, dismissively.

"You and Roy had a fight, didn't you?" Alma said, peering at her from beneath the bangs of her wig. "I could always tell when something was bothering you."

Meg felt her mother's eyes bore into her forehead as though trying to read her mind, and suddenly craved a cigarette.

"Nothing's bothering me," she said.

"Henry, make her tell us what's wrong," Alma demanded.

He covered his daughter's hand with his. His eyes were gentle. "It's okay, baby. You can tell us anything."

Meg felt a lump in her throat. She'd always been a daddy's girl, preferring farm work and stocking shelves at the store to the mindless list of chores her mother gave her. She realized everybody was watching her.

"Actually—" She paused, then told herself it was time to get it all out in the open. Her mother would wear her down eventually; she had a knack. "We split up," she said.

Alma looked shocked. "You're separated?"

"Divorced."

"Oh, my!" Alma's hand went to her mouth, and she looked at her husband as though she expected him to fix it somehow. He merely shrugged.

"I'm sorry," Meg said. "I know you don't believe in divorce, but it couldn't be helped."

"Your father and I have been married forty-one years now," Alma said. "It wasn't always easy; in fact, there were times I wanted to throw my hands in the air and walk out. I'm sure your father felt the same. But we couldn't walk away when we'd vowed to stay together till death."

"Alma, I don't think this is the time to discuss Meg's personal affairs," Henry said, picking up a plate of biscuits and passing them to his wife.

"This family has always shared everything," she replied. "Besides, my daughter shows up after a three-year absence and tells me she's divorced, and I'm not supposed to react or ask questions? You know how I feel about young people just throwing away their marriage over nothing."

Meg felt her temper flare. "Oh, you have it all wrong, Mama," she said. "I would have gladly spent the rest of my life with Roy had I not discovered he was a homosexual. See, that's the only reason he married me to begin with, so the other cops wouldn't find out he was a fairy."

Alma's face flamed a bright red. "Margaret, please—"

"And when Roy said he was going out with the boys, I had no idea he was going to gay bars. First time I ever saw him in drag I was envious as hell. I mean, the man knows his way around cosmetics."

Alma's jaw hung open so far that Meg could see the fillings in her molars. She tried to regain her composure. "This is *not* the time or the place—"

"Oh, but Mama, I want to be able to *share* my experiences with my family," Meg said. She could tell her father was enjoying the whole thing. As for Beryl, she simply sat there wide-eyed and silent while Travis chuckled and shoved food into his mouth. "You don't know what a relief it is to be able to talk about it openly."

"Margaret, that's enough!" Alma shouted.

Meg gave them a bright smile and shoved her chair from the table. "You're absolutely right, Mama. I didn't realize I was dominating the conversation. Y'all go on and eat. I'm going to step outside for a cigarette."

"You smoke?" Alma said weakly.

"Yes, Mama. I reckon I'm just hell bound."

Meg left the dining room, grabbed her jacket and purse from the kitchen counter, and made her way out the front door to the porch. She had half a mind to leave. She lit a cigarette and was contemplating doing just that when her father joined her.

"I didn't start it," she said without preamble.

He took her jacket and held it for her while she stuffed her arms in the sleeves. "No, but I wish you could just learn to ignore her."

Meg knew he was right, but it wasn't easy. "What's with the wig?"

"It's too ridiculous to discuss."

"Oh, I'm going to love this." She waited for him to tell her, but he didn't look so inclined. "You know how I get when I want my way."

"Aren't you a bit old for holding your breath?"

"Hey, if it works."

He sighed heavily. "Okay, here goes. I hired Fred Calloway's daughter, Mindy, to run the register at the store. Her husband ran off, left her with three younguns. She's desperate for money."

"So what's the problem?"

"Your mama swears we're having an affair. Every time she goes to town she comes back wearing a different wig. One day she's a blond, the next day she's a brunette."

"*Are* you having an affair with Mindy?" Meg couldn't resist teasing him.

He gave a snort. "What would a young girl like that want with an old goat like me?"

"I happen to think you're very handsome."

"Well, I'm not about to start cheating on your mother at my age. You got another one of those?" he said, motioning to the cigarette.

Meg handed him the pack and her lighter. "When did you start smoking?"

"When your mama started wearing those damn wigs." They both laughed. He reached for her hand and squeezed it. "It's good to have you home, baby."

Four

THE VISTA Campground was one of many tucked into the hollows of the Cherokee National Forest. A rustic sign meant to blend in with the environment suggested campers should pick out a site before paying the ranger. Meg followed a dirt road through the park, noting everything from pup tents to elaborate recreational vehicles. She was beginning to think she wouldn't find a site when she spied an empty space beneath a tangle of oaks at the widest part of the stream. She parked, climbed from the camper with her purse, and made for the camp store, where the ranger's office was located.

Although Alma had tried to convince Meg to stay in her old bedroom—insisting that serial killers lived in campgrounds and roadside parks—Meg had remained firm in her decision to have her own place. She was used to coming and going as she pleased. If she moved back home, even temporarily, her mother would probably assign her the same curfew she'd had at sixteen. Besides, Meg knew from experience that she and her mother would never last under the same roof.

The park ranger's office was located in a small room at the back of the camp store; Meg found the door open and knocked. Randy Bekins, as the nameplate on his desk read, was a handsome blond-haired man whom Meg suspected hadn't been out of college long. He wore a khaki uniform that gave him an official look, but the lazy grin he shot her told her he didn't take life too seriously.

"May I help you?"

"I'd like to rent site seventy-three," Meg told him.

He was still smiling as he motioned her to take the chair in front of his desk. "You came in the nick of time," he said. "The group before you had to leave on an emergency. All I had left was a couple of primitive sites. No sewer or electrical hookups." The smile broadened as he leaned back in his chair and regarded her. "You don't exactly look like the sort of woman who'd want to give up modern conveniences, if you don't mind my saying so."

"I'm tougher than I look, Mr. Bekins," Meg said in a no-nonsense voice. She pulled out a cigarette, tapped it against his desk, and lit it.

He reached into his middle desk drawer for a plastic ashtray that advertised the campground. "So how long you planning to stay, Mrs.—"

"It's *Ms*. Margaret Gentry," she said. "But my friends just call me plain ol' Meg."

"Begging your pardon, Meg," he said, ducking his head shyly, "but I could *never* call you plain."

She almost laughed, and was tempted to flirt right back, if for no other reason than to soothe her bruised ego. "You're too kind, Mr. Bekins," she said. "But I'm old enough to be your big sister. You'd best stick with the college babes. Now, what do you say we get down to business?"

"Younger isn't always better," he said. "Older women know what they want out of life and go after it."

"Is that so?" They may as well have been talking about the soybean market for all the enthusiasm she showed.

"I'll . . . uh . . . need identification of some kind."

Meg fumbled through her purse for her wallet and pulled out her driver's license. While he copied the information she tried not to look impatient, but she was in a hurry to get settled and make her new home as cozy as she could. It wouldn't be easy. Because the camper was attached to the cab, she would have to unhook the sewer, water, and electricity each time she went out. That meant her cabinets and doors and closets would have to be taped closed as well, so that everything she owned wouldn't fall out. She shook her head. Why hadn't she thought of that before she'd bought the damn thing?

Randy glanced up. "You're alone?"

"Any reason I shouldn't be?"

"I just figured"—he shrugged—"pretty thing like you all by yourself. Don't make much sense to me."

Meg put her cigarette out, already bored with the game. "What do I owe you for two weeks?"

"Won't take me long to find out," he said, reaching for his calculator. He figured the price and wrote her a receipt while she counted out her money.

"Thank you, Mr. Bekins." Meg stuffed the receipt in her purse and stood.

"I live in the cabin near the entrance. You can't miss it. There's a flagpole out front. If you need anything once the store closes, don't hesitate to drop by. I've always got a cold beer on hand."

Meg looked impressed. "No wonder this place is so popular," she said. "With that kind of hospitality, folks can't afford to pass it up."

He chuckled. "I don't exactly make that offer to everybody."

The guy refused to give up. Meg crossed her arms and leaned against the door frame. "Tell me something," she said. "Are you trying to win some Ranger-of-the-Year award, or are you just looking to get laid?"

He coughed and looked embarrassed. The telephone rang, and he snatched it up as if relieved to do so.

Meg made her way to the front of the store, where a couple of battered shopping carts had been shoved behind a rack of sweatshirts and hiking boots. After untangling the carts, she started down an aisle stocked with plastic coolers. Although there was a miniature refrigerator in her camper, she knew food would not stay cold when she was forced to unplug it and be on her way. She selected a cooler, grabbed a bag of ice, and bought only the necessities: coffee, sandwich meat, milk, and a variety of junk food. She grabbed a copy of the *Blalock Gazette* and a carton of cigarettes, and considered her shopping done.

Back at the camper, Meg hooked up her electrical, water, and sewer lines, then unloaded the few groceries she'd bought. She stood in her tiny adjoining living room–bedroom–kitchen combination and surveyed the area with a critical eye. The curtains were so old and dusty she feared they'd disintegrate if she touched them. The paneling probably hadn't been cleaned since man had landed on the moon, and she hated to think of all that had been spilled or dropped onto the carpet. She shook her head sadly.

"What have I done?" Meg asked herself, knowing she'd never be able to sleep in such a grungy place. She pulled her cleaning supplies from beneath the kitchen sink and went to work, scrubbing the bathroom and kitchen from top to bottom, washing the windows inside and out. After a quick cigarette break, she tackled the paneling with Murphy Oil Soap and used a foam cleaner on the carpet.

She carried a bucket outside to the back of the van. She experimented on Harley's artwork with a number of cleansers and an entire bottle of fingernail polish remover before finally grabbing a knife and scraping away the serpent and the expletive beside it. After more than an hour, she wiped away the last of the paint, as well as the avocado green beneath it. She stepped back to get a better look. And here she'd thought the camper couldn't look worse.

Meg was gathering her supplies and looking forward to showering and reading the newspaper when she suddenly glanced up sharply, half expecting to find the snake had reappeared, coiled and ready to strike. Nothing there. At least nothing the naked eye could see. But she sensed a presence regardless, as though something evil had been released into the air.

Oh, for heaven's sake, she thought. Something was in the air all right. She'd been breathing various fumes for several hours, and she obviously had a buzz going. Meg grabbed the rest of her supplies and hurried inside her camper, taking care to make sure everything was locked tight against the night.

Five

TRAVIS LYTLE had begun working for Bidwell Textiles when he was just thirteen, a shrimp of a boy who could barely manage a push broom. After twenty-two years, there wasn't a job he hadn't done or a problem he couldn't solve. Which is why he'd been promoted to operations manager the previous year. That, and the unexpected demise of J.T. Bidwell's son, a man with a penchant for hard liquor and fast cars. Bad combination when you lived in the mountains.

Nobody crossed Travis, not even J.T. himself, who, still grieving his only child, was more a figurehead. Travis Lytle ran the show. He might not have the salary or title of vice president yet—J.T. was loath to fill his late son's position—but Travis had the clout.

Power. He wore it well. The way he stood, the way he held his shoulders, only hinted at the enormous amount of pride he had in himself. He would continue subsidizing his income in other ways until J.T. decided to start paying him what he was worth. Besides, there were other perks— the conventions, the fancy hotels, the whores. Travis took advantage of them all. He figured anybody married to a woman as fat as Beryl had a right to screw around.

Travis entered the men's bathroom as he always did first thing in the morning, so he could check his appearance. He wasn't surprised to find Ray Edgewater standing at one of the urinals trying to eke out two or three drops of pee. Ray had been with Bidwell Textiles for thirty-five years and was currently experiencing prostate trouble. He was big on brawn but short on brains, which was why he hadn't advanced over the years.

Travis stepped up to the mirror and checked his dark hair from several angles. "Problems, Ray?" he asked.

The man turned red. "I'm fine," he muttered.

As usual, not a strand out of place. Travis sprayed his hair once each morning, and that did it for the day. His clothes were equally perfect. Tie straight, jacket unwrinkled, knife-edge crease in slacks, shoes polished. Beryl wasn't much good for anything else, but she kept his shoes shined like a new car. He pronounced himself ready.

"See ya, Ray," he said with a chuckle as he turned for the door. The man was still standing at the urinal wearing a pained look.

Travis went in search of Eugene Bless, Ray's immediate supervisor, a short man with bowed legs and skin so wrinkled it looked as if he'd come from a family of prunes. Eugene was talking to a young worker by the name of Purvis Dill, who'd been with the company several years now. Rumor had it he belonged to one of those snake-handling religions, so Travis stayed as far away from him as he could.

Dill walked away, and Eugene gave Travis his full attention. "You need something, Mr. Lytle?"

"Yeah. Ray Edgewater spends a lot of time in the can."

"He's having a few problems. Nothing serious."

"If I catch him hanging out in the bathroom many more times, he's getting a pink slip."

"But Mr. Lytle—"

"End of discussion, Eugene." He started to walk off. "By the way, how's that snake fellow doing? Aren't you afraid he'll put some kind of hex on you?" Travis wore a smirk.

"Ain't nary a thing wrong with that boy," Eugene replied. "Hardest worker we got. Next to Ray, that is."

Travis shrugged and walked off. As he made his way through the plant, he was aware that people watched him. They might not like him, but they had the common sense to keep it to themselves. After all, he held their livelihoods in his hands. Funny what you could get some of these women to do if they were afraid you'd take their job away from them.

Just the thought made Travis hard, and he automatically thought of his sister-in-law, Meg. Damned if she wasn't about the best thing he'd ever seen. And probably horny to boot, after living with that homo. He'd be more than happy to show her what she'd been missing all those years.

Yessiree, he was gonna have him some of that.

The *Blalock Gazette* was housed in a nondescript two-story building with a grimy picture window that looked out over the town square. Meg almost hoped there wasn't an opening.

With a sigh of resignation, she pushed through the front door and was greeted by the smell of burned coffee and stale cigarette smoke. She grinned. Who was she kidding? *This* was her kind of place. The main room was large, encompassing the reception area and a half-dozen desks, each bearing a computer that looked as though it had been picked up at a Radio Shack sidewalk sale. A plump, bald-headed man was feeding information into one. A door opened at the rear of the building, and Meg heard the sound of a printing press. A tall black man pushed a dolly through holding newspapers. He hefted a stack onto a worktable at the back of the room, in what appeared to be the mail area.

Meg stepped up to the reception desk, where a woman with big hair and lacquered midnight blue eyelashes was just getting off the phone. Melinda Giddings, her name-plate read.

"I'm Meg Gentry," she said, using the voice and smile

she saved for special occasions. "I have an appointment to see Bob Etheridge."

Melinda smiled back. "Down the hall, second-to-the-last door on the right. If you miss it, you'll be in the men's bathroom." She shuddered.

"Thanks for the warning." As Meg walked down the hall, she wondered what the big deal was over accidentally walking into the men's bathroom. Like she'd never seen a penis—or used the men's room, for that matter. Hell, she did it all the time at concerts and sports events. It was a whole lot better than waiting in line with a bunch of prissy women who, once they claimed a stall, took up housekeeping.

Meg stopped outside the appointed door and knocked. She heard a grunt from the other side and assumed that meant enter. Inside, she found a man with disheveled white hair and a scarred Tommy Lee Jones complexion. He was on the phone, giving somebody what appeared to be the browbeating of their life. He waggled a stubby finger at Meg, and she took it as permission to sit. He pointed to her résumé, and she handed it to him.

"Look, I don't give a goddamn about your so-called *hot item,* Murphy," he said, talking around a fat cigar. He opened Meg's résumé and glanced over it. "Bottom line is I'm pulling you off the paper for ninety days. You either get sober or you're out of here for good. And don't bother running to your wife, 'cause I'm not backing down on this one. Ninety days, you got that?"

He slammed the phone down and took a moment to compose himself. Finally, he stood and leaned across the desk to shake hands with Meg. "Bob Etheridge," he said, and reclaimed his seat. "Don't get me wrong. I don't have a thing against drinking. Keep a bottle in the bottom drawer of my desk, as a matter of fact. But when it starts getting in the way of your job, that's not good."

Meg nodded and hoped he never found out about her two-beers-before-bed ritual. "I agree," she said wholeheartedly.

He picked up her résumé and glanced through it quickly. "Why'd you leave the *Journal*?" he asked.

Meg shifted in her chair. "I got tired of big-city life," she said. "This is my hometown."

"I see you worked the crime beat. Pretty exciting stuff, huh?"

"Unless you have an aversion to seeing a person's brains splattered on the wall, or their intestines cut out and strung all over the living room. Other than that it's a real blast."

Etheridge looked thoughtful. "Okay, here's the deal. I've got a guy that's been with me for years. My managing editor, as a matter of fact. Handles local news, feature stories, and sports, plus he maintains a production schedule and supervises copy editors. He's got some personal problems."

"Is he the one with the hot item? 'Cause I'm here to tell you, I like hot items."

"Problem with this guy, he gets a pint of gin in him, and he thinks fly turds are big news." He leaned back in his chair and clasped his hands together. "We don't have a big staff. I serve as chief editor but pitch in where I'm most needed. Fred Garrison handles world news, business, and he takes care of the police beat. You might have to cover for him from time to time when he gets bogged down, and he'll do the same for you. Phil Jones is our production manager; we've got two part-time copy editors, and a part-time ad salesman. We also have people on rotating shifts to do outside printing jobs. So, what do you think?"

She blinked. "Are you offering me the job?"

"I can sign you on temporarily. Three months," he added. "If things don't work out for this guy, we'll discuss full-time employment. Matter of fact—" He paused and lit his cigar. Smoke billowed around him. "I can put you to work tonight if you're interested."

"Tonight?"

"Football game at Blalock High. They don't usually

have 'em on Monday night, but the last two were rained
out. You like football?''

''Love it.'' Actually, she didn't know jack shit about
it, but she wasn't about to tell him that.

He reached into the middle drawer and tossed her a
press card. ''Melinda will give you any other supplies you
need, including camera and film. We have a freelance
photographer. He's expensive, so we only call him out for
the big stories.''

''What do you consider big?''

He seemed to ponder it. ''Say some farmer finds
Noah's Ark while digging in his field. I'd probably call
this photographer, tell him to go get shots of it.''

''In other words, I'm responsible for my own pictures.
Even if it's an Elvis sighting. Are we going to discuss my
salary?''

''Not until I get a firm commitment from you. Oh, and
just because you worked for the *Journal,* don't be sa-
shaying around my reporters like you're hot stuff.''

''As long as they remember to curtsy, we'll get along
just fine.''

''So, do you want the job or not?''

Meg liked him. He was nothing like the troll she'd
worked for in Atlanta. That in itself was worth a cut in
salary. ''Yeah, I'll give it a whirl. Do I get to snoop
through what's-his-name's desk? You know, just in case
he really *was* working on something?''

''Don't waste your time. I've already looked.''

Six

DAN SMITH stood at the door of the Reverend Temple Beechum's bedroom and debated waking him. It was dark inside the small room. A piece of oilcloth covered the only window, but Dan was able to make out a shape on the cot against the wall.

"Temple, you awake?" he said. "I promised your girls I'd drop by. They's plum worried about you. Said you ain't put nothin' in your mouth for purt near a week. You know that ain't good for you."

The man on the cot slowly sat up. He was dressed in black, as though in mourning. His black hair fell into his face, which was pale and pinched looking. "The Lord God said we were to fast," he replied. "It humbles us, lest we become boastful."

Dan thought about it. "Folks around here are poor as dirt, Temple. That there keeps 'em pretty humble."

"Is that what you wanted to see me about?"

"No, I brung you a present from when I visited my brother in the Carolinas last week." He held up a quart-size mason jar. Holes had been gouged in the lid so the small snake inside could breathe.

Temple's eyes narrowed. "What is it?"

"You ever seen a pygmy rattlesnake? This'n is just a baby, probably won't get more'n a foot or two."

Temple took the jar and held it closer. The snake was small, no more than ten inches at best, with black-and-gray markings, and a reddish orange stripe running mid-dorsally. "He's nice."

"See that yeller tip on his tail? Means he young."

"Poisonous?"

"Naw. Probably'd cause you to get an infection if'n he wuz to bite you."

"You know a lot about snakes," Temple said.

"Yep. Been studyin' them all my life." Ben grabbed a straight-back chair, pulled it close, and sat down. "You shoulda seen me tryin' t'sneak him home on the Greyhound bus."

Temple smiled, but his eyes never left the jar. It was obvious he was fascinated. "Thank you for thinking of me, Brother Dan. I'll keep it as a pet."

"Well, I hope it makes you feel better, Reverend." He looked thoughtful. "You know, my brother has a buddy who raises eastern diamondbacks. Those suckers grow seven and eight feet long." He chuckled. "Makes our timber rattlers look plain sissified." He crossed one leg over the other and began swinging it. "Why, my brother says this fellow has a snake that measures over ten feet. I reckon a snake that big could bite you and dig your grave whilst you're dyin'."

"Ain't no snake big enough to kill you if the Lord's on your side," Temple replied. "But I wouldn't mind havin' me one of those. Sure keep unwanted visitors away," he added with a chuckle.

Ben nodded. "Tell you what, Reverend. You come in the kitchen and have something to eat, and we'll talk about it."

Meg was in and out of Wal-Mart in less than an hour, having selected rugs and curtains, among other items on her list. She was not the typical female shopper who combed the aisles for a good sale, and she absolutely hated trying on clothes in cramped dressing rooms with those full-length mirrors. She always suspected someone watched from the other side—a big woman with facial hair, dressed in men's trousers and rubber-soled work boots. After Wal-Mart, Meg purchased a cellular phone from Radio Shack and was hooked up in almost no time. She called the newspaper, gave her number to Melinda, and asked her to pass it on to Bob Etheridge.

When Meg arrived back at her campsite, she was stunned to find a familiar figure from her past sitting at her picnic table. Clay Skinner. Her heart seemed to skip a beat. She parked her camper, climbed out, and tried to think of something to say as she approached him. The minute he stood and smiled, her mind went blank. She just stared, thinking no man had a right to look that good.

"Well, well," he said, in a voice that would have coaxed a shy squirrel to take acorns from his palm. "Little Meggie Holcombe all grown up. And a sight for sore eyes, too."

He stepped closer, and his gaze caught and held hers. His eyes were just as she remembered, the color of hot cocoa, lightened with marshmallow cream. They were clear and observant, sharply assessing as they made a head-to-toe sweep of her. To her annoyance, Meg blushed.

"Are you finished?" she asked, unable to take her eyes off his deeply tanned face.

Clay smiled, showing healthy white teeth and fine laugh lines at the outer corners of his eyes. "For the time being. Just wanted to make sure you're still as pretty as I remembered."

Meg saw the humor lurking in his eyes. Same old Clay, only an older, taller version, with the widest shoulders she'd ever seen. "You don't look so bad yourself. How'd you know where to find me?"

"I ran into your mother at the hardware store. At first I didn't recognize her. Did she have long blond hair when we were dating?"

"She's experimenting with new styles."

He nodded as if it made sense. "She told me about your loss, and I came by to offer my condolences."

"My loss?"

"The death of your husband. I understand he was a detective, killed in the line of duty. You must've been very proud of him."

Proud wasn't exactly the word that came to mind when she thought of Roy. "My mother told you that?" Meg said.

"I hope you don't mind her sharing it with me. I know she did it out of concern for you and because we used to be so . . . close."

"My father put you up to this, didn't he?"

Clay's look of bafflement was all the answer she needed.

"Jesus Christ, she's crazy," Meg declared, a faint thread of hysteria running through her voice. "She's so goddamn crazy that she's dangerous. They should lock her up and melt the key so that it can never be duplicated."

"Who, your mother?"

"Of course, my mother," she almost shouted. "My husband, excuse me, *ex*-husband, wasn't killed. I left the son of a bitch because he was a homosexual."

"He's gay? Then why'd your mother give me that cock-'n'-bull story about you being newly widowed and all?"

Meg made her way around to the other side of her camper. She reached for one of the plugs, but Clay took it from her and began hooking up her utilities.

"She's convinced divorce is an unforgivable sin," she began, "right up there with wearing white shoes before Easter and charging full price for day-old bread." She gave a disgruntled sigh. "I suppose this means I'll spend eternity in some wretched place where you can't buy chocolate or decent toenail clippers." He grinned. "What's so funny?" she asked.

"Same old Meg."

That wasn't exactly what she wanted to hear. Meg liked to think of herself as being savvy and sophisticated after the years she'd spent away. But she didn't comment as she opened the door to the cab, climbed up on the step, and reached across the driver's seat for her purse, shopping bags, and jacket.

Clay eyed the form-fitting slacks she wore. Her hips were full and womanly, her waist small. Meg raised up, taking care not to hit her head, and turned around on the step. She looked surprised to find him there. "You've filled out," he said, reaching up for her sacks. "And in all the right places, I might add."

Meg wished he would step back, but he didn't look so inclined. With her purse in one hand and the other holding the door for support, she stepped down, and all but slid down the front of him. He was doing it on purpose, she told herself. Trying to see if the old physical attraction was still there. Well, she wouldn't give him the satisfaction of seeing her turn all goose-pimply and breathless. If he wanted heavy breathing, he could go home to his wife. With that in mind, she snatched her packages from his arms. "Would you please move out of my way?" He took a step back, and she marched to the front door of the camper.

Clay could feel a smile tugging his lips. She wasn't exactly happy to see him, but that was no reason to leave, as far as he was concerned. "Where are your keys?" he asked, when she came to a halt at her front door.

"My purse." She struggled with the sacks.

Without asking permission, he reached into what appeared to be a small burlap bag with sunflowers on it and pulled out a fuzzy, lime green key ring. The look on her face told him she didn't appreciate him going through her belongings without permission, but that only broadened his smile. He unlocked the door, opened it, and pulled out the metal step so she could climb up. "Here, let me help you," he said, supporting one elbow so she didn't fall as she stepped up. She stepped inside, thanked him, and kicked the screen door closed behind her.

Meg dropped her sacks on the sofa and tried to compose herself. Her encounter with Clay left her shaken, and she didn't like it. Not one bit. She was in the process of putting things away when she realized he was still standing outside, peering in. "Thank you for helping me," she called out. "I'm sure you have somewhere you need to be." Like home with your wife and kid, she thought.

"Aren't you going to invite me in?"

"Maybe some other time."

"Not even for a cup of coffee?"

Meg closed her eyes and counted to ten. When she opened them, she was just as flustered. She walked to the door and gazed out at Clay. It almost hurt to look at him. But that's because she'd been alone for so long. She had forgotten what it was like to have a man look at her the way Clay was looking at her this very instant. She couldn't remember what it was like to be held, but she ached for it just the same. Why had he come? To make things even more confusing for her? And why hadn't he mentioned his wife?

"Why should I let you in, Clay? You never once answered my letters after I went away to college. And how about all those times I came home for the holidays and tried to call you? You didn't even attend my college graduation, for Pete's sake! And don't tell me you didn't receive an invitation, because I mailed it certified mail." Though he didn't answer, Meg jerked the door open. "Okay, one cup of coffee and you leave."

Clay stepped inside, ducking so as not to hit his head. He gazed at Meg curiously. She was upset about something. Her pretty mouth was twisted into a grimace, and her movements were jerky. "What's wrong, Meggie?"

Her eyes stung at the pet name he'd given her all those years ago. That was twice now he'd used it. People got to where they depended on that sort of thing, and she didn't want to be one of them. She glanced at him. The camper seemed to have shrunk in size with his presence. "Please don't call me that."

"Sorry. Habit, I guess." He slid into the booth.

"We haven't seen one another in more than ten years. We don't have any habits between us."

He heard the catch in her voice, started to get up, decided against it. "Are you crying?"

She wiped her eyes. "Now, why would I be crying? I'm just . . . I'm a little self-conscious about my place, and I wasn't expecting company."

Clay glanced around. It was in sad shape, all right, but he didn't want to hurt her feelings. She was in a funny mood, but he figured she had a right, after discovering what she had about her husband. "What's wrong with it?"

Meg looked at him. You could put a man in a chicken coop, and he'd be perfectly content as long as there was a couch and TV and a refrigerator full of cold beer. "What do you mean what's wrong with it?" she almost shouted, then regretted it. What was wrong with *her*? She was so tense she thought her back would snap in half. "It needs sprucing up a bit," she said in a calmer tone. "I'm in the process of remodeling, in case you didn't notice."

"Maybe I can give you some pointers. I build houses for a living now."

She tried to sound excited for him. "No kidding."

"It's not so bad," he said, glancing around the compact area. "You could use some new carpet. I probably have some in my garage, left over from another job."

She did *not* want him doing nice things for her. "I bought a few throw rugs today," she said. "That should help." She began pulling masking tape from the cabinets so she could get to her coffeepot. "I have to tape everything when I go somewhere," she explained. "Otherwise the cabinet doors swing open, and stuff falls out."

"I can fix that," Clay said. "All you need are those kiddie locks. I installed them when my daughter was a toddler."

Meg, in the process of scooping coffee into a filter, paused and looked at him. The camper looked decidedly smaller with him in it. At the same time, he seemed to fit right in. "I heard you had a wife and daughter." So what the hell was he doing *here*? she wanted to shout. Maybe she was making a big deal out of it. Maybe he was just trying to make her feel welcome.

Clay nodded. "Cindy's six. Just started school this year."

She added water and turned on the pot. It made a gurgling sound. "So you and Becky Parker tied the knot, huh?" She gave a derisive snort. "No surprise there."

"What's that supposed to mean?"

"Well, damn, Clay, all the guys were hot for her. She had the biggest boobs of all the girls at Blalock High. Course, everybody knew she wore padded bras."

That amused light returned to his eyes. "Trust me, Becky doesn't need padded bras."

Meg's jaw dropped. "No shit?"

This time he laughed. "Anyway, Becky and I are divorced. Have been for a couple of years now."

Did he say divorced? Meg opened another cabinet and pulled out her nicest coffee cups. Since she owned only two, it wasn't difficult making the selection. "Divorced, huh? Guess big bazookas aren't everything."

"You sound envious. As I recall, you had very nice breasts yourself."

Meg felt a blush creep up her neck. The coffee had finished dripping through, and she poured two cups. "That was a long time ago. We were just a couple of kids with raging hormones. Thank God we grew up and came to our senses."

Clay studied her quietly. "You're saying you no longer have desires?" he asked. "I seem to remember a time when we couldn't get enough of one another. I knew if we ever made love we'd send up so many fireworks they'd have to call in the fire department. Surely you're not going to let one disappointment turn you into a bitter old crone." When she didn't answer, he couldn't resist ribbing her. "I'm sorry. That's not a question I should be asking a woman who just lost her husband to a man in silk hose.''

Meg shot him a dark look as she carried the cups to the table. ''You're going to get it for that one.''

''And I look forward to every minute of it.''

The look in his eyes caused her to stumble, and the coffee sloshed over the sides of the cups onto the table. ''See what you made me do,'' she said, turning for a towel. ''You're going to have to behave yourself, Clay Skinner, or I'll boot you out of here.'' She wiped up the mess, grabbed her cigarettes from her purse, and sat in the booth opposite Clay. She lit up and reached for an ashtray that advertised a tire company.

''When did you start smoking?'' he asked, stirring sugar into his coffee.

''Just now. You drove me to it.''

He watched her. ''No way. Anybody who can suck in that much smoke off one drag is a pro. What other bad habits did you pick up while you were away?''

She took another puff. ''We both know I picked up most of them from you. At the drive-in movie, if I remember correctly. Like the night you parked your car on the last row because it was a horror movie, and you didn't want me to see all that blood and gore. Neither of us watched the show.''

''I don't recall hearing any complaints from you. In fact, I believe I was the one who put on the brakes that particular evening.''

She almost shivered as she remembered how it'd been that night, lying across his lap with her jeans open, and his fingers teasing her until she thought she'd go crazy. He'd discovered where she was most sensitive, feather-flicking his thumb across that little nub until she'd climaxed.

''One day I'm going to touch you there with my tongue,'' he'd promised in a husky voice. They'd been seniors in high school at the time, with only weeks till graduation. Although Meg had allowed some heavy pet-ting now and then, she drew the line when it came to actual intercourse, terrified of becoming pregnant.

That night had been different. She had already been accepted into the journalism program at UNC, Chapel Hill, and she was waiting for the financing to come through. She'd wanted to give herself to him in hopes it would make a difference when the time came for her to leave. Maybe he'd go with her. But Clay had not taken what she had so freely offered, nor had he shown up at the bus station to say good-bye.

"Have you seen any of the old gang yet?" he asked.

Meg pushed the unpleasant thoughts aside and shook her head. "I haven't had a chance. I just got in yesterday, and I went job hunting first thing this morning."

"Did you find anything?"

"You're now looking at the new managing editor for the *Blalock Gazette*." At least for the next three months.

"You're taking Al Murphy's place?"

She'd forgotten what it was like living in a small town where everybody knew everybody else's business. She wasn't going to discuss the possibility of Al going into treatment. "Do you know Mr. Murphy?" she asked, avoiding his question with one of her own.

"We used to do a little fishing together."

"I hear he drinks."

Clay nodded. "Yeah, he can put it away. I hear he's getting worse."

"Makes you wonder how he can keep a job."

"Simple. His wife owns the newspaper."

"I guess that explains it." Meg took a final puff of her cigarette and put it out.

"We should celebrate your new job. How 'bout I take you to dinner this evening?"

"I have to work," she replied, thankful for an excuse to turn him down. She hadn't counted on Clay Skinner being divorced, or her still being attracted to him. The last thing she needed was another man in her life. "I'm covering the high school football game tonight. Did I mention that I know as much about football as I do about monster truck rallies?''

Clay shrugged. ''What's to know? The guy catches the ball and goes for a touchdown.''

''I think it's a little more involved than that. Like, why is that guy on the sidelines always dragging his tape measure out? You'd think he was planning to install wall-to-wall carpeting. I mean, aren't most football fields the same length? Except for the ones on TV, of course. They're smaller.'' She grinned at the look he shot her. ''Just kidding. I know they're not really smaller.''

Clay looked baffled. ''Are you talking about measuring for first downs? You really don't know anything about football—didn't your dad ever watch it?''

''He never had time, what with running the store and taking care of farm chores.''

Clay's smile bordered on tender. ''And you were usually right there with him.'' They stared at each other for a moment. Still watching her, he drained his cup and set it down. ''I'll go with you to the game if you like. I'll expect you to spring for the hot dogs, of course.''

Meg's heart lifted at the thought. Not because she looked forward to spending time with him, of course, but because she wanted her first article to be perfect. Yeah, right. ''You're a lifesaver, you know that?''

Clay slid from the booth and stood, the top of his head grazing the ceiling. ''I'll pick you up at six and give you a crash course on the way over.'' He started for the door and paused. ''Don't try to look sexy like you did in high school, or I won't be able to keep my mind on the game.''

''Don't worry, I don't own anything sexy. I gave it all away before I left Atlanta.''

As Meg watched him make his way toward a late-model pickup, she wondered if she was making a mistake. No, not as long as they both realized it was strictly business—and that's all it was.

So how come she had her eyes glued to his behind, and how come he had to look so good in a pair of faded, snug-fitting jeans? And what about those shoulders? Lord, you could hang half a dozen outlaws from those shoulders and still have room for more.

Listen to her—the ink hadn't dried on her divorce papers, and she was ogling another man's butt. What about her broken heart and wounded ego? What about her failed marriage? And Roy, to whom she had been so devoted before she'd seen him for what he was? Those things didn't go away overnight. It would take months, years probably, before she could get past the pain.

Clay turned and waved, and Meg sucked her breath in at the sight of him. It was just plain sinful to look that good.

"Oh, screw Roy," she muttered, and hurried to her pint-size bathroom for a quick shower.

Travis waited until the second shift clocked in, then decided to visit the nurse's office. Abby Merker was a petite brunette who'd never married. She made him laugh, at least when she was in a good mood, and he enjoyed bringing back little trinkets for her when he went away on business. He found her standing at a counter filling out a form when he entered. "Excuse me, Nurse, I'd like a pelvic exam."

"Go away, Travis. I'm busy."

He sat on the examining table. "Hey, where are those things I put my feet in? The stirrups?"

She shot him a look over her shoulder. "No wonder your poor wife takes Prozac."

"My wife takes Prozac because she can't stand herself. That's the only thing we have in common. We both hate her." Travis grinned. He liked sparring with Abby, and he wouldn't mind an occasional hump if she was so inclined. She wasn't pretty, but she had a nice, compact figure that made him itch to see more.

"Let me take you away from this dump, Abby," he

said. "We could fly off to one of those Caribbean islands and run naked on the beach."

She waved him off. "Now, Travis, you know I can't take the sun. It's Europe or nothing." She flipped through her stack of papers. "Did you hear someone from the dye room got sick today?"

"So? I wasn't going to invite him to come with us anyway."

She ignored him, "Red Barker came in before lunch complaining of chest pain. Says it's been bothering him for weeks now."

"Hell yeah, he's got chest pain. He smokes those non-filtered cigarettes to the tune of two packs a day."

"I had someone else from that area complain last week."

Travis slid off the table and approached her. "You know what you do with those complaint forms, don't you? Here, let me show you." He snatched one of the forms and, despite her protests, scrunched it into a tight ball and tossed it into the trash can.

"*That* was a very mature thing to do," she said. "Now I have to start completely over."

"If Red comes back in here complaining, tell him to call the tobacco company. It's not our fault he's got lung cancer." He paused and grinned. "Now, back to us. When are you going to let me set you up in a nice place? I can have you moved out of that dumpy trailer in no time." He was only half kidding. The thought of having somewhere else to go at the end of the day excited him, and he could afford to do it at this point. And Abby would be so grateful that she'd be willing to do anything for him. Anything.

Abby regarded him. "Travis Lytle, you talk more shit than a manure salesman. How are you going to afford to give me this lavish lifestyle when you've got a mortgage and a family to support? Besides, my trailer isn't a dump, and I'm tired of you saying so."

"I can take care of you, Abby. See, I have this little side job."

"You got a paper route, Travis?" She laughed. "I can just see you out at five A.M. on your kid's bicycle. I hope it has reflectors. What would these poor souls do if something happened to you? And what about poor J.T.? He'd have to close down the plant."

"No, I don't have no goddamn paper route. This is a serious business and I'm talking serious money. As far as J.T. is concerned, I done forgot more about the textile business than he ever knew."

"So where are you hiding this money?"

"In a place nobody would ever think to look. Not in a million years," he added smugly.

"You're stashing it in the toe of your sock?"

Travis could see she was making fun of him, and he didn't like it. He'd been the butt of many jokes growing up, simply because he'd been poor. Well, he had money and position now, and he insisted on being treated with respect.

"Watch it, Abby," he said. "You're not a pretty woman. My offer is probably going to be the best thing you ever get." He turned and walked out.

Purvis Dill sat in his truck in the factory parking lot and entered the day's events into his notebook. His light brown hair glinted with red highlights in the pale afternoon sun. One lock fell forward, and he brushed it back without a thought and went back to writing. He took care not to smudge the page with the grease he'd gotten on his hands while working on a piece of machinery. He'd washed up in the men's room, but the soap hadn't come close to getting him clean. He knew why. For months he'd kept his eyes open and his mouth shut, and by doing so he'd learned things. Now he had to figure out what to do with the information. He entered the date and time at the bottom of the sheet, then checked to make sure it looked neat and professional. No telling who'd end up seeing it.

He closed the book, then slipped his key into the ignition. As he turned on the engine, he glanced up and saw Travis Lytle standing at one of the windows. His mood veered sharply to anger. "It won't be long, you bastard." It was a promise he intended to keep.

It was after nine o'clock when Meg and Clay left the football game, Blalock's Howling Wolves having won a victory over the visiting team. Meg was glad she'd worn her jacket. The temperature had dropped during the past hour, but she felt rejuvenated by the mountain air.

"See, that wasn't so bad now, was it?" Clay asked as he pulled onto the main road.

She shrugged. "It's more interesting when you have an idea what's going on, but I'm not likely to become a football fanatic." She looked at him. "Thanks for all your help. And for giving me a list of questions to ask the coach. I probably would have asked him something dumb like why they stopped putting chili on the hot dogs, or who was the artist responsible for painting those white lines on the field."

"You handled yourself like a pro. Now, how about a cup of coffee at my place? I'd like to show you my house. Built it myself."

Meg wavered, suddenly very aware of him now that they were alone. Oh, what the hell. It wasn't like he was asking her to take a shower with him. "Yeah, sure." Besides, she was curious to see what kind of place he lived in.

He soon pulled into the driveway of a sprawling cedar ranch, surrounded by tall pines. A black Lab loped toward them as they climbed out of the truck.

"He's harmless," Clay said when Meg quickly sidled up to him. "But don't let that stop you from getting as close to me as you want." The dog sniffed Meg's feet, moved up her calves and finally to her crotch. Clay pushed him away. "Mind your manners, Bo," he said, then grinned at Meg. "He got that from me, you know."

Meg shook her head but couldn't help smiling. "It wouldn't surprise me."

The smell of new wood and lemon polish greeted Meg as she stepped inside the house and followed clay into a large living room done in tongue-and-groove paneling. The sofa and chairs were covered in a heavy woven plaid of navy, dark red, and hunter green, and braided throw rugs adorned the heart-of-pine floor. Clay looked very much at home in his jeans and thick ribbed sweater, worn over a plaid shirt. Meg could imagine him sitting on the sofa, reading the Sunday paper before a cozy fire, feet propped on the coffee table. She could almost picture herself beside him, reading the comics.

She took that thought and mentally tossed it, like she'd seen the players do earlier with the football. She suddenly realized she knew as much about relationships as she did sports.

"My place looks like a dump compared to this," Meg said. She gave a grunt. "What am I saying? My place *is* a dump."

"It's not so bad," Clay said, going into the kitchen. Meg followed and found herself in a large kitchen painted a deep hunter green with white cabinets. A light oak table and chairs sat before a bay window. "It's very striking," she said. "This is where I'd spend all my time."

Clay glanced up as he spooned coffee into a clean filter. "Are you asking to move in?"

She sat on a stool at the counter. "Excuse me, but do I have the word *imbecile* written across my forehead? Why would I move in with you when I'm still considering hiring a paid killer to knock off the last man?" She shook her head emphatically. "No, I think I'd rather keep my little house on wheels. That way if things don't work out, I can be a dot on the horizon in an hour."

"Sounds like the Meg I used to know," he said. "Here one minute, gone the next."

Was that bitterness in his voice? Meg changed the subject. "Did Becky decorate the place for you?"

He shook his head. "My ex-wife has never been invited inside. I practically had to sign away everything I owned to get her to agree to a divorce. Now that I finally have my own place, I'm very particular about who I let in."

She detected a sour note, but that handsome face gave nothing away. "So why'd you split up?" she asked, unable to resist prying.

He partially filled the coffeepot with water and poured it into the top of the coffeemaker. "It just didn't work out. I don't think it was anybody's fault, really."

"When a man says it wasn't anybody's fault, it usually means *he* was to blame. Did you cheat on her?"

He looked surprised by the question. "No, I didn't cheat on her." He turned on the coffeemaker and faced her, planting his hands on the counter. "Why are you allowing this Roy to taint your opinion of all men?" he asked.

Meg was staring at his hands. They were big and brown with long, sturdy fingers. His nails were clean and clipped short. She glanced up and found him watching her, studying her, actually. His eyes were speculative, and as the silence lengthened between them, she felt a fist of tension squeeze her stomach. It had been a mistake to come. If they had been drawn irresistibly to each other as teenagers, they would probably be more so as adults.

Meg tried to speak but found her mouth was dry. She wished the coffee would hurry. "I don't hate all men because of my bad experience," she said. "It's just going to be more difficult for me to trust them. Who knows, I may never trust again." She remembered some of the awful things she'd witnessed while working at the *Journal*. "Not just men, everybody."

"That's too bad."

At the censure in his voice, her ire sprang to life. "I'm sorry if you don't approve, but my happiness doesn't depend on your approval."

"I liked you better before you became such a hard-ass."

His gaze impaled her; she felt vulnerable and exposed. The barriers she'd constructed to keep her safe would never work with him, because he knew her too well. He would figure out the truth: She talked tough, but inside she was as confused and uncertain as the next person.

"Don't sit in judgment of me, Clay Skinner," she said. "You've got problems of your own."

"Such as?"

"Maybe you're holding a grudge because your ex-wife screwed you financially."

His expression didn't falter. "Sounds like you're the one holding the grudge because I got married in the first place."

She bristled. "Oh, give me a break!"

"You can't stop thinking about Becky and me together, can you?"

She refused to meet his gaze. "You're right. It keeps me awake nights."

He noted her heightened color, the rapid rise and fall of her breasts. She could continue this Herculean act of hers, but he'd glimpsed the raw hurt and loneliness in her eyes, and he knew better. "It bothers you that I was married to another woman, that she carried my baby."

The fist in Meg's stomach squeezed harder. "Made no difference to me. I was long gone by then."

"But you wondered what it was like between us. The sex, I mean. Well, let me tell you, Becky was hell on wheels in the sack."

"Thanks for letting me know. If I ever decide to become a lesbian, I'll give her a call." What with all the rotten men in the world, she was beginning to think lesbians were onto something.

Clay leaned closer. "She still is."

Meg's head snapped up, and she saw the satisfied light in his eyes. She gave a choked, bitter laugh. "You're not as smart as I thought," she said with a smirk.

"How do you figure?"

"If she was so damn good, why'd you leave her?" She stood and turned for the living room. "Please take me home."

He was beside her in an instant, blocking her. "We haven't discussed you and Roy yet."

"And we're not going to."

He backed her against the wall. "Fine. Let's discuss your first lover. The one who succeeded where I failed."

"What's wrong with you? Are you crazy, or are you just mean as hell?"

He stepped closer, his lower body pressed flush against hers. "No, babe, I'm resentful. I put up with your kissy-face routine for two years because you were hung up on remaining a virgin." His mouth twisted into a mocking smile. "Boy, your mother must've convinced you your cherry was worth gold. I walked around horny as a stud bull in a pen full of heifers all that time, just so you could keep your precious hymen intact, and for what? I'll bet you put out to the first college boy that looked at you. And here I was, led to believe I'd have to marry you to have it."

Meg could feel the moisture gathering in her eyes, but she wasn't about to let him see her cry. "Is this why you invited me here, Clay? So you could get back at me for wanting to do something with my life?"

"You make it sound so simple, but it wasn't. We'd made plans; we'd decided on how many kids we were going to have, what kind of house we wanted."

"*You* decided, Clay. And you didn't much care how I felt about it." Meg couldn't hold back her tears any longer. "You refused to listen to what I wanted! I would gladly have married you once I got my degree, but with you it was now or never. So go ahead and hate me for the rest of my life, for wanting to see something more than these mountains. And because I wanted to do something with my life," she added.

Clay closed his eyes for a moment, and when he opened

them once more, he was calm. "I don't hate you," he said in a somber tone, "although it would be easier if I did. Come on, I'll take you home."

They made the drive to the campground in silence. Meg tried to start up a conversation once or twice, but Clay didn't seem to be in a talkative mood. It was just as well, since she was still smarting from the things he'd said. She was glad it'd happened, though. It proved they couldn't be friends. There were simply too many hurt feelings and grudges that, combined with the strong attraction they felt for one another, could only lead to more heartache.

Clay pulled up beside her camper and Meg climbed out, drawing comfort from the fact she wouldn't have to deal with him again. He was a shithead for saying what he had, and her only regret was not slapping him silly at the time. "Thanks again for helping me with my article," she said, keeping her voice light when what she really longed to do was push his truck off the side of a mountain with him in it. Then she closed the car door and watched him drive away. She really was going to have to break down and buy a gun.

Meg turned toward the camper in the pitch black, irritated with herself for not leaving the outside light on. With the help of her cigarette lighter, she stumbled toward her front door and searched for her keys. Stepping inside the camper a moment later, she closed the door and reached for the light switch. Nothing happened; the bulb was obviously burned out. Damn, damn, damn. She started for the sink, remembering she'd recently put a new bulb in the fixture over it.

She sensed a presence a split second before she felt someone reach around and cover her mouth. She didn't even have time to scream.

Seven

"DON'T MAKE a sound," a voice whispered. "Not even a peep, or I'll hurt you. Understand?"

Meg thought her heart would burst in her chest from the adrenaline rush of fear. She nodded dutifully.

"Good girl. You do as I say, and I'll treat you right. I'm going to take my hand away, and you're going to stay quiet. Right?"

She knew that voice, despite his attempts to disguise himself. Once more she nodded, and he removed his hand. He reached past her and turned on the small light over the kitchen sink.

Finally, he turned her around so that she was facing him. "Why do you think I'm here?" he said.

Meg tried to keep her voice steady. "You're going to rape me."

He reached up and squeezed her breast hard. "Rape is a strong word," he said. "It doesn't have to be that way."

"Oh, I think it does, Travis," she said, " 'cause that's the only way you're going to get in *this* girl's pants." She reached out and jerked a drawer open beside the sink. A blade flashed in the light.

"What the hell are you doing?" he demanded, stepping away.

She offered him the knife. "You'll need this. Most rapists carry some sort of weapon, you know."

"I'm not a damn rapist," he snapped. "I don't have to rape when I know plenty of women who are willing to give it to me."

"You're not a rapist?" she said, looking genuinely confused. "Gee, you certainly *looked* like one. I mean, you break into my place, then hide here in the dark until I come home so you can force sex on me. I don't know, Travis; it smells like rape to me."

He grabbed the knife from her. "What is this, some kind of sick act you picked up from your fag husband?"

"Go ahead and kill me," she prodded. "After what I've been through the past six months, you'll be doing me a favor. Course, that means you'll be having sex with a dead body." She chuckled. "It'll change your whole image, Travis. Folks'll have to stop accusing you of sleeping with anything that has a pulse."

She'd barely gotten the words out before he slapped her hard across the mouth.

Tears stung the backs of her eyes and bright dots danced before her, but Meg laughed regardless. "Oh, so you're into S and M as well as rape. What was that, foreplay?"

He raised his hand to strike her again but thought better of it. "You're not worth the effort," he said. "I can tell you're a lousy lay just by looking at you." He shoved her hard against the cabinet, tossed the knife into the sink, and made for the door.

Meg laughed again, this time bordering on hysteria. "Does this mean you've lost interest? I was just trying to play hard to get."

He turned. "You're a real comedian, aren't you, Meg? Everything's a big joke. Well, this ought to give you a good chuckle. Now that you've pissed me off, I'm going home and take it out on your fat sister."

She tossed her head back defiantly, blood trickling from her lip. "Beryl isn't going to put up with that kind of treatment."

"Wrong. Your sister's pregnant, and I'm her meal

ticket." He reached for the door handle, then shot her a contemptuous look. "By the way, you might want to call her in the morning just to check on her. She's had two miscarriages in the past eighteen months, and she's worried sick about losing this one."

Meg began to tremble as frightening images invaded her mind, and she felt sick to her stomach. "You bastard!"

He laughed. "Maybe you'll be nicer to me next time."

"Or maybe I'll slit your goddamn throat."

He tossed her a cocky smile and let himself out.

Meg locked the door behind him and slid the chain in place. Then she sank to the floor, buried her face in her hands, and cried.

Meg awoke early the next morning, still wearing her clothes from the night before. She'd slept very little, and now she was exhausted. Wrung out. She glanced at her watch. Beryl would be waking the children for school about now; she would have to wait to call.

She stepped into her doll-size bathroom and groaned when she spied her reflection in the mirror. Her eyes were puffy from crying, and her top lip cut and swollen, compliments of Travis. *Shit.*

What was it about her that brought out the beast in men?

She should have cut his gizzard out with that butcher knife. No, what she should have done was report him to the cops for breaking and entering and attempted rape. Let the whole town see what a lowlife he was.

But she wouldn't do that to Beryl and the kids, and he knew it.

She added Travis's name to the list of men she'd like to see buried alive in wet cement.

Meg reached the *Gazette* before seven-thirty. Suspecting the office staff wouldn't arrive for another hour, she entered through a back door and found the printing press already running, spitting out copies of a full-page advertisement for Wal-Mart. She nodded to the men, grabbed a copy of the ad, and noticed the rugs she'd purchased the day before were half price. It figured.

Inside the office, she was able to locate her desk right away, thanks to the empty drawers standing open and a trash can spilling over. She rifled through it in record time, and found nothing that would hint at what Al Murphy may have been working on. Several steno books proved just as worthless. Finally, she went to work on the antiquated computer. Once she'd drafted the football article, she dialed her sister. It rang seven times before a groggy Beryl answered.

"I woke you, didn't I?"

"Oh, Meg, hi," Beryl said, yawning. "I must've overslept. I had a bad night."

Meg felt her anxiety level rise. If Travis *had* followed through with his threat, she would probably end up doing something that would get her twenty years to life. "What happened?"

"Jimmy was up half the night throwing up. He's got a stomach virus. And to tell you the truth, I don't feel so good myself. So, how are you? Is anything wrong?"

Meg wished she and her sister had been closer growing up. "Oh, no, everything's fine." She told her about the new job.

"Boy, you didn't waste any time," Beryl said. "When you see something you want, you go right after it. I've always admired that in you."

Meg was touched by the comment. "I have to admit I feel like a new person," she said. "The people in this office are so friendly, and there's a lot less stress. Of course, the best thing I did for myself was divorce Roy. That's what really made a difference in my life."

"It's a good thing y'all didn't have children. I've heard divorce is always harder on kids."

"I don't know, Beryl. I think I would've gotten out sooner had there been children. No sense putting them through all that misery."

Beryl didn't respond right away. "Meg, honey, have you looked up your old friends since you got back?"

"No, I've been too busy. Why?"

"You sound like you need someone to talk to," she said. "You've been through some major changes. Why don't we get together over lunch in a few days? Once this bug has passed," she added. "I'm a good listener, and I won't repeat anything you tell me."

"Oh, but, Beryl—"

"Jimmy's sick again, hon. Got to go. Call me later."

Meg stared at the phone in her hand. "Well, now, that was a productive call," she mumbled under her breath.

The daily staff meeting was brief because they were on deadline. Bob Etheridge introduced Meg to the group and said she was filling in for Al Murphy, who was on leave. "I hope you'll stop by Meg's desk when you get a chance and say hello. Also, she's used to working on a large newspaper and a daily, so this'll take some time getting used to. Please answer her questions and help her if you can." The employees smiled and nodded, and Meg was warmed by their welcome.

"That's all for now," Etheridge said. "Everybody's present and accounted for. Let's get moving." He looked at Meg. "You got the story on last night's game?" When she nodded, he looked pleased. "Grab yourself a cup of coffee and bring it to my office."

Meg knocked on his door five minutes later. "What happened to your lip?" Etheridge said. "Your boyfriend hit you?"

"I cut myself shaving."

"Uh-huh."

"I have a little mustache problem. All the women in my family have facial hair," she added.

"Sounds attractive."

"It's in the genes; what can you do?"

"I hope it doesn't happen again. I don't like to see my employees come to work looking battered. Especially the females." He began reading her copy, making minimal changes.

"Not bad for a city girl," he said. "I only have one suggestion."

"I'm listening."

"Your story starts off with Coach Steve Tindal leading the Howling Wolves to another victory. You covered all the big plays and which player was involved, but you could've given me something more colorful."

"Colorful?"

"Like, for instance, a little update on the coach and his family. Everybody knows his wife is battling cancer, but she still insists on attending all the games and watching their oldest boy play football. Sometimes she's so weak she has to watch from the car, but she refuses to miss. Folks not only want to know how the game went, they're interested in Mrs. Tindal's health as well."

"I didn't even know the coach was married," Meg said.

"You do now. Wife's name is Elinor. Write it down so you don't forget."

Meg did as he said. "Got it."

"And Mike Fuller, the quarterback, was injured halfway through the season last year and had knee surgery. Naturally, everybody is curious to see if he's going to be able to play as well as he did before he was hurt."

"I understand what you're saying," Meg replied. "When I covered the crime beat, I tended to depersonalize the victims in my mind. I laid out the facts, but I tried very hard not to get emotionally involved."

"I'd think most people have to do it that way," Etheridge said. "In the Lifestyles section, your stories will be more upbeat. You need to know who the movers and shakers are in town. Attend a few chamber meetings and town socials. Who knows, you may even meet a nice man," he added, gazing at her injured lip.

Meg stared at him. He obviously didn't know her track record.

"I assume you're single," he said. "I don't see a ring."

"I'm divorced. I took my ring to a pawn shop and traded it for a weed eater."

"Must've been hard on you."

"You're right. I was actually looking for a hedge trimmer."

He looked amused as he handed her a three-by-five slip of paper. "Here's several leads I want you to check out. There's no need for you to hang around here; we have all the help we need."

"Oh, somebody's getting married?" Meg said, reading his messy scrawl. "What a lucky break for them."

"Yes, indeedy. She's the daughter of the president of First Bank. Ben Fisher and his wife, Hildy, are well liked in this town. The wedding is this Sunday. I'd like you to get a couple of pictures and do a write-up. Do *not* try to talk her out of it in the meantime."

Meg pretended to zip her lips. "Anything else?"

"Yeah." He handed her another piece of paper. "Some blind guy up in the hills got struck by lightning some weeks back and claims he can see now."

"No kidding? Was he declared legally blind before it happened?"

"Gee, I don't know, Meg," he said, leaning forward and clasping his hands together. "I was sort of hoping you might drive up there and find out for us."

She gave him a look. "My last boss had a smart mouth, too, before his accident."

Etheridge reached for a stack of papers on his desk. "Get out of here so I can get some work done."

Meg returned to her desk. First she called the Fisher residence and spoke to the bride's harried mother to let her know she'd be covering her daughter's wedding. Then she checked the phone book for a Jarrod Renfree, the man whose sight had been restored after he was struck by lightning. Nothing there. She noted the address Etheridge had given her, and made her way to the mail area, where a wall map had been taped over the postage meter. She found what she was looking for and jotted down the directions. Grabbing her purse, notebook, and camera, she paused at the receptionist's desk and signed out. Melinda Giddings was in the process of painting her nails.

"You be careful way up there in those mountains," she warned, once she read where Meg was going. "You never know what you'll run into."

Meg pushed through the glass door leading outside and almost ran into Clay Skinner on his way in. In her surprise, she dropped her notebook, which he retrieved immediately. "What are you doing here?" she demanded.

"I stopped by to see if you wanted to go to breakfast. What happened to your lip?"

"Someone tried to take my parking place, and I kicked the shit out of them. Good-bye."

"I wasn't aware parking was such a problem in this town."

"I'm working, Clay. I don't have time—"

"Okay, forget breakfast," he said, "but I still want to know who hit you. I'm not leaving till you answer some questions."

"Someone was waiting for me when I arrived home last night."

Clay's jaw tensed. "Did he hurt you?"

"Just my lip and my pride."

"I hope he's sitting in jail right now."

"I didn't press charges."

"What? Why are you protecting this person?"

"I'm not. He can rot in hell for all I care. I'm trying to protect someone else I love very much."

"He'll come back. You know he will."

"I'm putting alarms on my doors and windows." She glanced at her wristwatch. "I really do have to go now," she said.

"Aren't you going to give me a chance to apologize?" he said. "I don't know what got into me last night, but I feel miserable about the way I acted. I couldn't even sleep last night for worrying.''

She smiled sweetly. ''I think I prefer you miserable and unable to sleep. Have a nice day.'' She turned and made for her camper.

He watched her walk swiftly toward the vehicle, hips swinging from side to side. Damned if she didn't look as good from the back as she did the front. He knew that she wasn't likely to forgive him any time soon. What he needed to do was appeal to her soft, generous side, and ask for a second chance.

And he knew just how to go about it: that fancy Italian restaurant on the edge of town. Dark, with candlelight and mood music, it would be the perfect spot for her to let go of all that anger and realize what a good guy he was. Women just naturally went for that sort of thing.

''Hey, Meg,'' he called out across the parking lot. ''You wouldn't happen to be free for dinner tonight?''

Without turning or breaking her stride, Meg raised her middle finger and flipped him off.

BOOK TWO

Eight

MEG FOLLOWED the two-lane highway that looped around the mountain like a ribbon. She could feel the pressure in her ears build as she climbed upward, reaching an elevation of four thousand feet. Here and there she passed a mobile home or small clapboard house where dingy sheets and towels hung from a clothesline.

She thought of her mother, who had gone to such lengths to keep her linens white: boiling them with lemon or adding several drops of turpentine to the wash. Lace was whitened by soaking it in sour milk. Nothing was allowed to hang on the Holcombe clothesline until it sparkled like something from an Ivory Snow commercial.

Meg replayed her conversation with Beryl and shook her head sadly. How could she help? What if her sister resented her sticking her nose in her business? She was so absorbed in her thoughts that she almost missed her turn.

Jarrod Renfree was a crusty-looking fellow with a snaggled salt-and-pepper beard and stumpy, bowed legs. Standing beside him was a blue-tick hound who didn't look any happier to see Meg than his master.

"Does your dog bite?" she asked, trying not to let her anxiety show. She'd become wary of dogs when that ill-mannered pit bull had chased her and her cameraman through an Atlanta junkyard while they were doing a story on stolen vehicles.

"Depends. You a bill collector?"

"I'm from the *Gazette,* Mr. Renfree." She noted that his facial hair had been singed and was just now growing back. His fingertips and the end of his nose were a dark gray, as though they'd been charred. "I'd like to talk to you about that accident you had some weeks back. When you were struck by lightning."

"Weren't no accident. 'Twas a sign from God." He continued to study her. "Yer not from around these parts, are you?"

Meg wondered what'd made him say that. Had city life left an indelible stamp on her? "I was born and raised in Blalock, as a matter of fact. My parents are Henry and Alma Holcombe. They own a small grocery store near the foothills. I've been away for a while."

Something in his look changed. "Yer pa buys eggs from me. He's a fair man." He looked at the dog. "Down, boy." The animal slid to the porch floor and closed his eyes.

The screen door was suddenly flung open by a squatty, auburn-haired woman in a floral housedress. She patted her hair self-consciously. "I didn't knowed we had comp'ny."

"This here's m'wife, Edith," he said. "Edith, this is Meg Gentry. She's a reporter come to ask questions about my miracle."

"I understand it was quite an event," Meg said to the woman, after declining her offer of coffee.

Edith pulled a rickety chair close. "It was. See, Jarrod's been blind since the Vietnam War. He was wounded purty bad over yonder."

"Got me a buncha medals t'prove it," he tossed in.

Edith nodded. "Anyways, his sight came right back after the accident."

"Dang it, Edith, I done tole you and tole you it weren't no accident. The Lord knew exactly what he'uz doing."

The dog had started to snore.

"Can you tell me a little about your, uh, miracle?" Meg asked.

"He don't remember much," Edith said.

"Would you please let *me* tell it," Jarrod snapped. He turned to Meg. "I don't remember much."

"Okay, just tell me what you *do* remember," she said.

"Happened a couple o' weeks back," he said. "I was out feedin' the dogs. I didn't let my blindness get in the way of my chores. I could tell it was fixin' to come a storm 'cause o' the way the air smelt. Well, it come up s'fast I didn't even have time to think about it. I started back fer the house, but some way or 'nuther I got turned around and didn't know which way I'uz going."

"You were disoriented?" Meg asked.

He paused. Finally, he nodded. "I reckon that's what you'd call it. I'uz just wanderin' around, bumpin' into trees like I'uz drunk or somethin'."

"I thought he'uz in the house," Edith said. "I had one o' my bad headaches, and I'uz layin' down."

"Anyways, all at once, I felt somethin' hit m'body like a stick of dynamite. Blam! Didn't know what it was, but it knocked me fer a loop."

"I heard 'im scream," his wife said, "and at first I thought a wild animal had got 'im." Her eyes welled with tears as she said it. "I grabbed the shotgun and went runnin' out o' the house and there he was flat o' his back, smoke comin' offa him like he'd been in a fire. I thought he'uz dead."

"What'd you do then?" Meg said, taking notes.

"Wasn't much I could do 'cept run fer the road. We ain't got no phone or car. So I stood out there tills I sees a car comin' and I waved it down. Was three o' them holy rollers from up the way."

"Holy rollers?" Meg inquired.

The woman looked embarrassed. "That's what we call 'em. They's from that holiness church that believes in holding snakes and drinkin' poison and such. We ain't never had nothin' to do with 'em, but they'uz real con-

cerned when I told 'em 'bout Jarrod. There'uz a little
blond-headed gal no bigger'n a minute, and she asked me
if I wanted her to pray for him. I said that would be fine,
but I still wanted them to take him to the emergency
room.''

"Holy rollers don't believe in doctors," Jarrod said.
"They believe in—" He looked to his wife.

"Divine intervention," she supplied. "Anyways, they
took Jarrod to the hospital like I asked, and the whole
time we'uz in the car, this little blond gal has her hand
on Jarrod's forehead and she's prayin' up a storm. Just as
we pulled up in front of the emergency entrance, this girl
told me my husband'uz goin' to live to see his new grand-
baby. I knowed my eyeballs 'bout fell out of my head,
'cause I hadn't told her Jarrod was blind or that our oldest
daughter was expectin'.''

Tears suddenly welled up in the woman's eyes. "I still
get emotional when I think about it. For the first few days,
they barely kept Jarrod alive. They said it was like all his
internal organs had been fried, and even if he lived his
brain would never be right. Said he'd be a vegetable.''

Jarrod picked up the conversation. "But I showed 'em
all, didn't I, Edith? When I woke up, there'uz nothin'
wrong with me, and I had my sight back t'boot.''

"I still say that little blond girl had something to do
with it," Edith said. "I'll bet she could do something for
your poor lip.''

Meg blushed and touched her lip self-consciously.
"Oh, it's fine," she said. "Do you know the name of this
church or where it's located?''

Husband and wife looked at one another. "I don't
know the name," Jarrod said, "but if you get back on the
main road and head up the mountain a mile or so, it's on
the right.''

Meg chatted with them a few minutes more and took
several pictures. Then, just as she was about to leave,
Jarrod sent Edith inside for a jar of her watermelon pick-
les. "Tell yer pa to try these," he said. "I can sell 'im

as many jars as he needs. Give 'im a good price, too.''

"I brought you a little salve as well," Edith whispered. "You'll be like new in no time."

Meg thanked them and left. She pulled out onto the road and drove until she found herself in front of a cinder-block building with a hand-painted sign over the door that read JESUS CHRIST HOLINESS CHURCH.

She parked, climbed out of her camper, and made her way to the rough-hewn door. It was locked. She went around back, hoping to find the blond woman Edith Renfree had told her about, but there wasn't a soul in sight. She retraced her steps, paused beside a smaller sign nailed to the front door, and copied the days and hours of worship. Not only did they have a Sunday morning service, they met on Friday and Saturday nights as well.

She planned to be at the next service.

Nine

AT FIRST Meg wasn't able to confirm Jarrod Renfree's hospital stay because the information was confidential, and she didn't have a signed release form from the patient. She hit pay dirt when she discovered the woman in medical records was an old school pal. She and Betti Bootle had been inseparable until Clay came into Meg's life. They chatted for a few minutes, playing catch-up, before Meg explained what she needed.

Betti didn't hesitate. "Let me check the files, and I'll get back to you. Just give me your fax number, kiddo, and I'll send you what you need."

Meg thanked her and hung up. She muttered a cuss word under her breath when she noted the time. She had to hurry if she was going to make the women's auxiliary meeting. She grabbed her jacket and purse and hurried toward the front door, asking Melinda to sign her out.

The ladies of the auxiliary were putting together a cookbook for charity. Meg chatted with a number of the women after the meeting and learned of other events taking place in the near future. When she left, having passed her cellular number out to several members, she felt confident she would build up a list of contacts in no time.

She bought a tuna sandwich from a convenience store and drove back to the office, where Melinda handed her several messages. Her mother had called to invite her to dinner that evening, Beryl wanted to know if she was feeling better, and Betti Bootle had faxed a letter confirming Jarrod Renfree's story, along with dates and doctor's comments.

Meg drafted the article and put it on Etheridge's desk, then made a note to send Betti a thank-you card. Finally, she carried her lunch to the morgue, where she planned to scan old newspapers for story ideas while she ate. One bite of the tuna sandwich convinced her she was better off hungry. She tossed it in the trash and reached for her cigarettes.

An hour later, Meg had just about decided that nothing exciting ever happened in Blalock, when she came across the headline, SNAKE-HANDLING MINISTER ARRESTED. She read the article twice, then studied the photo, which showed the reverend being led away in handcuffs by sheriff's deputies. One witness claimed the deputies were forced to kill a dozen timber rattlers before the Reverend Temple Beechum could be apprehended. She was so intent on the story that she didn't hear Etheridge come into the room.

"Jesus, it's like a fog in here," he said, pulling out the chair opposite her. "You need to carry an exhaust fan with you."

Meg saw that her ashtray was overflowing. "You're one to talk. People can smell your cigars two blocks away."

"Yes, but I'm making an honest effort to cut back."

"Well, I'm too busy to quit smoking right now. I'll just have to worry about that tomorrow, Rhett, honey."

"Right. So, has your day been productive?"

"Uh-huh. I got some good stuff from the women's auxiliary group this morning and from looking at past issues of the paper. I even came up with a couple of story ideas from interviewing Mr. Renfree."

"Your article was good. You believe all that business about faith healing?"

"I'll let you know. I plan to attend the next service and

ask for breast enlargements and more manageable hair.''

He chuckled. ''What do you have there?'' he asked, nodding at the open newspaper.

''I was just reading about the holiness church minister who was fined and forced to spend thirty days in jail for having snakes at his services. The unidentified girl, whom Mrs. Renfree claims saved her husband's life, attends the same church. I think most readers would find the whole thing fascinating.''

Etheridge skimmed the article. ''We've done bits and pieces on them before, usually when there's an arrest. Some of the bigger newspapers came in a couple of years back and wrote articles. Caught a lot of attention. Folks started coming in from all over the country looking to be healed. Still do, from what I understand.''

''I'd like to interview Reverend Beechum,'' Meg said.

''You'll never get in the door,'' he told her. ''Last year we had a reporter come in from *Newsweek* who wrote a scathing piece on them. Called the members freaks and fanatics, suggested they were mentally unbalanced. The reverend threatened to sue the magazine, but nothing ever came of it. Nevertheless, the media were barred from coming back.''

''I won't tell them I'm a reporter.''

''You looking to be the next Geraldo?''

''I have no intention of exploiting these people; I'm merely trying to understand them and perhaps give the public a better understanding. People shouldn't be labeled freaks or lunatics just because their beliefs differ from the mainstream. I'd also like to interview some of the people who go there for healing. Think what it must feel like to have a doctor tell you there's no hope. Anybody in his right mind would look for alternative healing.''

Meg had to pause to catch her breath. She could tell he was unmoved by her spiel. ''You're not going to let me do it, are you?''

He took a long time answering. ''What would you do if I said no?''

Meg shrugged. "What I always do when I want my way," she said. "I'd either hold my breath till I turned blue, or I'd cry." She smiled. "But don't let any of that interfere with your decision."

Blalock High was still as Meg remembered it: scarred wood floors, dun-colored walls with white enamel doors and transom windows. She found the home economics teacher, Clara White, going through a rack of dresses, snipping threads and checking buttons and zippers.

Meg introduced herself, and they shook hands. Clara was an older woman, no doubt approaching retirement, but her figure was trim and her beehive hairdo perfect. She peered at Meg from over the rims of harlequin glasses that boasted a rhinestone in each corner, as she talked of the upcoming fashion show.

"About half of my class isn't much interested in what I teach," she said. "Cooking and sewing, well, the whole thing is a drag as far as they're concerned." She smiled. "And the last thing they want to think about is becoming a homemaker. I'm talking about girls whose parents can afford to send them to college when they graduate. Sure, they want to get married and have a family one day, but that's way off in the future as far as they're concerned."

"Do you have a problem with that?" Meg asked.

"Of course not, dear. Back in my day, it was almost unheard of for girls to go away to college. At least in this part of the country. But I was determined." She pulled off her glasses and wiped them with a tissue. "I don't care what you do with your life, you need to be able to take care of yourself. You should know how to cook, how to sew on a button or hem a skirt.

"I'm more concerned with the poor mountain girls." She paused and shook her head. "Their lives are already mapped out for them. Most of them marry young and have large families. Not only do they need to know how to cook and sew and care for an infant, they have to learn to grow and preserve their own food without risk of contamination. You and I both know there's a world of difference between those living in the foothills and the families in higher elevations. I've seen some changes over the years, but mountain people stick close to tradition. I hope to instill a sense of pride in these young women by having them make their own dresses.'' She showed Meg some of the outfits. "The cloth store in town offers discounts to the students taking my class.''

"What about the girls who can't afford to pay at all?'' Meg asked.

"Oh, I try to help any way I can,'' she said. "I've got a closet full of material at home. Every time I see a sale, I buy more. Some people collect dolls or carousel horses, I collect cloth.'' She chuckled. "Drives my husband crazy.''

Meg smiled. "You're a good teacher, Mrs. White.''

The woman looked surprised by the compliment. "Well, my goodness, that's very kind of you to say so.'' She smoothed her beehive and changed the subject. "I'll look forward to seeing you Friday night at the fashion show.''

Meg left the school and drove to the Wal-Mart, where she purchased alarms for her door and the two windows on either side that were large enough to accommodate a trespasser.

When she arrived back at the office, she found an unusually subdued staff. Even Melinda, who was usually quite talkative, offered a solemn nod and went back to work. Fred Garrison refused to make eye contact. Meg's first thought was that she'd been fired. She barely had time to put her purse away before Etheridge peered out from his half-closed door and called her in.

"Have a seat,'' he said, once she stepped inside his cluttered office. He closed the door and sat down behind his desk.

Meg spied the bottle of Jack Daniel's on his credenza and noticed that his hair was even more disheveled than usual. Yep, he was going to give her her walking papers.

"You want a drink?"

"Not unless you can make me a piña colada with one of those cute umbrellas in it."

His smile was bland. "Sorry, I'm fresh out of umbrellas."

"Mr. Etheridge, is this about that story I wanted to do on the holiness church?" she asked. "I wasn't really going to hold my breath till I turned blue. Sometimes, people don't know how to take me. I guess I come off kind of strong."

"Meg—"

"I know I'm mouthy at times—"

"You're mouthy *all* the time," he said. "Could you just shut up for two minutes?"

"I don't really *have* to be."

He sighed. "I didn't call you in here to fire you. I'm offering you a permanent position with the paper as managing editor. I want you to know, I first offered the job to Fred Garrison, but he's happy with what he's doing. Although you'll officially be over Fred, he knows the paper inside out and will be a big help to you."

"As long as there are no hard feelings," she said.

He went on as though he hadn't heard her. "You'll get an increase in salary, of course, and you'll be eligible for benefits. I'll put it all together first chance I get. Since I never came up with a salary when I hired you, I'll make this offer retroactive from your first day." He paused. "What do you say?"

Meg was elated with the news, but she could tell from his demeanor that something wasn't right. "What about Mr. Murphy?" she asked. "Has he decided not to return after all?"

Etheridge's eyes clouded. "Al won't be coming back." He sat there for a moment, then took a deep breath. "He died last night."

Meg stared at him disbelievingly. "He's dead? Was he in some sort of accident?" The first thought that came to her mind was a drunk Al Murphy behind the wheel of his car, slamming into a station wagon full of kids.

Etheridge leaned back in his chair and wiped his hands down his face. Then he plunged his fingers through his hair and scratched his head, making small tufts of white hair stand up like tiny snow-capped mountains. Finally, he regarded her wearily.

"I suppose there's no use trying to keep it a secret," he said, his tone resigned but sad. "News like this travels fast. Al drank a fifth of gin last night and put a gun to his head."

Ten

CLAY SKINNER was waiting for Meg when she parked the camper at her site. He immediately went about hooking up her water and electricity.

"Why are you here?" she demanded, juggling her Wal-Mart bag, grocery sack, purse, and a multicolored carryall she used instead of a briefcase.

"I was worried about you. Here, let me take that."

"I don't need your help," she said, backing away, "and I don't need you worrying about me. Just leave me alone." She walked to the opposite side of the camper and set her things down while she unlocked her door. Inside, she kicked off her shoes and dumped her bags on the kitchen table.

She turned to close the screen door and found Clay standing there. "Look, I've had a shit day, and I'm not in the mood for company. The only way I know to make it any clearer for you is to surround the place with sharp-shooters." She closed the screen door, leaving the heavy door open so she could air out the place and enjoy the late afternoon breeze. She went about unloading her groceries.

"You don't really mean that." Much to her surprise, Clay opened the door and stepped in. "Besides, I brought dinner." He held up two sacks bearing the name of a popular chicken place. "I'll bet you haven't eaten yet."

Meg gaped at him. "I don't believe this. What makes

you think you can just walk into my home uninvited?"
she said, fists on hips. "Who the hell do you think you
are?"

"I even remembered you prefer dark meat. How's that
for a great memory?"

"I'm not hungry." Actually, she was so hungry she
would've gladly eaten the tuna sandwich she'd thrown
away earlier. But she wasn't up to sharing another evening
with Clay Skinner. "Thanks, anyway. Now, would you
kindly close the door on your way out."

He brushed past her and set the bags on the table. "Listen, Meg, I don't blame you for being mad at me, but you
still have to eat. Why don't we have a cold beer and call
a truce? I'm willing to forgive and forget if you are." He
smiled.

Meg bristled. If he weren't so damn good-looking, she
would have thrown him out on his ass. He could charm
his way inside the pearly gates. "I don't recall asking for
your forgiveness."

"And you probably never will, so I'll be the bigger
person and forgive you anyway." He leaned over, opened
the ice chest, and pulled out two beers. "Mind if I sit?"

"Would it matter if I did?"

He slid into the booth and opened both beers. "Aren't
you going to join me?"

"I'm busy." She finished unloading the groceries. It
was awkward having him there, watching her every move.
She felt self-conscious and clumsy, dropping things, hitting her head on a cabinet. Finally, she grabbed her cigarettes and ashtray and sat in the booth opposite him.

"So, you had a rough day, huh? Did it have anything
to do with the bastard who broke in here last night?"

The concern in Clay's eyes would have touched her,
had she not suspected he had an ulterior motive. Was he
hanging around, hoping he'd get her in bed, just to prove
to himself once and for all that he could? Or was he really
trying to help? She couldn't tell. She'd obviously lost her
ability to read people.

"I got promoted today," she said, and although her voice was calm, bitterness spilled over and gave her words an edge. "I'm now the permanent managing editor of the *Gazette*. Naturally, it means more money."

"Well, no wonder you're pissed. I'd be furious." He took a sip of his beer. "Just wait'll I see Etheridge. I'll teach that son of a bitch to give you a raise and promotion on your second day of work."

Her expression was deadpan. "Very funny, Clay. Aren't you the least bit curious as to *why* I got promoted?"

He thought for a minute. "I know it's a shot in the dark, but could it have something to do with your talent and drive, and a damn good background in newspaper reporting?"

"Al Murphy killed himself last night."

The teasing look in his smile faded. "No way."

"It's true. He shot himself in the head."

Clay just sat there, looking at her as though expecting the punch line to a very bad joke. "That can't be. Al had no reason to do something that crazy."

"He was a drunk, and he was about to lose his job."

"Al didn't have to work. His wife is loaded. He only did it to get out of the house."

"Did he and his wife not get along?"

"He claimed Natalie tended to smother him. She was older than he was, and I think it made her a little insecure at times." He shook his head. "I can't believe this."

"Did she nag him about his drinking?"

"Not often. Al was a happy drunk. Funny as hell. The only time Natalie got riled was when he started flirting with other women."

"Was he faithful to her?"

Clay frowned. "I think he tried to be. Why are you asking me all these questions?"

"Because you seem convinced he wouldn't have taken his own life," she said.

"I guess I didn't know him as well as I thought I did."

"Or maybe he didn't kill himself."

He gave her a funny look. "What's that supposed to mean?"

"Read between the lines, Clay," Meg said, impatient now. "Somebody could have killed him."

"Who?"

"How the hell should I know? I never even met the man."

They drank their beers in silence. Finally, Clay spoke. "I can't think of anybody who'd want to kill Al."

"Did he ever talk about his work? Do you know if he might have been working on something big? Or maybe he was going to do a story that someone else didn't want to get out?"

Clay shook his head. "Like I said, Al and I stopped hanging around together several years ago. He didn't talk about his job much back then, except to remind me over and over how much he hated Bob Etheridge. I think Bob felt the same way."

This surprised her. "So why did Etheridge keep him on?"

"Like I said, his wife owns the paper. She even had that Fred fellow demoted so Al could be managing editor. She probably saw it as a way to keep him busy and out of trouble."

"You mean out of other women's beds."

He shrugged. "If you want to know the truth, I think Bob pretty much rewrote everything Al turned in. I don't know why he put up with it as long as he did. Job security, I suppose."

Meg was thoughtful as she pulled the food out of the bags. "Do you think Etheridge will lose his job over this?"

"Natalie's not stupid. Bob's done a lot for that paper, and she knows it. Let's eat."

Meg took the hint that he didn't want to discuss it any further, and she set his chicken before him. "Everything looks so good," she said. "Do you need a fresh beer, or would you rather have a soft drink?"

"I'm fine." He bit into a french fry. "How's your lip?"

"Better. I put this salve on it, and I can already tell a difference."

"When are we going to talk about what happened?"

"We're not."

"Why are you protecting him?"

"I'm not protecting *him*. I'm trying to keep from hurting someone I love."

Clay put down his food and wiped his hands on a napkin. "That's not wise, Meg. As long as he knows you won't talk, he'll be back."

"I purchased alarms for the door and windows today."

"Look at me."

She raised her eyes to his. "What?"

"Did he rape you?"

"No."

"But that was his intent."

"Take a look around you, Clay. Do you think he was after my valuables?"

"I think he was after something extremely valuable. Something precious."

She opened the lid to her coleslaw. "Oh, yeah? What?"

"You."

Meg looked up, half afraid her eyes would start tearing. She hadn't felt valued or treasured in so long that she'd completely forgotten what it was like. She cleared her throat. "Thank you, Clay. That was a very kind thing to say."

"I'm scared for you. I could stay tonight, in case he returns."

She looked amused. "Nice try, Clay."

He frowned. "I'm in a generous mood tonight, so I won't take offense. As a matter of fact, I'll even put the alarms on after we eat."

Meg was immensely relieved, since she'd read the directions on the alarms and decided it would be easier to just nail the door and windows closed, then pry them open when she needed to go to work or air the place out.

"Unless you're one of those women who gets offended when a man offers to do something that was traditionally considered a man's job," Clay added.

He was probably one of those men who offered to do something, then failed to carry through. "On the contrary, Clay. I feel secure enough in who and what I am as a woman that I don't concern myself with role reversals."

His smile was slow and lazy, and Meg decided it was the sexiest thing she'd ever seen.

"What you're really saying is you don't know shit when it comes to stuff like that."

"I just figured it was the least you could do since I'm planning on taking you out Saturday night."

He blinked. "Come again?"

"Well, now that we've reestablished our friendship, I thought maybe you'd like to go on assignment with me. We could have dinner afterward, my treat."

"What kind of assignment?"

"I thought it would be more fun if I kept it a surprise."

"No surprises, Meg. You either tell me or you ask someone else."

"You used to be more adventuresome."

"I was eighteen at the time. So, what's the assignment?"

She pushed her food aside and lit a cigarette. "Are you familar with the Jesus Christ Holiness Church?"

The lines in his forehead bunched together in a deep frown. "You mean that church way up in the mountains? The one where somebody's always dying from snakebites or poisonings? *That's* your assignment? Is Bob Etheridge crazy?"

Meg wasn't about to tell him it was her idea. "So what you're really trying to say is you're afraid of the place."

"Good one, Meggie. I might have fallen for it in high school, but I'm a little wiser now. You have no business going into that church. What do you hope to accomplish?''

''I'm just trying to gain a better understanding of the people and their practices.'' She repeated what she'd told Etheridge.

''So it wasn't his idea. I should have known this was something you cooked up. I just can't believe Bob's going along with it.''

''Say what you like, Clay, but I'm going, with or without you.''

''I'll go under one condition: Tell me why you're inviting me. I know you wouldn't have a problem going alone.''

''I was hoping you'd take an interest in my work,'' she said, ''especially now that we've developed a friendship.''

''That's crap, and you know it.''

She was fast becoming irritated. ''Okay, I'll tell you the truth, since you're so determined to have everything your way. The reverend is very paranoid—''

''As he should be, since his members are dropping like flies.''

''And I'll never get inside if they suspect I'm a reporter. If we go as husband and wife, I'll have a better chance of getting in.''

''Husband and wife, huh? Does this mean we get to come home and have wild sex afterward?''

The idea of coming back and having wild sex with Clay was the most appealing thought she'd had in ages. But Meg knew how she was; one night in his arms and she'd fall in love with him all over again. And Clay wouldn't think twice about breaking her heart; in fact, that would even the score between them, as far as he was concerned.

''I suppose I'm to take your silence as a no,'' he said, reaching for the Wal-Mart bag.

Meg studied Clay as he read the directions on the alarms. She wished she could let herself confide in him. She remembered a time when she'd told him everything, even the dumb stuff that people often kept to themselves. She'd trusted him and everybody else.

That was before she'd seen what terrible things people did to one another, before Roy had made a fool of her and she knew there was no trusting anyone.

"I need to have a look at your tools," Clay said.

Meg pulled a drawer open next to the sink and reached inside. She handed him a screwdriver and a hammer.

Clay just looked at them. "You're kidding, right?"

"Do I look like a maintenance man?"

He slid from the booth. "I'll grab some tools from my truck."

Meg straightened the camper while Clay affixed the alarms to the door and windows. "You're supposed to be able to hear the alarm for two city blocks," he told her.

She laughed. "Travis'll piss all over himself." She didn't realize what she'd said until the words were already out. A feeling of dread washed over her, and she turned and looked at Clay.

He seemed to transform right in front of her eyes. "I should've known that fucker would come after you. He's never been able to keep his dick in his pants."

"Clay—"

"I'll rip his throat out with my teeth." He tossed the screwdriver aside and turned for the door.

Meg could feel the panic rising in her chest as she tried to block him. "Clay, wait! This is why I didn't tell you in the first place. I was afraid you'd do something crazy."

"Meg, please step aside."

She could feel his anger by the way his chest heaved against hers. "If you go against my wishes on this, I swear to God, I'll never trust you with anything as long as I live."

He grabbed her arms and shook her. "Why the hell are you covering for him?" he yelled, so loud the sound seemed to ricochet off the walls.

Meg was so startled she could only stare back at him. Tears stung the backs of her eyes. Something blocked her throat and made swallowing impossible. "I'm not," she managed at last, "covering for him."

He released her. "Sure looks that way to me," he said, just as loud as before. "Maybe you're hoping he'll come back."

Meg's anger flared into rage and she took a swing at him, but he caught her by the wrist. Before she knew it, she was flat against the wall, both arms pinned behind her. "Let me go," she said, between gritted teeth. Tears streamed down her cheeks.

"You're the one who wanted to play rough," he said, his face an inch from hers. "So why are you crying?"

She almost shivered as his warm breath caressed her cheek. His voice was deep and husky, his body rock solid as it pressed into hers. "You've never done anything nice for anybody in your life," she said. "How could you possibly understand?"

"Try me." It wasn't a request; it was an order.

"Beryl's pregnant, okay?" Meg said, on a sob that had just as much anger in it as pain. "She's already had a couple of miscarriages. I just don't think this is the perfect time to tell her she's married to the world's biggest prick. I thought I'd save it for the baby shower. How's that?"

"She probably already knows, Meg. Not the part about Travis coming over here, but your sister's no dummy. As bad as it sounds, I don't think a miscarriage is the worst that can happen to her. Sounds like she needs to get the hell out."

Tears were still streaming down Meg's face. "I don't think either of us is in the position to judge Beryl. We've made our share of mistakes."

"You know something, Meggie? You're beautiful even when you cry."

She noticed his voice had dropped an octave. "Don't start that nonsense with me, Clay Skinner. I've seen what I look like after a crying jag. Now, would you mind releasing this death grip you have on me? I'm in pain."

"You're not in pain; you're just incapacitated. And I

have no intention of letting you go, because you'll slug me the minute I do.''

"I'm not going to hit you." She saw the doubt in his eyes. "I swear."

"You'll swear to anything. Besides, if I let go you won't let me kiss you."

"Damn right I won't." She said it convincingly, but it was all she could do to disguise the shiver that followed.

"So I'm going to take my kiss first."

He'd no sooner got the words out before he leaned forward and touched her lips, taking care not to hurt the area that had been cut. He ran his tongue along her bottom lip, then drew it gently between his teeth. Meg felt a tugging sensation low in her stomach. He released her arms, and his hands appeared on either side of her head, as though anchoring it in place so he could do with her as he wished.

Meg couldn't have stopped him had she wanted to. In fact, when he raised his head, it was all she could do not to cry out in protest.

"I'd make love to you right now if I thought you were ready."

She thought the bottom would fall out of her stomach right there and humiliate her forever. "Assuming I would let you," she replied.

He brushed away the damp tracks left by her tears. He kissed each corner of her mouth, then her wound. "I think you could be persuaded." He nibbled her chin and moved down her throat.

Meg closed her eyes. She could not remember when kissing had felt so good. "In your dreams, Skinner."

He chuckled softly, and she felt a sudden damp hiss of air at her pulse point. The tiny hairs along the back of her neck seemed to quiver in anticipation. Her body was heating up fast; she felt flushed and dizzy. She could feel her nipples drawing in, tightening. She tried to calm herself. The last thing she wanted was to appear overly eager—

but it wasn't easy for someone who had sex less often than an ugly nun.

"Clay?" Her voice was unsteady. She just wasn't used to this much pleasure. They either needed to get on with it or stop all together.

He pulled back. "Yeah, I know. I'd better go."

She looked at him. Of all the choices they had, he'd picked the dumbest. She sighed. "You're probably right."

"We're still on for Saturday night, right?"

"Of course."

"Don't forget to wear something plain and kinda shabby," he said. "Leave the makeup and jewelry at home. Women aren't supposed to wear anything that'll make a man desire them."

"How 'bout I just dunk my face in battery acid and be done with it?"

"And don't even think about firing up a cigarette where anybody can see you."

"Gee, Clay, you certainly seem to know a lot about the women. Are you sure you haven't dated one or two?"

"Cute, Meg. Real cute."

"Anything else I need to know?"

He grinned. "Oh, yeah. Women are supposed to be submissive, so there'll be no talking back when I tell you what to do."

"Then I'd suggest you not try to tell me what to do, pal."

"And I'm not sure about this one, but I think the women are supposed to walk behind their husbands. You know, sort of hang back a couple of feet? That's to show respect."

"I can do that," she said sweetly. "Just watch your back."

Eleven

THE REVEREND Temple Beechum studied the neat column of figures in the ledger with the close attention of a man who had to work hard to understand what he was seeing. A single line creased his forehead, beginning at the top of his nose, where a pair of thick sable brows almost touched, and running straight up and disappearing into a widow's peak. He had never been very good with numbers, so he counted on Purvis Dill, the associate pastor, to take care of the church's financial affairs. Purvis could whip through a column of figures like there was nothing to it. And he could be trusted not to discuss church business with others.

"You're smart as a whip," Temple said with pride. The young man was like a son to him. "You're wasting your time in that mill."

"I have to earn a living," Purvis said. "Besides, the work isn't bad, and I like the people. Most of them," he added, thinking of Travis Lytle.

"I hear you've been pulling double shifts."

"Folks're passing around some kind of virus. I don't mind the extra hours."

"I hope you're not getting greedy, Son. The Good Book teaches us to store our treasures in heaven, not on earth."

"I've been having problems with my truck, and the water heater at home is busted," Purvis said.

"Worldly problems," Temple said, dismissing them with a wave of his hand. "You're not concentrating on what's important."

"I do my best."

The older man regarded him thoughtfully. "What's wrong, boy?" he asked gently. "I know something's troubling you; you haven't been yourself for weeks."

"Nothing's wrong," Purvis said. "I've just got things on my mind."

"You've always been able to talk to me before. How many times you reckon we've gotten down on our knees and prayed together over a problem? Ain't no problem or sin too big for the Lord, you know."

"What makes you think I've sinned?" Purvis asked quickly.

"I wasn't accusing you. Besides, only God knows what's in our hearts." He was quiet for a moment. "But I've known you all your life, and I can tell when you're unhappy. You need to lay down your burdens."

Purvis clasped his hands together and looked down at the floor. "I don't have your faith, Reverend."

"I'm more than twice your age. I've had more practice, is all." He closed the ledger and passed it across his desk to Purvis, who stood and walked to one corner of the room and lifted a slat in the floor. A combination safe had been partially buried in the ground beneath it. He opened the safe and stuck the book inside, where neat rows of cash had been stacked and bound together with rubber bands. He pushed the slat in place and covered it with a bookcase. When he returned to the desk, he looked weary.

"Will there be anything else, Reverend?" he asked. "I'm feeling kinda tired tonight."

Temple locked gazes with him. "You're not thinking of leaving the church, are you, boy?"

Purvis hadn't been expecting it, but he should have. There was plenty bothering him these days, and the reverend would be the first to notice. He tried to swallow, but there wasn't a drop of spit to be found. There would be no spit in hell, either, the reverend often preached.

"Leave the church?" Purvis said, as though he couldn't imagine such a thing. "Why, no sir!" He averted his gaze. He wasn't good at lying. Leaving the church was all he thought about these days.

Twelve

AT THE staff meeting the following morning, Meg
noted Bob Etheridge's bloodshot eyes and the weary
look on his face, and wondered if he'd slept the night
before. Was he feeling guilty over Al Murphy's death?
She longed to assure him it wasn't his fault, but he seemed
distant, unapproachable. She knew he was assisting Al's
wife with funeral and business matters, but that's about
all she knew.

Fred Garrison hurried in, apologized for being late, and
took the chair next to Meg's. She didn't miss the look of
concern on his face as he studied his boss.

"Okay," Etheridge said, his tone suggesting it was
business as usual. Still, his voice was strained and distant.
"We've got two days to get the paper out, and I'm going
to be gone much of that time. I'm counting on everybody
to pitch in." He turned to Fred. "Since you know what's
involved in getting the paper to print, I want you to stay
close and concentrate on that. Meg can cover for you if
something comes up."

"Be glad to," Fred replied.

The next half hour passed quickly as they tried to cover
as much as they could. Etheridge kept looking at his wristwatch as if he had to be somewhere. Finally, he reached
for his jacket.

"Before I forget," he said, "Meg has agreed to join us
permanently as managing editor. She brings a great deal

of experience with her; I hope you'll join me in welcoming her to the paper.'' He paused. ''Now, before the rumors start circulating, let's set the record straight. I offered the position to Fred first, since that's the job he was originally hired for. He's assured me he's happy where he is. Okay, let's go to work.''

Two hours later, Fred hurried over to Meg's desk. ''We've got a body.''

She looked up from her work. For a minute she thought she was back in Atlanta. ''Come again?''

He looked harried, and the bald area near the front of his skull was damp with sweat. ''Actually, it sounds like skeletal remains. Some contractor was digging a basement out in Rolling Hills Subdivision, and he came across it. Can you let go of what you're doing?''

''Gee, Fred, I don't know. Edwina Thompson's championship Maltese is missing, and she's trying to rally volunteers for a search party. There's even a substantial reward for the safe return of little Moppet.'' She was already reaching for her purse. ''To tell you the truth, I was thinking of taking the day off and looking for the dog myself.''

He stood there for a moment, mouth agape.

''I'm kidding, okay? Of course, I'll go.''

''I should warn you,'' Fred told her on her way out. ''The sheriff can be a jerk when he wants to.''

''Hey, jerks are my specialty.''

Meg was headed toward the outskirts of Blalock. She was about two miles shy of the interstate when she spied the sign for Rolling Hills Subdivision. She turned in and found herself in a neat, middle-class neighborhood. A narrow road led through a wooded section and dead-ended at a site surrounded by several cars from the sheriff's department, an emergency vehicle, and a larger-than-average station wagon. Yellow crime-scene tape was stretched around a gaping hole in the earth, but deputies were still working to keep curious neighbors at bay.

Meg parked and climbed out. She spotted Clay almost immediately and realized he must've reported the incident. He was talking to Sheriff Nate Overton, a tall heavyset man who had been in office for as long as Meg could remember. Nate's hair was almost completely gray now, and he'd put on a good sixty to seventy pounds since she'd last seen him. His khaki shirt strained so hard against his big belly that she couldn't help but wonder what kept the buttons from popping off.

Clay looked pleased to see her. "I see the newspaper sent their best reporter," he said.

She smiled and looked at Overton. "What have you got, Sheriff?"

He frowned. "Do I know you?" he asked in a gruff voice.

"Meg Gentry," she said, offering her hand. "Used to be Holcombe. I've been away for a while."

"Henry Holcombe's daughter," Clay added. "She just started with the *Gazette*. Before that, she worked the crime beat for that big Atlanta paper."

The sheriff ignored her outstretched hand and regarded her with a look of indifference. "Where's Fred Garrison?"

She lowered her hand. "Fred couldn't make it. Is that the medical examiner?" she asked, nodding toward a shaggy-haired man with wire-rimmed glasses.

Clay nodded. "His name is Dr. Grimes. Folks call him Dr. Grim behind his back, on account of what he does for a living."

"He's busy right now," the sheriff said. "Don't bother him."

Meg turned to Clay. The smile on his face told her he found the whole thing amusing. She, on the other hand, did not. "Who actually discovered the bones?" she asked.

"I did," Clay said. "I was watching one of my men dig a basement with a backhoe when I spotted what looked like bones protruding from some kind of cloth. It was real eerie climbing down there, curious as to what else I'd find, but dreading it at the same time. I took a shovel and tried to remove some of the dirt, then told myself I'd better call the authorities. So I—''

''Excuse me for interrupting, but what exactly does a backhoe do?''

Sheriff Overton gave a snort of disgust and walked away.

''Just as I thought,'' Meg muttered. ''He's crazy about me.''

''You did that on purpose.'' He stepped closer. ''You're looking mighty fine this morning.''

She gazed back at him, thinking he didn't look so bad himself with the sun glinting off his dark hair. There was a ruggedness about him that she found very appealing. ''I'm not allowed to flirt on company time,'' she said. ''Do you have anything to add to your story?''

''I'll make something up if you'll meet me for lunch.''

''I can't. We're on deadline and Etheridge is out.''

''Another time, then.''

Meg caught up with the sheriff a few minutes later. He didn't look happy to see her. ''Sheriff, is there anything you can give me on the remains that were discovered earlier?''

''Nope. That's the coroner's job. You know that as well as I do.''

''Yes, but the medical examiner seems to be busy at the moment, and you look like you've got some time on your hands.''

He glared at her. ''I'll tell you one thing, Miss Gentry. Nobody knows what we've got over there, and I'm going to be mad as hell if you go and stir folks up by planting wild ideas in their head about a dead body. That could be the remains of somebody's dog, for all we know.''

''Thank you, Sheriff; I'll certainly keep that in mind. Is it okay if I take a look?''

''No!''

''Oh, let her have a quick peek, Nate,'' Clay said. ''What can it hurt?''

"She ain't going to see nothing but a few dirty bones wrapped in rotten cloth. Besides, I don't need her to come in and bungle up my crime scene."

"I've never botched a crime scene in my life," Meg said. "But I have watched a few cops run roughshod over pertinent evidence."

Meg left the two men arguing and hurried over to where the action was taking place. Nate was right; there wasn't much to see at the moment, and she'd be wasting good film if she tried to get a picture. Dr. Grimes and a younger man were deep in discussion, but she couldn't make out what they were saying.

"What are they doing?" she whispered to a black female deputy whose job seemed to be keeping the neighbors and other curiosity seekers at bay. The deputy glanced at Meg's press badge.

"It's okay," Meg told her. "The sheriff said I could take a look."

The woman nodded. She looked young. Her name tag read JENKINS. "Dr. Grimes is trying to bring up the remains without disturbing the integrity of the scene," she said, as though reciting it from a text book on forensics. "After that, they're going to sift through the dirt to make sure nothing is left behind. That part might take awhile."

"Has he indicated whether or not he thinks the bones are human?"

"No, but they sure look human to me."

The doctor's assistant walked over. "We're going to bring it up now," he told the deputy. "Can you try to get these people out of the way so we have a clear path to the wagon?"

"Sure." The deputy went back to work.

Meg rejoined Clay and the sheriff, who were sipping coffee. "Your deputy seems to think the bones are human," she told Overton.

Nate gave a snort of disgust. "Who, Jenkins? Hell, she can't even clean her gun unless someone's in the room to make sure she don't shoot her foot off."

Meg lit a cigarette and waited for Dr. Grimes to finish his business so she could question him. She was only vaguely aware of the story Nate was sharing with Clay.

". . . so finally, I sent over half a dozen of my men to run those fanatics off. Confiscated a bunch of timber rattlers while they were at it, and all of it taking place right smack-dab in the middle of the courthouse square. Can you believe it?''

Meg suddenly perked at the mention of snakes, but she stepped away and closely watched the goings-on at the dig site. If Nate Overton thought she was interested in what he had to say about the holiness people, he'd clam up immediately.

". . . what they do behind closed doors is their business as far as I'm concerned. Course, the mayor don't see it that way. He's just gunnin' to close 'em down. Good thing he was home sick that day or the whole bunch woulda been run outta town. I say, let 'em be. It's not like I don't already have enough work to do.''

Meg wondered at Nate's remark. He did not strike her as a tolerant man—unless there was something in it for him. She saw they were bringing up a stretcher, and hurried toward Dr. Grimes, who was headed in the direction of the oversize station wagon—or meat wagon, as his assistant had callously referred to it.

"Excuse me, Doctor," she called out. "Dr. Grimes?'' He paused and looked up. She stepped closer. "I'm Meg Gentry with the *Gazette*—''

He acknowledged her with a brief smile. If he disliked the media like most MEs, he didn't show it. "I'm afraid I don't have anything for you right now, Miss Gentry," he said politely.

"I know it's too soon to tell much," she said. "Would you mind if I called you in a couple of days? When it's convenient, of course.''

"That's fine." He handed her a card and walked the rest of the way to his car, where he opened the door and reached inside for a clipboard. He looked up after a moment as though he could feel her watching him. "Was there anything else?"

"Huh?" Meg flushed. "Oh, no. It's just"—she paused—"I'm fascinated with your line of work."

He studied her a moment as though trying to figure out if she was serious or just pulling his leg. "Fascinated, huh? That's a new one. Most people don't like to think about what I do for a living."

Meg stepped closer. "I've often wondered if I could handle watching an autopsy," she said quietly, as though confiding in him. "Not that it should bother me, what with all the gore I've *already* seen in my life." At his questioning look, she went on. "I worked the crime beat several years for the *Atlanta Journal and Constitution*."

"Yes, then I would imagine you've just about seen it all."

"You wouldn't believe the shoddy work that goes on in the ME's office there," she said, deciding it was okay to lie if it served in building a solid relationship with Dr. Grimes. "I've heard how meticulous you are. You would put those bozos to shame." She slapped her hand over her mouth. "Oh, I can't believe I said that. Sometimes words just spew from my mouth without getting clearance from my brain."

He coughed as though embarrassed. "Yes, well, I'm sure you meant no harm. I can't even imagine what it would be like working in a city that size; the number of bodies coming in must be staggering. I can afford to be a bit fastidious in my work, because I don't have as much going on."

"I didn't think of that," Meg replied.

"Of course, I'd imagine they have an army of personnel," he added, "and I have to assume their equipment is state of the art."

"Yes, it's very sophisticated," she said, although she didn't have a clue.

"That's why they're so good at solving crimes," he told her. "They should try working with the antiques I use.'' He squared his shoulders. ''Nice talking to you, Miss Gentry.''

Meg shrugged and started for her camper, where she found Clay waiting for her. Nate was standing at the hole watching the deputies sift dirt.

''Did you get what you needed?'' Clay asked.

''Oh, yeah. It just doesn't get any better than this. What bug crawled up the sheriff's behind?''

''He's got problems.''

''Right—like he's the only one. I can't believe I left a big, important story to come down here and be insulted by some sour-faced bigot.''

''His wife is mentally ill.''

''Damn right she is. Can you imagine a sane woman marrying him?''

''I'm serious. Cut him some slack, okay?''

She held her hands up as though surrendering. ''Okay. But I'm not going to let the guy push me around.''

Clay moved aside, reached for the door handle, and opened it so she could step into the cab. He waited until she was settled. ''I trust none of your alarms went off last night.''

''It was a quiet evening,'' she replied, still feeling the sting of his remark. If Clay expected her to kowtow to a bullying sheriff, then he could take his charm and good looks elsewhere.

The sound of a car made them look up. Dr. Grimes pulled beside Meg's camper. He gave it the once-over. ''Those your wheels?'' he asked.

''It's a loaner,'' she said. ''My Harley's in the shop.''

He seemed to think that was funny. ''Since you have such an interest in forensics, you might be interested in seeing what we do with bones. How about I give you a holler at the office in a day or so?''

Her luck seemed to be changing. ''Sounds great, Doctor. I look forward to it.'' She waved as he drove away.

''What's that about?'' Clay asked.

''Oh, I just proved once again that flattery can get you everywhere.''

Thirteen

BACK AT the office, Meg glanced through her messages and discovered her mother had called. She dialed her parents' number while she waited for the computer to warm up. Alma Holcombe answered on the first ring.

"How come you never call?" she accused, the minute Meg identified herself.

"I've been busy. We're short staffed here." She knew no excuse would be good enough.

"I heard about that young man taking his own life. And they're going to bury him right in the family plot, on consecrated ground. In my day, that was unheard of. Which explains why your great-aunt Beatrice was buried across the street from the cemetery. They found her with her head in a gas oven."

Meg sometimes wondered if her mother made stuff up to torment her. She'd never even heard of an aunt Beatrice. "Was there something you wanted, Mom?" she asked, knowing she had an article to get out.

"I didn't know I needed a reason to call my own daughter, but yes, I wanted to invite you to dinner tonight."

"I have to work late," she replied. "Like I said, we're short on people, and we're on deadline to boot."

"You still have to eat, Margaret. Besides, the paper isn't due out till Sunday morning. This is Thursday."

"There's a lot to do in the meantime, Mom. Could we plan dinner for another night?"

"I suppose," Alma said in a weak, tortured voice that Meg knew was meant to make her feel selfish and guilty until she was old enough to collect Social Security.

Fred Garrison shot her a questioning look. "Look, Mom, I really do have to go." She hung up after promising to call first chance she got.

Meg typed her article, which amounted to only four paragraphs even though she'd stretched it as far as she could. "This is all I have for now," she said, handing it to Fred once she'd printed it out. He read it quickly.

"So we don't know if the remains are human?" he asked.

"Dr. Grimes promised to call me. He even invited me to watch some kind of procedure. If you don't mind, I'd like to follow up on it. I sort of have a personal interest in it now."

Fred looked amused. "Don't tell me you've already grown bored writing about garden parties and weddings."

"Nothing wrong with a little variety now and then. Not that I'd even consider giving up the Lifestyles section. I get a charge being on the cutting edge of news. Speaking of which, has anyone heard from Moppet, the missing Maltese?"

Fred chuckled. "Edwina Thompson called while you were out. The animal shelter has had the dog the whole time. Seems she lost her collar in flight, got her lustrous coat dirty and tangled, and was picked up as a plain ol' stray. Edwina's having a fit, claiming the shelter mistreated Moppet by locking her in a cage for three days and giving her dry food."

"Sounds like they should have put Edwina in a cage." They both laughed.

"As for the bone story, you're welcome to it," Fred told her. "I've got enough on my platter. By the way, I'm glad you've signed on permanently."

"Um, about the job—I feel like it should have been

yours. I wasn't looking for something with paperwork."

"Listen, I'll tell you like I told Etheridge. I've been in the newspaper business a long time, and I've had all the recognition and glory I want. Not that you're going to get those things on a paper this size," he added quickly. "I've suffered one heart attack, and I don't need the stress or headaches that come with a bunch of administrative duties." He patted her on the shoulder. "You have my blessings."

Meg knew she was going to enjoy working with him. "Now that we've cleared the air, let me tell you, Sheriff Overton was a royal pain in the ass."

Fred shook his head sadly. "Nate's personal problems have gotten to him. He's still a good sheriff if you can overlook the sour disposition. Which isn't always easy," he said.

"Have you heard from Etheridge?"

"No, but we called the funeral home. Services are at ten Saturday morning, open to the immediate family only. We're all chipping in on flowers. See Melinda if you're interested in donating anything."

They worked well into the evening. By seven o'clock, most of the office staff had gone home, but Meg and Fred stayed behind and worked with Phil Jones, the production manager, deciding layout on stories that had been assigned in advance and allotting space for late-breaking items. They finished up at nine o'clock, and Fred began turning out lights as Phil went out the back way.

"Are you hungry?" he asked Meg as they walked to the front door.

"Starved."

"The E&M Restaurant is running their Salisbury steak special tonight. I usually go there every night, since I don't trust my own cooking. You're welcome to join me. It's only a five-minute walk from here."

"And here I was looking forward to the stale pimento cheese sandwich in my desk," she said.

They left the building a few minutes later and started

down the well-lit sidewalk at a leisurely pace. Meg shoved her hands into the pockets of her jacket. The air was nippy, but it felt good to be out after having been stuck inside for so long.

"This part of town looks almost exactly as it did when I was a kid," she said.

"You grew up here?" Fred asked.

She nodded. "Back then I thought it was the most boring place in the world to live."

"What about now?"

"So far, I haven't had time to be bored, but I look forward to it."

The E&M hadn't changed much in the years Meg had been gone. The walls were still a dark beige, and although the booths looked relatively new, they were the same color red they'd been before. Meg was warmed by the sameness.

They were seated right away by the owner's wife, who had acquired more wrinkles and gray hair, and maybe a pound or two of flesh, but her smile was the same. She hugged Meg when she saw her, and asked about her family.

A slender middle-aged waitress with reddish brown hair and cute freckles waited on them. Her name tag read SUE. She set a small dish of pickled beets before them and offered menus, but they ordered the special.

"What would y'all like to drink?" Sue asked.

"I'll have tea," Meg said.

"What would you like, Frank?" the waitress asked.

Meg glanced at Fred and saw that he was staring at the waitress. When he continued to sit there and stare, she kicked him under the table.

He looked startled. "Huh?"

"What do you want to drink?"

"Uh, tea."

Sue thanked them and walked away. Meg stared at him. "What was *that* all about?"

"What?"

"You were giving that waitress goo-goo eyes."

He blushed. "I was not."

"I was sitting right here watching you, Fred. I thought you were going to spontaneously combust. What's the deal here?"

"I sort of have a crush on her," he said under his breath, "and she can't even remember my name." He slid lower in his seat.

"So change your name. How much can it cost?" She saw the look of misery in his eyes. "Boy, you've got it bad. How long has this been going on?"

"She just started working here a couple of months ago. I try to get a table in her station when I come in, and I always leave a good tip."

"So this is why you come here every night. Tell me something. Have you ever been married?"

"Me? Oh, yes, I was married for thirty years. My wife died three years ago."

"I'm sorry. Do you have children?"

"Four daughters. And nine grandchildren," he added, almost whispering the words. "I don't want Sue to know about the grandchildren just yet. Some people tend to think you're old the minute they hear you're a grandparent. They think you can't, uh, you know."

"What?"

"Cut the mustard."

Sue brought their beverages and set them down. Fred got so flustered he dropped his fork. She promised to bring him another one.

Meg lit a cigarette. "Do your children live in Blalock?" she asked, trying to draw him into conversation.

"Oh, no. They're in Asheville. That's where I'm from. Bob Etheridge called me to offer his condolences when my wife died—we went to college together, you see—anyway, it was sheer coincidence that he had an opening at the *Gazette*. I took an early retirement at the Asheville paper, and here I am."

"Do you miss your girls?"

"Yeah, but they were driving me crazy. They thought I needed looking after once their mother died."

Sue delivered their food and handed Fred a clean fork. He dropped his spoon. She returned with two of everything. "I keep telling Frank he needs Velcro," she said to Meg.

"Great idea," Meg told her.

"How am I going to get her to notice me?" Fred asked, once the waitress hurried off to another table.

"Drop that fork again, and I'll stab you in the heart with it," Meg said. "That should get her attention. Just kidding, Fred," she added quickly when he looked horrified. "Don't worry, I'll think of something. Before long, ol' Sue'll be hanging off you like an orangutan."

"From your lips to God's ears."

Meg gave him the thumbs-up sign and finished her meal. Sue carried their dishes away and brought them coffee. Although Fred seemed more relaxed now, Meg got a little nervous each time he picked up his cup.

"How well did you know Al Murphy?" she asked

"Al?" Fred shrugged and stared into his cup. "I knew him well enough to know he had no business working in a newspaper office. He would have done better selling advertising, but his wife wanted him to have a job with a little prestige."

"Didn't you resent it when he ended up with your job?"

Fred looked surprised. "Has Melinda been gossiping again? She had the hots for Al, you know. Wouldn't surprise me if there was a little hanky-panky going on at the time. I've heard him promise more than one woman that he was going to leave his wife for her."

"Do you know if he was working on anything important when he died?"

"A fifth of gin, most likely."

Sue returned and refilled their coffee. Meg waited until she'd walked away, and Fred gave her his attention once more. "I take it ol' Al wasn't on your Christmas gift list."

"Bob and I both got tired of rewriting the crap he brought in. I'll give Al credit for one thing, though. He had a nose for news. He picked up a lot of gossip while hanging out in bars, and he followed through on it. Unfortunately, he didn't know the first thing about journalism."

"Do you think he really committed suicide?"

"That's what they're calling it. Personally, I think he got caught with somebody's wife. The sheriff told me they found him way up in the mountains, parked on the side of the road with his head—" He paused. "Well, never mind."

"Don't worry, I know what it looks like." She sighed. "I wish I could get my hands on any notes or files he might have had with him."

"The car was clean. Nate said they tore it apart looking for a suicide note. Nothing has turned up at his house either. If he was working on something, we'll probably never know."

They left the restaurant a few minutes later, once Fred tucked a generous tip beneath the edge of his plate. "So, have you figured out a way I can win Sue over?" he asked as they stepped outside the front door.

Meg answered with a question of her own. "When's the last time you bought clothes?"

"My wife used to buy all my clothes before she got sick. I guess it's been a few years."

"There you go. You need a new wardrobe." She studied him from beneath a streetlight. E&M customers came and went. "And lose the sweaters, Fred. They make you look older."

"What am I supposed to wear?"

"Go to a menswear store and pick up a couple of sports jackets. Lean toward casual. You own any denim?"

"Just what I wore in college."

"No, Fred, you'll need something a little more recent than Vietnam. Buy stonewashed jeans, and get yourself some of those new canvas pants. For dressier occasions, you'll need pleated twill trousers, and—''

''I don't know what any of that is,'' he said helplessly. ''Would you go with me? There's a midnight madness sale going on tonight at the Belk Simpson department store on the highway. I got a coupon book in the mail yesterday. It's in my car.''

''You mean go tonight?''

''We could be in and out in an hour,'' he said. ''I'll treat you to dinner at the E&M next week.''

Meg was tired, and she didn't think she could sit through another dinner with him at the E&M. But she saw the hopeful look on his face and knew she had to help. ''Okay, okay.''

She started to turn, but the sound of childish laughter caught her attention. From out of the shadows, Clay suddenly appeared, holding a small girl's hand. Meg smiled and raised her hand to wave, then decided against it when a blond, buxom woman hurried up from the rear. Becky Parker looked even better than she had in her high school days. Clay pulled the door open to the restaurant and held it for his ex-wife and daughter, and they stepped inside. He was just about to follow when something made him look up. His gaze landed on Meg.

''Come on, Fred,'' she muttered. ''Let's get the hell out of here.''

''Is something wrong?'' Fred asked, rushing to catch up with her.

Meg shook her head. ''No. For a minute, I thought I saw someone I knew.''

Fourteen

SARA BEECHUM glanced at the clock on her bedside table and saw that it was late. She was still upset over the argument she'd had with her father, and couldn't sleep. In the next bed, her older sister, Maybelline, already slept peacefully. Sara knew she would regret this loss of sleep come morning, when the alarm sounded at five-thirty. After a quick cup of coffee, she and Maybelline would begin their chores: tending the hogs and chickens, weeding the winter garden, cleaning the house, washing clothes, and cooking.

Somewhere in their busy schedule, they would have to prepare for three individual services to be held at the Jesus Christ Holiness Church that weekend. Once their father wrote his sermons, it was up to Maybelline and her to choose the scripture and hymns to go with them. There would not be time for much else. There never was.

In the beginning, Sara had been more than willing to meet the challenges of the church. She knew the Bible well—it was the only thing she and her sister were allowed to read, other than school books. Temple Beechum did not permit television, magazines, or newspapers in the house because he felt the only news they should be concerned with was the Lord's. Sara carefully practiced reading Scriptures in front of the bathroom mirror, the only mirror allowed in the house because Temple feared his daughters would become vain like the girls in town. Like his wife had, before she'd abandoned the family. Sara had been told more than once she resembled her mother, "Tiny" Beechum, as they'd called her because she had been so small. Perhaps that's why her father watched her so closely.

Sara seldom left the house unless he was with her, and she knew his reasons. He firmly believed she was a Chosen One, handpicked by God to do His work and perform miracles. With this being the case, she must remain pure and chaste. She would never be permitted to marry or have children. Maybelline could visit friends now and then, but Sara's outings were limited to sickbeds and wakes, and, of course, church services. If a young man even so much as looked in her direction, the deacons ousted him from the community.

Sara had finally worked up the nerve, that very evening, to tell her father how she felt. He'd been in the living room, sitting in the old recliner resting his eyes, when she'd approached him with her decision to leave the mountains for a time and go to college. She planned to be a social worker.

His eyes had almost bugged out of his head. "Where do you plan to get the money?"

"I could get a student loan. Or apply for scholarships." They'd had this discussion in her senior year of high school, when her guidance counselor had encouraged her to continue her education.

"We already got us a social worker," he'd replied.

"Nobody likes Mrs. Beasley, Pa. You know how mountain people feel about city folks. There's more women dying of cervical cancer in Appalachia than anywhere else in this country because they don't get checkups like they should. Young mothers refuse to get prenatal care because they don't trust doctors. And what's worse, they're not immunizing their babies. They don't know the first thing about preventive medicine; the only time they see a doctor is in the emergency room, and by then it's usually too late."

"Our faith teaches divine intervention, Sara," Temple had pointed out. "Maybe you should get some of these women to attend church more often. I'm more concerned about these people's souls, daughter. Life is a drop in the bucket compared to eternity. God told Adam and Eve there would be hardships when they ate of the forbidden fruit.

"Now, go on about your chores so I can rest. There'll be no more talk of you goin' off to some college where young people drink and take drugs and have sex with whoever they want to. You call that gettin' an education?" He gave a grunt. "I call that Sodom and Gomorrah."

He rubbed his eyes and leaned back in his chair. "I'm still tryin' to live down the shame your mother brung upon this here family. I'll not have a daughter of mine living the life of a harlot."

"But, Pa—"

"The subject is closed," he'd told her with a look of finality that had left no room for argument. "We will not speak of it again."

She had known it was useless to argue. It didn't matter that she was of legal age and could do as she pleased. She'd never once crossed her pa; the mere thought scared her to death.

Now, as Sara tried to fall asleep, she knew it wasn't likely her pa would ever change his mind. She would never escape these mountains.

Fifteen

ETHERIDGE SHOWED up late Friday afternoon, his forehead so deeply creased it appeared as though the lines were permanent. Meg offered him a bright smile and received a grunt in return. "Are the part-time copy editors here?" he asked.

She nodded. "They're in the conference room going over the paper word for word."

"I need about fifteen minutes at my computer," he said. "So I can finish my editorial."

"What's it about?" the production manager asked. "I can start working on a headline."

"It lists all the things Mayor Bradley promised at the last election but never followed through with." He held up a piece of paper. "I've been making notes all along. Also, it gives reasons why he should never be allowed to serve another term. I'm tired of these no-talents getting jobs they don't deserve. Other people always suffer."

Meg noted the anger in his voice, and the sudden tension that followed. Etheridge wasn't just pissed over the mayor.

The production manager snapped his fingers. "Okay, how about calling it 'Mayor Bradley Is a Lying Piece of Shit and Should Die'?"

"Naw, too vague," Etheridge said. "I want something the voters will remember come election time."

"The reason he can't get things done is because the

city council hates him," Fred said. "If he voted for clean drinking water, they'd want dirty."

Etheridge glanced at him, then did a double take at his Calvin Klein jeans, hiking boots, and new leather bomber jacket. The jacket was unzipped and revealed a bright rugby shirt. "Who the hell are you supposed to be?" he asked. "A fashion model?"

Meg, who didn't want Fred's feelings hurt, jumped in. "Just start a nasty rumor about the mayor," she said. "This time next year, folks won't be able to think of anything else when they go to vote."

"Just title it 'Mayor Doesn't Live Up to Promises,' " Etheridge said, and disappeared into his office.

It was coming up to six when Etheridge came out and handed his article to Fred. "See if you think it's too strong," he said. "Like where I suggest we put a bomb in his car." He motioned for Meg, and she followed him inside his office.

"You doing okay?" he asked, once he'd closed the door and they'd both seated themselves. "I feel like I've abandoned you."

"You had no choice," she said. "Fred's been a big help."

"So what's the deal with those clothes?"

"I picked them out for him," she said. "He's kind of sweet on somebody, and I thought a few new outfits might help. Please don't say anything to embarrass him."

Etheridge shook his head and reached into his desk drawer for his bottle and a glass. He poured a hefty shot and tossed it back in one clean gulp. He poured a second one and held it. He noticed Meg was staring. "What?"

"You look awful."

"I haven't slept well the past couple of nights."

"How's Mr. Murphy's wife?"

He stared into his glass. "Not good. She blames me for what happened. I suppose in some ways I am to blame. I hired Al even though he wasn't qualified, gave him Fred's job, then had Fred rewrite everything he handed in. Mental health professionals would label me an enabler.''

"His wife owned the paper."

"Not good enough, Meg. I should have stood up to her, but I was scared. Where would I find another job at my age?"

Meg could see that he was deeply hurt, but what worried her most was the look of total exhaustion. "Why don't you go home and get some sleep," she said. "I've got to run over to the high school to snap pictures of the girls' fashion show, but I'm coming back. I'll stay as long as I'm needed."

He downed his drink, and they walked out together. "You'd think Fred would get hot in that jacket," he said.

Meg grabbed her purse and coat and stopped by Melinda's desk, where she signed out. "Don't you remember what it was like falling in love?" she asked her boss as they'd exited the building and found themselves standing in the chilly night air.

"Are you kidding? At my age, I don't even remember if I'm wearing clean underwear."

Travis was mad enough to spit. Beryl had known for days he was supposed to go out of town tonight, but the damn woman hadn't so much as packed a pair of socks for him. She was downstairs studying for some goofball course she was taking at the community college. Probably basket weaving or cake decorating. And here he was supposed to be in Chattanooga by nine o'clock that evening.

The conference didn't start till Monday, of course, but Travis knew there'd be two days' worth of partying for those lucky enough to get away. Boy, was he looking forward to a little downtime. He checked his closet for clean shirts and found none.

"Beryl, goddammit!" he yelled. "Did you iron my dress shirts like I told you?" He closed his eyes and counted to ten. It was times such as these that he wished murder weren't a capital offense. "Beryl, get up here this minute!" He'd barely gotten the words out of his mouth before she was standing in the doorway holding his dress shirts. "Jesus, where were you?"

"I was getting your dress shirts, Travis, like you told me to," she said calmly. "Why do you let yourself get all bent out of shape over little things?"

"This happens to concern my job," he said. "Which I can't afford to lose since you've become accustomed to a certain lifestyle."

"Travis, I talked to Dee Abbott today, and she said the conference doesn't start till Monday."

"You're so dense, Beryl. Dee's husband is just a supervisor. I'm manager of operations. The executive meetings begin tomorrow morning."

"Oh, well, I didn't think of that."

"That's the problem with you, Beryl, you *never* think."

"You have a nice time, Travis. Try not to work too hard, and I'll see you when you return."

He watched her leave the room. She knew he was lying, and she didn't even care. It was easier for her to just accept the lies than confront him and be forced into making a decision. Well, that was fine with him. As long as she kept his clothes washed and ironed, his house clean, and his children well tended, he would put up with her. One day, though, and it wouldn't be long, he was going to convince J.T. to make him vice president of Bidwell Textiles. He'd want a good-looking woman on his arm then.

Travis carried his suitcase downstairs and set it beside the front door. He could hear Beryl in the kitchen cooking dinner, and the kids doing homework at the table. Moving quickly, he grabbed a stepladder from the utility room and carried it to the fireplace in the den, where a mounted bull moose head looked over the room as though guarding it. He'd bagged it on a hunting expedition in Vermont. Beryl hated it with a passion, which is one of the reasons he kept it. That, and the fact that it served a purpose. He climbed the ladder, pulled the head from an oversize nail, and stuck his hand inside.

Sort of like dipping into a honey pot, he thought.

Sixteen

ON SATURDAY, Meg visited a thrift store and purchased a simple cotton dress, a shabby sweater, and a pair of badly scuffed flats to wear to the holiness church services that evening. She scrubbed the makeup from her face and pulled her hair back. Studying her reflection in the bathroom mirror, she wondered if she was making a huge mistake by letting Clay see her without all the fixings.

Not that she was half bad to look at, mind you, but a little mascara and blush went a long way toward helping a woman look her best. Girls seemed to learn this early nowadays, she thought, as she remembered the painted faces of the high school girls the night before.

As Meg stood there taking in her reflection, she reminded herself that Clay Skinner might not even show. He and Becky may have patched things up. They certainly had appeared to be happy at the E&M. Probably, it wasn't an easy thing to walk away from a woman with breasts the size of cantaloupes. Meg turned and viewed her own breasts from a side angle. Of course, the most damaging evidence against Clay was the fact that he hadn't called to explain.

"Explain what?" Meg said aloud to her fairly flat-chested reflection. "You don't have any hold on him. He doesn't owe you an explanation; he doesn't owe you a damn thing. Get a grip."

By the time Meg heard Clay's truck pull up, she had pretty much gotten herself in hand. She grabbed her purse and keys and stepped out of the camper as he approached. He didn't look any different, except that his clothes looked old. To a casual observer they would appear to be simple mountain people, struggling like the rest of their neighbors.

"I wasn't sure you'd show," she said, despite the ten-minute lecture she'd given herself in front of the bathroom mirror and the vow she'd made not to bring up Thursday night.

"I said I'd be here."

His tone was cool, or maybe cautious was the better word. Yes, he sounded like a man who'd just reunited with his ex-wife but felt he should take care of his remaining obligations.

"Perhaps this isn't such a good idea," Meg told him. "I really don't mind going by myself."

"Meg, let's not argue. Just get in the truck, okay? We can talk on the way."

She followed him to his pickup. Neither of them said anything until Clay had left the campground and turned onto the highway leading up the mountain.

"Okay, I know what you're thinking."

"You *don't* know what I'm thinking," she snapped. "If you did, you would have been too scared to show up today."

"You can raise as much hell as you want, Meg, but I'm not going to apologize when it comes to my daughter. She had a recital last night, which I attended, and afterward I offered to take her and her mother to dinner."

"You're dating your ex-wife?"

"Don't be ridiculous."

"Just forget it," she mumbled, feeling silly for making such a big deal out of it when it really wasn't any of her business what Clay did. As he drove in silence, she kept her distance, hugging the passenger door and staring out the window as if it held the answer to some riddle.

"Meg, do you remember how close you were to your dad when you were growing up?" Clay asked after a while. "That's how it is with Cindy and me. She came into the world weighing less than three pounds. She was premature, you see. I thought I was going to lose her.

"I told my dad how I felt, and I'll never forget what he said because it hurt me so bad. He said there'd be other children, that Becky and I were both young. But as I looked down at Cindy, hooked up to all sorts of gadgets, I knew there would be no replacing her. I knew if I lost her, I was going to be missing out on something important and meaningful in my life. I remembered feeling the same way when you left."

Meg softened toward him. Yes, she knew what it was like for a little girl to love her daddy, because she'd been crazy about hers for as long as she could remember.

She was startled from her thoughts when Clay hit a pothole. She glanced at him. "I'm sorry I overreacted," she said. "Cindy's very lucky to have a daddy who loves her as much as you do." She smiled. "Just try not to spoil her like my daddy did me."

Clay grinned and reached for her hand, then kissed her palm. "I'd like to spoil you. If you belonged to me, I'd pamper you and give you everything your little heart desired."

"Take me, I'm yours," she said matter-of-factly.

"When I think you're ready, I might just do that." He suddenly let go of her hand. "You're going to have to help me out on directions. I haven't been up this far in years."

Meg saw they had gone a long way in a very short time; at least, it seemed that way compared to the speed at which her camper traveled. "Keep going," she said. "It's just up the road."

They hadn't gone far before the road became lined with cars. "Oh, Lord," Meg said, noting what seemed like hundreds of people walking toward the church and milling about the front yard. "I'm not sure we're going to get inside."

Clay stopped in front. "See if you can find us a seat," he said, "while I park."

Sara and Maybelline Beechum welcomed their father's congregation as they'd been taught since childhood, kissing the women and giving the men and boys a warm handshake. It would not be proper to kiss someone of the opposite sex, lest the devil cause your heart to be filled with lust. Lust was a bad thing—as were gossip, lying, bad language, and the use of tobacco and alcohol or any other mind altering drug.

There were many rules at the Jesus Christ Holiness Church, and the members were expected to abide by them faithfully. Women did not wear slacks or short skirts; makeup and jewelry, except for wedding rings, were also forbidden. Women were never to cut their hair. The only ones allowed to do so were the men, and they were expected to keep it above their collars. Facial hair of any kind was not permitted.

Sara noted the pretty young visitor in the crowd and watched her as she tried to make her way closer. Though her clothes could have been pulled from Sara's own closet, the woman was definitely not one of them. Her shoulder-length hair, pulled back demurely, was streaked blond with some sort of hair dye, which was not permitted in their faith. Was she a local woman coming for the first time? Sara wondered. As the woman stepped up to her, she smelled something that reminded her of a spring day, after a drenching rain. Fresh and clean, with only a hint of sweetness.

Sara smiled. Her father would think the hair dye and perfume an abomination, but she loved pretty things and nice smells, and she imagined the Heavenly Father did as well. "Welcome to the Lord's house," she said, and kissed the visitor on the cheek. The woman returned Sara's smile, and her face became quite beautiful.

Next Sara welcomed a family from North Carolina. She watched them take their seats along the back row, where most visitors sat, people who had no idea what to expect and were anxious about being there. Anxious but desperate.

''We'd best get up front,'' Sara told her sister once she saw the associate pastor, Purvis Dill, take his place at the altar. They quickly made their way up the aisle.

The little church was filled to bursting inside, and much too warm due to the mass of bodies, despite the partially raised windows that permitted those on the outside to see in but obviously let very little of the cool night air in. The Jesus Christ Holiness Church did not offer smooth, highly polished oak pews like the big Baptist church in town; folks had to sit on boards. Cinder blocks made up the walls of the church, and a tin roof covered the structure. There was a tiny unisex bathroom, and a small office on the other side of the wall that ran behind the stage. The stage itself was nothing more than a raised platform that had been roped off. It encompassed the altar and offered space for the musicians, who were presently tuning their instruments.

As Sara reached the front, she saw that Purvis was still dressed in his work clothes. He'd obviously had to work overtime again, probably hadn't eaten a bite since lunch. His brownish red hair was longer than most, but Sara knew it wasn't intentional. He probably hadn't had time to get a haircut, what with all the long hours he worked at the mill, not to mention the time he spent assisting her pa. She would offer to trim it for him first chance she got. If he'd let her. He'd been acting strange toward her lately.

Sara took her place at the podium, introduced herself, and welcomed members and guests. When the band was ready, she sang an old hymn that her grandmother had taught her long ago. She'd been singing solo in her daddy's church since she was fourteen years old. He jokingly referred to her as his opening act, but those who'd known her all her life couldn't get over the changes in her. Most were awed when they witnessed the healing brought on by her touch, and no matter how many times she tried to explain it was the Lord working through her, they couldn't grasp it.

Sara had grown accustomed to living with the unexplained. It had always been that way for her.

Seventeen

THE MINUTE Meg spied the small blond woman on the steps of the church, she knew it was the same one who'd placed healing hands on Jarrod Renfree after he'd been struck by lightning. She wasn't sure *how* she knew, only that she did. And when the young woman looked into her eyes and kissed her cheek in welcome, Meg felt humbled, as though she had stumbled upon something sacred. This woman was no impostor.

"Good evenin', folks," Sara said, once her song had ended. "Welcome to the Jesus Christ Holiness Church. For those of you who're visiting for the first time, I'm Sara Beechum. My sister, Maybelline, is at the piano, and this young man sitting nearby is our associate pastor, Purvis Dill. We'd like to welcome you and apologize for the lack of space. As many of you know, we hope to build a new church in the next couple of years. Until then, I hope you nice people will continue to worship with us, despite the inconvenience. We're always happy to have visitors."

Sara glanced at the woman at the piano, who nodded in return. "I'd like to sing another hymn which is a favorite of mine," she said. "It has to do with prayer. Sometimes it doesn't feel as though the Lord is listening to us when we pray. Especially when we're asking for something important and feeling impatient about it," she added. "But I believe Jesus hears all our prayers and answers them in good time." She paused, and her smile faltered for a split second before she went on. "Sometimes, though, we have to be prepared for how the Lord chooses to answer our prayers, since He knows more than we do what's best for us."

Meg watched Sara as she spoke, and wondered if she personally had a prayer that she was waiting to have answered. But as she started to sing, Meg forgot all else but the sound of Sara's voice, rich and full and unbelievably lovely. The small woman held the congregation rapt with her song, and Meg found herself wishing it would never end. She was so transfixed that she didn't see Clay trying to make his way through the crowd, and she was startled when she looked up and found him standing beside her.

"Bet you thought I wouldn't make it," he whispered. "Only an amoeba could get through this crowd."

Meg nodded, but her attention was still focused on Sara. When the last note faded away, Purvis Dill stood and opened the service with a prayer. Meg studied him as she had Sara Beechum. He looked perfectly normal, as did the others. They certainly didn't look like the sort of people she imagined handled snakes and drank poison.

"... and if there are those among us who have not accepted the Lord as his or her personal savior," Purvis prayed, "let them do so tonight. In Jesus' name. Amen."

The band struck up another hymn, this time a lively tune, and Sara grabbed a tambourine. Meg was surprised at how good they were. In almost no time they had the congregation swaying and clapping their hands. At the back of the platform a door opened, and a tall, black-haired man stepped out. Meg knew immediately he was the Reverend Temple Beechum. She felt a sense of drama about to unfold as Sara Beechum handed him the microphone and backed away.

Meg studied him closely, the gaunt face and angular body, and she wondered what it was about him that gave him such presence. He wasn't handsome; the bones in his face were much too prominent, but he was oddly striking.

"Welcome, brothers and sisters," he said into the microphone. His voice was both commanding and self-assured, but thick with the mountain twang so common to the area. "I am genuinely pleased to see we have so many here with us tonight. We're always grateful for visitors."

Clay leaned closer to Meg. "That's because he's getting rich off them," he whispered.

Meg shivered as his warm breath fell on her ear. "He certainly doesn't appear rich," she said softly, noting his simple clothes.

"Probably stashing it in a Swiss bank account."

"Brethren, I believe I heard my sweet daughter mention the church we're plannin' to build. I know I can count on your continued support to see this dream become a reality. It's going to be like nothing else we've ever had in these parts, a monument to our Lord Jesus Christ."

"More like a monument to himself," Clay whispered, and a big man in overalls turned and shot him a dark look.

Meg's own look was a warning to be quiet.

Clay put on a sober face.

The reverend raised his hands to the ceiling and stared straight up as though expecting the roof to peel away and the heavens to part for him. "Lord, have mercy on us sinners and make our hearts pure as freshly fallen snow. Strengthen our faith so that we might bear witness for you."

He pulled down his arms and gazed across at the congregation. "Jesus said our faith only had to be the size of a mustard seed to move mountains. How strong is your faith, brethren?" He looked across the crowd. "Do you believe that God Almighty has the power to heal you, or do you run to the doctor every time you're struck down by sickness? What about it, brothers and sisters? Do you believe that any doctor can save you when your Father has decided to call you home?" His voice became louder. "Let me tell you, friends, there is *no* medicine powerful enough to save you when Jesus Christ calls you to his bosom, just as there is nothing in this world that can kill you until the Lord feels you have served your purpose here on earth, amen.

"Don't put your trust in these great new wonder drugs or these high-priced specialists who think just because they spent eight or ten years in medical school they can play God. I *tell* you," he said, pounding one fist into his palm, "only our Creator knows when our time has come, and it is not up to these heart doctors or cancer research people! And what about these transplant doctors? Who would ever have thought we'd be cutting one man's heart out and putting it into another man's body? And how do they decide who shall live? I'll tell you *exactly* who. The rich man. The man who can afford to donate a new hospital wing or buy millions of dollars of equipment."

There was a rumble among the crowd, and the people nodded in agreement. Temple Beechum walked over to a young woman holding an infant. He touched the baby on its head, and when he spoke his voice was solemn. "Let me tell you what these great medical geniuses are doing to our newborns. They're taking premature babies and hooking them up to every kind of machine and . . . and apparatus you can imagine just to keep them alive. These tiny beings don't weigh more than a pound or two, and they're poking 'em and jabbing 'em with needles, and you know why? Because they think they have the right." He raised his voice again. "And the whole time they're doing it, they're bleeding the poor parents for every dime they can get!

"And what do you suppose becomes of these babies they're able to save? I'll tell you what becomes of them, brethren. They suffer health problems for the rest of their lives." He suddenly looked angry. "Either their hearts or lungs never developed right, or there's something bad wrong with their kidneys, and they have to spend day after day on dialysis."

Meg could feel Clay tensing beside her. She glanced in

his direction. His jaw was hard, his lips pulled tight in an affronted frown.

"They don't get to live a normal childhood, and both parents end up working two or three jobs to keep up with the medical bills. The family disintegrates under the stress, and the mama and daddy end up in divorce court. Why? All because some doctor decided he had the right to play God!

"And while we're on the subject, brothers and sisters, think about what they're doing to our senior citizens. It's no different. A man cain't die in peace nowadays; he has to suffer a thousand indignities first. They shove tubes up his nose and down his throat and heaven only knows where else. He cain't even go to the bathroom on his own, and every time something shuts down in his body, they pull out another gadget to keep that body part going until finally he looks like Frankenstein lying there. Is that how you want to remember your loved ones, brothers and sisters? Is that how you want them to remember you?"

People in the crowd shook their heads emphatically.

The reverend's eyes suddenly filled with tears, which slid down his bony cheeks. "These doctors might be smart, m'friends, but they don't know what we know. They don't know how beautiful it is to watch a Christian leave this sinful world behind. How wonderful it is to let go of a sick and diseased body and wake up in heaven with our Lord, Jesus Christ."

"Amen to that, Reverend," someone said.

"So, I tell you, brothers and sisters. We believe in miracles. I'll be the first one to arrive at a sick person's house and pray for healing, but there are times we have to put our life *and* our death in the hands of our savior. Amen and amen. Let us pray."

Meg bowed her head respectfully as the reverend led the congregation in prayer. She chanced a look in Clay's direction. As he met her gaze, she wondered if he was as impressed with Temple Beechum's sermon as she was. Not that she agreed with everything the man said, but he was a powerful orator nonetheless. As the praying continued, she realized some of those around her were speaking gibberish, and it hit her that they were talking in tongues. She felt the hair on the back of her neck stand, and she scooted closer to Clay, who grinned and took her hand.

"Glad I came with you?" he whispered.

She nodded.

"Brethren, there are many Christians today who are being persecuted for their beliefs and practices, just as they were in Jesus' time. This nation was founded on religious freedom. Our Constitution guarantees it, but we are still hounded by politicians and lawmakers who want to make a name for themselves." Several in the crowd nodded and mumbled to themselves.

"Now, I ain't got nothin' against the law," he said. "We have to have laws in order to live in a civilized world. But—" He held one finger up, and when he spoke again his voice was loud and full of conviction. "If I have to choose between God's laws and man's laws, I'll choose God's every time. Amen!"

A number of people clapped and cheered, and Temple was silent for a moment as he waited for the noise to die down. "Jesus said, 'In my name shall they cast out devils; they shall speak with new tongues. . . . They shall take up serpents; and if they drink any deadly thing, it shall not hurt them; they shall lay hands on the sick, and they shall recover.' "

"Hallelujah!" a deacon called out.

"I believe that with my whole heart, brothers and sisters, amen. And if there is someone here who is suffering from emotional or physical distress, I say let this be the night you receive your miracle."

The crowd went wild. Even those outside the building who couldn't actually see the service were being swept up by the reverend's words.

"Brothers and sisters, we have a number of timber rattlers in here tonight, and Brother Dan Smith has brought a fruit jar of Red Devil lye. For those members who would like to participate fully in the services, let him or her partake, but only if you feel moved to do so and only when you are fully anointed. Amen. We don't encourage visitors to take part unless they are sincere and feel the Spirit upon them. We do things in a decent manner here; we don't believe in forcing folks to follow our practice.''

Meg tried to see what was going on at the front of the church. Two men in the front row had stood at the mention of snakes, but she couldn't tell what they were doing because of the crowd that separated her from the altar. Finally the men reappeared beside the reverend, each holding a wooden box over his head.

The musicians began playing again as Temple took one of the boxes and held it up for everyone to see. ''Remember, folks, with Jesus Christ anything is possible, but you can't rush sanctification. The Lord will tell you when you're ready.''

The congregation was becoming more excited. A number of people had joined Reverend Beechum on the platform, dancing and hugging one another. As the music swelled, the atmosphere became more and more frenzied.

Meg opened her purse and pulled out her camera. She was taking a chance, but she simply couldn't pass up the opportunity. Just as she was about to snap a picture, though, she heard someone scream from the back of the church.

At first Meg thought she'd imagined it; it would've been difficult hearing even a gun go off with all the ruckus. Then she suddenly noticed she wasn't the only one looking for the origin of the sound. She tapped Clay on the shoulder. ''Did you hear someone scream?''

He didn't have time to answer before several women began screaming all at once. Meg could see the crowd being jostled. The musicians stopped playing, and even Temple was trying to find out what was going on.

''Is there a problem?'' he asked, only to be answered by hearty male laughter.

"He's got a rattlesnake!" someone shouted. "A diamondback!"

"Hell, I thought you people liked snakes," a male voice said, slurring his words badly. "Me'n my brother paid twenty-five bucks fer this'n."

With a chill, Meg recognized the voice, then caught sight of two men moving toward the front of the church. Harley and Bert Attaway. They'd managed to do the impossible: cut a six-foot-wide path down the center aisle. Meg felt a chill race up her backbone when she noted the long metal rod in Harley's gloved hand, from which hung the largest snake she'd ever seen. Suddenly, there was chaos, men shoving their wives and children toward the door, folks scrambling this way and that to escape.

Temple Beechum seemed to grow paler under the bright lights. "What do you boys think you're doing, coming into the Lord's house intoxicated?"

Bert grinned. "We ain't 'toxicated, Rev'rend. We're plumb drunk on our asses."

Purvis Dill stepped forward. "What d'you want, Attaway?" he said, his gaze resting on Harley. "Can't you see we're trying to hold services?"

"Hell, Purvis, that's why we're here," Harley said, dangling the snake closer. "We heared tell how crazy y'all was 'bout snakes, so we brung ya a gift. This here's Gus. He's a pure diamondback straight outta North Carolina. We figured it'uz time you folks stopped pussyfootin' around with those lit'l timber rattlers and take on the real thing. What d'ya say, Rev?" He looked at Temple.

Meg felt Clay tug her hand. "Let's get out of here," he whispered, "before the trouble starts." She glanced around. People were still spilling out the door. Someone had shoved a couple of windows up higher, and the men were passing children out.

"We should let the young people get out first," she whispered.

"You were wrong to bring that snake through a crowd of innocent bystanders," Temple said. "You could've hurt one óf the children. Now, take him away.''

Harley looked surprised. ''What the hell's goin' on?'' he demanded. ''Everybody knows y'all ain't nuthin' but a buncha snake worshipin' fools.'' He moved the rod closer, and the snake writhed as though trying to break free. Its rattle was less than a foot from Beechum's face. ''Or maybe the rumors we been hearin' is right. Some folks say you milk your snakes before you handle 'em. Iz that right, preacher man?''

''Nobody in this church handles snakes or takes part in *any* of our practices until we are fully anointed. Only then do we—''

''I think you're full of horseshit, Reverend,'' Harley said, glancing around at the room. He laughed when he saw the people trying to get out. ''And I think the whole bunch of you is pussies.''

Meg lifted her camera again. She started to edge closer, but Clay grasped her upper arm. Her look was pleading. ''Fine, it's your funeral,'' he whispered, but made a point to stay right at her side.

''Tell you what, preacher man,'' Harley said, reaching into his pocket and pulling out a pistol. ''I'm goin' t'give you to the count of three to take this snake before I start shootin' up the place.''

''Get out of here, Harley,'' Purvis said, looking angry now, ''or you're both going to spend the night in jail.''

''On second thought, maybe *you'd* like to hold ol' Gus,'' Harley said, aiming the pole at the younger man until the snake was right above his head. ''What d'ya say I drop him right on yer noggin', dumb ass?''

''Stop this!'' Purvis's father, Amos Dill, rushed forward, just as one of the other deacons grabbed Harley from behind and yet another reached for the pole. Harley released the catch, and the snake fell on Purvis's shoulder. It coiled, and Purvis braced himself for the bite. Amos tried to slap the snake aside. With split-second precision, it turned and sank its fangs into the older man's cheek.

Eighteen

MEG AUTOMATICALLY began snapping pictures. The men tried to pull the snake free, amid Amos Dill's agonizing cries. "It's like trying to get a fish hook out," one of them said. A fight had ensued between the Attaway brothers and several deacons, and Purvis was doing his level best to calm his father. One of the deacons wrestled the gun from Harley, took aim from the side, and fired at the snake. He missed and aimed again. Meg held her breath. The second shot found its target, and the snake's head exploded, spewing blood and gray matter across Amos's face. The diamondback's long, scaly body fell to the floor with a thud. Amos fainted, and was immediately caught up by Purvis and Temple, who very gently laid him down on the platform.

Sara Beechum, who'd remained frozen to her spot during the ordeal, ran to them. "I need clean rags," she shouted, "and some soap and hot water."

"I'll get the water," Purvis said, heading toward the bathroom. Several people offered Sara fresh handkerchiefs, and she took them, pressing one of them against Amos's wound. With the soapy water, she cleaned him up as best she could. "Pa, it's bad," she said. "We need to get him to a hospital."

"He don't need no hospital," Temple said.

"He'll die." Sara looked at Purvis. "He will."

Purvis looked torn. "I don't know what to do."

"Listen to me," Temple said, his voice low so that only those close by could hear. "This is the very foundation on which our religion is based. Your father is a deacon in this church. How will it look to members of the congregation if we take him to the hospital?" He turned to his daughter, and his anger was palpable. "You have no right condemning this man to the grave," he said. "Only the Lord, Jesus Christ knows if it's Amos's time."

Purvis looked around. The church had cleared out, but people watched from the doorway and windows. Temple was right. How *would* it look if the associate pastor went against their teachings and demanded medical attention? "We'll take him home," he said.

"I'll pull my truck up front," one of the deacons offered, and raced from the building.

Temple motioned to several church members. "Clear a path so we can carry Brother Dill out." He suddenly swung his gaze in Meg's direction. "And *you*," he said, pointing a finger at her. "We do not permit pictures to be taken inside our sanctuary. You have no business bringing that camera into our place of worship."

Meg opened her mouth to protest, but both her purse and camera were snatched from her hands by a big man in overalls. Clay tried to retrieve them, but he was rushed by several other men who were determined to keep Meg's things away from him.

"Who do you think you are, going through my personal belongings!" Meg demanded as the man rifled through the items in her pocketbook. He pulled out a press card and held it up. "She's from the *Gazette*."

"Get them out of here now!" Temple yelled, then glared at the Attaway brothers, who were being held in a clinch by several men. "And take that white trash out of here, too!" he said, pointing to the Attaway brothers.

"Hey, we didn't mean nuthin'," Harley replied, looking genuinely frightened. "We was just messin' with you."

"Shut up, pond scum," a man said, popping the back

of Harley's head. "Where do you want us to take 'em, Reverend?"

"For a long ride down a deserted road," Temple said. "Won't hurt to let them spend a night out in the cold. That's where wild animals belong."

The Attaway brothers were roughly escorted from the building by several large church members. Meg and Clay were surrounded by another group of men, whose intent to see them out was clear. "Reverend, wait!" Meg cried. "You can't actually mean to send that poor man home without medical attention when you know he's going to die."

Temple glared at her but didn't respond.

Someone gripped her upper arm. "Let's go, miss."

"Take your hands off her," Clay ordered, struggling to pull free from the men who held him. "We're capable of seeing ourselves out." Meg was released, and Clay took her hand. "Let's get out of here."

Meg opened her mouth to argue, but the look on Clay's face shut her up. Her purse was thrust into her hands, and Clay propelled her toward the door.

"Deacon Pitts's truck is here," someone called from the front door. Meg and Clay were forced to pause while the injured man was rushed through the door, Sara Beechum still tending him.

Meg followed Clay out the door and down the front steps as the pickup carrying Amos Dill pulled away. The crowd lingered on the church lawn and along the side of the road, but she paid them no mind. Several minutes later she was sitting in Clay's pickup, smoking a cigarette and trembling badly.

"You okay?" Clay asked, starting the engine.

"I think it's an outrage that they won't help that poor man," she said. "We have to report this."

"He'll be dead before they can process the paperwork," Clay said. "Don't forget, the man is a member of a church that practices serpent handling, and his son refused to take him to the hospital."

Clay pulled onto the narrow road and started down the mountain. "It's none of our business, Meg. These people believe in what they're doing. They've gone to jail over it, and they've paid large fines. You're not going to change their minds."

"You heard that young woman, Sara, try to convince her father to take the man to the hospital."

"She'll probably be reprimanded for it."

Meg leaned back in the seat and closed her eyes. She felt empty inside, desolate. It was as though all the good things had been sucked out of her, and she had to find a way to put some of it back. Maybe she'd buy a puppy, she thought. Something she could love, and maybe derive comfort from.

They arrived at her camper before she knew it. "You want to come in?" Meg asked.

He nodded. "I'd like that very much," he said. "But if I do, I want it understood I won't be leaving any time soon."

All at once, her chest felt tight. She met his gaze. To hell with the puppy, she thought, suddenly realizing what she really needed at the moment. "It's understood," she said.

Nineteen

"YOU WANT a beer?" Meg asked.

"No thanks."

She opened the door to her miniature refrigerator and peered in for no reason other than to have something to do. "How about a soft drink?"

"I'm not thirsty. Are you?"

She closed the door. "Not really."

She heard movement and realized he'd stepped closer. She could almost feel the heat from his body. Her heart pounded, and she struggled for her next breath. If this was any indication what *real* sex was like, she didn't know if she'd survive it.

"Meg, please look at me."

She took a deep, steadying breath and turned around. Clay was only inches away. She raised her eyes to his, and he stepped closer, placing his hands on her shoulders. They felt unusually warm through the thin fabric of her dress. His gaze, when she met it, was intense.

"You're nervous," he said.

"No shit."

He smiled and kissed her on the forehead. "You have no reason to be. Not with me. We've known each other too many years."

"This is different."

"Not really," he said gently. "I've made love to you a million times in my mind." When she glanced away, he hooked one thumb beneath her chin and tilted her face so that he was looking into her eyes once more. "Did you ever think about me that way?"

She could already feel her body responding. Something inside quickened. "Yes."

He looked pleased. Without releasing her, he leaned forward and nibbled an earlobe. "What was it like?"

Meg shivered as his breath warmed her cheek. "It was . . . always good."

"So you thought of me more than once?"

"Yes."

Clay's lips followed the line of her jaw and moved to the hollow of her throat. He took her hands and placed them around his neck, then pressed against her intimately. She could feel him straining against his jeans, and she suddenly had the urge to run off and smoke a cigarette.

"Is that where you sleep?" he said, nodding to the mattress

"Yeah. Not much of a bed, huh?" She had a thought. "We can take the table down and make a bed from the booth. That's probably what we should do." She slipped from his arms and began clearing the table. While Meg grabbed clean sheets and a couple of pillows from an overhead cabinet, Clay turned the booth into a double bed. Meg put the cushions in place and covered them with the bottom sheet.

"Not very long," she said. "Your feet will probably hang off."

He shrugged. "We've made out in worse places." He sat down and gave a small bounce as though to test the cushions. He smiled and patted the spot next to him. "Come here."

Meg joined him. He started to put his arm around her, and the movement startled her so badly she jumped.

"Hey, take it easy. You're as edgy as a long-tail cat on a porch full of rocking chairs," he said, hoping his teasing would calm her down. He leaned closer and nuzzled her neck, pulling her hair free as he did so and combing it with his fingers.

Meg leaned in the opposite direction. "Clay, wait—" He looked more surprised than anything.

"What is it, babe?"

"I have something important to tell you. I've been meaning to tell you from the beginning, but the time never seemed right. Now that we're about to become . . . uh . . . *intimate,* I have no choice."

A small frown marred his forehead. "You don't have herpes, do you?"

"What?" She blinked, then laughed. "Oh, no, nothing like that. Damn, Clay, I can't believe you asked me that."

"Well, you're starting to worry me."

"I just want to explain why I sometimes act kind of . . . you know . . . tough."

He arched one brow. "You do?"

"I'm trying to be serious here," she insisted. "I'm not really like that inside. I just had to appear that way because of my job in Atlanta and because of what happened with Roy."

Clay toyed with her hair. "I'm listening," he said.

"Well, my self-esteem went to hell over Roy. I thought something was wrong with me."

"But if you knew he was gay—"

"I didn't find out until the end. By then I'd convinced myself I was either abnormal, deformed, or that I had a serious case of BO."

Clay shook his head sadly and turned her around so that she was facing him. "Listen to me, Meggie," he said. "The first time I laid eyes on you I felt like someone had kicked me in the gut. I thought you were the most beautiful thing I'd ever seen. I still feel that way. There's nothing wrong with you, babe." He kissed her tenderly. "Give me half a chance and I'll show you how beautiful you are."

"There's one other thing. I'm fresh out of rubbers."

He grinned and kissed her again. "I gotcha covered," he said against her lips.

"Maybe I should have had that beer."

He pushed her back on the bed and plunged his fingers through her hair. Eyes closed, Meg gave in to the sheer pleasure of his embrace. Her scalp tingled as his fingers massaged it, drawing imaginary circles that sent shivers through her. When he broke the kiss, they both sucked in air. "I can't believe you still taste the same after all these years," he said, dropping dewy kisses on her eyelids.

Meg didn't have a chance to respond as his lips descended once more. He pulled his hands from her hair, and she felt him reach behind her for the buttons on her dress. She shifted on the cushions to give him easy access, and the next thing she knew he'd pulled the dress over her head. Clay tossed the garment aside, as he did her half slip. He fixed his gaze on her in matching ivory-colored bra and panties, and the sight almost took his breath away.

Meg had always had beautiful skin, and ten years hadn't changed that. It was still silky smooth. A faint tan line showed above the lacy cups of her bra, and he remembered the lazy summers they'd spent at Willow Lake, him rubbing her down with suntan oil and tasting it on her shoulder later when he kissed her there. Her bathing suit had been modest compared to most; the Holcombe girls didn't wear bikinis. But no matter how hard Alma Holcombe tried, she could not conceal her youngest daughter's lovely figure.

He reached for the clasp at the front of her bra, unhooked it, and marveled that her breasts were still as gorgeous as he remembered. They were fuller, but still pert and youthful looking. Ripe. He pulled off his own clothes, and Meg could only gaze back at him in silence, and wonder what she'd ever done to deserve a second chance with him. Clay didn't give her time to ruminate; he buried his face against her breasts.

Meg's mind shut down. Her body responded to his every touch, his lips tugging and suckling, his wet tongue swirling around her nipple, causing it to draw up and become erect. He kissed her lips once more, slowly, deeply, and as his mouth made love to hers, his hands did the same to her body. Each gentle massage stirred something deep inside, and her body awakened as though from a long thaw. Finally, he moved over her and stroked her legs apart, and she gasped when he entered her. The rest of the world faded away, and her entire reason for being suddenly became centered on the man atop her—the feel and smell of him, the way his hair-roughened chest scratched and tickled her breasts. Low in her belly, the tension built until she could stand it no longer.

They climaxed together, the pleasure so intense for Meg that she cried out. Clay soothed her with tender words and kisses, and, afterward, held her close as though he feared she'd escape if he didn't. Meg drifted off to sleep in his arms, secure in the knowledge that she still loved him.

Clay left early the next morning after giving Meg a long, lingering kiss and promising to call later that day. He was trying to finish up a job so the people could close on their loan the following week, and he had a crew working seven days a week to meet the deadline. Meg pulled on a pair of sweats and walked to the camp store for a pound of coffee, wondering if the world had somehow turned more beautiful during the night, or if her mood had simply improved. She even smiled and waved at Ranger Bekins and received a cool nod in return. He obviously didn't share her joyous mood.

Alma and Henry Holcombe chatted on the front lawn of the church for a good twenty minutes before climbing into their car for the drive home. Alma was wearing her blond wig and a salmon-colored suit with matching shoes. She had wanted to dress especially nice today. She glanced over at Henry, who was still handsome in his dark blue suit, after all these years.

"I have a little surprise," she said, as her husband

pulled away from the church. He looked at her, and she went on. "I made some of my special fried chicken yesterday, and I packed a picnic basket this morning. I hid it in the trunk of the car while you were showering. What would you think about taking a drive to one of those state parks and finding a nice place by a stream—"

Henry frowned. "Alma, why are you doing this to me?" he demanded. "Yesterday, you told me you wanted me to come home early, so I closed the store at five o'clock and hurried home. The truck had just come by and unloaded a ton of stock, but I left it sitting there in the middle of the floor. I figured I could go by after church and put everything away."

"Why can't you do it Monday?"

"'Cause Monday I'm going to have to sweep and mop, since I couldn't do it yesterday."

"Fine," she snapped. "You always have an excuse not to spend time with me. Just take me home."

"Alma, I'm not trying to find reasons to stay away from you. Maybe we could have the picnic later." She didn't say anything, and he didn't push. They arrived back home, and Alma stormed into the house. Henry went into their bedroom and changed into work clothes, then climbed into his truck and made the short drive to the store. He unlocked the door and froze at the sight inside. The stock had been put away. Even the boxes were gone.

"Hi, there." A cute face bobbed up from behind a set of shelves.

"Mindy, what in tarnation are you doing here?"

"I knew you'd worry yourself silly about putting this stock away, so I thought I'd surprise you."

"Hon, that's real sweet of you, but I don't expect you to give up your only day off. I'll pay you extra, of course."

"I don't expect pay, Mr. Holcombe. It's just my way of saying thank you for all the kindness you've shown. You gave me a job, and you never give me any grief if one of my kids gets sick. Shoot, I can walk to work 'cause it's so close. Now, why don't you go on home and watch TV or something? I can have this place swept and mopped in no time.''

"Oh, Mindy, what am I going to do with you?" he said, gazing down at her. He tweaked her nose. Maybe he could take Alma on that picnic after all. *If* she was speaking to him. "At least let me get the mop bucket ready. And when you're finished with it, just push it to the back of the store, and I'll dump it first thing in the morning. I don't want you lifting it, you hear? Puny thing like you . . . you're liable to end up in the hospital." He chuckled.

"Who are you calling puny?" she said. "I'll have you know I gave birth to a ten-pound son, and I didn't so much as ask for an aspirin. Try doing *that* some time."

Henry laughed. "No, I don't think that's an experience I care to go through. I can't even get my teeth cleaned without Novocain."

They were still laughing when Alma pushed through the door. "Well, this is a nice surprise," she said. "I came to help you put your stock away so we could have that picnic, but I see you're already having one. Excuse me for interrupting."

"Alma, wait—" Henry started for the door, then glanced over at Mindy. "Would you mind locking up?" he said.

"Sure, Mr. Holcombe," she said. "Hey, I thought your wife was a redhead."

He didn't answer. He hurried to his truck and climbed in.

Twenty

THE FISHER wedding was held at two o'clock at the Methodist church. Julie Fisher was a plump, freckle-faced redhead who wore no makeup and made a liar out of the person who'd said all brides are beautiful. Beau Simms, the groom, was fighting a battle with acne and losing. Ben and Hildy Fisher, the bride's parents, were on the pudgy side themselves, making Meg wonder if the Fishers shared a sluggish metabolism or were big on fried foods and rich desserts. Meg sat on the back pew, wearing a navy linen coatdress that was one size too large and had a tendency to gape open at the collar, but had been a bargain at half price. As she listened to the couple exchange vows, she searched through her purse for a safety pin and wondered what the future held for her and Clay. Probably not wise to look too far into the future, she thought, unable to find a pin. Julie and Beau were pronounced man and wife, and Meg was still trying to figure out what to do about her dress.

Once the couple shared a chaste kiss and started down the aisle, Meg snapped a couple of pictures, then hurried out for a quick smoke. The reception was held in the basement, and although the food was by no means fancy, it looked tempting and there was plenty of it. She was standing in line at the buffet table when she happened to look up and see her sister, Beryl, making her way through the crowd toward her. "Hi," Beryl said. "If I'd known you were coming, we could have driven out together. Oh, you must be covering the wedding for the *Gazette*," she said, noting the camera. "Will I be in your way?"

"Of course not," Meg told her, thinking her sister had never looked lovelier, in a mint green silk tunic and matching skirt. "Beryl, you look wonderful," she said. "Have you lost weight?"

The other woman beamed. "Seven pounds. But do you think Travis noticed?"

"Does it matter?"

The question seemed to startle Beryl, as though she'd been taken off guard. Finally, she laughed. "No, not really." She leaned close. "Your brassiere is showing," she whispered. "We need to visit the ladies' room."

"And lose my place in line?" Meg asked.

Beryl dragged Meg in the direction of the ladies' room and produced a safety pin as if by magic. "You need to grow some boobs," she said, as she pinned Meg's jacket. "I'd gladly give you some of mine, but I'd insist that you take some of the extra padding around my hips as well. There now," she said, stepping back to get a better look at her handiwork. "That'll do for the time being, but it really needs to be taken in. If you bring it by the house sometime, I can do it."

"Thanks. I'll probably take you up on that. Where's Travis?"

"At a convention."

"So, are you feeling okay these days? Everything all right at home?"

"Same as always. Why are you asking all these questions?"

Meg shrugged. "I'm a reporter; that's what I do best." She opened the bathroom door and they stepped out.

On their way back to the buffet table, Beryl stopped several times to speak to people, introducing Meg each time. After waiting in the slow-moving line and filling their plates, they found a place to sit. Beryl told Meg about the various accounting courses she was taking.

"Are you thinking of going back to work?" Meg asked, hoping that was the case. Beryl needed to spend time with nice people who appreciated her, instead of devoting her energies to some louse.

"I've been wanting to for quite a while," Beryl said. "It's just, I didn't feel I was qualified to do much. Then I remembered how much I liked math, so I thought maybe I should see if I like accounting."

A woman in a gawdy hat hurried over, and Beryl introduced Meg to Mrs. Payne and explained they attended the same church. "Would you like to join us?" Beryl asked, her apologetic glance at Meg making it obvious she didn't want to hurt the woman's feelings. Mrs. Payne sat down, and the conversation turned to children and grandchildren. She talked nonstop. It was some time before the sisters could extricate themselves.

"I'm sorry," Beryl said once they reached the parking lot. "I shouldn't have invited her to sit with us. I had no idea the woman talked so much. Where's your Bitchmobile?"

"I hid it in back of the church. I scraped the bad word off."

"So why are you hiding it?"

Meg looked at her. "You've seen it. You still have to ask?" They both burst into laughter.

"Here, let me give you a ride to your coach," Beryl said, unlocking the door to her car. "Hop in." Once they were inside Beryl's economy station wagon, she turned to Meg. "You should follow me out to the house. We can catch up on things. The kids won't be home till this evening," she added, "so it'll just be the two of us. Unless you have plans."

Meg saw that her sister looked as though she needed to talk to someone. "I'd love to come over."

Meg followed Beryl through town and up the mountain a short distance, then pulled into the driveway of an attractive bi-level home that she and Travis had purchased some five years prior. What Meg appreciated most was the fact they didn't have neighbors close by. She parked in the driveway next to her sister, gathered her purse and keys, and climbed out. Beryl hurried up to her.

"I want to see the inside of your camper," she said.

"Oh, it's nothing special," Meg told her. "Actually, it needs a lot of work."

"I still want to see it."

Meg sighed. At least it was clean. "Okay, okay. But don't expect much."

"I don't," Beryl said, grinning.

"And don't be a smart-ass or I'll charge you for the tour."

"I'll be good," Beryl promised.

Meg unlocked the door, pulled the metal step out, and motioned her sister inside first. "Oh, Meg, this is nice," Beryl said. "I thought it was going to be . . . you know—"

"A dump?" Meg said, joining her.

"No, nothing like that. I just never expected it to be so cute. And cozy. Why do you have everything taped?"

Meg explained how the cabinets and drawers tended to fly open while traveling. "A friend of mine has offered to put special locks on them so I won't have to go through all that trouble."

Beryl slid into the booth. "That friend wouldn't happen to be Clay Skinner, would it?" She chuckled. "Mom said she ran into him."

Meg sat opposite her. "Did she bother telling you the story she made up about my ex-husband?" When Beryl shook her head, Meg filled her in.

"That's scary," Beryl said. "She's so damn worried about what other people think that she doesn't care what she puts her family through. But she's always acted weird where you were concerned, Meg."

Meg couldn't help but show her surprise. "I thought I was the only one who felt that way."

"Oh, no. It's not like she wasn't obvious. Dad blamed her when you left right after high school. Said she made your life miserable and that's why you got out first chance. Would you happen to have anything cold to drink?"

Meg reached into her cooler and blushed when all she had was a grape soda and several beers. "I'm afraid I don't have much to offer."

"I'll take a beer," Beryl said. "But only if you drink one with me."

Meg shrugged. She wasn't really in the mood for one, but she'd drink dog piss just to watch her goody-two-shoes sister toss back a cold one. "Sure," she said, pulling out two icy cans and wiping them off with a dish towel. She passed one to Beryl, who popped it open like an expert.

"I sometimes sneak one of Travis's Budweisers when he's out of town on business," she confessed. "Or should I say, when he's out of town on *monkey* business."

Meg, who was in the process of taking a gulp, almost choked. She coughed several times.

"Sorry," Beryl said. "I figured you knew. Everybody else in town does."

Meg lit a cigarette. "I supposed I've suspected from time to time."

"Is that why you came on to him the other day in town?" Beryl said, giving her a knowing smile.

At first Meg was too shocked to say anything. She forced herself to remain calm. Travis had told her she would be sorry for what she'd done; he'd obviously meant what he said. "Is that what he told you?"

"I'm not supposed to say anything, of course. He just wanted me to know what kind of woman you are."

Meg took a drag of her cigarette. She was so angry she was trembling. So that's why Beryl had invited her over. "That's not the way it happened," she said.

Beryl drained her beer and set it on the table. "Why don't you hand me another beer and tell me your side of it."

Meg regarded her sister thoughtfully. "Should you be drinking in your condition?"

"What condition?"

Meg suddenly felt very foolish. "That bastard lied and told me you were pregnant. He figured that way I wouldn't tell you."

"Tell me what, Meg?"

"Why do you stay with him, Beryl? Do you still love him?"

"I haven't loved Travis in years, dear. I stayed with him because I was insecure about being able to make enough money to support me and the kids and"—she paused—"just a whole bunch of things." She took another sip of her beer. "The shit-ass doesn't deserve it."

Meg blinked and wondered if her sister was getting drunk. "You're right about that," she said. "He doesn't deserve *you*."

"So tell me."

Meg sighed and told her what had occurred that night. As she talked, her sister continued to drink, but the look on her face was hard to read. Finally, Beryl slammed her can down.

"That pig! I'll kill him."

"He's not worth it, Beryl."

"You're right, he isn't. But I'd like to kill him anyway. Why didn't you *tell* me?"

Meg shook her head. "I didn't know what to do."

Beryl suddenly stood, somewhat unsteadily, and made for the door. "I'm going to make him wish he'd never been born." She opened the door, stepped out, and started across the yard for the house.

"Wait, Beryl. What are you going to do?"

Beryl didn't answer. She took her key from her purse and unlocked the front door, then made her way down the stairs to the den. Meg followed. When she reached the den, she found Beryl getting into Travis's gun cabinet.

"Beryl what the hell—?" She swallowed when she

saw her sister pull out a rifle. "That thing's not loaded, is it?"

"Of course it's loaded. You don't think Travis cares anything about gun safety. Now, stand back. I'm doing what I should've done years ago."

"You're drunk. You don't know what you're doing."

"I know *exactly* what I'm doing." She took aim.

Meg considered trying to get the rifle away from Beryl, but was afraid they'd both end up seriously injured. She glanced up to see what her sister intended to shoot, and saw it was a large moose head that had been mounted over the fireplace. Meg jammed her fingers in her ears and closed her eyes as Beryl fired.

The sound was deafening. The moose head exploded as though a bomb had gone off inside. When Meg opened her eyes, it looked as though someone had emptied a bank vault through a hole in the ceiling. Wordlessly, both women stared as one-hundred-dollar bills rained down and floated around them.

"Damn," Meg said. "Does Travis have any more of these things mounted? I'd like to shoot the next one."

An hour later the sisters had cleaned up the mess and counted the money. "Do you realize there's almost a quarter of a million dollars here?" Meg said, motioning to the stacks of money on Beryl's kitchen table.

Beryl looked to be in shock. "Maybe we miscounted."

"We counted it three times."

"You think it's counterfeit?"

"No, it's not counterfeit. These are all new bills." She showed her sister how to tell if they were the real thing. "I had to write an article about it when the Treasury Department first released them." Meg sat back in the chair and grinned. "You know, Beryl. You won't have to feel financially insecure now about leaving Travis. You've got yourself a little nest egg here."

The other woman just looked at her. "Are you saying I should *take* the money?" she asked. "What if Travis came by it illegally?"

"Of course he came by it illegally," Meg said. "Unless Bidwell Textiles gave him one helluva raise."

"But he'll kill me if he finds out I took it."

"So, you don't tell him."

It was some hours later when Meg and Beryl carried out a number of large garbage bags, boxes, and a set of golf clubs to Meg's camper. Next, Meg took a hammer and screwdriver to the back door and busted the lock.

"There, now. Do you think you can remember everything we discussed?" she asked.

Beryl nodded. "I won't forget."

The sisters hugged and Meg hurried to her camper. She needed to find a good spot to unload her cargo.

Beryl threw her a kiss and went inside the house. She walked to the kitchen phone and dialed 911. "Hello," she said in a strained, high-pitched voice. "This is Beryl Lytle on Highpoint Road. I'm calling to report a burglary."

BOOK THREE

Twenty-one

AFTER HAVING found a place to dump the items she and Beryl had put in her camper, Meg was not surprised to find herself sitting in front of the Jesus Christ Holiness Church. She tried the front door, but it was locked. In the next yard, a man was working in his flowerbed. She hurried over and questioned him.

"I don't know nothin' about those holy rollers," he said, waving her off. "Don't *want* to know nothin'. But the preacher man don't live far from here." He gave her directions, and Meg thanked him.

The Beechum house was less than half a mile away, down a narrow, pockmarked road. There was no vehicle in the drive, but Meg decided to try knocking anyway. As she went up the narrow walk, she couldn't help but notice how neat everything looked. A big iron pot near the front steps held bright yellow mums, and the yard was free of clutter. The house had been painted recently, as had the navy blue shutters. The glass sparkled in the windows. Meg started up the steps as a rangy-looking mutt rounded the house and barked once.

"Nice doggie," she said nervously. She was tempted to run for her camper, but knew that could incite the dog further. Had these people never heard of leash laws? "Good boy," she added, although she had no idea what sex the animal was.

"He won't bite," a voice said.

Meg snapped her head up and found Sara Beechum standing at the door in a simple cotton shift. She hadn't even heard it open. "Oh, hi there," she said, still eyeing the dog.

"Butchy, go!" Sara said, pointing toward the backyard. The dog hung his head and slunk away. She turned her attention to Meg. "You're the lady my pa threw out of church."

Meg introduced herself. "I hope you don't mind my stopping by. I just wanted to check on that poor man's condition. The one who was bitten by the snake last night. Is he—"

"They're still holding a prayer vigil for Brother Dill," Sara said. "I was there all night and most of today. I hate to sound rude, Miss Gentry, but my pa will be home soon. You won't be doing yourself any favor if he catches you here."

"You don't suppose there's a way I can get my film back?"

"If that's why you're here, then you're wasting your time. It's probably been destroyed." She started to close the door.

"I also wanted to talk to you. Maybe we could meet somewhere. When's a good time?" she asked, glancing over her shoulder anxiously.

The younger woman paused. "Why?"

"Well—" She struggled for the right words. "I'd hoped to get to know you better. I sort of got the feeling you were unhappy."

"Have you been appointed to help me?"

"Help you?"

"I've been praying a long time. I thought maybe the Lord sent you."

Meg didn't quite know how to respond. "Well, I've been accused of many things," she said, giving a short laugh, "but nobody's ever mistaken me for a messenger from the Lord."

"This is not a laughing matter, Miss Gentry," Sara

replied coolly. "I'm afraid I misunderstood your reason for being here. I hope you won't repeat this conversation." She closed the door.

"Wait!" But it was too late. Meg heard the click of a dead bolt and realized she'd blown it. She knocked anyway. "Sara, I'm sorry if I offended you." There was no answer. "Sara, would you please open the door?" She waited. Nothing. She glanced toward the road and decided she'd better go before it was too late.

Meg didn't breathe a sigh of relief until she was well down the mountain, but she did manage to chain-smoke three cigarettes on the way. She had no desire to run into the Reverend Temple Beechum and cause Sara more problems. She wondered about the sad, haunted look she'd seen in the girl's eyes, wondered what she was trying to escape from. And why had Sara asked *her*, a complete stranger, for help?

Her cell phone rang, and Meg snatched it up.

"I just wanted to let you know I can't see you tonight," Clay said. "Something's come up."

Meg felt her hopes sink at the news. "Is there a problem?" she asked.

"Cindy's got a viral infection. Her asthma is acting up."

"She has asthma?"

"Yeah. Anyway, one of Becky's old friends is in town, and they've made plans, but Becky doesn't want to leave Cindy with a sitter in case she gets worse. I figured I'd pick up a couple of children's books and read to her."

"You're a good daddy, Clay," she said, trying to hide her disappointment. She'd hoped to spend the evening with him, but it didn't look like that was going to happen.

"Thanks for understanding, babe," he said. "Let's plan on dinner tomorrow. I'll take you somewhere fancy. I know a place where you can get great submarine sandwiches." They chatted a few minutes, and he promised to call later.

Meg continued on her way. She was going to have to get used to being second in Clay's life. If she tried to compete with his daughter, she'd lose every time. She saw the sign for the campground and slowed to turn when the phone rang again. She snatched it up, hoping it was Clay calling back.

Dr. Grimes identified himself from the other end. "I thought you might like to see what we're doing with these bones, Miss Gentry."

Meg perked up. "You betcha. When?"

"Now, if it's convenient. An old colleague of mine is helping me piece things together. I think you'll find it interesting. My office is in the basement of the hospital."

"I'm on my way."

The drive to Blalock Memorial took about twenty minutes. Meg was escorted downstairs by a security guard; Dr. Grimes met her at the elevator and led her to the autopsy suite. Two stainless-steel tables and a four-door refrigeration unit dominated the room.

"Promise me you won't open any of those doors," Meg said.

The doctor laughed. "Is this the same woman who voiced an interest in watching an autopsy when we first met?"

Meg noticed various jars sitting on counters and tables, each containing samples of organ tissue, which she couldn't identify and didn't want to. "I've changed my mind." They entered another room with a long worktable, where a middle-aged brunette sat in a white lab coat. Behind her were shelves holding skulls and other bones; nearby, a desk supported a large microscope.

"Meg Gentry, meet Dr. Janet Coleman." Meg smiled and shook the woman's hand, but she was more interested in the two dozen or so bones laid out on the table before them. At the other end was what looked to be part of a rotted quilt. "Janet is a forensic anthropologist," Grimes said, "and a close personal friend. When I told her what

I had, she offered to help. Please, sit down,'' he said, indicating a chair.

"This all looks very interesting," Meg said. "Have you been able to come up with any clues?"

"Oh, yes," Grimes said. "You'd be surprised the stories bones tell. But Janet's the expert; I'll let *her* tell you."

"Could I just ask one question?" Meg said. "As much as I appreciate your letting me in on this, why *are* you?"

Grimes smiled. "Because you're going to help us catch the killer."

Twenty-two

Meg looked from one doctor to the other. "I don't mean to sound rude, but if y'all are counting on me to solve a murder, we're in a shitload of trouble. I can't even solve a crossword puzzle without a dictionary."

Dr. Coleman chuckled. "Alan told me I'd like you, Meg. No, we don't expect you to solve a murder; we just need your help in seeing that our clues reach as many newspapers as possible. First, let me explain exactly what it is that I do," she said. "Besides working in anthropology, I do forensic sculpting as well. Which means—"

"You build faces?"

"Right. I make a plaster cast from the victim's skull, *if* the skull is still intact, and then I perform facial reconstruction. The skull was in good condition in this case, so I shouldn't have any trouble."

Although Meg had heard of this sort of thing before, she'd never seen an actual model. "You mean you're able to re-create this person's face exactly?"

"It won't be a perfect match, but the resemblance can be strong enough for close friends or relatives to recognize. *But* they have to see it, and that's where you come in. Once we have a likeness, we'd like you to run it in the local paper. If we don't get a hit, we'll probably ask you to put something together for the *Atlanta Journal*. I understand you used to work there."

Meg nodded. "Yes, and I'm sure they'd be very interested in what you're doing. Is it okay if I take notes?"

"By all means," Grimes said. "If we come across information we don't wish to share with the public just yet, we'll let you know."

"Before we get started," Meg said, "can you give me an update on Al Murphy?"

"I'll tell you what I told the sheriff," he said. "Evidence indicates that the gun was fired by the victim. If it wasn't suicide, somebody went to a lot of trouble to make it appear so, and we know appearances can be deceiving. I've told the sheriff not to rule out homicide. The body has been sent to Asheville for further testing. We should know more in a couple of weeks, but rest assured the investigation is continuing."

"Did someone search Mr. Murphy's car?"

"My assistant vacuumed it for fiber and other trace evidence. The only items in the car were a foam coffee cup and several matchbooks bearing the names of our local watering holes. I'm sure the sheriff will be glad to address your questions."

He motioned to the table. "So, Miss Gentry. Tell me what you see."

Reaching into her purse for her notepad, Meg studied the bones, which had been arranged according to their placement on a human body. "It looks to be the skeletal remains of a child," she said.

"It would appear so at first glance," Janet Coleman said. "But once you look more closely, you'll see they belonged to a young woman. Someone in her mid-twenties," the doctor added.

"A very *small* woman," Grimes said. "I suspected she was of Asian origin at first, since their bone structures tend to be dainty, but Janet has convinced me otherwise."

"I'll just tell you what I know about this victim so far," Coleman said. "Like I said, the remains belonged to a young woman. If you compare this skull to that of a male—" She turned and reached for another skull on a shelf behind her. "This is a man's skull, by the way. See the difference in the forehead?"

Meg saw it right away. The skull was larger and appeared heavier, and the forehead was slanted. "What about race?"

"Definitely Caucasian. There's a vast difference between Caucasian and Negroid skulls."

"How do you know the bones belong to a woman and not a young girl?" Meg asked.

"There are a number of ways," she said. "Without getting technical, let me just say that we know approximately at what age bones change and mature. As for knowing the sex, all I had to do was examine the pubic bones, located in front of the pelvis. The angle of this bone will be wider in a woman, to accommodate childbearing." She paused and smiled. "Now, you're going to find this fascinating," she said. "Look closely at the depression left on this pubic bone."

Meg nodded. "What caused it?"

"A woman's pubic bones separate during labor, then go back together afterward. Once a woman births two babies, a small indention is left. This woman had at least two children."

"We don't have near all the bones," Dr. Grimes said. "I still have people sifting through dirt, but wild animals could have gotten to her."

"You keep referring to this woman as a victim," Meg said. "Does that mean you suspect foul play?"

Dr. Coleman nodded. "There were no bullet holes or fractures to the skull to suggest a fatal head injury, but one of the bones in the center of the throat was broken. This one." She pointed to a small U-shaped bone. "It's called the hyoid bone. I think our Jane Doe was strangled to death."

Meg repressed a shiver. "Can you tell from your evidence when the murder occurred?"

Dr. Coleman looked sad. "Unfortunately, we don't have any way of testing the age of bones—unless they are prehistoric, in which case carbon dating is used. We've gone over what's left of the quilt she was wrapped in, looking for fibers or other trace evidence. Sadly, we didn't find much. We'll try to date the fabric used in the quilt, of course, but that probably isn't going to help us. The quilt could've been twenty or thirty years old when the victim was buried with it.''

"What about dental records?'' Meg asked.

Grimes shook his head. "This woman never had any dental work.'' He glanced at Dr. Coleman. "Janet is usually called in as a last resort, but she agreed to reconstruct the face as a personal favor to me since I've always been interested in forensic sculpturing.''

The other doctor nodded. "I had two weeks' vacation coming. It was either spend it with my seventy-year-old mother, who's a habitual complainer, or come here. I've always wanted to visit Appalachia, but Alan only just recently got around to inviting me.''

"When do you plan to get started?''

"First thing in the morning,'' Dr. Coleman told her. "It usually takes several days from start to finish.''

"You're welcome to come by anytime,'' Grimes said. "I plan to take pictures of the entire process, and I'll have an extra set made for you.''

Meg thanked him. "So what are our chances of finding out who this woman was, and who killed her?''

Dr. Coleman looked thoughtful. "Not as good as I'd like them to be. But with your help, we can improve those odds.''

"Count me in,'' Meg told them.

The following morning, Meg met with Etheridge to discuss various story ideas, including the holiness people and Dr. Coleman's attempt to reconstruct the face of the skeleton they'd found the previous week.

Although it was obvious his thoughts were elsewhere, Etheridge seemed intrigued by both stories. "For someone who wanted to get out of crime reporting and all the gore associated with it, you certainly seem to have gotten yourself smack-dab in the middle of it.''

"You have to admit the Jane Doe skeleton is exciting,'' Meg said. "She's been out there all those years, just waiting for somebody to find her.''

"We're talking homicide, right?''

"Right. Evidence points to strangulation.''

"And you plan to follow the procedure and take pictures.''

"Uh-huh. When this forensic sculptor is finished, she'd like us to run a picture of the woman in the paper to see if anyone recognizes her.''

Etheridge nodded. "Sounds good to me. Go for it.''

Meg started to ask him how he was doing when a knock came at his door. Melinda peeked in.

"Meg, you have a visitor. A Miss Beechum.''

Meg and her boss exchanged surprised looks. "Uh-oh, the snake people,'' he said. "Better talk to her in the parking lot.''

Meg shot him an amused look as she stood. Melinda's usually bored expression suddenly became wary.

"What's he mean by that?'' she asked Meg as they exited the office.

"I'll explain later.'' Meg hurried toward the front of the building. She was disappointed to see that it was the older Beechum sister, and not Sara. Nevertheless, she offered the woman a pleasant smile. "Hello, Miss Beechum. You wished to see me?''

"Call me Maybelline,'' she said, her mountain twang more pronounced that her sister's. "Is there someplace we can talk? In private?'' she added, eyes darting toward Melinda.

Meg could see by the expression on Melinda's face she didn't appreciate the comment one bit. "We could find a bench in the courthouse square,'' she said. "Just give me a second to grab my jacket.''

Meg made small talk as she and Maybelline walked the short distance to the park. Because it was not yet lunchtime, there were several empty benches. They selected one in the sun.

"How's Mr. Dill?" Meg asked once they were seated.

Maybelline clasped her hands together in her lap and stared at her feet. "I'm sorry to report that Brother Dill passed away before dawn this mornin'," she said softly. "His body is bein' prepared for the wake, and a church member has already started on his coffin. Once Mr. Mott from the funeral parlor gets the body ready, they'll bring him home till it's time for burial."

"Oh." Meg could feel herself becoming angry, but she knew the woman before her wasn't responsible for the decisions made in the holiness church. The Reverend Temple Beechum was in charge. "Did Mr. Dill go peacefully?" she asked.

Maybelline clenched her hands tighter, so tight it looked as though her knuckles would pop through her skin. "I'm afraid he suffered a great deal, Miss Gentry."

"Call me Meg."

"Call me Maybelline. I don't know why the Lord saw fit to let Amos die such a horrible death. He was a good man, a *godly* man."

"Maybelline, pardon me if I sound rude, but I don't see what the Lord had to do with Mr. Dill's demise. Certainly no one asked the Lord whether or not the poor man should be taken to the hospital."

"I'm not goin' to try to convert you to our ways, Meg," Maybelline said. "I, too, am having a trouble dealin' with Brother Dill's death. He was like family."

Meg knew it would be useless to argue. "What will happen now?" she asked.

"Well, the sheriff arrested my pa about an hour ago. He'll prob'bly have to pay a fine and spend time behind bars, even though he didn't have anythin' to do with bringing the snake in. The mayor says Pa is guilty because everyone knows he encourages snakes in the worship service. Mayor Bradley's had it in for Pa a long time."

"What about the Attaway brothers?" Meg asked.

"There's warrants out for their arrest. Those two skunks is prob'bly hidin' out in the woods somewheres, survivin' on beetles."

Meg shuddered at the thought.

"But that's not why I came to see you," Maybelline said. "I'm here 'cause of my sister."

"Go on."

Maybelline didn't say anything for a moment. "We need you to help Sara escape."

At first Meg didn't think she'd heard right. "Escape?" Maybelline nodded. "Escape from who?" she asked. "Or what?"

"Pa." The woman glanced around as though to make sure no one would overhear the conversation. "Pa believes Sara is the Chosen One."

"Chosen for what?"

"He thinks the Lord is usin' her as a vessel to perform miracles and spread His word. See, our little church was nothin' in the early days. We only had a handful of members, barely collected enough to pay the electric bill. Then Sara got involved, and the money started rollin' in. She's a healer, y'see."

Meg nodded. She'd seen TV evangelists order the crippled to toss away their canes and walk, and she'd watched them restore hearing and cure various other ailments. She was convinced it was a hoax. "I'm listening," she said.

"Our granny had the gift, and she passed it on to Sara before she died. Granny could cure thrush in babies and take the fire outta burns. She could even stop the flow of blood." Maybelline chuckled softly. "Wouldn't a soul let her anywhere near a hog killin', 'cause they couldn't bleed it properly once they stuck it. Same with Sara, only her gift is more powerful. You wouldn't believe the things I've seen."

"What things?" Meg asked.

"I've seen her snatch folks right outta death's grip. That's no lie," she added, then paused abruptly as two

men in business suits passed. She scooted closer to Meg.
"There was this baby once. Could'na been more'n a few
months old, and he'd been sick for days. 'Twas the dead
of winter, and his pa walked I don't know how many
miles in the freezin' cold to find Sara. By the time she
got there it was too late."

"The baby was dead?"

Maybelline hesitated. "He sure 'nuff *looked* that way.
His little body was already blue, and when I held a mirror
to his nose there weren't a whisper of breath comin' from
him. His mama had already sent her oldest boy to ask a
neighbor to start buildin' a coffin.

"Well, Sara weren't about to give up without a fight.
She laid that baby out on the kitchen table and started
CPR. Nobody ever trained her to do it; she just *knew*. She
was prayin' and carryin' on somethin' fierce. She was
beggin' God not to take the child."

Maybelline paused. "I'll tell you the honest-to-
goodness truth, that little fella suddenly gasped and made
these mewin' sounds, and I thought my heart would fly
right outta m'chest. 'Fore long he was kicking and flailin'
his arms and cryin' to be fed. His mama got down on her
knees and started thankin' God right there on the spot."

A chill shimmied up Meg's spine as she listened.
"Sometimes a person can slip into a coma and *appear*
dead," she said, her voice little more than a whisper.

"I'm just tellin' you what I saw," Maybelline said.
"By mornin' his color was back to normal. His mama
says he ain't been sick a day in his life since, and every
fall his pa brings us a big load of firewood. That's the
way folks do things 'round here. We gets plenty of eggs
and fresh vegetables. Stuff like that. Course Pa makes us
give most of it away."

Meg was confused. "You say Sara wants to escape.
Doesn't she feel some sense of mission with what she's
doing?"

"Sara wants to go to college to become a social worker,
so's she can teach families about good hygiene and the

proper way to care for their babies and such. She and Pa don't always agree on our practice of divine healin'. She thinks babies should be vaccinated and women should get checkups every year. We got a lot of women dyin' from cancer in their female parts 'cause they don't never visit a doctor. And even though Sara has a lot of success with healin', some people wait till it's too late before they call her.''

''And your father is against Sara getting an education?''

''Dead set against it. He's not interested in what goes on in this life; he says folks should be more concerned where they're goin' to spend eternity. Pa believes the more you suffer, the better your chances of goin' to heaven.''

''But he doesn't mind the fact your sister's able to bring more money into the church.''

''Oh, he don't use that money for personal gain. We're just as poor as the rest of our neighbors.''

''So how does your sister plan on paying for college?''

''I reckon she'll have to get government loans. She's smart as a whip and was offered all kinds of scholarships in high school. But Pa wouldn't think of letting her go. He believes Sara'll just run wild like—'' Maybelline glanced away quickly, as though afraid she'd said too much.

''What were you going to say?'' Meg asked.

The other woman blushed. ''Our mama was a sinful woman. She, uh, ran off when I was four years old. Pa's convinced that me and Sara have some of her bad blood in us. That's why he watches Sara so closely. As the Chosen One, she must remain pure and chaste.''

''What about when she marries?''

''She won't. Not as long as Pa's alive. She's to devote herself to the church and God's work. Which is a sad thing, 'cause Sara loves children and wants a family one day.''

Meg was thoughtful. ''How old is your sister?''

"Oh, she's of legal age to leave, if that's what you're asking. But Pa seldom lets her out of his sight. She's trapped. That's why we need your help."

"You really love your sister, don't you?"

Maybelline nodded. "She's all I got. And I—" She paused, and for a moment it looked like she might cry. "I can't stand to see her mistreated."

Meg felt her stomach muscles tense. "Who mistreats her? Your father?"

Maybelline stood. "I've already said more than I should have. Will you help her?"

Meg suspected she wasn't going to get anything else out of the woman today. She stood, and they started walking. Meg's mind was already racing for solutions to Sara's problem, even though she didn't know what it was. She had her suspicions, but that's all they were. All she knew for certain was that something was terribly wrong. The sisters had to be desperate to come to a complete stranger for help.

"How come you haven't gone to the sheriff with this, Maybelline?" she asked.

Maybelline stopped walking. "You cain't breathe a word of this to him," she said. "Pa pays Sheriff Overton to keep his nose out of church business."

"Are you telling me the sheriff is taking bribes?"

"Yes. You have to realize, the only reason Pa's in jail is because the mayor got involved. Sheriff Overton would've found a way to get him off. If you was to go to the sheriff with this, he'd tell Pa, and Sara would suffer twice as much."

"How soon is she wanting to leave?"

"The sooner the better. This would be a good time, with Pa locked up and all."

Meg nodded. "Give me a couple of days to think about it. I'll be in touch."

Maybelline thanked her and hurried away. As Meg started back for the newspaper office, she wondered what she was getting into. Whatever it was, it couldn't be good.

Twenty-three

DRS. COLEMAN and Grimes were hard at work on the plaster skull when Meg arrived shortly after her meeting with Maybelline, bearing coffee and Danish from the E&M. "Alan, we're going to have to adopt Ms. Gentry," Dr. Coleman said. "She's so good to us."

After they finished their pastries, they went back to work. "Let me explain what I'm doing, Ms. Gentry," Dr. Coleman said, pointing to a series of rubber pegs that she was in the process of gluing to the face of the model.

"Please call me Meg."

"And you can call me Janet," the other woman said. "No need to be formal."

Dr. Grimes saluted Meg with his coffee cup. "And you can call me anything you like. Just don't call me late for cocktails."

Meg smiled and reached into her purse for her notebook. "I'm ready when you are."

"Before we get started, let me explain one thing," Janet said. "I can't guarantee that we'll hit pay dirt with this. Forensic sculpturing, as we know it now, is more an art form than an exact science. Fortunately, we have a young doctor in Tennessee, working on a grant, who claims he can come up with more exact data by using a computer. As it stands, much of what I do is guesswork."

"So you're saying it's a long shot."

"Precisely."

172

"It may be a long shot," Grimes said, "but it's all we've got at the moment. The authorities don't have anything else to go on—no missing person who fits this profile, nothing. Unfortunately, many counties, and this is one of them, can't afford to pay someone like Janet to come in."

"Lucky for me, Alan's a gourmet cook," Janet said. "His offer of free lodging and fine food are payment enough." They shared a private look before Janet turned her attention once more to her work. "Now, then, you're probably wondering what all these little pegs are about," she said to Meg. "You'll note they've been cut in different lengths."

The pegs ranged from about an eighth of an inch to a full inch in length. "They look like pencil erasers," Meg said.

"That's what they are," Janet told her. "They're called landmarks, and they represent tissue thicknesses on the face."

"How do you know how thick a person's soft tissue is to begin with?" Meg asked.

"I use a chart. It's a compilation of tissue depths for men and women of various ages. I've cut thirty pegs and have glued them according to length at different points on the face." She fixed the last one in place and waited for Grimes to take pictures.

"Next, I'll use modeling clay. You'll note I've already cut the clay into strips of different thicknesses. I connect the pegs, or landmarks, then fill in the areas and smooth the clay so that when I'm finished, the facial area is fleshed out. That process will take another couple of days." She paused and reached for a stack of snapshots. "These are models I've worked on in the past," she said, handing Meg the pictures. "The face on the left is the finished sculpture, and the face on the right is a picture of the victim we were able to identify."

"You even added eyes and hair," Meg said. She studied the photos. While there were indeed similarities between the models and pictures taken of the victims before their disappearance, they were not exact. "What's your success rate, if you don't mind my asking?"

Janet looked thoughtful. "Well, out of the last ten models, I've managed to identify about three victims. I'm hoping we can improve on that number once we're computerized and the process becomes more exact."

"Janet's success rate depends a lot on the public," Grimes said. "Someone who knew the victim has to see a picture of the model and recognize her."

"Are you going to work on the model for the rest of the day?" Meg asked.

Grimes answered for her. "Janet's been at it since five A.M.," he said. "We'll probably take off early. After all, she's supposed to be on vacation."

Dr. Coleman smiled. "Alan knows how obsessed I become when I'm working. I forget to eat or sleep."

"I don't know how you've managed to stay healthy, my dear," he said. "You obviously need someone to look after you."

Meg suddenly felt like a third wheel, and stood. "I'm going back to the office and type out my notes while they're still fresh in my mind. I'll call before I come by tomorrow." They exchanged good-byes, and she exited the autopsy suite. As she waited for the elevator, she couldn't help but wonder if they would end up together permanently.

That made her think of Clay. Her stomach fluttered just thinking about how they'd spent their last evening together. What did their future hold? she wondered.

Several messages were waiting for Meg when she returned to the office. Her mother had called; no surprise there. Meg wondered what had taken her so long. Clay had called to cancel their dinner plans, saying he was tied up. That made her frown. She wondered if it was business or if his daughter had taken a turn for the worse. She wouldn't call, and she wasn't going to wait by the phone until he called. She was not desperate.

As Meg waited for her computer to warm up, she dialed her parents' number.

"You called me more when you lived in Atlanta," Alma Holcombe said.

Meg knew the routine. "I've been busy."

"Well, if you can stop thinking about work long enough, I have some bad news for you."

Meg knew her mother enjoyed passing on bad news. "What is it?"

"Your sister's house was burglarized yesterday. She and the kids weren't home at the time, thank God, but she's terribly shaken. Your father insisted they stay here until the sheriff's department catches whoever did it. I think you should come for dinner. Beryl needs her family right now."

"You're right," Meg replied. "I'll be there."

Twenty-four

MEG ARRIVED at her parents' house shortly before six. As if watching for her from a window, her mother hurried out the front door, red wig jostling about on her head, apron flapping in the breeze. She wore a mournful look, and as Meg climbed from the camper and closed the door, she knew she was in for some high drama.

"I'm so glad you came," Alma said, whispering despite the fact nobody was around. "Beryl needs us. She's trying so hard to be brave for the children, but I know she's crushed."

"That's Beryl for you," Meg said. "Laughing on the outside, crying on the inside. What a trooper."

"I didn't tell you the worst part. The burglars took her and Travis's wedding album."

Meg stopped dead in her tracks. "Say you don't mean it!"

"But like I told her, nobody can steal your memories. She'll always have those."

"I know Beryl will cherish that thought for the rest of her life."

Inside, Meg found her sister setting the table. "Oh, Beryl," she said sorrowfully. "I feel so bad for you." They hugged. "Has the sheriff's office learned anything?"

"No, I'm afraid not. Other than it was a forced entry.

176

The back door had been pried open with a screwdriver."
She shook her head. "Travis is going to be sick when I
tell him. The burglars took all his guns and his fishing
equipment, and his golf clubs. They even took his beautiful moose head that was mounted over the fireplace."

Meg shook her head. "The things people will stoop to
these days."

"That moose head was his pride and joy. I suppose
you could say it was worth its weight in gold as far as
Travis was concerned. Oh—" She paused and dragged in
a long shaky breath. "And they took his mama's china."

"The set with the baby chicks on it?" Meg asked.

"Uh-huh. You know how poor his family was. That
china was the only thing they had that was real quality.
His mama saved her S and H green stamps for years to
be able to get it."

Alma frowned. "I thought you hated that china. I distinctly remember that big fight y'all had 'cause you had
guests coming and he wanted you to use it."

Beryl gave her mother a tremulous smile. "Mama,
when you love a man like I love Travis, you learn to
appreciate the things he likes."

"Are there no limits to what people will do?" Meg
said.

Beryl choked back a sob. "Would y'all excuse me?"
she said. "I need to be alone for a few minutes." She
hurried out of the room.

"She's trying not to fall apart in front of the children,"
Alma whispered. "Luckily, whoever did this awful thing
didn't take the children's photo albums or baby books. At
least she still has that. You know, it's almost as if the
burglar had it in for Travis. It was mostly his stuff that
was taken."

"But who could possibly have anything against
Travis?" Meg said.

Alma looked around to see that they were alone.
"Some woman's husband, maybe?"

"Don't tell Beryl. She thinks the sun rises and sets in that man."

Dinner was a subdued affair. Alma had allowed Jimmy and Amy to eat on a TV tray in the living room so the adults could discuss Beryl's situation. Henry didn't see the need for a discussion; he'd decided Beryl and the kids were going to stay right where they were until they found the burglar.

Meg knew her sister had no desire to stay with their parents. One week with Alma, and Meg would have to draw up commitment papers for Beryl. She took her sister's hand. "Listen, honey, I know you're probably going to think this is a crazy idea," she began, "but I think you and the kids should get an apartment in town. At least temporarily. Statistics show that once you've been burglarized, your chances of being robbed again are even greater."

"I didn't know that," Beryl said, stuffing a fist in her mouth as though to keep from crying out. "You mean those evil people could come back?"

Meg nodded. "I saw it all the time when I was working the police beat. Next time, you might not be so lucky. What if you and the kids are there all alone when he or *they* return? With Travis rotating shifts and going to conventions like he does, you never know." She made a tsking sound. "You could even rent something furnished on a short-term basis. Those new Vista Villas are nice," she added.

"The Vista Villas!" Alma said. "Do you have any idea what they rent for? And what, pray tell, does your sister need with a swimming pool, a hot tub, and tennis courts? I hear there's even an arcade on the premises and a clubhouse where they have weekly social gatherings. What does a married woman need with a social club?"

"Mama's right," Beryl said. "I don't need anything fancy. Just something clean, near school and church."

"She needs a place where there are other Christian women like herself. I hear the Vista Villas have a lot of single and divorced men. Why, they might try to take advantage of Beryl's innocent nature.''

''You're missing the point,'' Meg said. ''The Vista Villas has a security gate. Think how safe you'll feel knowing the place is watched twenty-four hours a day.''

''Meg's certainly right about that,'' Alma said. It was the first time Meg could recall her mother agreeing with her about anything. ''But what about Travis?'' she asked suddenly.

''Oh, he isn't going to leave that house,'' Beryl said. ''He'll just have to visit us when he can. Hopefully, they'll catch this burglar soon. But I'm not going back until they do, and that's final.'' She was quiet for a minute. ''How will I ever afford that kind of rent?'' she asked, turning to Meg. They both knew she had the money, but that had to be their secret.

Henry started to say something, but Meg cut him off. ''I can loan you the money, Beryl. I made quite a bit off the sale of my house in Atlanta.''

''Oh, thank you, Meg. You're a lifesaver. And I'll see that Travis pays back every penny of it.''

It was still early, not even eight o'clock when Meg left, and the thought of going back to the campsite and sitting by herself was not the least bit tempting.

She found herself in front of Clay's house twenty minutes later. It was dark; no one home. She gave a dejected sigh as she backed out of the drive and headed back toward town. She drove around for a bit, past the drive-in where she and Clay had exchanged some heated kisses in the backseat of his car, past the Royal Castle where they'd hung out with friends. The building looked much the same, but the parking lot was deserted. Still restless, Meg drove to the office, made a pot of coffee, and worked on various small articles she'd been assigned. She polished them, printed them out, and dropped them on Etheridge's desk.

She spent the next few hours in the morgue guzzling coffee, chain-smoking, and sifting through old newspapers, searching for story ideas and fresh angles. She came across a handful of articles concerning the holiness church, made copies for her file, and went about putting things away.

It was by sheer accident that she spied an engagement picture of Clay and Becky Parker. She studied the picture closely. They were a striking couple, Clay dark and handsome, Becky pretty and fair-haired. On a whim, she grabbed the phone directory and scanned the listings for a Becky Skinner and saw that she lived on Apple Orchard Lane, less than ten minutes away.

It was after eleven when Meg reached the upper-middle-class neighborhood where Jeep Cherokees and Ford Blazers, plus a couple of Broncos, were the vehicles of choice. She stopped in front of a neat, two-story frame house with black shutters. It was dark; those inside were obviously snug in bed. Meg didn't have to check the mailbox to see if it was Becky's house. Clay's pickup parked in the driveway was proof enough.

Twenty-five

IT WAS after midnight by the time the last visitor left the Dill house. Sara washed the coffee cups and set them on a dish towel to dry, then went about straightening the place. Purvis was still slumped in the fake leather recliner next to his pa's casket, looking forlorn and utterly lost. She knew he was consumed with guilt; his pa had died trying to protect him. Nothing anyone said seemed to help.

"Why don't you try to rest now?" she said, putting her hand on his shoulder. "I can sit up with your pa."

Purvis raised red-rimmed eyes to hers. Sara looked like an angel standing there, her eyes big and worried. A small frown creased her forehead. Was this a sign from God? Had He sent Sara to ease his grief? He gazed about the room and saw they were alone except for the stiff figure that had once been his father, in the casket. When had the others left?

"I'm too wound up to sleep," he said. "You should have gone home with Maybelline."

"We've already agreed on this, Purvis. I'll watch over the body tonight, and Maybelline'll stay tomorrow night."

"Why do people feel they need to sit with the body anyway?" Purvis asked. "It's not like he's going anywhere."

"That's just the way we've always done things." Sara reached for a straight-back chair and pulled it closer to him. She sat down and took Purvis's hand. It felt as cold and lifeless as Amos's. She felt Purvis stiffen and wondered why he was so uncomfortable with her lately. Had she offended him somehow? She released his hand and clasped her fingers together, trying to think of something to say.

"Pa once told me there was a time when the family took care of the dearly departed, and we didn't have to worry about sending the body to a funeral home. He said the family bathed and dressed their loved one and saw to the laying out of the body. It sounds so much nicer than how we do things today. I'd much rather have a family member or close friend tend to me than some stranger."

Purvis shuddered at the thought of having to bathe and dress a loved one who'd passed on. He'd heard tell how folks'd have to break the arms and legs of the deceased, once rigor mortis set in. He'd even heard of dead folks being stored in barns or on front porches when the ground was too frozen to bury them.

He was not comfortable with death; in fact, it frightened him worse than anything else he could think of. He hated touching a dead person, hated kissing them good-bye, as was custom. And the smell. That sickly sweet scent that no amount of embalming fluid could erase. He hadn't yet kissed his father good-bye. He would be expected to do that at the funeral. His stomach churned with anxiety at the thought. Temple viewed the death of a Christian as a joyous occasion to be celebrated, not mourned. He believed the minute a man took his last breath, he woke up in God's arms. Purvis was not so sure. What if it was all just a big hoax?

Finally, Purvis could sit still no longer. He tried not to think how his father would look in a couple of days or a week from now, after they'd closed the coffin forever. He tried not to think of his poor daddy sealed tightly inside without air or sunlight, but the thoughts came regardless.

Sara noticed his pained expression. "Purvis? You okay?"

He tugged at the collar on his shirt; he couldn't seem to catch his breath. All he could think of was being closed up in a black vacuum, his cells screaming for oxygen. Without warning, he raced to the door and bolted from the house. The night air was cold; he sucked it in. Suddenly, he couldn't get enough. In and out. Gasping. Panting like a dog. He gripped the porch rail for support. He was only vaguely aware that Sara had followed him out.

"Purvis, stop that!" she cried. "You're going to hyperventilate." She rubbed his back. He flinched and edged away. "Stop running from me, for heaven's sake," Sara said. "Let me help you." She'd barely gotten the words out of her mouth before he turned and grasped both of her arms.

Purvis shook her. "Help me? You're the one who's tormenting me!" he shouted.

"What have I done?" she asked, eyes tearing. "Whatever it is, I'll stop."

"Can't you see how I feel about you? How I've felt for some time now?" He saw the tears spilling from her eyes, and he hated himself for being the cause. "I love you, Sara."

A sob caught in her throat. "Well, I love you, too, Purvis. I always have."

"Not that kind of love, Sara," he said, his frustration clear. "Not the kind you feel for a close friend or family member. I'm talking about the love shared between a man and a woman." He watched her mouth, that beautiful, perfect mouth, form a small O of surprise.

"How could you not know?" he asked. Purvis didn't give her a chance to answer. His own mouth came down on hers, hard and demanding. He tasted her lips, and he knew it was probably the closest he'd ever come to reaching heaven. When he raised his head, he found her cheeks wet with tears. "Oh, Sara," he said, releasing her. "I didn't mean to make you cry. I should have kept my feelings to myself."

"I—I thought you hated me," she confessed. "The

way you've been acting toward me lately.''

''I could never hate you, sweet Sara. If I've been acting strange, it's only because I've been agonizing over this for months. Your father would never permit anything between us, even if you were so inclined, which I know you're not. I know how desperate you are to escape these mountains.''

Sara still tasted his kiss—the *only* kiss she'd ever shared with a man, hard as it was to believe at her age. ''I never said I wanted to escape from *you*.'' She touched his sleeve. ''You could come with me.''

Purvis looked stunned. ''Come with you?'' He considered it for a moment as he gazed down at her, heart overflowing with love. Did that mean she felt something for him as well? A shimmer of hope went through him.

''I'm leaving, with or without Pa's blessing,'' she said. ''I'll never have a life outside the church if I stay, never a moment's freedom. Besides, I can't condone building a new church of the magnitude Pa's talking about. We don't have that many members, and who knows how long we're going to attract these crowds? We could end up with this elaborate church, big enough to seat half the town of Blalock, and only twenty or thirty people attending.

''In the meantime we have people going hungry, several families crowding into one flimsy shack that looks as though it's going to fall with the next strong breeze. They nail newspapers to the walls to keep the cold from slipping through the cracks, and their windows are covered with plastic because they can't afford to buy new ones.

''We have children walking around with no shoes on their feet or coats on their backs, and nobody seems to care. I'm not talking about abandoning these people, Purvis. I have all intentions of coming back once I get my degree. Then I'll be in a better position to help them, *fight* for them. Right now I'm just an ignorant mountain girl. Who's going to listen to me?'' Sara took his hand. ''You could make a difference, too, Purvis. Look how you take up for the mill workers. Let Pa worry about everybody's souls; we need to be concerned about jobs and schooling and health. We need to fight the alcohol and drug abuse and family violence. And incest,'' she added softly. ''Folks can deny it exists all they want, but it's happening.'' She shook her head sadly.

''Only in the most remote areas,'' Purvis said.

''What difference does it make? We're talking about human beings committing terrible acts against one another. We're talking about schoolgirls bearing babies that belong to their pas or their brothers. And you know as well as I do that these babies have problems. They're not normal.''

Sara suddenly jumped at hearing a rustle in the bushes. ''Is anybody there?'' she called. Maybe someone from the church had decided to return and sit with them through the night—though they would've come up the path openly. Nobody answered, and she told herself it was only the wind. She was just letting herself get spooked because of Amos's wake.

But Purvis had heard the noise, too. ''Let's go inside,'' he said, knowing wild animals still roamed the mountains freely at night. ''We can talk of this later. After the funeral, when I can think clearly.'' He paused and looked into her face. ''Don't tell anyone about what we've discussed here tonight, Sara. Let's keep it between the two of us. Promise?''

She nodded, and Purvis ushered her inside.

Neither of them saw the face peering at them through the leafy vines of a wild honeysuckle bush, its expression twisted into a grimace of jealous rage.

Twenty-six

WHEN SARA opened her eyes the following morning, the sun was just coming up, sending a murky gray light through the window over Amos's coffin. Nearby, Purvis was sleeping soundly, probably the only decent sleep he'd had since his father's death. Sara raised up from the sofa, grabbed her small purse, and tiptoed to the tiny bathroom. When she came out, her face and teeth were clean, and her long hair had been brushed and pulled back with a strip of material. Using care not to waken Purvis, she scribbled a quick note, slipped out the back door, and started home. There was much to do in preparation for Brother Dill's funeral.

Sara hadn't gone very far before she heard the sounds: twigs snapping, leaves rustling. Footsteps? Was someone following her? She glanced around. "Purvis, is that you?" she called, wondering if he'd awakened, found her gone, and come in search of her. Perhaps he'd overlooked her note. "Purvis?" she repeated.

There was no answer—nothing but a thick silence that went unbroken by the sound of a whippoorwill or an occasional owl. The forest was shrouded in a gray mist that fell cold and damp on her cheek. She shivered and moved on. Her house was less than twenty minutes away on foot; she and her sister had taken this same route many times. She passed a stand of white pines and veered left, knowing she was at the halfway mark. Suddenly, she heard the sounds again. There *was* someone following her.

Sara swung around. "Who's there?" she demanded. "Purvis, is that you?" she repeated. She remembered the childish pranks he'd pulled on her and Maybelline when they were kids. "If you're trying to spook me, it won't work, so stop hiding and come out." She'd barely gotten the words out of her mouth before a shotgun blasted, an ear-splitting crack that couldn't have come from more than a hundred feet away. Someone was shooting at her! Hunters or poachers, most likely, and probably drunk to boot. "Don't shoot!" she cried, but another shot rang out, the bullet ricocheting off a tall poplar.

Panicked, Sara whipped around and took off, running fast as she could through the thick woods. Adrenaline rushed through her veins like a wild river, making her sweat despite the cold. She dodged trees and bushes and jumped fallen logs as she raced like a scared rabbit, tall grass and briars slapping and biting her bare legs. Another shot, and this time she actually heard the bullet whiz past her! The person was either stone crazy or out to kill her. Who hated her that much?

The forest floor became a sharp incline, and Sara knew she'd never be able to outrun the person after her. She spied a dense cluster of rhododendrons ahead and knew it was her only hope. She scrambled between the branches, hit the ground and prayed.

Meg called Melinda that morning to tell her she was checking out a story and would be in later. With a coffee cup in one hand, cigarette in the other, she climbed behind the wheel of her camper and headed up the mountain to the Beechum house. She saw Maybelline standing at the edge of the woods brandishing some sort of rifle. Damn these mountain women and their guns. It was worse than Atlanta.

Meg climbed from the cab of the camper and hurried toward the woman. "What's wrong?"

"Someone's shooting," she said. "Close by. Probably

those stinkin' Attaway brothers out poaching. If they set foot on this property, they're going to have a surprise waiting for them."

"Where's Sara?"

"She spent the night at the Dill house."

They stood there several minutes listening. "I don't hear anything," Meg said.

"Could be I scared them off." She relaxed after a moment. "You want a cup of coffee?"

"Yeah, sure." Meg followed Maybelline toward the house. "When do you expect Sara home?"

"She said she'd be home early. There's lots to do in preparation for Brother Dill's funeral. She'll have to cut through those woods. That's why I don't like hearin' shots."

"You think she's okay?"

"Actually, I was thinkin' of going after her," Maybelline replied.

"I'll go with you."

"No, you'll just end up gettin' lost and I'll have to look for you, too."

Meg opened her mouth to protest when she suddenly heard a noise, something like a sob. Both women glanced up as the bushes parted and Sara stumbled into the clearing, her face and legs scratched and bleeding.

Maybelline rushed forward. "Sara, what on earth happened to you?"

"Someone was . . . shooting at me," she gasped.

Still holding the rifle, Maybelline put one arm around the sobbing girl. "I heard them," she said. "I was fixin' to come looking for you, but you're always fussin' how I treat you like a child. Are you sure it wasn't poachers?"

"I called out to let whoever it was know I was there. They fired anyway."

Maybelline looked angry. "I'm willin' to bet my last dime it was Harley and Bert Attaway tryin' to get even."

"We should call the sheriff," Meg said.

"Nate Overton isn't going to help us," Sara said, wiping tears from her eyes. "His wife is blood kin to that bunch."

"Sara's right," Maybelline said. "Why do you think we just let 'em go the night they brought that rattlesnake in that killed Amos? Nate's wife ain't right in the head, and he's not about to do anything to upset her. Besides, if we get Nate riled up, it's likely to make things harder on Pa."

"This is all so unbelievable," Meg says. "A sheriff who takes bribes and won't arrest anyone who's related to him. Why do people stand for this?"

Maybelline prodded Sara in the direction of the house. "We're the only ones who know how crooked he is," she said, "but we cain't say anythin' 'cause he'll shut down the church. Our hands is tied."

They got Sara inside. Meg helped her out of her jacket while Maybelline searched for something to clean her wounds. "It's hotter'n a pistol in here," Maybelline said, cracking a couple of windows so some fresh air could get in. "I've been bakin' all morning." She saw to Sara's scratches, then poured each of them a cup of coffee.

"I may be able to help you with your problem," Meg told Sara, once they were settled at the kitchen table.

Sara and Maybelline exchanged looks. "You mean you can help me escape this place?" the younger sister asked.

Meg nodded. "I called a friend of mine last night. She helped me through a tough time, and she's agreed to put you up until you can find a job and save enough money of your own. She can probably assist you in locating college funds."

"Is this for real?" Sara asked, unable to believe what she was hearing.

"I know you're desperate," Meg said, glancing at Maybelline. She pulled an envelope from her purse. "There's enough money in here to buy a bus ticket and take care of any personal needs you might have."

The sisters looked at each other, then back at Meg. Sara's eyes misted. "I don't know what to say . . . how to thank you. I'll pay you back as soon as I can."

"There's a bus leaving for Atlanta tonight."

"Tonight?" Sara thought of Purvis. "I'll need a day or two."

Maybelline's jaw fell open. "What do you mean you need a day or two? Here's the chance you've been waitin' for, and with Pa in jail it'll be easier to get away."

Sara chewed her bottom lip. She wanted to tell them about her conversation with Purvis, but she'd promised not to, and even though she'd never kept anything from her sister, she couldn't go back on her word. She had to let Purvis know where she would be in case he decided to join her. "I have to wait until after Brother Dill's funeral," she said. She looked at Maybelline. "We've been friends with Purvis too long for me to walk away in the middle of burying his pa."

Her older sister suddenly looked frustrated. "Don't you think Purvis would understand?" she asked. "Good grief, Sara, you've got to think of yourself for once."

"I can't leave tonight," Sara said.

"When's the funeral?" Meg asked.

"Tomorrow morning at eleven."

"Okay, there's another bus leaving at two-thirty," Meg said. "Sara, you can still attend the funeral, but you have to be back here, packed and ready, no later than one forty-five."

"I can do that," Sara said, knowing it would give her time to tell Purvis what was going on. "Can you tell me where I'll be staying?"

Meg reached into her purse. "As long as you don't let it get in the wrong hands. I don't want your father starting trouble with my friend." She handed Sara the slip of paper with Libby's address.

"I'll personally wring her neck if she tells anybody," Maybelline said. "And I want you to stick that money in your bra, Sara, and don't take it out till you get to the bus station." Sara did as she said. "Lordy, look at the time," Maybelline said. "Brother Thomas is supposed to pick me up at noon to carry me to the Dill house, and I still have to fry up these here chickens to take with me. Once I heard those shots, I dropped everythin' and—'' She paused and looked at her sister. ''I can't leave you alone tonight. Not if there's a chance someone's out to hurt you. I'll have to ask somebody else to sit with Purvis.''

''I'll keep the doors locked,'' Sara said.

Maybelline shook her head. ''That's not going to stop the Attaways if that's who's after you. They'll kick the door down and, well, no tellin' what.'' She glanced at Meg, and it was obvious what she feared most.

Meg had no desire to stay at the Beechum house, especially if there was a chance Bert and Harley would show up. Of course, they could all be overreacting, but she wasn't about to take a chance. ''Sara can stay with me tonight. It'll be a tight squeeze, but she's more than welcome. The campground is less than twenty minutes from here. I can run her up here first thing in the morning, then go back to my office until it's time to pick her up to go to the bus station.''

Maybelline looked relieved. ''I'll try to get someone to take over sittin' with Purvis bright and early,'' she said. ''That way Sara won't have to come home to an empty house, and Purvis'll have somebody with him when they come for his daddy's body.'' She looked at Meg. ''I'll rest easier knowin' Sara's with you.''

Twenty-seven

THE DAY dragged for Purvis, who welcomed one guest after another into his house and listened to various accounts of his father's life. He'd not slept more than a few hours in the last twenty-four, and he could feel his eyes sagging. Maybelline had seen to feeding everyone and cleaning up after them, but Sara had not stopped by once. She'd slipped out that morning while he was still asleep, leaving him with this leaden feeling in his gut that hadn't gone away. It was approaching dark by the time the last visitor left. He turned to Maybelline reluctantly.

"I don't mean to hurt your feelings," he said, "but I'd rather be alone tonight if you don't mind."

Maybelline glanced up from wiping down the kitchen table. "Save your breath, Purvis; I'm not leavin' you at a time like this."

He regarded her. She had never been pretty, nor was she dainty like her sister. She was a big woman, tall and raw-boned and capable. Her ample bosom tempted him, made him wish he could bury his face against it and escape this overwhelming sense of loss that had overtaken him the minute his father had slipped away. He was instantly ashamed. How could he love one woman as much as he did Sara and harbor such thoughts about another? What kind of man was he?

"What you need is somethin' to make you relax,"

Maybelline said. "How else do you plan to make it through the funeral tomorrow?"

He shook his head, feeling too weary to argue. He didn't want her to take care of him; he didn't want to be surrounded by friends and well-wishers. He longed for solitude, so he could mourn his father's passing in privacy and give in to his fears. He was tired of pretending to be brave. "Maybelline, please—"

"Tell you what I'll do," she said. "I'm goin' to make you some chamomile tea. My granny used to make it for me and Sara when we couldn't sleep. I keep a little haw-thorne in my purse," she said, reaching for her bag. "Set-tles the nerves. Granny taught me all kinds of tricks." She filled a kettle with water and put it on to boil. When Purvis started to object, she shushed him. "You have to keep up your strength, honey. How's it going to look if you fall apart—"

"I'm not going to fall apart, Maybelline," he said, al-though lately he feared he would. It was this thing he had about death. What if he *did* crack up tomorrow in front of everybody while trying to preside over his own father's funeral? And what would he do when they closed the coffin and shut off all the light and oxygen? He took a deep breath. The room seemed to be closing in on him. The reverend was so much better dealing with this sort of thing. Of all times for him to be in jail.

"I could ask one of the deacons to take care of the service. Every single one of 'em loved your pa dearly."

"I don't want a deacon handling it," Purvis said sharply, knowing most of them didn't use good English or read past second- or third-grade level. They didn't have the presence Temple Beechum had; they'd botch up the whole thing. "My father deserves better."

"Here, Purvis, drink this." Maybelline set a cup of piping hot tea in front of him. "Why don't I fix you a sandwich? You haven't eaten all day."

"I'm not hungry." He sank heavily onto a kitchen chair and reached for the cup. The tea was good, and it warmed his belly. Maybe it would take the chill away. "I wish your father was here. I feel—'' He stopped. He'd almost told her how lost he felt. How would that look for the associate pastor? It was his job to take over when Reverend Beechum couldn't be there, and he was failing miserably. "I'm thinking of trying to bail him out of jail tomorrow," he said, his voice little more than a croak. "He should be in charge of the funeral." He wanted to make her understand they were expecting too much from him.

Maybelline shook her head sadly. "They're not going to let Pa out. He's lookin' at thirty days minimum. Could be closer to sixty this time."

He took another sip of the tea. "Nate's greedy. He'll let him out if the price is right."

Maybelline regarded him. "Where do you plan to get the money?"

Purvis could feel the sweat popping out on his forehead and upper lip. He ran a hand over his face and found it slick. "From the church funds. The reverend will just have to understand." He suspected Reverend Beechum would pitch a fit for spending money meant for the new church, even if it was to get him out of jail.

"Well, you might get Nate to agree to lettin' him out, but Mayor Bradley won't go for it."

Purvis took a deep, shaky breath and drained the tea. He knew the mayor couldn't be bought. He was an honest man, a strict Baptist, who talked family values and bad-mouthed the rich and greedy. He would fire Nate Overton in a second if he knew the man was taking bribes. Bradley'd won his last election by promising to create more jobs, fight for higher standards of education, and offer incentive programs for kids to stay in school. So far, the only thing he'd accomplished was getting a handful of computers into the high school, but the dropout rate was the same, and he hadn't made much progress in the job department either. Those who weren't able to commute to larger cities for work ended up taking what they could get in Blalock. Competition was stiff; employers had the upper hand. Purvis figured the mayor needed a new cause if he was to win the next year's election.

Perhaps Mayor Bradley's new platform should be job reform. Purvis thought about the notebook he kept hidden beneath the seat in his truck. *The book.* It listed every single offense, every safety violation at the factory; it even gave the date, the names of those involved, and the witnesses. For months he'd wondered what to do with it.

Now he knew.

"Purvis, you don't look well," Maybelline said. "Why don't you lay down for a spell?"

"Huh?" He looked up, having forgotten for a minute she was in the room. He saw the worry in her eyes and felt guilty. Did she know him so well that she could sense the fear in him? One deacon was dead, and the church minister was behind bars. What would happen if he couldn't cut the mustard, if he collapsed in the face of death when he'd told so many they had to be strong? He needed the reverend, and Mayor Bradley was his only hope.

Right now, he was much too tired to figure everything out. "I think I'll rest," he said at last.

Meg had never felt so tired in her life. She had spent the day helping Sara. There was wood to be chopped, hogs to be slopped, chickens to be fed, and a multitude of household chores that had kept them busy until late afternoon. The time had passed quickly, though. Sara was a wealth of information on mountain life—she knew everything there was to know about home remedies, midwifery, burial customs, planting by the signs, you name it. She'd also answered questions about the holiness practice. For dinner, Sara dropped a fist-size mound of lard into a hot iron skillet, in which she fried a mixture of potatoes, squash, and onions. She served it with canned tomatoes and cracklin' bread. Meg learned cracklin' came from boiled-down hog fat.

"We don't throw away anything when we slaughter our hogs," Sara said. "The feet, the skin, the tail, even the head."

Meg looked up. "The head?"

"Yeah, we call it souse meat or headcheese. We cut out the eyes, of course. Then we scrape off the hairs and soak the whole head in a pot of water to get the blood out and cook it till the meat falls off the bones. Run it through a grinder, add your seasoning and cornmeal, and there you have it. I'm not crazy about it. Tastes like fish. Pa doesn't like it either. He says he doesn't want to eat anything off a hog that tastes fishy. Most folks in these parts love it. I guess some people will eat anything. You ever heard of hog's head stew?" When Meg merely wrinkled her nose, she went on. "Now, that's not so bad. My granny used to can sixty to seventy quarts of that every year come fall."

Meg listened as Sara gave her the ingredients. She grinned at the thought of Libby, who shopped at health food stores and was always on the lookout for new ways to use kale, sprouts, and bean curd, and who would have instantly paled at the sight of solidified fat, which seemed to be the mainstay of the Beechums' diet. "You're going to have to share your recipes with my friend from Atlanta," she told Sara.

Meg cleaned the small kitchen while Sara packed a suitcase and hid it at the back of her closet. As Meg washed the dishes, she glanced out the window above the sink several times. It was after seven o'clock, and she'd planned to be gone before dark. Maybelline had left the rifle behind, claiming Sara was a better shot than most, but Meg had no desire to witness the young woman's expertise. She'd thought the only people who carried weapons wherever they went were thieves and drug dealers, but the mountain people seemed to have a code of their own. Maybe it had something to do with having a sheriff who was on the take.

"We need to get going," Meg called out as soon as she'd dried the last dish and put it away.

Sara came hurrying out of the bedroom with a paper sack. "I'm taking a nightgown, my toothbrush, and a change of clothes. I can dress for the funeral in the morning."

They stepped outside a few minutes later and stood under a naked bulb on the porch while Sara locked up. Meg didn't breathe easy until they were both in the cab of her camper and on their way down the mountain. She noticed Sara was unusually quiet.

"Are you nervous about tomorrow?"

The other woman nodded. "I've never been out of these mountains. I don't know anything about Atlanta. I once saw a postcard of it." She gave a nervous laugh. "There's a lot of tall buildings. I guess that shouldn't frighten me, since I'm surrounded by tall mountains, huh?"

"Are you sure you want to go through with it?" Meg asked, hearing the doubt in Sara's voice.

Sara looked out the window. "I've never been more sure of anything in my whole life." She glanced at Meg. "That doesn't mean I don't plan on returning one day. I *do* aim to come back once I get my education."

"I hope your father doesn't give you any trouble," Meg told her. They rode in silence for a while, each of them caught up in her own thoughts.

"I need to write a couple of letters before I turn in tonight."

Meg tossed her a smile. "A boyfriend?"

Sara was thoughtful for a minute. "I'm not sure." She shifted in her seat. "He and I grew up together. I've always thought of him as a brother—till lately," she added. "Are you married?"

Meg shook her head. "Not anymore."

"Do you have someone here you might wish to marry one day?"

"If I could have a wish, I'd ask for one of those whirlpool tubs,'' Meg said. ''I hate taking a shower in this thing.''

''Where would you put a tub that size?''

''I'd have to leave that up to the genie. I'm too busy to be bothered with every little detail.'' Meg followed the winding road through the campground. It was a cozy scene, people sitting around campfires. She almost wished she hadn't chased off Randy Bekins; he had to be pretty good at building a fire. Then Meg spied Clay's pickup truck sitting beside her site.

Twenty-eight

"**W**HAT THE hell do you mean, we were robbed?" Travis demanded over the phone from his motel room. He was freshly showered and dressed and already ten minutes late for his date with this sweet little thing he'd met the night before at some cowboy bar.

"There's no need to shout," Beryl said. "At least be thankful that me and the kids weren't home when it happened. We could have been killed. Which is why I'm staying with my parents right now. I refuse to set foot in that house until they find the burglar."

"Does the sheriff have any leads?"

"Not a one." She paused. "Travis, I've been thinking maybe the kids and me ought to get us a little place in town. Just temporarily, mind you. Until they find this person."

"And just where do you think the money's going to come from?"

Beryl knew darn good and well where it was coming from, but she wasn't about to tell him. "You know how difficult my mother can be," she said. "I'm already a nervous wreck as it is. The poor kids are having nightmares."

"Look, everything's insured. What the hell did they take?"

"Well, your guns and fishing supplies for one thing,"

she said, then paused when he flew into a litany of cuss words. "All your sports equipment, as a matter of fact. Oh, and that old moose head from over the mantle."

Her words had the same effect on him as a syringe of ice water shot into his veins. Travis started to tremble; he suddenly felt sick. "Beryl, what the fuck are you talking about?"

She almost shivered. Never in all their years of marriage had she heard him use that tone. "I'm sorry, Travis. I know how much it meant to you."

Travis hung up the telephone without another word. He was still shaking with shock, was chilled to the bone. He didn't even bother to kick off his shoes as he pulled the bed covers aside and climbed beneath them. He closed his eyes and concentrated on getting warm. All that money. Who could have taken it? Who the hell could have *known*? He would find out, by God, and they'd regret the day they were born!

Just like J.T.'s son, that nosy son of a bitch who'd come close to blowing the whistle on his lucrative business dealings. Easiest way in the world to get rid of somebody in these parts was to run 'em off the mountain.

Meg and Sara opened their doors simultaneously and stepped out of the camper's cab. Although Clay looked surprised to see Sara, he nodded politely and hurried around to hook up the utilities. Meg pulled out the metal step and unlocked the door. "Clay, you remember Sara Beechum," she said when he joined them. "Sara, this is Clay Skinner, an old high school buddy of mine."

"You were with Meg the other night at church," Sara said.

"Yes. I enjoyed hearing you sing." He turned to Meg. "Could I have a word with you?"

"Sara and I are very tired—"

"It won't take long."

Meg looked at the other woman, who seemed unsure what to do. "There's a box of stationery in the cabinet over the kitchen table," she said. "You can start on those letters you wanted to write. I'll be right in."

"Nice to see you again, Mr. Skinner," Sara said, and disappeared inside the camper.

"What's she doing here?" Clay asked in a quiet voice.

"Never mind that. What are *you* doing here? Last I heard, you'd moved back in with Becky."

He looked stunned. "Who the hell told you that?"

"I saw it with my own eyes."

"You were *spying* on me?"

"Call it what you like. I was looking after my emotional well-being. I've already been screwed once."

"So what'd you see, Meg?" he asked. "Or better yet, what do you *think* you saw?"

"I saw your car parked in Becky's driveway at midnight. All the lights were off."

"And you just naturally assumed I was sharing my ex-wife's bed as well. Thanks for the vote of confidence."

"I figured you'd try to deny it."

"Why should I deny it when you've already found me guilty?" he snapped. "Look, I'm not going to stand here arguing about this. I've had a crappy couple of days, and I don't deserve to be accused of something I didn't do. And I'm damn sure not going to keep walking on eggshells because another man took a shit on you. Have a good life, Meg." He turned for his truck.

She panicked at the thought of him walking away. "Then you tell me what the hell you were doing over there that time of night," she said, wishing she didn't sound like one of those jealous wives in pink foam hair curlers and quilted bathrobes.

He paused and turned. "My daughter happened to be very sick, so I spent the night in a sleeping bag in her bedroom. Had you bothered to hang around till about two A.M., you would have witnessed Becky and me rushing her to the emergency room, where she spent the night."

Meg's first impulse was not to believe him. How did

she know he wasn't just pulling one over on her? She'd certainly been gullible in the past.

"I still carry Cindy on my insurance plan, and I have her discharge papers. I'll show them to you if that's what it takes, but I refuse to keep going on like this. If my word isn't good enough—" He shrugged.

Meg's eyes smarted with tears, but she turned her head so he wouldn't suspect. She walked over to the picnic table and sat down. "I sometimes have a problem with trust," she confessed.

"One would never know," he said dryly. He joined her at the table and took her hand in his. "Meg"—he sighed heavily—"I was in love with you once. When you left, I got angry. I even hated you for a long time. But I never fell out of love with you. It doesn't matter that you were gone from my life ten years, or that you were married to another man. My feelings haven't changed—except to grow stronger.

"I'm going out on a limb here by telling you this, because I don't know what your plans are, or where you're going to be a month from now. But I'm willing to risk it. I still love you, Meg. I don't want another woman. I never have."

She felt the back of her throat grow thick, and her eyes misted. She raised her hand to his cheek and touched it lightly. She could feel the stubble of his beard. "That's so . . . sweet."

"I'm not trying to be sweet; I'm trying to tell you how I feel about you." He paused once more. "But as much as I care, I can't just walk away from my other obligations. If something happens to my daughter, I have to go. It's always going to be that way."

She waited for him to say more, but he didn't. "And Becky?"

"Becky knows about you."

"How?"

"It's a small town; word travels fast. She asked me if

it was serious, and I told her it was for me, but I couldn't speak for you.''

"How did she take it?''

"She took it very well." He shrugged. "What's she going to do? We're divorced. She's the mother of my child, but that's the extent of our relationship. Do you believe what I'm telling you?''

She leaned against him. "Yes. But you're going to have to be patient with me. I have to get used to the idea of sharing you.''

He slipped his arms around her waist. "What we have between us can't be shared; that's *ours*. The fact that I love my daughter doesn't make me love you less.''

Meg felt the lump in her throat the size of a goose egg. "I love you, too, Clay," she said.

He pulled her into his arms and kissed her deeply, then held her in his arms for a long time. Finally, he released her. "I don't mean to change the subject, but what is that girl doing here?''

"Her sister fears she's in danger." Meg went on to explain about the shots fired at Sara in the woods.

"Jesus, Meg, why are you getting mixed up in it? If she's in danger then she could be putting *you* in danger.''

"How can I be in danger? Only a couple of people know where I'm staying.''

"Suppose you were followed. Did you bother to check?''

"You're being paranoid.''

Clay stood and shoved his hands in his pockets. "One of us needs to be. What do you even know about this girl? If somebody's shooting at her, they're not going to stop until she's dead. I don't like it, Meg. Why did you even get involved with these people to begin with?''

She stood as well. "I'm a big girl, Clay. If I choose to befriend Sara Beechum, that's my business.''

"No, babe. I just poured my heart out to you. It's my business, too." He gave her a knowing look. "You're trying to get a story out of this, aren't you?''

She felt herself blush. "It started out that way. But Sara needs my help. She's trying to escape from her father. He's cruel to her, Clay. He keeps her a prisoner in their own home."

He shook his head in disbelief. "Do you know what you're doing, Meg? This church group could be nothing more than another one of those cults. If somebody suspects one of the members of trying to defect, they'll stop at nothing to get to her. And if they think you're involved, you could end up dead on the side of the road."

"You're making too much of this," she said, although she was beginning to worry as well. It hadn't occurred to her that someone had possibly learned of Sara's plan to escape, and was determined to stop her. She wasn't just *any* member—she was the main attraction. Without her, the church would fold.

"You can't stay here tonight," Clay said. "You'll have to sleep at my place."

"Oh, won't that be cozy," she said. "Sorry, Clay, I'm not leaving Sara."

"You misunderstood me, babe. I'm not trying to seduce you; I'm trying to save your neck. Yours *and* Sara's. Now, be a good girl and pack a bag."

She looked at him. "I just don't want you to think I can't take care of myself."

"That thought never crossed my mind. Tell you what, I'll even let you smoke in my house."

She pondered it. "You wouldn't happen to have one of those whirlpool tubs, would you?"

Twenty-nine

BY THE time Meg climbed out of Clay's Jacuzzi, she felt as limp and wilted as a vase of old flowers. She pulled on a nightshirt and panties and stepped out barefoot into Clay's bedroom. He was lying, fully clothed, on a pine sleigh bed that looked as inviting as the man on it. He was watching TV, with the phone tucked between his head and the pillow. He mumbled something into it and hung up.

"Feel better?" he asked.

Meg wondered if he'd been talking to Becky. She wouldn't ask. "I'm not cut out for chopping wood and slopping hogs," she said. "When I grow up, I'm going to buy a condo surrounded by an asphalt parking lot. That way, I won't even have to mow the grass."

Clay gazed back at her lazily. He could see the question in her eyes. It would have been easier to just tell her that he'd been talking to one of his subcontractors, but he wasn't going to get into the habit of explaining his every move. He smiled at her. She looked squeaky clean, her wet hair curling about her face, her skin pink and flushed from her bath. Her nipples poked through the thin fabric of her thigh-length T-shirt. Her legs were the stuff men dreamed about.

"You already look grown-up to me," he said.

"On the outside, maybe. Inside"—she pointed to her head—"I'm just as confused as ever."

He patted the mattress. "Come tell Papa."

Meg hesitated a moment before crossing the room and sitting on the edge of the bed. "There's not much to tell," she said, avoiding eye contact. "I guess I'm just trying to sort through things."

He reached for a strand of her hair and toyed with it. He caught the honeysuckle scent of her shampoo. "I hope you're not confused about us." He let his hand drop to her thigh and tried not to notice how smooth it was. It wasn't easy, now that he knew how smooth she was all over.

"I suppose I'm going to have to let go of some of my resentments. And maybe learn to trust again," she added.

"Would it help to know that I've no intention of hurting you?"

"I'm something of a coward when it comes to matters of the heart."

He reached up, cupped the back of her head with his palm, and pulled her down for a long kiss. Finally, he released her. "You don't ever have to be afraid again."

"I wish I could sleep with you."

"That makes two of us."

"I just wouldn't feel right. Not with Sara in the next room."

"There's always next time."

She kissed him good night and reluctantly made her way from the room.

Meg found Sara sitting on one of the twin beds, flipping through a magazine, when she came into the guest room. The younger woman had showered and braided her long hair. She wore a faded, oversize flannel gown that touched her ankles. "I figured you'd already be asleep," Meg said.

"No, I'm still looking through these magazines I brought from your place. You don't know what a treat it is for me. Pa won't let us have them in the house."

Meg took the opposite bed. She was debating grabbing her cigarettes and stepping outside for a quick smoke, but it would mean putting on her shoes and jacket, and she didn't have the energy for it. "I hardly think you'll find anything sinful in *Good Housekeeping*," she said.

"We're only allowed to read the Lord's word," Sara replied without elaborating. She studied the page before her. "Actually, I was looking at this article on quilting. They've even got different patterns listed." She looked up. "When my granny was alive, she kept a quilting frame in the living room at all times. She and her friends, must've been eight or ten of them, they could sew a quilt in less than a week. Sometimes they'd give it to someone who was getting married, or they'd sell it and use the money to buy food for someone who was down on his luck. Poor Granny tried to teach me, but I couldn't have sewn a straight stitch if my life'd depended on it."

"I'm not real handy with a needle myself," Meg said. Maybe she could just pull on her socks and step out on the patio for two or three quick puffs, just enough nicotine to settle her nerves and make her forget about Clay sleeping in that big bed all by himself. Of course, she risked being mauled by Clay's dog. At least the mauling was done out of affection, though, and not out of some primal need to taste human blood.

"Oh, if you could only see some of the fine work she did," Sara went on, almost wistfully. "Her quilts were very detailed, her stitches precise. In these parts, a good seamstress is considered good wife material."

"Then I'm out of luck," Meg said. "I can't even hem a skirt without botching it up." The hell with it, she thought, climbing beneath the sheets. She'd just smoke twice as much tomorrow to make up for not smoking tonight.

"And it didn't hardly cost nothing to make them. See, folks saved every scrap of material they could. Granny had the lady at the fabric store save her scraps, and then, of course, what scraps she was able to get from the mill. We'd get all kinds of pretty colors and designs. That material was for the front of the quilt. They used cotton batting for the filling, and they lined them with unbleached muslin. Won't nothing keep you warmer in the winter than a good thick quilt.''

Meg could think of one thing warmer than a quilt. She hoped Sara wasn't in a talkative mood; already, her eyes were beginning to glaze over from this chitchat.

''My granny had this special pattern she came up with all on her own, that she gave to newly married couples she was close to. She only made a few of them, and they were her pride. It was called Passion Flower.'' Sara laughed. ''She wouldn't give anyone else the pattern. She signed those quilts by placing her initials inside a hand-stitched wedding ring that was tucked inside the beak of a dove. The dove was to promote peace in the world, and the passion flower, which resembled an orchid, was supposed to make a couple more fertile.''

Meg noticed Sara was fidgeting with her hands. ''What's wrong, Sara?'' she asked. ''You look anxious.''

''My mind's racing. And I can't stop thinking of someone.''

''Who is he?''

Sara didn't quite meet her gaze. ''Purvis Dill, our associate pastor. Last night he told me he was in love with me. I'm still shocked.''

''How do you feel about him?''

Sara met her gaze. ''I'm a little confused. I don't really know what it feels like to be in love. I mean, I had crushes on boys back in high school, but nothing ever came of it since Pa refused to let me date.''

''Sometimes falling in love can be scary,'' Meg said, then realized she had actually said out loud what she'd been thinking. ''For some people,'' she added quickly.

They were quiet for a moment. ''I never really thought of Purvis in a romantic way before,'' Sara confessed. ''Like I said, we grew up together. Our folks were real close at one time. I guess it was before my mother left. I knew even then that Purvis wanted to be a minister.

''We had our own little church. At least that's what we pretended it to be. It was really an abandoned shack way out in the woods. We cleaned it up and held church services there. Purvis was handling snakes even then. Maybelline and I would sit on the floor and listen to him preach.'' She chuckled. ''Every now and then one of us would pretend to be lame or deaf, and Purvis would heal us.''

Sara was quiet for a moment. ''I still go there once in a while when I can get away. I didn't think anyone knew about it, but the last time I went I found a couple of old blankets. I figure vagrants must've taken it over.'' She yawned suddenly. ''Law me, I'm full of words tonight, aren't I?'' she said. ''I guess I'm edgy about tomorrow, too.'' She put the magazine on the nightstand and climbed beneath the sheets.

''You're going to be okay, Sara,'' Meg told her, as she reached to turn off the light. She pulled the covers to her chin. The sheets were crisp and smelled brand-new, as though they'd been pulled from their package and put on the bed without laundering. She smiled. It would never occur to Clay to wash them first.

She turned over and closed her eyes, but hard as she tried, her mind refused to close down for the night. She almost resented the fact that Sara had drifted off so easily. She entertained thoughts of sneaking into Clay's room and slipping into his bed naked, then decided against it. She didn't want to run the risk of Sara waking and hearing the whole thing.

Finally, Meg grabbed her purse and tiptoed from the room. She smoked three cigarettes in Clay's garage before returning to bed. But as she drifted off to sleep, his face was the last thing she saw.

Thirty

THE PICKUP truck turned into the Vista Campground and moved slowly along the winding road. Meg Gentry's camper wasn't hard to find, thanks to a full moon that gave the night a soft glow. That same full moon could also make it more difficult to do the job at hand.

The camper was dark; its occupants would be fast asleep by now.

The driver smiled. *They'll never know what hit 'em.*

Randy Bekins was drunk, and a little bit stoned from the joint he'd shared with the woman next to him. He was going to feel like shit come morning. He raised up on the bed, and the RV bedroom seemed to spin. He waited for his head to clear.

"You're not leaving, are you, sweetie?"

"Got to," he said, searching through the bedclothes for his underwear. He found it and stepped into the leg openings. "My boss is due to arrive tomorrow afternoon, and I've got to have this place in tiptop shape." He noted the time on the alarm clock. It was after two. Shit. He'd get only about four hours sleep if he was going to put the campground in order.

He reached for his jeans and shirt. It was his own fault he was behind. He'd been lax in his duties of late, ever since Mary Wilson had arrived in her spiffy new RV with its own miniature satellite dish, wet bar, Jacuzzi, and every other luxury one could think of.

"Why don't you drop by in the morning once you get caught up," Mary said, talking around a wide yawn. "I'll make you my famous blueberry pancakes."

"I'll probably be tied up most of the day," he said. He saw her frown. "Hey, I gotta make a living."

"You could drop by at the end of the day," she said. "I'll make you a nice dinner."

Randy didn't doubt it for a minute as he stepped into his jeans and zipped them. She had only arrived two days before, and he'd probably put on ten pounds, thanks to her gourmet cooking and a bar fully stocked with only brand name liquors. It didn't matter that she was twice his age. They still had a lot in common. She was lonely; he was bored. She had money; he was always in need of it.

Randy stepped out of the camper a few minutes later, turned on his flashlight, and started down the road. The night air was cold, and he sorely regretted having to leave Mary's comfortable bed with its scented sheets. He sucked in a deep breath and tried to clear his head, but he knew it would be awhile before the booze and pot wore off completely.

Down the road, a pickup truck idled. Randy frowned. He hoped there hadn't been an emergency while he was partying with Mary. That wouldn't look good to his boss. But damn, he couldn't be on the job twenty-four hours a day. Still, he'd have to check it out.

He was coming up on Meg Gentry's camper when he saw something move in the shadows. What the hell was Meg doing hunkered down beside the camper? Probably one of her lines had come loose. Snobby bitch. He had half a mind to pass right by her. Knowing her kind, she'd probably tell his boss. He aimed his flashlight in that direction, and discovered it wasn't Meg at all.

The person looked startled to see him.

"What the hell do you think you're doing?" Randy

asked. He'd barely gotten the words out of his mouth before he saw the flames. A burning rag had been stuffed inside the opening of a gas can.

"Jesus Christ, are you crazy?" Randy dropped to his knees and reached beneath the camper. He didn't want to think what would happen if the fire reached the gas. There was no time to think; he had to pull the burning rag free. He tugged at it several times, burning himself with each attempt.

He never thought to yell out to Meg.

He never saw the log come down on his head—or felt the explosion that followed.

Thirty-one

MEG FROWNED at the sound and resisted waking, but the noise continued. She heard Clay call her name, and realized he was knocking on the bedroom door.

In the next bed, Sara sat up. "Meg, are you awake?" she said. "Clay's at the door."

Grumbling to herself, Meg climbed from bed and staggered to the door. She opened it and found Clay standing on the other side in jeans and T-shirt. "What's going on?" she said groggily.

"Something's happened. I need to talk to you."

She suddenly looked alarmed. "What—?"

"It's not your family," he said. "Let's talk in the kitchen."

"Sure, give me a second." Meg grabbed her purse from a nearby dresser. She glanced over her shoulder and saw that Sara was awake. "I'll let you know if it's important," she said, closing the door softly behind her.

In the kitchen, she found Clay pouring coffee into stoneware mugs. A quick glance at the wall clock told her in wasn't yet six A.M. "This better be good," she said, dropping onto a stool at the counter.

"It's not. Your father just called. Your camper was destroyed by a fire during the night."

Meg felt her jaw drop. "What?"

"The sheriff's department went through the records at the campground so they could find out whose camper it was, but once they put the fire out and didn't find traces of a body inside, they called your next of kin. Your father was frantic when he called me to see if I'd heard from you. I told him you were here and explained the situation, so he's okay now. But I'm afraid your camper is gone.''

Meg sat there for a moment, trying to absorb all he'd just told her. "*Everything* burned?'' she said, going through a mental list of what she'd lost.

Clay felt bad for her. "I'm afraid so." He reached across the counter and took her hand. "It can all be replaced, babe. I just thank God you're safe."

"Safe but homeless," she said.

"Your home is here with me."

She was so touched that it brought on tears. "Do they know how the fire started?"

"Arson. The sheriff's department found a badly burned gas can beneath it. Once it reached your propane, the whole place went up." He paused. "There was a fatality, Meg. The park ranger, a fellow by the name of Bekins. The deputies questioned a woman who claimed he'd just left her place when it happened. They think he may have seen the fire and was trying to put it out when it exploded."

Meg suddenly felt sick to her stomach. She choked on a sob. "God, he was so young. A kid, really."

Clay rounded the counter and put his arms around her. He reached for a box of tissues and handed her a couple, then held her while she cried. Once her tears had subsided, he kissed her swollen eyes.

"Listen to me, Meggie," he said. "Another camper said he heard what sounded like a pickup truck speed away only seconds after the explosion. This person is probably going to try again, once word gets out you're alive."

She was still crying softly. "I should have been nicer to poor Randy Bekins."

Clay shook her slightly. "You're not paying attention," he said.

She looked up, startled, then angry. "Excuse me if I'm a little distracted right now."

The look on her face made him sad, but he didn't have time to feel sorry for her. She needed protecting. "Do you think Travis would do something like this?"

"I think Travis is capable of anything," she said. If he suspected Beryl and her of taking that moose head, he'd probably kill them both with his bare hands. She didn't think this was a good time to worry Clay with that. "But he's out of town," she added.

"I'm going to ask the sheriff's department to check on that," Clay said. He dropped his voice to a whisper. "I think this has something to do with Sara."

Meg suddenly looked up and found Sara standing in the doorway in an old bathrobe. "How much did you hear?" she asked.

"Most of it. I wasn't trying to eavesdrop, but I suspected Clay had bad news, and I wanted to help." She looked as though she might cry as well. "This is all my fault." She stepped closer and put a hand on Meg's shoulder. "I should never have dragged you into my problems."

Meg wiped her eyes and faced her. "Don't be ridiculous," she said. "We don't know who's behind this. Nevertheless, I'm more determined than ever to help you escape."

"Do you have any ideas, Sara?" Clay asked. "Can you think of anyone who might want to hurt you?"

The girl shook her head, looking sad. "I didn't know anyone hated me that much."

"Who has the most to lose if you leave the church?" he asked.

"My pa. But he's in jail."

"Who knows you're leaving?"

"Just my sister and Purvis Dill, our associate pastor. They've been trying to convince Pa to let me go for months. They wouldn't tell a soul." She was thoughtful. "I just can't imagine anyone wanting to see me dead."

"It's simple, Sara," Meg said. "You're leaving the church. How do you think that will affect the collection plate?"

"Who knew you were going to Meg's tonight?" Clay asked.

"My sister. She didn't want me staying by myself after someone shot at me today."

"Did you see the person who shot at you?"

Sara shook her head. "I didn't see anything. We just assumed it was the Attaway brothers. They're always causing trouble for us. They're lucky Maybelline didn't catch up with them. As much as she hates them, she would have killed them both on the spot."

"I assume you reported it to the sheriff."

Meg and Sara exchanged looks. "I don't tell Nate Overton anything."

"What's the deal with Nate?" Clay asked. "Is he taking bribes?"

"Pa gives him money to keep his nose out of church business. Otherwise, he'd be barging in on every service, killing snakes, taking folks away in handcuffs."

"So why is your father sitting in jail right now?"

"The sheriff doesn't have much choice but to arrest him if there's a death."

Clay was quiet for a moment. He was disappointed to hear that Nate Overton could be bought. "How does your sister feel about your leaving?" he asked.

"She thinks I should have done it a long time ago. She says it's unhealthy the way Pa watches over me."

"Her sister is the one who asked me to help get Sara out."

"And this Purvis?" Clay asked. "What does he think of you leaving?"

Sara blushed. "Actually, he might come with me." She looked thoughtful. "You know, with Pa in jail, it wouldn't surprise me if he had one or two of his deacons watching me. If they knew I was leaving, they might try to scare me, but I can't imagine them trying to kill me."

Clay looked at Meg. "What's the game plan?"

She hesitated. "You won't try to stop me?"

"Has anyone ever been able to stop you once your mind was made up? I'm just trying to see that you live to a ripe old age."

"I'm taking Sara home this morning so she can attend Mr. Dill's funeral at eleven. There's a bus leaving for Atlanta at two-thirty. She's going to be on it. I've already found her a place to stay once she gets there."

Clay nodded. "Okay, but I'm coming with you." When Meg looked like she might object, he went on. "You don't have much of a choice, now that your ride has been blown to smithereens."

"There's a motorcycle in your garage," she said. "I saw it when I was on my smoke break."

"Forget it. It's way too heavy for you to handle."

"I wasn't talking about me. You can use the bike, and I could use your truck."

"No way. I'm going to stick to you like rubber cement over the next few days. Whether you like it or not," he added. "Besides, I promised Nate I'd run you by the sheriff's office first thing this morning. They want to ask you a few questions."

"I can't tell them the truth," she said, adamantly. "I'm not going to say anything that will screw up Sara's chance for escape."

"Let me remind you, we're talking murder and attempted murder here."

"I'll talk when I'm convinced she's safe." She looked at Sara. "I won't tell them where you are."

Clay glanced at the clock on the wall. "You need to call your parents and let them know you're really okay," he said. "Then, it might be a good idea to try and grab another hour of shut eye. We've got a busy day ahead of us."

Meg reached for the phone. She reassured her father

she was fine, and listened to her mother bemoan the fact that her reputation was shot now that she'd spent the night under Clay Skinner's roof.

"You're right, Mom," she said. "I should have stayed in my camper like a good girl and been blown to hell and back." She hung up before her mother had a chance to respond.

Meg grabbed a quick smoke in Clay's garage, although he insisted it wasn't necessary, then returned to bed only to spend the next hour tossing and fighting more tears. All she could think of was poor Randy Bekins, who'd been much too young to die.

Thirty-two

PURVIS WAS up and dressed before seven. He found Maybelline at the kitchen table, sipping coffee and fighting to keep her eyes open. She gave him a weary smile, and he returned it, although it was forced.

"Have a seat," she said, pushing herself from the chair. "I'll get your coffee."

He sat. Already his mind was at work on how to get rid of her. He had things to do, and she would only be in his way. Maybelline returned with his coffee and set it before him. He thanked her. She reclaimed her chair.

"How'd you sleep?" she asked.

"Good. I'm sorry I abandoned you last night. I guess I was more tired than I thought."

"That's why I'm here for, Purvis."

"Anyway, I feel much better this morning." He was lying. His stomach was giving him fits; he felt like he'd fly apart if someone so much as tapped him on the shoulder. "You need to go home. Try to rest before the funeral. I'm going to be counting on you, you know." That seemed to please her. He knew there wasn't anything she wouldn't do for him.

Maybelline nodded. "I do need to get back," she said, "even though I know I won't be able to rest till afterward. We've had some problems at the house and—"

"What kinds of problems?"

"I didn't want to tell you, but Sara thinks somebody

219

might have been shootin' at her yesterday morning, after she left here.''

He looked startled. "Shooting at her! Is she okay?"

"Of course she's okay."

He paled at the thought of someone hurting Sara. His Sara. "You should have said something sooner, Maybelline. I would never have agreed to you leaving her."

"I've been takin' care of Sara since she was a toddler, Purvis," she said irritably. "Do you think I'd go and leave her by herself if I thought she was in danger? She's stayin' with a friend."

"Who would do such a thing? Why, everybody loves her."

"I figure it's those sorry Attaway brothers. I don't know why they don't just leave us alone."

"Or it could be someone from the church has found out she's planning to leave."

"I haven't breathed a word to anybody. Have you?"

"You shouldn't even have to ask that question." He stood, hoping it would bring Maybelline to her feet as well. He would leave a note on the door for the funeral home, telling them to go ahead and take the body to the church. He didn't have time to waste.

She rose and gathered her things. Purvis followed her through the small house. She paused at the coffin and gazed down at his father. "Thank you for always being good to him," he said. Suddenly, he looked concerned. "I should take you home. How do you know you won't have trouble like Sara did?" he asked.

Maybelline waved the statement aside. "I ain't scared of no Attaway. Besides, I brought protection." She opened the small closet near the front door and pulled out her rifle. "They mess with me, and I'll blow 'em to kingdom come."

Purvis was awed by the strength he saw on her face and wished he could draw from it. When had he become so afraid? He suspected it had something to do with the many deaths he'd witnessed, those like his father who'd writhed in agony from snakebites or poison before the grave finally claimed them. He had made a mistake by agreeing to be the associate pastor.

"I'll ask someone from the congregation to come for you and Sara around a quarter till eleven," he said. "No sense you two having to walk to the funeral."

"Isn't that just like you?" she said, shaking her head. "Here you are grieving over your pa, but you're concerned about me and Sara. You are somethin' else, Purvis. Somethin' else indeed."

Purvis watched Maybelline go. He wondered if she suspected his feelings for her sister, then told himself there was no way she could know, no way *anybody* could, for that matter. He'd been very careful around Sara, so careful that not even she had guessed how he'd felt until he'd finally blurted it out the night before. He was thankful Sara was getting out, even more grateful she had asked him to go with her.

Reverend Beechum would not take it well; in fact, he would probably look for them. In a way, Purvis felt guilty. After all, the reverend had spent a number of years training him. Yet if he stayed, he would be expected to participate in the same ritual that'd killed his father. He would have to deal with the fear every time they let the snakes out or passed around the mason jar of water laced with strychnine. And that fear would ultimately kill him because it proved his lack of faith, the main ingredient he needed to stay alive. And how many more deaths would he have to witness before his own? How many deathbeds would he have to visit before his own bed was prepared?

All at once, a thought hit him. He or Sara could be the very next victim. A chill ran through him at the thought of watching his beloved suffer as his father had. "No!" The sound shattered the quiet in the cabin as though someone had thrown a brick through one of the windows. His gaze fell to his father, and the horrible scar that left one side of his face looking like something out of a bad dream. That could have been Sara.

Panic gripped him. He had to help Sara escape while there was still time. First, though, he had to bail the reverend out of jail so he could take his rightful place as head of the church.

Purvis left the house a few minutes later, once he'd scribbled a brief message to the funeral home and taped it to the front door. He had his notebook with him. He would need that. He would also need money.

The church was only five minutes away. Purvis parked in back and unlocked the door to the office. Inside, he pulled the bookcase aside and lifted the loose board that covered the safe. He tried the combination, but his fingers trembled so badly, he missed the first time. He took a deep breath, tried again, and the door opened.

As always, Purvis was amazed at the amount of money hidden away. He grabbed several bundles before closing the safe and putting everything back in place. Then he stuffed the money in the pockets of his jacket and started from the room, only to come to a dead stop. What if his plan didn't work? What if the mayor turned down his request, despite the information he had? What if Nate Overton refused to cooperate?

He couldn't take that chance.

Purvis rounded the desk and sat in Temple's chair. He found the key pressed against the magnet that Temple Beechum had affixed to the bottom of the center drawer. Of course, the reverend had no idea anyone knew about the key, and Purvis'd never had any cause to use it before.

Now he did.

Purvis unlocked the middle drawer and pulled it open. He could not believe the clutter: pens, paper clips, rubber bands, thumbtacks, toothpicks, candy bars. Scrap paper containing ideas for sermons and various scriptures.

Not what he wanted. He was looking for a large envelope. The pictures inside were certain to win Reverend Beechum's freedom, if the safety violations and sexual misconduct at Bidwell Textiles didn't. Mayor Bradley needed some kind of soapbox if he hoped to win the next election. All he had to do was clean up one workplace, and hopefully make an example of Travis Lytle, and he would have factory and textile workers all over the country on his side.

The photos of Nate Overton accepting bribes would be Purvis's insurance policy, in case he ran into problems. The mayor didn't need the embarrassment.

Purvis felt relief when he found the envelope in the bottom right-hand drawer. He'd never once figured on using blackmail to get what he wanted, but he was desperate. He started to close the drawer, then noticed the coffee can at the back. Had Temple taken to chewing tobacco? Surely not, since his followers were forbidden to touch it. Curious, he reached for the can and looked inside.

He expected to find a black, tarry substance, but the reverend hadn't been using the can as a spitoon. What Purvis saw was white. He knew its source. Harley Attaway's words came back to him.

"Maybe the rumors we been hearin' is right. Some folks say you milk your snakes."

Stunned, Purvis returned the can to its place and tried to make sense out of the whole thing. He didn't like what he was thinking. Did this mean the reverend didn't believe what he preached? And if that was the case, if he truly was milking the snakes, then how come they'd had deaths over the years? None of it added up.

Unless the deaths were planned.

Purvis grabbed the envelope, locked the drawer, and let himself out, taking care to lock the door behind. He climbed into his truck and started for town. It was after eight o'clock when he parked in front of City Hall and made his way inside. He found the mayor's office easy enough. A stout woman with gray hair and a friendly smile greeted him.

"I need to see Mayor Bradley," he said.

"Do you have an appointment, sir?"

Purvis shook his head. "No, but he'll see me. You might say I'm here to make a campaign contribution."

Thirty-three

J.T. BIDWELL was on the telephone when Travis stepped into his office. He motioned him to sit in one of the leather chairs in front of his desk. As J.T. scribbled notes on a pad, Travis studied the man who'd been his boss for so many years. J.T. was completely bald, his skull shiny and speckled with liver spots. Travis hoped he died before he ever got that old and ugly.

J.T. hung up. "Thank you for coming right up," he said. "We've got problems."

Travis noted the sharp tone and sat taller in his chair. "I'm sure it's nothing I can't correct, sir," he replied, suspecting the man was just annoyed because he had to stop playing with his train set.

"Three employees from the graveyard shift were rushed to the hospital shortly before dawn this morning, with severe allergic reactions. All three worked in the dye room. I spoke with Oliver in Safety, and he hasn't a clue. I thought maybe you could shed some light on the matter."

Travis had learned a long time ago not to show emotion, and he was thankful for that talent now. "What's the condition of the workers?"

J.T. massaged his temples as though his head ached. "I just got an update from the hospital. Two of the men will probably be released within the next forty-eight hours. The third man, Dirk Hodges, isn't doing so well. A chest

X ray showed damage to the mucus lining of his lungs. There's damage to his sinuses as well. The hospital is running additional tests, of course. OSHA's sending someone over late tomorrow afternoon. In the meantime, I want a list of all the chemicals used in our dyes.''

Travis tugged at the collar of his shirt. He wondered what it'd cost him this time to keep Jim Frank, from OSHA, quiet; then he remembered that his stash was missing. Jim would just have to wait until Travis had the cash. ''They're sending the usual guy, right?''

''Mr. Frank had a death in the family. They're sending in a new guy, but they can't get him here till tomorrow because they're looking into an accident near Cherokee. This guy's name is Dan Thompson. He's fresh out of college, and he'll be in charge of the investigation. Please see that he has all he needs.''

Travis pondered it. A college boy. Piece of cake.

Thirty-four

MAYBELLINE STEPPED out onto the front porch when Clay pulled up in his pickup truck, with Sara and Meg in the front seat. She started down the porch steps as they made their way toward the house. She looked anxious. "I'm glad you're here, little sister," she said. "Jerome Hawkins stopped by not ten minutes ago to tell me Brandy was in labor all night and—" She paused abruptly. "What's wrong?"

"Meg's camper burned to the ground last night," Sara said. "A man died trying to put it out."

Maybelline looked as though she might faint. Clay quickly grabbed her and forced her to sit on one of the porch steps. Tears sprang to her eyes as she reached for Sara's hand. "How did you manage to get out alive?" she asked.

"We stayed at Clay's house last night," Meg said. "Once I told him Sara suspected someone was shooting at her in the woods yesterday, he insisted we go with him."

"Thank God," Maybelline said, even though the tears continued to fall. She mopped them with the hem of her apron. Finally, she looked at Meg. "Somebody other than us had to know you were taking Sara to your place," she said.

"Did you tell anyone where Sara was staying last night?" Clay asked.

Maybelline shook her head. "Nobody even told *me*," she said. "Course, it wouldn't take a smart person to figure out it was one of the campgrounds close by, but I had no idea which one. I guess I had so much on my mind yesterday that I forgot to ask."

"Do you think someone could have overheard us talking about it yesterday?" Sara asked. "What if the person who shot at me followed me home and somehow managed to overhear our conversation?"

"The windows were open." Maybelline looked worried. "Remember, I opened them because the kitchen was so hot from baking. Somebody could have been listening."

"Or maybe we were followed," Meg said. "Once this person discovered where we were staying, he probably left, figuring he'd come back later when most folks would be asleep. Which is why he didn't see us leave with Clay."

Maybelline looked at her sister. "You have no choice but to leave now."

"I plan to attend Amos Dill's funeral," Sara said. "And I have to say good-bye to Purvis."

"I'll say good-bye to Purvis for you," Maybelline told her. "He's so upset over losin' his pa, he ain't even thinkin' straight."

"Which is why I can't just walk away without a word."

Maybelline suddenly looked annoyed. "Suit yourself, Sara, but you're bein' selfish, expectin' everybody to stop what they're doing and guard you every minute. You coulda been long gone if you'd taken that earlier bus, like Meg said. I don't even know if I'm going to be at the funeral, what with Brandy fixin' to have a baby and her bein' my best friend."

"Why doesn't someone just take her to the hospital?" Clay asked.

"You don't know how it is up here," Maybelline said. "Folks are scared of hospitals and doctors. They have to be bad off before they'll go. Anyway, I've delivered more babies than most of those high-priced quacks." She looked at Sara. "If you decide to stay for the funeral, then you'll have to go with me so I can keep an eye on you."

Sara was hurt and more than a little embarrassed over the dressing down. For years now, all she'd done was take care of other people's needs. Although she knew Maybelline was lashing out at her in fear and concern, she was not going to let her sister make her feel guilty for having a few needs of her own.

"I can take care of myself," Sara said. "Just leave the rifle."

Maybelline threw up her arms in frustration. She stood and regarded Meg. "Well, it's obvious I can't talk to her."

Meg was torn over leaving Sara. "Do you know how to use a gun?" she asked.

"You won't find a better shot in these mountains," she said. Sara glanced at her sister, but Maybelline looked angry. She was probably exhausted after sitting up with Amos Dill's body all night, and now she had to birth a baby. No telling how long that would last. All Sara could do was try to settle Maybelline's mind until the funeral was over and she climbed on that bus.

"I'll keep the rifle with me at all times, and I'll make sure the doors and windows are locked. Besides, the person who started the fire last night probably thinks I'm dead. If it's a member of the church, he won't know I'm still alive until he sees me at the funeral. He certainly won't come after me there."

"I hadn't thought of that," Meg said.

"We'll go ahead as planned," Sara said, as though she had suddenly been placed in charge. "I'll have my bag packed and waiting beside the front door. If you can pick me up after the funeral and run me back here, it won't take a minute to grab them."

"There's only one problem with that idea," Maybelline said. "Folks're going to see who you ride off with, and they'll be able to describe the car and the people in it to Pa.'' She focused her attention on Meg. ''He'll hound you night and day until he finds out where Sara is. Or worse,'' she added.

''How much luggage do you have?'' Clay asked.

Sara looked at him. ''One small suitcase is all.''

''I'll pick you up after the funeral on my motorcycle,'' he said. ''I'll be wearing a black-and-silver helmet and a black leather jacket. Nobody will recognize me. Just tell me where to meet you.''

They worked out the details. Meg suspected she wouldn't see the woman again, since Clay would be coming for her, so they hugged and Sara promised to write. Meg had tears in her eyes as she followed Clay to the truck and rode away.

Travis sat on the sofa in his den, trying to get through his second cup of coffee, but it was all he could do to hold it down. He'd called J.T. at home two hours earlier to say he'd be late coming in, due to personal business. He'd let him think it had something to do with the burglary. The man had sounded preoccupied, almost cold—something probably broke down on the old buzzard's train set.

Just as he had last night, Travis stared at the bare spot over the fireplace and wondered who could have taken his moose head. Who would even want it? The only reason he'd kept the damn thing to begin with was because he'd personally bagged the animal. And because Beryl had pitched such a fit when he'd brought it into the house. What he should've done was mount it on the front door.

Travis had a nagging thought. It didn't make much sense that a burglar would drag in a stepladder and take somebody's hunting trophy, unless they knew there was something valuable inside. He was almost certain Beryl didn't know about his stash. But what if she'd seen the burglary as a way to finally get rid of it? Damn thing could be sitting in a Dumpster somewhere, empty.

That would explain how she could afford one of those

fancy new apartments in town. She claimed Meg had loaned her the money, but he couldn't imagine his sister-in-law having much cash if she was living in that ugly camper. No telling what they were up to if Meg was involved.

Hell, they could have burglarized the place themselves.

The thought startled him so badly he spilled some of his coffee. Beryl would never do such a thing on her own, but with her smart-ass sister beside her, no telling what they'd cook up. He would find out. And if he did, they would pay dearly.

Travis decided to chew on it awhile. He had more pressing business. Grabbing the portable phone beside him, he dialed the hospital, and asked for the woman he'd spoken to the day before. "This is Travis Lytle from Bidwell Textiles," he said, once she'd picked up. "I'm calling to check the status of Dirk Hodges."

The woman hesitated. "Oh, Mr. Lytle, I'm so sorry. I'm afraid we lost Mr. Hodges about forty-five minutes ago."

Thirty-five

SHERIFF NATE Overton's uniform was streaked with soot and grime, and he looked as though he hadn't slept in a week. Meg would have felt sorry for him had she not known about the bribes.

"Mind telling me why someone'd want to light your place up like a giant firecracker and kill a man in the process?" he asked as soon as she and Clay were seated in his office.

Meg forced herself to concentrate, but she was terribly worried about Sara. "I've no idea, Sheriff," she said. "I really haven't been here long enough to make many enemies." She shook her head sadly. "I'm sorry as I can be about Randy Bekins. He was so young." She hesitated before asking the question that'd been nagging her. "Do you think he suffered?"

Nate reached for his bottle of antacid tablets. He could feel the sausage he'd eaten for breakfast churning in his gut and spewing acid straight up his esophagus to his throat. Reminded him of that volcano movie he'd watched last year. He popped a pill.

"Dr. Grimes seems to think Ranger Bekins died on impact. Me and the fire chief figure the killer rigged it so that when the gas can exploded, your propane tank would go up as well. One of my deputies found a piece of hose from the tank with a hole in it, so that pretty much proves our theory, that propane leaking." He leaned back in his chair. "So the answer to your question is no. Bekins never knew what hit him."

"I suppose his family has been notified."

Clay took her hand and squeezed it. "Meg, you're going to have to stop blaming yourself. That park ranger was just doing his job."

Nate seemed to ponder the situation. "So you have absolutely no reason to believe someone might be out to hurt you?" he asked her.

She shook her head. "No. Most people are crazy about me the minute they meet me."

"Then how come you stayed at Clay Skinner's house last night?"

"You're getting a little personal, aren't you, Nate?" Clay said. "Can't a man and woman spend time together simply because they enjoy one another's company?"

Nate gazed at Meg steadily. "You and your sister are certainly having your share of bad luck these days, seein' how her place was burglarized and yours burned to the ground. Don't you think that's a coincidence?"

Meg fidgeted with her hands. Finally, she looked at Clay. "Should I tell him?"

Clay looked at her, wondering what the hell she was up to. "You have to do what you think is right," he said.

Meg cleared her throat. "Well, Sheriff, there is one person I think might be capable of something like this. I'm sure you know my brother-in-law, Travis Lytle?"

"I know *of* him."

She told him about Travis breaking into her camper with the intent of raping her. "I fought him off," she said. "I have special defense training, you see. Ol' Travis didn't stand a chance."

"Did he or did he not rape you?" Nate asked.

"No, he didn't. That's just the point: He's probably trying to get even after I beat the crap out of him. Plus, he could've been trying to shut me up just in case I decided to report him."

"Why didn't you report it?"

"I couldn't. He—" She paused when tears suddenly filled her eyes. Nate handed her tissue, and she thanked him. She realized Clay was watching her, a strange look on his face. "Travis threatened to hurt my sister. She's suffered a couple of miscarriages in the last eighteen months. Travis led me to believe he'd caused them."

"I never liked that punk anyway," Nate told Clay as he dumped several antacids into his palm and tossed them into his mouth.

"As for the burglary," Meg said, "wouldn't surprise me one bit if Travis did it himself or paid someone to do it so he could collect on the insurance."

"You plannin' to press charges?" Nate asked.

Meg sniffled. "I have to discuss it with my sister first."

"Don't take too long," the sheriff said. "You don't want him trying the same thing on somebody else." He scribbled something on a yellow legal pad. "I'm going to let you go on back to work, Ms. Gentry. We can talk again when you're not so upset." He stood, rounded the desk, and shook her hand. "Everything's going to be okay."

Meg and Clay left the building, and Clay didn't speak until after they were in his truck. "You're good," he said, giving Meg an amused look.

"Thanks," she said. "I don't consider it my finest work, but it'll do in a pinch."

Sara was dressed and ready to leave for the funeral by ten. Her bag sat beside the front door. She tried to think what she might be forgetting. She checked her purse; the letter she'd written to Purvis was tucked inside. She would have to slip it to him somehow. Leaving Purvis and Maybelline behind would be the hardest thing. And Meg, of course. She felt as though she might cry just thinking about her new friend.

With more than an hour to wait for her ride, Sara decided to straighten the kitchen. They'd done so much cooking the past couple of days that they'd be hard-pressed to find a clean pan in the house. She grabbed her apron and went to work, trying to get as much done as she could so Maybelline wouldn't have to return to a dirty house. Birthing babies was no small task. Sometimes it took all day and night; other times, the baby came after only a few contractions.

Sara jumped when she heard a knock at the door. Her ride was early, but she hoped it would give her time to speak with Purvis. She'd managed to get most of the kitchen in order, she saw, as she pulled off the apron and tossed it aside. She hurried toward the door, not even thinking about the rifle she'd promised to keep with her. Fixing a pleasant smile to her face, she opened the door.

The smile faded abruptly as she looked into her father's face.

Thirty-six

"DON'T YOU have to work?" Meg asked Clay as they pulled out of the parking lot.

"I took the day off," he said. "I'm more concerned with keeping you safe." He started down the main road. "Where to? You need to go by the office?"

Meg shook her head. "I've already checked in. Actually, I need to run by the morgue."

"Come again?"

"I'm doing a story about those bones you dug up."

"Yeah, they've still got the place surrounded by crime-scene tape. Which explains why I can afford to take a day off."

"You've got other jobs going, don't you?"

He nodded. "I've got a crew framing one house this week, and a guy putting wood floors in another. I'd just be in the way." He offered her a smile. "So you're stuck with me for the next day or two. The morgue, huh? And here I thought there weren't any romantic places to go in this town."

She pulled out her cigarettes. "You sure it's okay if I smoke in your truck?"

"Go ahead," he mumbled.

"I won't if it bothers you."

He stopped at a red light and looked at her. "Maybe you should see what my kid goes through when she can't catch her breath. Then you'd feel pretty stupid about what you're doing to your lungs."

"Clay, don't start guilt-tripping me. If you don't want me to smoke in your truck, I won't."

"I don't care if you smoke," he said begrudgingly, "as long as you don't do it around Cindy."

Meg lit up. "I doubt I'm going to be spending any time with her."

"Yes, you will. Becky told her I had a girlfriend, so she wants to meet you."

Meg almost choked on her own smoke. "What?"

"Becky and I had a long talk the night I stayed over there. She said there's been times she's let Cindy think we'd get back together because she didn't want to disappoint her. But after talking with the child psychologist, she realized she was doing more harm than good by avoiding the truth. The psychologist told her that kids take their cues from their parents. If we're upset and tense around each other, Cindy's going to sense it, and she'll get upset, too. And that could bring on an asthma attack. So Becky and I are going to try and be more civil toward one another."

"What if Cindy doesn't like me?"

He looked at her. "What's not to like?"

She grinned. "That's true."

"So you'll make an honest effort to cut back?"

"That's not fair. You didn't even tell me you were switching to another subject. Besides, why are you suddenly trying to change me? You don't see me doing that to you."

"I don't have any bad habits." He smiled.

"Oh, brother!"

"Well, nothing that affects my health and life expectancy." He sighed. "Never mind. It sounds like I'm trying to tell you what to do, but that's not it at all. The truth is, I love you just the way you are. I just want to make sure you're around for a long time."

Meg didn't know what to say. "Okay, Clay, maybe we

can work out some kind of compromise. What if I promise to cut down? What if I make a genuine effort to cut my smoking in half?''

"In half?''

"From two packs a day to one pack.''

It was a start, he told himself. "I'll settle for that,'' he said.

"And you'll quit razzing me?''

"I guess so.''

"Okay, on to the next problem.''

He glanced at her. "I didn't know we were having problems.''

"Not us, me. I don't want to have to move in with my parents—''

"I've already told you, my place is yours.''

"What kind of arrangement are we discussing here?''

"How about marriage?''

"Isn't that a bit fast?''

He shrugged. "Not when you know what you want. But if you need more time, I'll give it to you. Just don't expect me to be the one who breaks the news to your mother. No telling what she's going to say when I tell her you'd rather live in sin than marry me.''

"You fight dirty, you know that?''

They were still discussing the situation when they entered the hospital and took the elevator to the basement. She found Drs. Grimes and Coleman sitting in his office; they looked pleased to see her. She introduced Clay, and the three of them shook hands.

"So what's new?'' Meg asked.

"I finished the sculpture late last night,'' Janet said. "Want to see it?''

"I'd love to. Is it okay if Clay comes?''

Janet nodded. "That's fine.''

Dr. Grimes led them across the hall and unlocked the door to the autopsy suite. Meg saw Clay glance at the stainless-steel table and the refrigeration unit, and she smiled. They walked into the next room where the large worktable sat, and Meg came to an abrupt halt at the sight before her. The skull now had skin, hair, teeth, and eyes. It was affixed to a small wooden base; there was even a scarf tied around what was supposed to be the neck.

"Wow," she said. "It looks so real. I mean, *she* looks so real."

Dr. Grimes beamed. "Like I said, Janet's the best forensic sculptor in the country. Probably in the whole world."

Janet Coleman blushed. "Your opinion is completely unbiased, I presume?"

Clay, too, was impressed. "This is actually the skull that we dug up?"

When both doctors looked confused, Meg went on. "Clay's the one who found the skull to begin with."

"What will you do with it now?" he asked.

"Meg is going to run it in the newspaper," Dr. Grimes said. "Hopefully, someone will recognize the likeness. He reached for a stack of photos and handed them to Meg. She noted the pictures were numbered and showed each step of reconstruction. He also handed her a sheet of paper that explained the process.

"What happened to the quilt?" Meg asked.

"We had it messengered to a master quilter and curator for the Museum for Appalachian Studies in Elizabethton, and she's already given us a lot to go on. Although she claims the design and signature is not one she recognizes, she's quite familiar with the fabric. Bidwell Textiles started producing double knit in the early seventies because it was so popular. The thing about double knit is, you can't get rid of it. The damn stuff refuses to decompose. Anyway, this woman was able to match some of the double knit in the quilt to what was being produced at the mill here.

"The material next to the victim's body was unbleached muslin. Most of it decomposed because of the acid in the victim's body, but there was still enough left to identify it, and Bidwell had been manufacturing muslin for years."

"So we know the quilt was made here, and we know the murder is at least twenty years old," Meg said.

"That's as close as we can get at the moment," Janet told her.

Meg noticed the time—they needed to get back to Clay's house if he was going to change and pick Sara up from the funeral on time. "I'll discuss this with my boss when I get back to the newspaper," Meg said, putting the photos and notes in a side pocket of her purse. "I'm sure it'll receive top priority."

She thanked them, and they shook hands again. As the doctors escorted them through the main autopsy room, Clay pointed to the refrigeration unit. "Got any customers in there?"

Dr. Grimes looked amused. "Yes, we do, as a matter of fact. Eighty-seven-year-old grandmother who died in her sleep. Relatives didn't find her for a week. She was under an electric blanket the whole time. Care to have a look?"

"I'll pass," Clay said, picking up his pace.

"Me, too," Meg replied, suppressing a shudder.

Sara's knees felt rubbery; it was all she could do to remain standing. "Pa, what are *you* doing here?"

"I live here. Least I did last time I checked." He tried to step through the door, but Sara blocked his way. He gave a sigh of exasperation. "Have you turned into a pillar of salt, child? Would you kindly move so I can enter my own house? I only have long enough to clean up before Purvis comes back for me."

Sara stepped aside so her pa could come in. She glanced out the door in time to see Purvis pull away in his truck. She was as good as dead.

Temple saw the suitcase and knew what it was about. Just as he'd suspected: Even with all the people he had watching her, which included someone at the bus station, he'd figured Sara would try to run. Which was the *only* reason he'd allowed Purvis to use church funds to bail him out of jail.

"Isn't this just great?" he said, indicating the luggage. "It's not bad enough that Nate Overton locked me up like an animal and demanded a king's ransom for my release. Then, I have to deal with Purvis sniveling about how he's unsure of his faith—" His voice choked off as his anger rose. "Never mind that I spent years training him and grooming him to take my place one day."

Temple could barely hear his own voice over the blood rushing through his head. He paced, fists clenched. He could feel his control slipping. Not good. He knew where it could lead. He gritted his teeth. "Now you, the one person I thought I could trust, have gone and stuck a knife in my back. A modern-day Judas, that's what you are."

"Pa, please let me explain," Sara said, stepping closer.

All at once, Temple raised his hand and landed a blow along his daughter's cheek. Sara cried out and sank to the floor. "You're no different than your mother," he shouted. "You're not fit to be called a child of God!"

Sara's ears rang, and she half feared the bones in her cheek were broken. It wasn't the first time Temple had hit her. She huddled into a tight ball and remained perfectly still.

"Where were you going to get the money to leave on?" Temple asked, his booming voice echoing off the walls. "Was some man helping you? Answer me!" Temple went to kick her in the stomach, but she moved to fend off the blow, and the toe of his boot glanced her jaw. She cried out. He knew she would be carrying bruises. Good—let his congregation see what happened to those who tried to turn away from the church.

Temple spied Sara's pocketbook on the sofa and rifled through it. Where was her money to leave? He took great care to see that she never had more than a couple of dollars. Same with Maybelline. He knew his older daughter wouldn't hesitate to help Sara escape, and he knew the reason why. Instead of finding cash, though, he found an envelope addressed to Purvis. He stuffed it in his pocket and tossed the purse to the floor.

"Go to your room," he ordered in barely checked rage. "I'll deal with you later." When Sara didn't make a move, he pulled her up and slapped her hard across the face. "Do as I say! And don't even think about trying to get away, because I'm taking your suitcase with me."

Feeling broken up inside, Sara moved toward her bedroom. He *would* deal with her later. In the meantime, she'd be forced to wait and wonder what lay ahead. Experience had taught her there was no limit to his wrath. She closed the door softly and walked the short distance to her bed, then fell on it in a wounded heap. It's over, she thought in despair. She'd never get away now.

Temple knew he had to calm down before he disciplined his daughter; otherwise he might go too far. He'd done it before. He would go to his office and lock himself inside. Nobody would know he was there; they would be too busy mourning Amos Dill's passing.

He hoped Amos Dill rotted in hell.

He grabbed Sara's suitcase and purse and locked them in his room, then made for the door. Suddenly, he remembered the letter and pulled it from his pocket. He tore open the envelope and scanned the page. Sara and Purvis? The thought left a bitter taste in his mouth. The two people he'd trusted most. No doubt they'd been planning to run off for some time; Sara'd even promised to wait for him to join her. Had Purvis bedded her? Was she no longer pure?

The thought heightened Temple's rage. He knew who Purvis was presently sleeping with, and even though the thought had sickened him, he'd kept quiet. All along, he had hoped and prayed that Purvis would see the error of his ways and confess his awful sin. Purvis would burn right beside his father; that much was certain. But by the time Temple was finished with him, he would think he was already in hell.

As for Sara, he would see that no man ever looked at her again.

BOOK FOUR

Thirty-seven

TEMPLE LEFT the woods and stepped into the clearing where his church and a small cemetery sat, enclosed within a waist-high wrought-iron fence that'd long ago gone to rust. A freshly dug grave waited to receive Amos Dill's remains, and a dozen folded chairs sat beneath a patched tent for those closest to the newly departed. From where he stood, Temple couldn't see the front parking lot, but he assumed the funeral home had probably already delivered Amos's body. Taking care to be extra quiet, he pulled his key from his pocket and unlocked the back door leading into his office.

The room was dark; there were no windows to let in the morning light Temple pulled the door closed, locked it, and reached for the light switch. He jumped when he found Purvis slouched in a chair in front of the desk.

"What are you doing here?" he demanded.

The younger man looked surprised to see him. "Just killing time till I come back for you. Why aren't you dressed?"

Temple seated himself behind his desk and regarded the man before him with a look of disgust. He reached into his shirt pocket, pulled out the envelope, and tossed it to him. It fell to the floor. With a questioning look, Purvis reached for it. "What's this?" he said.

"Read it."

Purvis pulled the sheet of paper out. He recognized

Sara's handwriting immediately; the small neat letters reminded him of the woman herself. He glanced at Temple and found the reverend watching him speculatively. Finally, he began to read.

Dearest Purvis:

By the time you read this, I'll be on a bus to Atlanta. I have a place to stay, so don't worry about me. I've been thinking about what you said, and I realized, yes, I do love you, and I want to spend the rest of my life with you. Please join me as soon as you can.

All my love,
Sara

Purvis folded the letter carefully and returned it to the envelope. He was so touched by Sara's words that he almost forgot about Temple. He hoped she'd gotten away safely. He tucked the letter into the pocket of his jacket and regarded the man in front of him. "Now you know," he said simply.

"Is that all you have to say for yourself?"

"I love your daughter, and she loves me. I'm sorry if you don't share our happiness."

"Sara has been punished for trying to run," he said.

Purvis clenched his fists in sudden anger. "What did you do to her?"

"I'm her father," Temple said. "I do as I please, and I don't need permission from you."

Purvis feared the worst. Had the man beaten her? He would know before long, and he hoped for Temple's sake she was okay. He hitched his chin high. "I love Sara, and I plan to marry her."

Temple gave a grunt of disgust. "I'll see you in hell first."

Purvis knew it wouldn't be easy convincing Temple,

but the hate he saw in the man's eyes startled him. "Reverend, my intentions toward your daughter are honorable. I will do everything in my power to be a good husband. I—"

"Do you think for one minute I'd let *my* Sara marry a known fornicator?"

Purvis felt his heart skip a beat. He knew! Shame filled him. "I wanted to come to you, but I—"

"But you were too much of a coward," Temple finished for him. "I had to hear it from a member of my congregation. Did the two of you think you could wallow in sin forever without getting caught?"

"I wasn't thinking at all. I haven't . . . uh . . . met with her in some weeks now. I've prayed for forgiveness. I know I've sinned."

"You don't know the half of it," Temple said in a voice filled with contempt. He stood and glared at the younger man. "You were nothing until I took you under my wing and molded you into the man you are today. I could have made you into a great evangelist. This is how you thank me? By bedding your own sister?"

Purvis snapped his head up. "What are you talking about?"

"Actually, she's your half sister. But incest is incest, isn't it, boy? And don't think for one minute I won't tell Sara. She'll despise you."

Purvis shook his head blindly. It was too wild to imagine. "What are you talking about? How did something like this happen in the first place?" he asked, trying to put the pieces together.

"Ask *her*."

"You mean . . . she *knows*?"

"She's known all along. I told her if it didn't stop I was going to see that the two of you paid. And pay you will," he added. "I expect the both of you to leave the church immediately. You might consider leaving the area as well."

Purvis could only stare back at Temple in fixed horror.

Did the man think for one minute that he would leave without taking Sara with him? He felt a sinking sensation. Would Sara even want to go, once she'd found out what he'd done?

"I will inform the congregation at the next service. The two of you will never be able to show your face again." He offered the younger man a menacing smile. "Now, I suggest you pull yourself together, go out front, and see to burying your father. After today, you will never set foot in this church again. Or any other if I have anything to do with it," he added.

Purvis stood on trembling knees. He was not ready to go out front yet. He needed time to come to grips with all he'd been told. He would find a way to get Sara out, no matter what. He went to the back door and opened it, then glanced over his shoulder at the man sitting behind the desk.

"You're not a man of God," he said, and saw Temple's shoulders stiffen. "Otherwise, you wouldn't keep Sara a prisoner like you do. No wonder your poor wife ran off. How does it feel to know the only way to keep your family from leaving is to have people watch them? Pretty sad, if you ask me."

"Get out of my office," Temple ordered.

Purvis gave a nasty laugh. "By the way, I know you milk your snakes." He slammed the door.

Finally, Temple was alone. He drooped in his chair and propped his long legs on the desk. He was dog tired from having lost so much sleep in jail, and his argument with Purvis had sucked everything right out of him. Milking snakes, indeed, he thought. Had Purvis lost his mind?

He still had Sara. Once he told her what Purvis had done, she would turn away in disgust. Probably cry for a week as well. Perhaps that was punishment enough. But how would he keep something like this from happening again? After all, she was her mother's daughter.

There was one way. He knew of a woman who could cut away that part of a female's sexual organs that was responsible for sinful thoughts. Circumcision, it was called. This woman had told him it was a religious practice where she came from, and that she had performed it on little girls as young as four years old. She left her country when a number of her patients had died and the parents had threatened her life.

He wished he'd had it performed on his wife.

Yes, something like that would keep Sara in line. It didn't matter that the procedure was dangerous; he'd prefer seeing his daughter dead than repeating her mother's mistakes. He would go see that woman. Finally, exhaustion overcame him, and he drifted off.

Thirty-eight

THE BACK door to the office inched open slowly, allowing a sliver of light across the floor as the person peered in and found Temple sleeping soundly. The sliver fanned outward, and a shadow loomed. The person waited, but the only sounds coming from the reverend were his deep snores.

Temple mumbled something in his sleep, and the person froze. And waited some more. One hand clutched a wooden box with a wire mesh front, in which several timber rattlers slithered about restlessly. The other hand grasped a crowbar. It was a simple plan. Setting the wooden box on the floor, the person squeezed the crowbar with two hands. It arched high in the air.

The first blow sprayed blood on the desk, wood floor, and walls, and left a gaping wound in Reverend Beechum's skull.

The second blow crushed a portion of his head completely.

The third blow wasn't even necessary; he was already dead.

One by one, the snakes were draped across the reverend's shoulders.

Stepping back, the person studied the final image. Temple Beechum looked like something that had crawled out from the pits of hell.

Thirty-nine

PURVIS TRIED to hide his rising panic as he stood on the church steps, welcoming members of the congregation. His lips felt numb as he thanked people for the nice things they said about his father. At the moment, he was trying very hard not to have a breakdown.

He had put off going inside as long as he could. Somehow, he would have to walk down that aisle, stand before his friends and neighbors, and say good things about the man who'd raised him. Somehow. It didn't feel as though his legs could carry him that far.

Finally, Purvis turned to go inside when he heard someone call his name. Maybelline burst through the trees and ran toward him. He forced a sad smile and a greeting he didn't feel.

"Sorry I'm late," she said, pausing at the bottom of the steps to catch her breath. "Brandy Hawkins just had a baby boy. Barely had time to smack his behind and clean him up before I threw my clothes on and raced over."

"Have you been home?"

"No, I changed at Brandy's and cut through the woods to get here." She started up the steps, then paused. "Somethin's wrong. What is it?"

"I bailed your father out of jail this morning." At her look of surprise, he went on. "I told you last night I planned to try."

"Yeah, but I never in a million years thought they'd let him go." She suddenly looked frightened. "You didn't take Pa home, did you? Please tell me you didn't, Purvis."

"Yes, I did."

Maybelline closed her eyes. "Oh, dear Jesus."

He leaned closer. "It would've been nice if you'd told me Sara was planning to leave today."

"I figured you had enough on your mind. How did you convince them to let him out?"

"It doesn't matter now. I think you need to go home and see about your sister. There's no telling what he did to her. You can take my truck." He fumbled in his pants pocket for his keys. "I must've left them on the desk in the reverend's office."

Maybelline started down the steps. "I'll go the back way."

"He's in a rage."

"He can't pin anythin' on me," she said. "I was at Brandy's all morning, bringin' little Seth Hawkins into the world. I'll tell him I didn't know Sara was plannin' to run. Law me, now we're back to square one, and I'd planned everythin' so carefully." She paused and tossed a suspicious look at Purvis. "If I didn't know better, I'd think you messed everythin' up on purpose."

Purvis shrugged. Let her think what she wanted. He had to bury his father. Taking a deep breath, he squared his shoulders and went inside, then walked down the aisle toward the altar, where his father waited in his simple wooden box.

At the podium, Purvis glanced out at the sad faces, many of whom had taken time off work to be there. "Brothers and sisters, welcome," he began timidly. "Today, we're here to mourn the passing of a man who meant many things to many people."

Purvis wondered which of his parents had committed adultery and created this terrible situation.

He opened his mouth to continue, but his words were

cut off by a sudden, high-pitched scream that startled him
so badly he dropped his Bible. People in the congregation
glanced at one another in surprise. A man in the front row
jumped up.

"It came from back yonder," he said, pointing to the
door that led into Temple Beechum's office. Another
scream, this one louder. Purvis crossed the stage and tried
the door that led into the office. It was locked, and he'd
left his keys inside.

"You don't have a key?" the man from the front row
asked, when yet another scream sounded and caused several of the ladies to hurry out of the church. Purvis shook
his head frantically. "Then I reckon we're going to have
to break the door down." Another man joined him, and
they took turns slamming their shoulders against the door.
It gave on the third try, splintering wood and tearing at
the door frame.

"Holy Jesus," one of the men said, looking inside.

Purvis wedged between them, and his insides took a
sickening swoop the minute he saw Reverend Beechum.
He was so horrified at the sight that he was only vaguely
aware that Maybelline was still screaming.

Forty

SHERIFF NATE Overton sat in the last row of the Jesus Christ Holiness Church and waited for his deputies to clear the back office of snakes. He hoped they didn't disturb the murder scene too much in the process. In the row before him, a church deacon tried to comfort Purvis Dill and Maybelline Beechum. Nate was there on the pretense of questioning them, but the truth of the matter was, he was scared of snakes. *Any* kind of snake. Hell, they didn't even have to be poisonous to scare the bejesus out of him. He had what his wife's fancy psychiatrist called a *phobia*. He'd looked the word up in a dictionary and decided yep, that's sure as shit what he had, 'cause he'd rather face a man-eating mountain lion than come across a garter snake in the road.

Course he wasn't about to let his deputies know that and have them think he was chickenshit.

Nate leaned to one side and fished an antacid from his pants, only to discover it was his last. An early lunch of two chili dogs and a large order of onion rings had left him with a miserable case of heartburn. He had an economy-size bottle of pills on his desk, but it wasn't doing him a damn bit of good there. He popped the large tablet in his mouth and chewed, hoping it would bring him some relief. He always worried when he had indigestion because the symptoms sometimes resembled a heart attack, and he'd already had two of those. The doctor had gone to great lengths to explain the differences, but he still got confused sometimes and didn't know whether to pop an antacid or a nitroglycerin pill.

"Mind if I ask the two of you a few more questions?" Nate said, pushing his thoughts aside and trying to buy a little more time before he went in back. He suspected by all the whoopin' and hollerin' goin' on that his boys hadn't caught all the snakes. "I know you have to bury your pa, son," he said, giving Purvis Dill a sympathetic look, "but I need just a minute more of your time."

"I don't know what more I can tell you," Purvis said, his patience wearing thin. The funeral home had moved his father's body to the small cemetery out back, and everyone was waiting for him so they could finish the service.

Maybelline turned in her seat. Nate could see how red and swollen her eyes were; looked like she'd been crying a week. She really wasn't a bad-looking woman, 'cept for the fact she carried a good thirty or forty pounds more than she should. Not that he was in a position to judge; he carried twice that much.

"Sheriff, do your men *have* to use that kind of language?" she asked. "We *are* in the Lord's house, after all."

Nate scratched his head. "They're just excited, Miss Beechum. They don't mean no disrespect. Besides, we don't share a fondness for snakes like the rest of you, so you'll have to bear with us." He was tempted to tell her to get off her fat ass and go catch them herself, but he thought better of it. Nate glanced at his notes and saw he didn't have much to go on. "Can either of you tell me if Reverend Beechum had any enemies?" he asked.

"Only those who didn't share his religious beliefs," Purvis said, glancing over his shoulder. He began to list them. "Law enforcement, public officials, other clergymen. His friends and neighbors loved him."

Nate wondered if the man was trying to be a smart-ass. "Did either of you speak with the reverend today?"

"I did," Purvis said.

"And what was the basis for your conversation?"

He shrugged. "Church business. Same as usual."

"What was his mood?"

"A bit crabby. He'd just gotten out of jail, as you recall. Took a chunk out of the new church fund, as you can imagine."

Nate was beginning to get crabby, too, thanks to his indigestion and the other man's mouth. He decided to ignore him. "What about you, Miss Beechum? Did you talk to your father today?"

She shook her head. "I was gone much of the day to deliver a baby. I finished up only minutes before Brother Dill's funeral was to begin."

"And you're the one who found him?"

"I've already told you that."

"You have a sister, don't you?" Nate asked, remembering seeing a small blond woman from time to time. Quite a looker, too.

"Yes. She wasn't feeling well today, so she stayed home."

"Sheriff?" Purvis checked his wristwatch.

"Okay, you can go now. Both of you. You'll call me if you think of something else?"

They nodded and slipped from the pew. As if acting on cue, one of his deputies, a man named Guthrie, stepped out from the back office. "We got 'em, Sheriff," he said, grinning like a Boy Scout who'd just earned his first badge. "You want me to take 'em to the edge of the woods and let 'em go?"

"Take 'em out back and kill 'em," Nate said.

"But, Sheriff—"

"I don't care how you do it; shoot 'em in the head if you have to. Just don't let Jenkins do it. She'll go through a six-month supply of bullets and won't come close to hitting one." He noted the bewildered look on Guthrie's face, but he didn't budge. "Go on, do what I said."

Nate waited a good five minutes. His stomach felt like

a furnace. He headed toward the church office where Reverend Beechum had died so violently. "Looks like the reverend had a bad day," he said from the doorway.

"Someone pert near busted his brains out," another one of the deputies said. Ray Jones had been with the department for years and knew his stuff. He was in the process of opening a homicide kit.

Deputy Jenkins came in the back door carrying her radio. The black woman was still a thorn in Nate's side, but he tolerated her because he was expected to hire a certain number of minorities. He only wished he'd gotten someone with brains.

"Dr. Grimes is on his way, Sheriff," she said.

"Okay. Jones, you can start dusting for prints," Nate said. "Just don't go messin' with the body. I don't want Grimes chewing on my ass." The deputy nodded and went about his work.

Jenkins stared at the dead man. Nate noticed she'd taken on a greenish tint. "I've never seen anything like it," she said softly. "Why, he don't even look human."

"Well, if you're gonna get sick, do it outside," Nate told her. Several shots were fired from out back. There was a brief pause, followed by two more shots, then silence. Nate breathed a sigh of relief. He stepped closer to the reverend, his eyes scanning the floor just in case his men had missed one or two timber rattlers. When he was convinced it was safe, he studied the dead man more closely.

His skull was crushed; gray matter spilled from the opening like stuffing from an old sofa. He had bite marks on his arms, neck, and face. Jenkins was right; he didn't look human.

Guthrie came in. "I took care of 'em, Sheriff. Throw'd 'em in the trash and stashed the box in the trunk of your patrol car for evidence." Nate nodded, and the man went on. "Listen, some guy keeps driving back and forth on his motorcycle. Wearin' a black leather jacket and a black-and-silver helmet. He looks like one of those biker dudes from out in California. Think I should pull him?''

"Has he broken the law?"

"Not so far as I can tell."

Nate hated dumb questions. He figured they only added to his level of stress, and that made his health worse. With folks knowing about his stomach and heart problems, one would think they would stop asking dumb questions. "Well, if he's not doing anything wrong, why would you want to pull him over, Guthrie?" he asked in such a way one would've thought he was talking to a two-year-old. "Don't you think we've got enough to keep us busy for the time being?"

The deputy nodded. "I reckon you're right, Sheriff."

Nate shook his head. Between Jenkins and Guthrie, he didn't stand a chance. Damn, his stomach hurt.

When Sara opened her eyes, she felt as though she'd dozed for some time. She checked the clock on her night table and saw that it was almost one. The funeral would be over by now, and Clay would have come and gone. She sighed. Nothing had gone according to plan.

Pushing her sore body from the bed, she went into the bathroom and stared at her battered reflection. No surprise there. It was not the first time her pa had left his mark. And knowing him like she did, it wouldn't be the last.

Sara decided then and there she couldn't take it anymore. She was over twenty-one, plenty old enough to be on her own. She was tired of being ruled by fear and intimidation. Hitching her chin high, she marched into the kitchen and searched through several drawers until she found an ice pick. She went to her father's bedroom door and jabbed the pick into the tiny hole in the doorknob until the lock clicked. She opened the door, and smiled when she found her suitcase and purse.

Five minutes later, she stepped out onto the front porch and listened for sounds of an approaching vehicle. There were none. She hurried down the steps and sprinted across the road, then disappeared in the woods. She knew a shortcut to the highway.

It was after one-thirty, and Clay had not seen the first sign of Sara. He *had* seen a number of patrol cars, and that worried him. What was going on? The funeral was over. That much he knew from riding by the church a number of times and watching people climb into their cars and pull away. He couldn't keep going by; one of the deputies was beginning to stare at him. Where the hell could she be? Her bus left in an hour,

Clay decided to ride out to the Beechum house and see if Sara was there. When he arrived, the place looked deserted, but he knocked on the front door and waited. No answer. He knocked again, harder this time, then went around back and called out for her.

Something wasn't right. He wondered if it had something to do with the sheriff's department being at the church, or were they there because of the funeral? He decided to take the main road down the mountain in case Sara had become anxious and started for town on foot.

Forty-one

"OKAY, WE got us one helluva hole in the ol' noggin," Alan Grimes said, looking closely at Reverend Beechum's skull injuries.

"I wish you wouldn't use that sophisticated medical jargon, Doc," Nate said irritably. "You know how it flies right over my head."

"That's why I use it, Nate. To keep the rest of you guessing."

"Yeah, well, it doesn't help when I have to fill out my report."

"Okay, okay. I'll have to open him up first, but I'm willing to bet my best bottle of scotch that death was caused by epidural hemorrhages resulting from traumatic skull fractures by a blunt instrument. How's that?"

"Not so fast," Nate said, trying to get it all down in his notebook.

Grimes paused. "In other words, somebody knocked the slop out of him."

The sheriff shook his head. If he didn't know better, he'd think the doctor was getting laid these days. He'd never seen the man in such a good mood. "What about the snakebites?"

Grimes looked at the sheriff. "Those bites didn't kill him. From the looks of them, they're dry bites."

"Dry bites?" The sheriff looked confused.

"He means they didn't release any venom," Deputy Jenkins said.

"I know that the hell it means," Nate snapped, making the woman jump. He looked at the doctor once more.

"There could be some residual venom," Grimes said. "But not enough to kill him. Like I said, cause of death was this big crater in his head." He poked a hole in Reverend Beechum's shirt and inserted a needle-nosed thermometer beneath the man's right rib cage so he could register the temperature of his liver. Jenkins, in the process of dusting for prints, shuddered. Grimes looked amused. "I can either do it this way or we can flip him over, drag his pants down, and shove a thermometer up his rectum."

"Don't mind me, Dr. Grimes," she said. "You just go about your job and I'll go about mine."

"How long you figure he's been dead, Doc?" Nate asked.

Grimes checked the reading. "He's fresh. An hour. No more than two." He looked at the sheriff. "You got a weapon?"

"Still looking. We spent the first half hour chasing goddamn snakes. That's why we don't have the crime-scene tape up yet."

"Well, it's a bona fide homicide," Grimes said, "but I'm sure you've already figured that one out all by yourself. You got any suspects?"

Nate shook his head. "We're questioning people." He stepped closer. "Look, if you don't need me, I'm going to run to the store real quick and grab something for my heartburn."

Grimes didn't look up from his work. "D'you hit the pizza bar at Ollie's again?"

"Naw. Chili dogs at Pete's."

Grimes shook his head. "Nate, Nate. You're not taking care of yourself. When are you going to start listening to your doctor?"

Nate chuckled. "Like I always say, I know more old

fat sheriffs than I do old doctors.'' He kept the smile in place as he let himself out the back door. He knew people who couldn't talk about anything else 'cept how bad they felt or what ached, but that's not the kind of man he was.

As Nate headed toward his patrol car, he saw that his men had finally put up the crime-scene tape. Thank goodness for that. People were already standing around gawking. Nothing like a grisly murder to keep folks' tongues wagging. "I'll be back d'rectly,'' he told one of his deputies. He climbed into his patrol car and drove away.

As he followed the winding mountain road downward, Nate couldn't help but note the odd feeling in his stomach. It was as though an old barn rat were sitting down there gnawing a hole in the bottom of it. With his luck, it was an ulcer. Probably he'd gotten it from worrying about his heart. Jesus. It was a never-ending cycle. If one thing didn't get you, another would. He often wondered how much pain he'd suffer when the Big One hit, the major heart attack that was going to take him out. After seeing Reverend Beechum, though, he decided there were worse ways to die.

As was often the case when he thought of death, he thought of his wife, Charmaine. Who would take care of her if something happened to him? Who would see that she took her medicine, and who would drive her to that high-priced psychiatrist in Elizabethton every week? Nate reached down and unbuttoned his pants because his waistband was cutting into his stomach. Charmaine had moved the button a few weeks ago, and he was already bustin' out of them. All because of stress. Some men drank when their troubles got to 'em; others cheated on their wives. He stuffed his face. What made it worse was the fact he didn't exercise. His doctor said he was a walking time bomb.

Nate grabbed a handkerchief from his back pocket and mopped the sweat from his brow. Like he needed another reason to be stressed. His wife's doctor bills and prescriptions were eating him up. His insurance plan was useless, certainly not worth the effort of filing a claim and having everyone in the department, not to mention the entire town, know how sick Charmaine was. He could just imagine the names they'd call her.

Which is why he'd worked out a plan with Temple Beechum. For what it cost to meet Charmaine's medical debts, he turned a blind eye to what was going on in that church. They could afford it, thanks to Sara Beechum's healing powers that brought folks from all over the country.

But Temple was dead now, and Nate had no idea how he'd manage in the future. He was still pondering it when he came out of the convenience store ten minutes later chewing antacids and drinking a carton of chocolate milk. A motorcycle went by, and Nate vaguely wondered if the man clad in the black leather jacket was the same one Guthrie had fretted over. Well, the deputy could take comfort in knowing the man wouldn't be giving them any trouble. He was headed down the mountain in the direction of town.

Nate finished his chocolate milk, tossed it in a nearby trash can, and climbed into his patrol car. He wondered what Charmaine was up to. She seemed to sleep way too much during the day and not nearly enough at night. She'd battled insomnia for as long as he'd known her. He wished that were her only problem.

Nate pulled out onto the highway and started up the mountain toward the holiness church. He was so absorbed in his thoughts that he almost missed seeing the petite blond woman step out of the woods beside the road. Curious, he slowed and watched her through his rearview mirror, noting the suitcases she carried. She seemed to be in a hurry. He knew of only one woman with hair that blond and that long.

Nate made a U-turn and went after her.

* * *

Sara was more than a little irritable after having fought her way through the woods to get to the main road. She hadn't saved much time taking the shortcut, but it had kept her from having to walk past her pa's church. She wondered what time it was, wondered if Clay was still looking for her. She started walking, taking great care to keep her head down in case a friend or neighbor drove by or, worse, someone from the congregation. She'd walked about five hundred feet before she heard a car pull up behind her. She glanced around and found Nate Overton sitting in his patrol car with the blue light flashing.

For a moment, she just stood there. Why was she being stopped? She started for the patrol car as Nate opened the door and stepped out. "Where's the truck?"

She glanced around. "What truck?"

"The one that hit you square in the face?"

"Oh, that." Sara had forgotten about her face. She looked down. "I know I'm a sight."

"Who's been knocking you around, hon?" Nate said.

She didn't look up. She wondered if she was bound by law to answer him, since he was the sheriff.

"Sara?"

She put her suitcase down and clasped her hands together in front of her. "My pa and I got into a fuss."

"That why you're running away?"

She hitched her chin up, finally meeting his gaze. "I'm not *running away*, Sheriff. I'm over twenty-one. I have every right to move out if I want to."

"Course you do. Can I give you a ride any place special?"

Her hopes soared. "The bus station?"

"Let me grab your bag." He reached for it, then paused. "You don't happen to have any snakes with you?"

"Of course not."

Nate winked. "Just kiddin'." As he put her bags in the back, she climbed into the passenger's side of the car. He joined her in the front a moment later and pulled onto the main road. "I can't believe I ran into you like I did. I was just talking to your sister, not five minutes ago. She told me you was home sick."

Sara looked at him. "Where'd you see my sister?" she asked, hoping Maybelline hadn't run into trouble delivering the Hawkins's baby.

"Back at the church," he said.

"Did you go to the funeral?" She couldn't imagine why.

"No, I had to go by for another reason." Nate braked at a four-way stop and glanced at her while he waited his turn. He was trying to get a fix on her, but it wasn't easy based on what he knew. He'd heard all kinds of things: Not only could she heal, she'd been rumored to raise the dead as well. Not that he believed that business with the dead, mind you, but it made him wonder about her now. Would a person so dedicated to healing be able to kill another human being?

The answer was staring him right in the face, of course. You only had to look at her to see that she'd been brutalized. Nate pulled off the road onto a scenic overlook.

Sara looked at him and wondered why he was acting so strangely. "Sheriff, my bus leaves at two-thirty."

He looked at her, and he suddenly felt very sad. If her face was evidence of Temple Beechum's handiwork, then he felt no sympathy for the man whose brains had been knocked out. And if she'd done it, he couldn't hardly blame her. But the law was the law, and although he'd tried to ignore his conscience when it came to taking that money for Charmaine, he couldn't turn his head where cold-blooded murder was concerned. Not even if it was justified.

"Sara, honey, I got some bad news for you. First of all, I just came from your daddy's church, where I found him dead in his office. He was murdered," he added, watching her face closely for a response. There was none. He shook his head sadly. "Now, I don't claim to be the best sheriff this town has ever had, but, honey, I'm afraid I'd be neglecting my duty if I let you get on that bus."

Forty-two

MEG STARED at the phone on her desk and decided she couldn't put off calling her parents regarding her relationship with Clay anymore. Luckily, her father answered. Explaining things to him was a breeze.

"Listen, honey, you're a big girl now. You can run naked down Main Street for all I care, and I'll still love you." There was silence. "Oh, no, I think your mother just fainted. Maybe you should wear a bathing suit." There was a muffled sound; then Alma came on the line.

"Are you okay, Margaret?" she asked

Meg heard a trembling in her voice. "I'm fine, Mom. I just want to let you know that Clay has offered me his guest room at a reasonable cost, and I've decided to take it." She was lying about him charging her for the room, of course, but it made it sound more like a business arrangement, and that's what she was shooting for. "I'll also pay half the groceries and utilities."

"I see," Alma said. "Well, that's a very modern way of doing things, but I suppose it's for the best. We're a bit crowded here right now anyway. Beryl's looking at apartments, but Travis says they can't afford to keep up two places. So Beryl said she'd get a job. I've been worried sick about what's going to happen. I've never seen a marriage split up over a burglary."

Meg could tell her mother was trying awfully hard to understand everything that was going on around her. "I just wanted to let you know I'll be okay. I'm in the middle of a story right now, but once I'm finished we'll plan to get together. How's that?"

"That would be nice," Alma said. "Give us a chance to talk."

Meg saw movement from the corner of her eye and was surprised to find Clay walking through the front door. The look on his face spelled trouble. "I have to go now, Mom," she said. "I'll call as soon as I can."

Clay closed the distance between them and didn't waste time on preliminaries. "She wasn't there."

"What?"

"I must've ridden by the church twenty times. I went out to the house, banged on the door, nothing."

"Where the hell is she?"

He shook his head. "Damned if I know."

Melinda, who hadn't taken her eyes off Clay since he'd walked in, answered the phone. "Meg, you got a call on line two. It's that Beechum woman that was here the other day?"

Dazed, Meg picked up the phone and spoke into it. She listened for a moment, mumbled a few words, and hung up. "Well, that solves that riddle," she said. "Sara's in jail. She's been charged with the murder of Reverend Temple Beechum."

Forty-three

MAYBELLINE AND Purvis were sitting in the lobby of the sheriff's office when Meg and Clay arrived. A chunky brunette wearing a 1960s hairstyle sat at a desk behind the counter reading a paperback novel. Meg noted Maybelline's puffy eyes; she'd obviously shed her share of tears that day.

"I'm so sorry about your father," she told the woman. "I thought he was in jail. Can you tell us what happened, and what's going on with Sara?"

Although Maybelline tried, Purvis ended up giving Meg and Clay most of the facts. "I didn't know Sara'd made arrangements to leave today," he said. "I bailed Temple out of jail this morning and dropped him off at his house." He shook his head sadly. "I reckon that's when he found out Sara was planning to go." He skipped the part about him and the reverend arguing. "Neither of us has seen Sara, but—" He paused and for a moment it looked like he might not be able to finish. "We assume Temple beat her pretty bad, because the sheriff tried to get her to go to the hospital and, well—" He looked away. "It's not the first time something like this has happened."

"That's why I came to you in the first place," Maybelline told Meg.

"This whole thing's been awful," Purvis said. "We'd already started the funeral service for my father when

Maybelline found Temple's body. We had to stop everything to answer a bunch of questions; then as soon as I got my father in the ground, one of the deputies informed us Sara'd been taken in and charged with murder.'' He shook his head as though he couldn't believe the whole thing.

''Will they let us see her?'' Meg asked.

''The sheriff says no,'' Maybelline replied, dabbing her eyes with a tissue. ''They're booking her now. We're just waiting to find out when they'll hold—'' She paused and looked at Purvis. ''What'd they call it?''

''The arraignment.''

''It's a preliminary hearing,'' Meg said. ''Sara will be taken before a judge, and he will decide if there's enough evidence to hold her.'' She focused on Maybelline. ''Do you know what kind of evidence the sheriff has against your sister?''

Maybelline shrugged and shook her head. ''They wouldn't tell us nothing.''

''Does she have a lawyer?''

''Don't know that either,'' Maybelline said.

Purvis leaned closer. ''I've got pictures of Nate taking bribes,'' he whispered. ''In case that's worth anything.''

A door opened in the hall, followed by the sound of footsteps. Nate Overton walked over to the receptionist and asked her to type something. Meg hurried over to the counter. ''Sheriff Overton, could I speak with you for a minute?'' she said.

He didn't look pleased to see her. ''Are you here on behalf of the newspaper, or do you have information regarding the fire that destroyed your camper?''

''I'm personally involved with the Beechum case.''

''Why doesn't that surprise me? I can see you for about two minutes; that's it.''

Clay shot Meg a look of warning as she hurried down the hall after Nate. She waited until they were both inside his office and the door was closed before she spoke.

"What evidence do you have against Sara Beechum?" she said.

The sheriff sat down behind his desk but didn't invite Meg to sit. "Why don't you attend her arraignment tomorrow morning and find out for yourself?"

"I plan to be there, but I just want to make sure you have reasonable cause to hold her, and that you're not just trying to satisfy some personal vendetta."

"What the hell are you talking about?"

Meg placed her palms flat on his desk and leaned toward him. "I know about the payoffs, Sheriff."

Nate sat back in his chair and regarded her in absolute silence. So those holy rollers had told her. "Where's your proof, Miss Gentry?"

"I have pictures," she said.

He reached for his economy-size bottle of antacid tablets. He unscrewed the cap and popped two into his mouth. "Are you trying to blackmail me?"

"Call it what you like. I'm here to see that you don't send an innocent girl to prison."

Nate leaned forward. "Okay, listen up," he said, holding one hand up and counting off on his fingers. "First, her daddy 'bout beats her to a pulp. The poor girl looks like she was run down by a produce truck. Then, we get a call about a murder. The body ain't even cold before I see Sara Beechum tryin' to hightail it to the bus station. Now, what does that look like to you?"

"We made plans to put Sara on a bus before Temple Beechum was murdered," Meg said.

"Right. And when Temple found out, he lost his temper and beat the hell out of her. She had every reason to seek revenge."

"Don't you want to know *why* Sara was trying to get away?" Meg asked.

"I'm not stupid, Miss Gentry. A person only has to look at Sara Beechum's face to know why."

"That's not the only reason, Sheriff," Meg said. "Sara was supposed to stay with me last night, and we both know what happened to my camper.'' She saw that she suddenly had his undivided attention. Meg sat in the chair in front of his desk. ''That same day, someone was shooting at her in the woods. They assumed it was Bert and Harley.''

''Bert and Harley Attaway are not capable of doing everything they've been accused of in this town, and I'm not saying that just because my wife is related to them.''

''I don't think the Attaways are involved either,'' Meg told him. ''I think someone from the church doesn't want to see Sara leave. She's the main event, the star attraction. She keeps the money coming in. If it's not a church member, then it's someone who stands to lose a lot when she goes.''

''Someone like me, Miz Gentry?'' he said.

''I wasn't accusing you.''

''But the thought crossed your mind, I'm sure.''

She shrugged. ''You might have a reason for trying to stop Sara from leaving, but you wouldn't stand to gain much by killing Reverend Beechum.''

''Okay, figure this one out,'' he said. ''I've got a woman in the next room who had every reason to kill Temple Beechum. She has no alibi for the time of the murder. I've got the mayor breathing down the back of my neck telling me to throw the book at her. Frankly, I wouldn't blame Miss Beechum if she *did* kill her father, and I don't think a jury is going to come down hard on her either once they see the pictures I took of her.''

''Do you really think Sara's capable of murder?''

He considered it. ''Miz Gentry, I believe we're all capable of the unthinkable when our backs are against the wall. But if what you're saying is true and somebody is really out to hurt Sara, this is the safest place at the moment. I'll see that she gets good meals, is treated well, and has a guard with her twenty-four hours a day. You won't find that kind of service anywhere else.''

When Meg came out of the sheriff's office a few

minutes later, she found Maybelline wringing her hands and both men pacing. Everybody stopped what they were doing and looked at her.

"Sheriff Overton is going to keep Sara," she said, deciding not to go into all that she and Nate had discussed, in case Maybelline or Purvis accidentally let something slip in front of the wrong person. "I think it's probably for the best, considering the threats on her life." She waited for everyone to absorb that. "The arraignment is tomorrow morning at nine."

"When will they decide whether or not to let her out on bond?" Purvis asked.

"That'll probably happen tomorrow," Meg said.

"I'll meet with the deacons this evening and ask them to approve using church funds to bail Sara out."

Maybelline looked shocked. "But Purvis, that money—"

He hushed her. "I know what that money's intended for, but right now we have an emergency on our hands. Besides, the deacons know Sara isn't capable of murder. She's a *healer*, for heaven's sake. That money will be secure."

Maybelline nodded. "What am I thinking? Of course we have to bail her out. I guess I'm just used to having to worry about what Pa will say."

"Temple's dead," Purvis said gently. "It's not up to him."

"Did the sheriff say when that Dr. Grimes would be releasing Pa's body?" Maybelline asked.

"I forgot to ask," Meg told her.

"I don't know why they have to do an autopsy when it's obvious what killed him." Maybelline looked weary. "I reckon we'll be planning another funeral."

"You'll have to discuss it with one of the deacons," Purvis said. "I won't be here."

She looked stunned. "You can't leave the church. Why, Pa raised you to take over once he was gone. How can you be so selfish?"

"I've given all I can, Maybelline." He stood and walked out the door.

She hurried after him. A few minutes later she was back. "He left me," she said in disbelief.

Meg and Clay stood as well. "I need to get back to my office," she told Maybelline. "You're welcome to use the phone there. Maybe you can find a ride home."

Clay dropped them off at the *Gazette* building after arranging a time to pick up Meg at the end of the day. Once inside, Meg showed Maybelline to her desk and told her to help herself with the phone.

"If you can't catch a ride, Clay and I can drive you home when we get off work," Meg told her.

"Thank you," Maybelline said, grabbing a tissue and blowing into it. Meg began unloading her notes and the photographs Drs. Grimes and Coleman had taken of the restored skull, so she could meet with Etheridge on what she had.

Maybelline reached for the phone but stopped midway when she saw the photos. "Who's that?" she asked.

"It used to be a woman that we think lived in this area. She died some time back, but we don't know exactly when. They found her skeletal remains, including her skull, and a special doctor managed to rebuild the woman's face. Pretty neat, huh?"

"What are you going to do with it now?"

"I'm going to run it in the newspaper and see if anybody recognizes her." Meg heard her name called, and glanced around to find Etheridge standing in the doorway of his office. She picked out several good photos and left the others lying on her desk.

"Excuse me, Maybelline," she said. "I need to meet with my boss. I hope you find a ride."

Meg hurried into Bob Etheridge's office. She closed the door, took the chair in front of his desk, and explained what she had.

"This is a fascinating story," Etheridge said, looking at the photos and glancing over her rough draft. "Can you have it ready for the Saturday edition?''

Meg nodded. ''Dr. Grimes is trying to get a fix on the signature at the bottom of the quilt the body was wrapped in. So far they think it's some kind of bird, maybe the Carolina wren.'' As she said that, she had a strange feeling about it, but she couldn't for the life of her figure out what was bothering her. ''I'm going to put all that in the article; maybe it'll jog somebody's memory. I also hope to have more on Temple Beechum's homicide by then as well.''

''Sounds good. Hey, I'm really sorry about what happened to your camper,'' he said. ''Do you have a place to stay?''

''I'm renting Clay's guest room.'' She studied him closely. ''How about you? How're you doing?''

''Things are beginning to calm down.''

''So you were able to convince Mrs. Murphy that you'd made the right decision by putting Al on probation in the first place?''

''Not exactly. I handed in my resignation.''

''What!''

''You should have seen the look on Natalie's face. It was obvious that was the last thing she'd expected. Suddenly, she couldn't do enough for me. She gave me a raise and a bonus to boot.''

''Did Fred and I get a raise?''

''No, just me.'' He went on. ''I tell you, I had her eating out of my hand. She even gave me a piece of the action.''

''You had sex with her?'' Meg said, unable to hide her surprise.

''You got a trash mind, you know that? No, Natalie is letting me buy into the newspaper at a very good price. We've already signed the paperwork. Oh, and she's having my office decorated.''

''What about Fred and me?''

''Your names never came up.''

Meg stood. ''Congratulations,'' she said. ''You deserve

every bit of it. I gotta go back to work now.'' She turned for the door.

''Hey, Meg?''

''What?'' She glanced at him from over her shoulder.

''Our new computers arrive next week. It's top-notch equipment. I picked them out myself.''

She grinned. ''Okay, forget all the nasty things I had planned to say behind your back.''

When Meg returned to her desk, Maybelline was gone. She questioned Melinda.

''She just split,'' the receptionist said. ''She was visibly upset. And very pale—looked like she'd seen a ghost.''

Forty-four

IT WAS coming up to eight o'clock when Nate Overton returned to his office, having polished off a meal of chicken fried steak, rice and gravy, and vegetables at the E&M Restaurant.

The owner was a friend, and always gave him extra helpings of everything. Not that he needed it. But while his mind said no, his belly said yes.

A quick glance at the old schoolhouse clock told him it was well past quittin' time. Nate unbuttoned his pants and sat in the chair behind his desk. He wasn't in a hurry to go home. Charmaine had started a new medication, and it seemed all she did was sleep. Maybe it was for the best. It gave her rest from the demons that haunted her.

Nate had just gotten comfortable in his chair when he saw an envelope on his desk with his name on it. He tore it open. Inside was a note and a small plastic bag containing white powder. He held the powder up to the light. *What the hell?* He read the note, then dropped it as though it had burned his fingers. What was this craziness? He hurried out of his office to the reception area where the dispatcher sat—a widow named Bertie, who'd never learned to face the night alone since the death of her husband. She worked the graveyard shift.

"Did you see anybody go into my office while I was out?" he asked.

The woman shook her head. "No, it's been real quiet this evenin'."

"Were you at your desk the whole time?"

"Well—" She looked thoughtful. "I went back for coffee once, and I had to use the ladies' room. I always turn the phone up loud so I can hear it when I'm away from my desk. It didn't ring. Like I said, it's been real quiet."

Nate took the elevators to the second floor, where the holding cells were. He found a deputy sitting at a desk working a crossword puzzle.

"Something wrong, Sheriff?"

"How's Sara Beechum doing?"

"Fine. She's a real sweet thing. Asked me if she could have an extra blanket. I figured that'd be okay. It gets cold up here at night. She's in number two."

Nate walked over to the cell that held Sara. She was already asleep, her small hands pressed together in a prayerful position and tucked between her cheek and pillow. The picture of innocence. He gazed at her for a long time. This girl was not capable of cold-blooded murder. Was someone trying to set her up? Who hated her enough to try and kill her? Did she know something about the holiness practice that they didn't want to get out?

Nate wished he'd never gotten involved with Temple Beechum. He walked back to the guard. "Has anyone tried to call or visit Miss Beechum?" he asked the deputy.

"No sir. I think she's upset about her father. She didn't touch her dinner. I thought I heard her crying later."

Nate nodded. "Listen," he said, almost in a whisper. "This girl might be in danger. I want her on CO status immediately, you got that?"

"Close Observation, yes sir."

"I don't want her eating or drinking anything unless someone from this department *personally* delivers it. She's not to have visitors, phone calls, or mail unless I approve it. Nobody steps inside that cell without me beside them, and if anything looks even *remotely* suspicious, I want to know about it. Any questions?"

"No sir."

"You can reach me at home if you need me."

Nate went back to his office, put the letter and envelope in one plastic bag and the white powder in another. He called for a deputy. "Take this over to the lab and ask 'em to check it out, ASAP."

Meg and Clay were sharing a pizza and drinking root beer in front of the fire in his living room. "This was a good idea," she said.

"I'm full of good ideas. Getting you to move in with me was the best one yet."

"Don't be too quick to judge. You haven't seen what a slob I am yet. Or how irritable I get when PMS hits."

"You're not a slob, you're a clutter freak. You've already got a zillion Post-it notes all over the kitchen counter. I'm going to buy you an organizer first chance I get."

"You should have mentioned you wanted a neat roommate."

"I'm not interested in having you as my roommate. I'm only doing it this way so you can get used to living in the same house with me. I think you know which direction we're headed."

"I'm still afraid we're rushing it. I just got divorced."

"You and Roy were separated for a long time." He saw that she still looked anxious about the subject. "I'm amazed that I can feel so certain about this relationship, while you still harbor so many doubts." He got up. "I'm going to take a shower." He started for his bedroom.

"Are you mad at me?"

He didn't bother to turn around. "No. Just confused."

Meg was still thinking about the conversation as she readied for bed. Clay was watching TV in his bedroom. Although his door was partially open, she didn't feel particularly welcome at the moment. She smoked a cigarette in the garage and went to bed, but it was still early, not even ten o'clock. She slipped into bed, leaving the light on so she could read until she got sleepy, and grabbed the top magazine from the stack she'd brought the night she and Sara had shared the room. The *Good Housekeeping* was open and folded back to the article on quilts. Meg stared at it without really reading, and the print began to blur as her mind searched.

Finally, she scrambled from the bed and made her way to the kitchen, where she scanned the phone book. She dialed. After the phone rang several times, an answering machine came on. "Dr. Grimes, this is Meg Gentry. I think I know who Jane Doe is."

Forty-five

Meg and Clay arrived at the courthouse shortly after nine. Meg had mentioned her suspicions concerning the skeleton he'd found, and Clay listened, but he was quieter than usual. Meg suspected they were going to have a long talk as soon as things settled down.

Inside the main courtroom, they joined Maybelline and Purvis near the front. The court had appointed Sara a lawyer, and the two were presently standing before the judge listening to the charges against her. Sara wore an oversize green jumpsuit, and her hair was braided and fell past her waist. Sheriff Nate Overton and two deputies, one a woman, waited nearby. "How do you plead, Miss Beechum?" the judge asked.

"Not guilty, Your Honor."

Meg glanced over at Maybelline, who looked as though she might shatter with the slightest provocation. "Are you okay?" she asked.

The woman nodded but didn't say anything.

Meg returned her attention to the front. Sara's attorney was discussing the issue of bail, listing various reasons why it should be granted. When Sara glanced over her shoulder, Meg felt as though someone had kicked her in the gut. The girl's face was covered in bruises. "All the evidence against my client is purely circumstantial, Your Honor," the lawyer continued. "Besides, Miss Beechum does not have a record; she's a veritable pillar of the community.''

''Bond is set at fifty thousand,'' the judge said, and slammed his gavel.

Nate paused to speak to them on the way out. ''Here's the name of a bondsman who can help you.'' He held out a white business card to Purvis. ''He's an honest guy. I work with him a lot.''

''He's honest?'' Maybelline said. ''Then how'd you come to know him?''

''Shhh!'' Purvis nudged her with his elbow.

Nate ignored the remark. ''Miz Gentry, I'd like to speak with you when you have a moment. Do you think you can drop by my office?''

''Sure.'' Meg nodded, wondering what was up.

''Why are you acting so nice to that double-talking sheriff?'' Maybelline asked Purvis. ''All he's done for years is rip us off! He's only trying to be nice now so we won't blow the whistle on him.''

''This is not the time to try and stir up trouble,'' Purvis told her. He looked at Meg. ''I need to go see this man right away,'' he said, indicating the business card. ''I spoke with the deacons last night, and they agreed we should help Sara.''

''A decision they'll regret once they learn you're leaving the church,'' Maybelline snapped. ''They'll probably demand the money back once you go, and Sara will be thrown back in jail.''

''You're leaving the church?'' Meg asked, more than a little surprised. She knew Purvis had been trained by the reverend himself to take over.

He looked embarrassed. ''Not immediately. I'll get all this other business out of the way first. Maybelline isn't happy with my decision. She thinks the church will collapse without me. I don't share that belief.''

Maybelline and Purvis left for the bondsman's office, and Meg and Clay walked the short distance to the sheriff's office. A small crowd had gathered out front. Meg

wondered if the people were members of Temple Beechum's congregation, or just interested members of the
public. Nate was waiting when they arrived.

"I don't want to get things stirred up," he said, once
they were all seated in the privacy of his office, "but
someone made a threat against Sara's life." He told them
about the note he'd found on his desk the night before.
"Could be a simple prank. I don't have the lab results
back on the substance that came with it, but the person
responsible could very well have tried to murder her."

Clay shook his head. "Who do you suppose it could
be?"

"Same person who blew up my camper," Meg said.
She eyed Nate. "Do you believe me now when I say Sara
is innocent?"

"I don't *dis*believe it," Nate said. "But if that's the
case, then the person who killed Temple Beechum is most
likely the same one after Sara. I just want to make you
aware of the danger she's in."

"She can't go home," Meg said. "Maybe I should take
her to a motel. Someplace out of town."

"I don't like that idea one bit," Clay said. "Besides,
what about your job?" He looked at Nate. "Sara can continue staying at my place. Nobody'll know."

"Somebody could follow us there when we leave,"
Meg said. "You saw the crowd out front."

"I think can we can divert their attention," Nate said.
"Where are you parked?"

"In back."

"Good. Once Mr. Dill bails her out, I'll send her out
the back door."

Meg nodded. "That's a good idea. What should we tell
Purvis and Maybelline?"

Nate didn't hesitate. "Tell them I'm taking her to an
undisclosed location. I don't want nobody to know where
she is, and I mean *nobody*."

Once Clay and Meg had managed to get Sara safely
inside his house, he checked all the windows to see that

they were locked, then brought in a firearm. "Now, I don't want to make either of you nervous," he said. "This is just an added precaution. Sara, I know you're somewhat familiar with guns, but why don't you hold it first, just to get the feel of it. I'll take you out back so you can practice."

"I probably won't need to practice," Sara said. "I've handled a lot of different shotguns and rifles."

He started to hand it to her, then hesitated. "First rule, of course, you never, *ever* point a gun at anybody." He didn't notice the amused look on Meg's face.

Sara nodded and took the gun. "Very nice," she said. "It's old, but I can tell you've taken good care of it."

"Belonged to my grandfather," Clay said, noting it was almost as long as Sara was tall. "Is it too heavy for you?"

"No, I can manage."

"What kind of gun is it?" Meg asked.

Clay started to answer but Sara beat him to it. "It's a twelve gauge double-barrel, side by side. I don't think they make many of them anymore. Nowadays, the barrels are one on top of the other. I prefer a twenty gauge myself 'cause it doesn't have such a kick to it, but this is good." She checked the barrel. "Needs cleaning," she said. "I'll be glad to do it for you. You got any shells?"

Clay just looked at her. "Guess you do know a little about guns."

"Killed my first coon when I was five years old."

"You need to keep this gun with you at all times," Clay told her. As he and Meg prepared to leave, he turned to Sara. "Help yourself to what's in the fridge, but don't eat anything that has green stuff on it."

"I promise," Sara told him.

"Are you sure you'll be okay?" Meg asked. "I hate leaving you like this, especially with your father just dying and all."

"I'm okay," Sara said. "I'm looking forward to spending some time alone. And please don't worry about me. I'm not as helpless as my sister makes me sound."

"We're not worried," Meg said, trying to sound confident. "Something'll break soon."

"You think she'll be okay?" Meg asked Clay, once they were on their way.

"I don't see why not. Nobody knows where she is, and she's got a shotgun to protect herself." He reached over and squeezed her hand. "Stop worrying, babe. You're going to get wrinkles, and then I'll have to trade you in on a younger model."

Meg looked at him. "Oh yeah? And what's she going to do with an old fart like you?"

Travis hadn't been able to think straight since he'd learned of Dirk Hodges's death. His stomach was still queasy from the booze he'd drunk the night before, and his head hurt like a son of a bitch. He wiped his forehead and found his brow damp. Everything seemed to be coming unraveled, slipping out of his control. He thought of Ray Edgewater standing at that urinal, dribbling, unable to do anything about his problem.

Finally, he picked up the phone and dialed. The voice on the other end was raspy, almost a whisper, as though the person behind it was used to talking in hushed tones.

"Travis Lytle here," he said. "I've got a problem."

"So write to Dear Abby."

"This is serious, man. The last batch of dye you sold me is making people sick. I need to know what's in it."

"What am I, a goddamn chemist?"

"Don't you know what you sold me?"

"All I know is I get you some hellacious deals, man. You're getting these goods for a fraction of what your regular supplier would charge you."

Travis undid his top button so he could breathe. "Can I get some kind of breakdown on the chemicals used in this particular batch?"

"Look, brother, one of the reasons you save so much money is because my suppliers don't have a bunch of government agencies running eight million tests and jacking up the price each time. You're on your own, pal.''

The next thing Travis heard was a dial tone.

He hung up the phone and muttered a curse. That young inspector was due any moment. Time to plan his itinerary.

First, Travis would convince him to put off the inspection until the following day. Then he'd take him to Mama Leona's Bar, a private, out-of-the-way place up in the mountains. You could watch two of Mama's girls get it on for less than what it'd take to fill your car with gas. For an additional fee, you could get someone to sit on your lap while the show was going on. Half the fun of doing it was watching the guy next to you go at it.

Yes sir, he knew how to show a guy a good time, but it was even more meaningful if captured on film, and Mama was only too happy to oblige. He still had the pictures Mama'd taken of the other OSHA inspector, Jim Frank, who'd paid extra to rent a bed with two women in it. Jim had wept when Travis had shown him those photos the next day. After that, there wasn't nothing the man wouldn't do for him.

There was a knock at his door, and Travis opened it. Standing on the other side was a young blond man, nothing more than a kid, really. ''Yes?''

The young man smiled and offered his hand. ''I'm Dan Thompson from OSHA. I'm sorry to be so late, but I got lost. I'm brand-new with OSHA, and I don't know the territory yet.'' He blushed. ''Excuse me for rambling. Are you Mr. Travis Lytle?''

Travis shook his hand, happily noting the guy didn't look old enough to be out of high school. And there was a wedding ring. It was almost too good to be true.

Forty-six

CLAY DROPPED Meg off at the newspaper building and drove to a job site on the outskirts of town. Melinda handed Meg several messages when she stepped in the door, one of them from Dr. Grimes. She called him back right away.

"Do you know what an orchid looks like?" she asked the doctor, once he'd answered.

"I should hope so," he said. "My mother raised them."

"Do you think the flowers in that quilt resembled orchids?"

"Hard to tell, since it's in such bad shape. Why do you ask?"

Meg told him what she knew. "The woman who designed the pattern—she called it Passion Flower, if my memory serves me—she signed it by placing her initials inside a wedding band that was carried by a dove."

"A dove! Damn," he muttered. "I've been checking state birds throughout Appalachia. Yes, it could pass for a dove. I thought that thing in its beak was a worm, but Janet said that was disgusting. I told her, hey, I can't always be witty and refined." He paused. "So, tell me, who is she?"

"This is just a wild guess," Meg said, "but I think she's Reverend Temple Beechum's long lost wife. She supposedly ran off some twenty years ago."

Grimes whistled into the phone. "Are we talking about the same Temple Beechum who's in my refrigerator this very minute?"

"Yep, that's him. Anyway, I've heard Mrs. Beechum was a small woman. That certainly matches with Jane Doe."

"Do you think you can get your hands on the original pattern for this quilt?" Grimes asked.

"You plan on putting me on the payroll for all the work I'm doing?"

"No, but I'll let you in on a little secret. Al Murphy did not commit suicide."

"No shit?"

"No shit. It was cold-blooded murder. I'm just now getting some of the tests back, so keep it to yourself. See how nice it is to have friends at the morgue? Now, how about that pattern?"

"I'll try," she said. "It might take me a few days. I still have my other job, you know."

He chuckled. "Atta girl."

Meg hung up the phone and jumped when she found Bob Etheridge standing right behind her. "Jesus, why don't you sneak up on me?"

"I just walked up, for Pete's sake. You seem a little edgy these days, kiddo. Is it that time of the month?"

"That was a very sexist remark, boss."

"Hey, I'm a very sexist guy. What d'ya got?"

She tried to hide her notes. "Some of it's top secret," she said.

"Top secret?" He looked amused.

"But I can tell you this: Dr. Grimes won't be releasing Reverend Beechum's body anytime soon. And I think that skeleton might belong to the late reverend's wife. She supposedly left him. I'll bet anything he's the one who killed her."

"You'll never get him to admit it. What about his daughter? The one who just got out of jail?"

"She's staying at an undisclosed location."

"I'll bet that makes for some romantic evenings with Clay."

"I never said she was at his house."

"You didn't have to. Hey, the pictures of that skull are going to look great. How long before you have something for me? Like in the way of an article?"

"Depends on how long you're going to hang around my desk."

"You realize once the paper comes out, our phones aren't going to stop ringing. It's going to be a real pain in the ass for you and Melinda."

She glared at him.

He leaned closer. "By the way, have you heard the news? Al Murphy didn't kill himself. He was murdered. What d'you think of that?"

Meg didn't hesitate. "I think I just figured out what number to list for people to call regarding the skull."

The morning and afternoon passed in a blur. Although Meg thought of Sara a couple of times, she didn't call. Clay had told the younger woman not to answer the phone for any reason, unless she heard one of them on the answering machine telling her to pick up. Sara had their phone numbers, and Nate Overton had promised to have a patrol car cruise the vicinity. Meg wondered if the sheriff was trying to protect Sara, or if he still considered her a suspect in Temple Beechum's murder.

Fred Garrison breezed in wearing his Calvin Klein jeans, a spiffy plaid shirt, and a yellow nylon jacket. He stopped by Meg's desk. "Guess who's agreed to go out with me?"

Meg couldn't help but show how pleased she was. "I knew Sue would wake up sooner or later. When's the big event?"

"Saturday night. I'll have my new car by then."

"New car?"

"It's a Mazda Miata. Bought it right off the showroom floor. I found it in Elizabethton. Built-in phone and everything. I'm hoping to pick it up tonight or first thing in the morning.''

"Well, you're moving right along," Meg said.

"Thanks to you." He glanced around. "I've, uh, decided to let her call me Frank. You've got to admit it sounds sexier than Fred."

"You go, Frank!" Meg gave him the thumbs-up sign. As he walked away, she noticed there was a bounce in his step.

It was after five by the time Clay picked up Meg. They were both starving, since neither one had taken time for lunch that day. "We can call out for pizza," he suggested as he drove home. "I know a place that delivers."

"Right now, I could eat a hog's head sandwich, I'm so hungry," she said.

He smiled at her. "I'd better tell them to put a rush on that pizza."

They pulled into his driveway fifteen minutes later. Clay unlocked the front door, and they went inside. The smell of food cooking made their mouths water. They walked into the living room, and they saw it was spotless, the furniture polished, windows cleaned. They moved to the dining room, then stared at the table, which had already been set.

"Wash up for dinner," Sara said. "I'm pulling everything out of the oven now."

Meg and Clay did as they were told and reappeared to find Sara had set out a meat loaf, a big bowl of mashed potatoes, green beans with chunks of bacon and onion, and glazed carrots. She'd made a salad of tomato, cucumber, and onion slices in Italian dressing. Tall glasses of iced tea sat at each plate. Sara returned with a basket of hot corn muffins, and blushed when she saw them staring.

"I hope it was okay to go ahead and cook," she said timidly.

Clay shook his head and gave her a stern look. "No,

Sara, we will not tolerate a clean house or supper on the table when we walk in the door."

"Dang, Clay," Meg said. "I think we're going to have to adopt her."

They sat down and passed the food. Meg tried to remember the last time she'd had homemade muffins with real butter.

"I cleaned the whole house," Sara said, beaming. Her smile looked out of place in among the bruises. "It's the least I could do after what you two have done for me. Tomorrow I'm going to do the ironing and mending."

"When do you think you'll get around to painting the house?" Clay asked.

"Don't you think you're overdoing things a bit?" Meg said.

"I like staying busy. Otherwise, I spend too much time thinking about things."

"Have you been thinking about your father, honey?" Meg asked gently.

Sara raised pain-stricken eyes. "Pa kept me a prisoner for years," she said. "He beat me worse than any animal." She clenched her fists on the table. "I hated him, and I'm glad somebody killed him, because otherwise I probably would have eventually."

Clay looked at Meg. "I believe the answer to your question is no."

"Sara, try not to be too bitter," Meg said. "You'll only end up hurting yourself. One day you're going to have to forgive your father. Whether he deserves it or not."

"Why?" she asked.

Meg shrugged. "For your own peace of mind, if nothing else."

"I'll *never* forgive him," Sara said. "And you know what? If I ever get out of this place alive, I'm never coming back!"

Meg saw the tears that threatened to spill, and placed a hand on Sara's. The young woman might pretend indifference to her father's death, but she was hurting nevertheless. And she was scared. They could hide her and give her a weapon to protect herself, but in the end the killer might still get to her.

Meg wondered if Sara had been safer in jail.

Forty-seven

NATE OVERTON entered his house through the back door as usual. The room was dim, save for a light burning over the stove. He shrugged off his coat and draped it over the back of a chair, then removed his cap and holster and placed them on top of the refrigerator. He noticed the dust and wished he could afford to hire someone to come in and thoroughly clean the place.

Charmaine had always been a fastidious housekeeper, at least until the last ten or twelve years, when her illness had progressed. As a new bride, she'd had dark moods, but nothing had prepared him for what was to come. He should have realized how sick she was.

He saw the note on the kitchen table, telling him she'd prepared his snack. No matter how bad she felt, Charmaine always had something waiting for him in the refrigerator. She didn't seem to notice how fat he was getting. Didn't seem to care. She called him her big teddy bear.

Her bottle of pills was next to the sink. An elephant would have trouble swallowing them, he thought, and wondered how his petite wife managed to get them down. Practice, he guessed.

He walked down the hall and peeked into the spare bedroom, where Charmaine had taken to sleeping because of her restlessness. He hated sleeping alone, but he knew she worried about disturbing him during the night. This new sleeping pill seemed to have done the trick; she was snoring gently as though in a deep sleep. He only hoped her doctor had finally found a drug her body could tolerate.

Nate leaned over and kissed his wife on the cheek before returning to the kitchen.

He found his snack in the refrigerator: a ham and cheese sandwich, a bag of chips, and two cookies. Charmaine had even poured him a glass of milk, although she'd forgotten to add the chocolate. He wouldn't think of drinking a glass of milk without chocolate; in fact, he and Charmaine had fought over that very thing shortly after they'd married. Funny, the things you fought over as newlyweds, he thought, as he carried the plate and glass to the kitchen table. But from that day on, Charmaine had never forgotten to buy his chocolate at the grocery store. Which is why he was a little hurt that she'd managed to forget now, he admitted to himself, as he pulled the tin of powered chocolate from the pantry and stirred a heaping tablespoonful into the glass. Probably the medicine had made her forget.

Nate wolfed down the sandwich, chips, and a couple of Twinkies, and drank his chocolate milk. He suddenly felt stuffed. No surprise, since he'd eaten a full dinner of liver and onions at the E&M only a couple of hours ago. He belched loudly. One of these days his heart was going to explode, and he would regret making such a pig of himself.

Exhaustion finally hit him, and even though he knew it was bad to go to bed on a full stomach, Nate found himself eager to get out of his uniform and climb beneath the covers. He went down the hall toward the bedroom he'd once shared with his wife, and switched on the lamp. Charmaine had turned the covers down for him and turned the electric blanket on low to take the chill out of the sheets. A fresh uniform hung on the back of the door; on the dresser were his socks, underwear, and a large bath towel for the morning. It meant a lot to him that Charmaine always saw to his needs, no matter how crummy she felt.

He was sinking fast, he realized, as he emptied his pants pocket of keys and loose change, and the small prescription bottle of nitroglycerin pills. He set the bottle on his night table, within reach, and shrugged out of his clothes. He hoped he wasn't catching the flu. He climbed beneath the covers, then realized he'd forgotten to turn off the lamp. Oh, well, he'd do it later. After he rested.

Henry Holcombe had fallen asleep in his recliner when the phone rang. He snatched it up before it rang a second time, hoping it didn't wake Alma. Mindy Calloway spoke from the other end. Henry blinked several times, trying to make sense of what she said. "Slow down, Mindy," he said. "I can't understand a word you're saying." She did as he'd asked, and he listened.

"You're broke down?" he said. "Is it your battery? Well, what in tarnation are you doing out at this hour anyway? Yeah, well, you're right about that. Younguns got to have milk for their cereal. Okay, tell me exactly where you are."

Five minutes later, Henry pulled out of the driveway. He'd scribbled a brief note to Alma in case she woke up while he was gone, but that wasn't likely, since Alma slept like the dead. He came upon Mindy some ten minutes later. Lucky for her she'd had car trouble within walking distance of Fletcher's Service Station. The station was closed, but there was a pay phone out front. Other than that, there wasn't a soul anywhere around.

He pulled his truck right up to Mindy's, so close their hoods nearly touched. As he climbed out he reached behind his seat for his jumper cables. He closed the door and barely had time to turn around before a sobbing Mindy threw herself in his arms.

"Oh, Mr. Holcombe, I'm so glad you're here," she said. "I was scared to death."

"It's okay, sugar," he said, patting her on the back, at

the same time noting how good she smelled. Even her hair. She must've bathed for bed when she realized she was out of milk. He tried to disentangle himself, but she clung tighter. "Mindy, for goodness' sake," he said, laughing out of embarrassment, "there's no cause for alarm."

She looked at him, and her eyes seemed to sparkle like jewels in the glow of his headlights. "What about that poor minister they just found murdered? There's a killer on the loose and—" She shuddered and pressed against him.

Henry stood there for a full minute wondering how to handle the situation. The girl acted like she was near to hysterical, but that just wasn't the Mindy he'd come to know. "Mindy, we need to get your car started so you can get home to your babies."

"Please don't let me go, Mr. Holcombe." She raised her face to his. "I've been afraid for so long. Don't let me go." Without warning, she pulled his head down and kissed him on the mouth.

Henry felt his body respond immediately, and he didn't know which shocked him more—that, or the fact Mindy was kissing him. He felt her pry his lips open with her tongue as she moved against him intimately. His shock suddenly turned to desire, and he was amazed to find himself harder than he'd been in years. The girl wanted him. Him! And here she was, young enough to be his daughter.

The thought had the same effect on him as if someone had dropped ice cubes down the front of his britches. He pulled away so quickly he almost sent Mindy toppling.

"Good grief, girl, what are you doing?" She reached for him again, and he stepped away. "Stop this nonsense, do you hear me!"

"I love you, Mr. Holcombe!" she cried, clasping her hands together as though that was the only way she could keep herself from touching him.

"*Love* me?" His expression was stunned. "An old man

like me? What's wrong with you, gal?'' He laughed, once again, to hide his discomfort.

Tears streamed down her cheeks. ''Don't make fun of me, dammit. I'm serious.''

He dropped his smile. ''So am I, Mindy. Now, I'm a married man with daughters close to your age. You need to meet a nice young man who can help you raise your children.''

The tears continued to fall. ''I'll never meet anyone as nice as you.''

He put his hands on her shoulders. ''Maybe you should stop looking in honky-tonks. You're not going to meet a good man there. Why don't you visit our church this Sunday? We've got a singles' group.'' She shrugged. ''Promise me you'll think about it, okay?'' Finally, she nodded. ''Good girl. Now let's get your car started.''

Mindy rolled her eyes. ''Silly man. There's nothing wrong with my car.''

Travis leaned back in his chair and regarded the younger man across the table from him, who was presently passed out cold. ''Shit, this was too easy.''

Mama Leona, a large, thick waisted woman with frizzy gray hair, shook her head sadly. ''How many drinks did he have before he arrived?''

''He split a six-pack with me on the ride up. And two scotches once we got here.''

''Some folks ain't got a tolerance for booze,'' Mama said. ''I gots a brother who can get sloppy drunk on half a beer. Must be some kinda enzyme thing. Anyway, I got the pictures you wanted,'' she said, handing him several Polaroids. ''I asked Desiree if he poked her, but she said he was too drunk to do anything more'n drool on her blouse.''

Travis studied the pictures. ''Doesn't matter. It *looks* like they're doing it. And ol' Dan here has been married less than a year. He won't want his pretty young wife to see these. *Or* his boss.'' He reached into his pocket and pulled out a wad of bills. It was more than he could afford, under the circumstances, but Mama Leona had never let him down, and she might just save his job.

"By the way, d'you hear my house was robbed?" he asked as he handed her the money.

Mama tucked the bills in her bra. "Yes, and I'm sure sorry for you."

Travis knew she was lying. She would have robbed him blind herself if she thought she could get away with it. "Have you heard anything?"

"Weren't nobody from around here did it. I'm usually the first to know."

Travis nodded and turned his attention back to the drunken OSHA inspector. "Can you get one of the boys to help me get Junior here to the car?"

"Do you know which motel he's stayin' at?" Mama said.

"No. I'll just take him to my place." Travis chuckled. "I want my face to be the first thing he sees when he opens his eyes in the morning. And the second thing he sees"—he paused and kissed one of the photos—"will be these."

Alma was sitting in his recliner when Henry returned. Her eyes were rimmed with red as though she'd been crying, but he knew she would never admit it. Alma was proud to a fault. She was also without her wig tonight, and Henry longed to tell her how pretty she looked in her own hair.

"I'm sorry if I woke you," he said, shrugging off his coat and hanging it on a rack near the door. "A friend called with car trouble."

Alma stood and faced him squarely. "That friend wouldn't happen to be Mindy Calloway, would it? I believe that's her shade of lipstick you're wearing."

Henry reached for his handkerchief and wiped all around his mouth. "I've never lied to you, Alma, and I'm not about to start. It *was* Mindy who called."

"I'll bet there wasn't a blasted thing wrong with her car."

He frowned and wondered if all women were privy to that trick. "No. Her car was fine."

"And?"

He looked at his wife. When had they drifted apart? He remembered a time when he couldn't get enough of her. Why, he even remembered when, on a slow day, they'd lock the door at the store, turn the sign around, and sneak into the supply room for a little lovin'. Maybe it was time he cut back on his hours, spent more time at home.

He saw that she was waiting for an answer. "Mindy won't be calling me again, Alma."

She didn't answer. Henry stepped closer and studied her for a long moment before threading his fingers through her hair. He pulled her head close and gazed into her eyes. They were bright with tears. Alma blinked, and the tears fell, and Henry wondered how many crying women he was going to have to deal with before the night was over.

He leaned forward and kissed her on the lips. "Alma, I'm sorry if I've made you feel unloved or unwanted. It was never my intention. And if you'll kindly step into our bedroom, I'll prove it."

She blushed.

He smiled.

They started down the hall holding hands. "And tomorrow," he began, "I'm going to burn all those ugly wigs."

Forty-eight

NATE JUMPED and opened his eyes, although he wasn't sure what woke him. His head felt thick, as though someone had stuffed it with cotton. That's what Charmaine said it was like waking up in the morning when she took all those pills that were supposed to make her feel better. Something moved beneath the covers. It brushed across his chest, grazed one thigh. What the hell?

Nate lifted the covers and froze at the sight. Timber rattlers! Jesus Christ, at least half a dozen of them. Squirming and wriggling, their tongues slipping in and out, in and out. Panic gripped him, and he opened his mouth to scream.

"Don't do it, Sheriff," a voice across the room said.

He looked up. He recognized the person sitting in his grandmother's old rocker. Why?

"Please . . . ," he whispered. Sweat beaded across his forehead and upper lip as he tried to make sense of what was happening.

"You should have given Sara that powder like you were told, Sheriff. You could have saved us both a lot of trouble."

Nate was only vaguely aware of the voice. The snake on his chest was coiled tightly, ready to strike, its devil tongue whipping in and out. In and out. Adrenaline gushed through his bloodstream, fed by the frantic beating of his heart. A sudden heaviness inside his rib cage, pressure building inside his chest. The pain. He knew that pain. His pills—they'd been moved to the far side of the night table. Out of reach.

"You want me to take away the snakes, Sheriff?" the voice asked.

"Y-yes." Barely a whisper.

"Tell me where Sara is. Tell me, and I'll take the snakes away."

The snakes moved all around him. Always moving. Cold scaly bodies brushing his arms and legs. Nate wet himself. In utter humiliation, he closed his eyes. "Clay Skinner's place."

"You sure about that?"

"Yes. Please—" That whining sound. Was it coming from him? The pain in his chest. Bad. Now in his shoulder. "My wife," he whispered.

"I know about your wife. This ought to send her right over the edge."

His jaw and teeth hurt. He was suddenly sick to his stomach, the urge to vomit so strong it made his jaw muscles ache. More pressure. Building, building. Like a boulder on his chest. He moaned. And no longer cared if he died.

"Know what I once heard, Sheriff?" the voice said. "I heard when you have a heart attack it feels like there's a tractor sitting on your chest. But you probably already know that 'cause this isn't your first one, is it?" The person reached for a crudely built box with a screen cover and carried it to the bed. Nate's eyes were wide and unblinking. He was past hearing. "But it's going to be your last."

The person threw back the covers and reached for the snakes, one by one, and dropped them into the box. Thick rubber gloves made clumsy work of the job, but they were a necessity for those who didn't like snakes, even snakes who'd been milked of all their venom and couldn't hurt you.

Poor, stupid Nate Overton.

Moving down the hall quietly, the person entered the kitchen and took Nate's empty milk glass from the sink. The glass was washed twice to make sure no trace of his wife's sleeping medicine was found. It was then dried and placed at the very back of the cabinet.

That was that.

Forty-nine

DAN THOMPSON stared at the photos, then dropped them on the kitchen table and buried his face in his hands. "Did I have sex with that woman?" he asked. "I don't remember much of what happened last night."

Travis was enjoying himself. It was the first time he could remember feeling halfway joyful since the burglary. "Certainly looks that way to me, old buddy. By the way, she said you were great. You young studs can go all night." Dan looked up. For a minute Travis thought he might actually cry.

"I should've told you, I don't really drink."

"Well, you made up for it last night, bub."

Dan suddenly looked scared. "We've got to get rid of those pictures. I'm a married man!" He reached for them, but Travis was faster.

"The pictures are my property, Danny boy. And I'm going to do everything in my power to make sure your sweet wife doesn't see them. In other words, I'm going to protect you."

Dan swallowed, and his Adam's apple bobbed. "Thank you," he managed. He gazed at Travis. "You want something in return, don't you? Does it have anything to do with my inspection of the mill?"

Travis patted him on the back. "You learn fast, boy."

*   *   *

Mayor Bradley arrived at his office earlier than usual. He liked to have breakfast with his family and spend time with them before he left for work, but this morning was different. Two deputies were shown in by Bradley's secretary.

"I was hoping Nate could be here," the mayor said. "We're not looking at a simple parking ticket. This is big."

One of the deputies gave an embarrassed cough. "I'm sorry, Mayor Bradley, but I don't think the sheriff was feeling well this morning. He hadn't come in by the time you called. Dispatch was trying to reach him when we left."

"Probably the flu bug," the other deputy said.

Bradley's secretary appeared in the doorway. She looked confused. "There are some men here from OSHA. And this other agency just called," she said, handing him a message slip. "Said they'd meet you at the mill."

The mayor smiled. "Very good. Tell the OSHA people I'll be right out." He picked up the phone and dialed. "Bob Etheridge, please." He waited. "Bob, Ed Bradley here. No, I'm not still mad about that editorial, but after today, folks'll know I mean what I say. I've got something big going, and I want you in on it."

Purvis arrived at work early, since the mayor had specifically requested it. He turned to Maybelline, who was sitting in the passenger's seat. "Don't forget to call me at noon in case something happens and I have to leave."

"They're *not* going to fire you, Purvis. Why, you managed to get more on that Travis fellow than that newspaperman, that Murphy fellow."

"That's not saying much, Maybelline," he said wryly. "Al Murphy was a drunk."

"Don't you see what you're doing for these people? You'll be a hero before it's over. They might even make you vice president or something. I'll bet you won't be in such a hurry to leave town then."

He stared out the window wordlessly. He missed Sara, and he dreaded the confrontation ahead. As for leaving town, he couldn't get out fast enough.

Maybelline gave an exasperated sigh. "Try not to look so miserable. I know you've been in a lot of pain lately, but so have I. They won't even let me bury my pa, for heaven's sake, and I'm constantly worried about Sara's safety."

"You knew," he said softly.

"What?" She leaned closer. "Did you say something, Purvis?"

He looked at Maybelline. He had too much on his mind at the moment to get into a fight with her, but he would have his say before it was over. "I have to go," he said. He opened the door, but she grasped him tight around the wrist before he could get out.

"Are you angry with me, Purvis, honey?" she asked sweetly.

He gritted his teeth. "Let me go, Maybelline." He pulled free and climbed from the truck, then made his way toward the mill entrance.

Charmaine Overton picked up the phone in the kitchen and dialed 911. She felt calm and composed, although still groggy from the sleeping pill she'd taken the night before. Nate always joked how she lost it over little things, but she was cool as a cucumber during emergencies. Later, she'd fall apart, and her doctor would have to up her tranquilizer dosage, but for now she would do what was necessary.

"This is Mrs. Nate Overton," she said to the voice on the other end. "I'm afraid my husband's heart gave out on him sometime during the night. Yes, I'm certain he's dead. It seems he went peacefully in his sleep. Could you please send an ambulance?" She hung up and waited.

Etheridge called Fred and Meg into his office and closed the door. He frowned at the other man's bold orange-and-black-striped shirt and leather vest. "Fred, you look like a goddamn Halloween decoration." He regarded Meg. "Did *you* pick that out?"

She shook her head emphatically. "Fred did some shopping on his own."

"Then he has no one but himself to blame."

"I think it looks good," Fred said. "You know, Bob, you're starting to look like an old man. If you're going to be a big newspaper tycoon, you need to take a second look at your clothes."

Etheridge gave him a droll look. "I'll take that into consideration." He became serious, almost reverent. "We've got a couple of situations on our hands. I just got a call from the sheriff's office. I'm afraid Nate Overton is dead."

Meg felt the blood drain from her cheeks. She simply stood there for a moment, wondering if she'd heard right. She tried to concentrate on what her boss was saying.

"They think it was a heart attack, but there's been a lot going on lately. I want to make sure this is on the up-and-up." Etheridge paused. "Meg, are you all right? I've never been able to talk this long without you interrupting me or saying something foul."

She nodded. "I'm fine." But she wasn't. The pressure behind her eyes was killing her. One would've thought she'd liked the sheriff.

Etheridge studied her for a moment. Finally, he looked convinced that she was okay. "Fred, I want you to see if you can get the deputies to talk while they're still emotional. Find out what they thought of Nate, what it was like working for him. They trust you; they shouldn't have any trouble opening up." He turned to Meg. "If you can get something out of Nate's wife, *anything,* it'll help. Just go easy on her."

He checked his wristwatch. "I have to run over to the textile mill. I have a feeling something is about to come down. If not, then the mayor's setting me up."

Meg suddenly perked. "My brother-in-law works there."

"Well, let's just hope it has nothing to do with him."

"If I know Travis, he's right in the middle of it."

All three stood. "Before I forget," Etheridge said, "Grimes got a hit on Jane Doe's picture. You were right, Meg. The caller says she's the spitting image of Reverend Beechum's wife, who disappeared twenty years ago. Grimes said they have to do a lot more checking before they confirm it."

Fred smiled at Meg. "That was fast."

"Yes, well, they had to sift through a number of crazies first," Etheridge said. "A couple of people saw a strong resemblance to Elvis. Be our luck, CBS'll come interview them, and they'll make the rest of us look bad." Etheridge suddenly grinned at Meg. "By the way, Grimes said to thank you for listing his number at the morgue with your article. Said he had about fifty calls yesterday."

"I should have been nicer to Sheriff Overton," Meg blurted. "It's like I have this curse following me around." She thought of Randy Bekins. And what about Temple Beechum? She hadn't particularly liked him either. "It's almost as if everyone I dislike ends up dead."

Both men just looked at her. "Trust me, Meg," Etheridge said. "You don't have that much power." He reached for his jacket and was gone.

"You'll be okay," Fred said, grabbing a box of tissue and taking Meg by the hand. He led her toward the door. "You get to ride in my new car. I'd put the top down if it weren't so cold." He led her out of the building and toward his Miata. "And when we finish at the sheriff's house, I'll take you out for ice cream."

"How come your license tag says Frank?" Meg asked.

He looked embarrassed. "Sue got me that. I've never had a personalized tag before, but she has a friend who works for the Department of Motor Vehicles, and they just happened to have one. Pure luck, that's what it was."

He unlocked his car and opened the door on the passenger's side.

Meg grinned. "You know, Fred. If this thing gets serious, you're going to have to tell her your real name."

Fifty

THE PARAMEDICS had already loaded Nate Overton's body into the ambulance when Meg and Fred arrived. Five deputies were on the scene, all appearing stunned and disbelieving. Meg saw the black female deputy named Jenkins standing inside the garage and hurried up to her. "Are you okay?"

The woman had tears in her eyes. "He acted like I was a big pain in the butt to him," she said, "but I really think it was all for show. I think he kinda liked me."

Meg was determined not to cry. "What happened, Officer Jenkins?"

"I guess it was his heart. He had a condition, you know." She made a sound that was somewhere between a hiccup and a laugh. "He always said I was going to be the cause of his next one. I'm proud to say"—more tears—"I'm proud to say I was nowhere near him when it happened."

Suddenly, there was a noise from inside the house. One of the deputies pushed through the screen door. "Quick, somebody grab a rake or a hoe," he yelled.

Without hesitating, Jenkins swung around and opened a door to a small storage closet. Within seconds, she'd found a hoe and passed it to the other lawman. There was the sound of running feet. Meg followed Fred and the officers inside a large country kitchen. A woman in a bathrobe sat at the kitchen table, crying quietly into a ball of tissue while another woman and an older gentleman holding a Bible tried to comfort her.

Finally, one of the deputies came down the hall holding the tail end of a four-foot-long timber rattler. Its head was almost completely severed, and only a thin piece of skin connected it to the trunk.

Meg did a double take at the sight.

"Oh, my God!" the woman at the table cried. "Where did you find *that*?"

The deputy paused. "In the bedroom, ma'am. One of our men almost stepped on it."

"How'n the world did it get in here?" she demanded, clearly agitated. "We've never *ever* had snakes in this house. Nate was terrified of them. Why, he would have *died* at the sight of one." She burst into tears. The man with the Bible tried to comfort her. "I want to know how that snake got in this house!" she screamed. "And don't try to tell me it was an accident."

Meg was shaken by the incident. She looked at Fred. "I'd also like to know how a poisonous timber rattler got inside." She looked thoughtful. "Did you know the sheriff had a heart problem?"

Fred nodded. "I reckon most of the town knew."

Meg tried to suppress a shudder as she watched the deputy carry the snake out the back door. Snakes seemed to be popping up everywhere these days. Coincidence? She didn't think so. "Do you mind if I use your car phone?" Meg asked. "I need to make a call."

"No problem," Fred said. "Help yourself."

Meg walked toward his car. Inside, she grabbed the phone and dialed Clay's home number. The answering machine clicked on. "Come on, Sara, be standing nearby," she said as she waited for Clay to give his spiel. There was a beep. "Sara, it's Meg. If you're standing there, would you please pick up? Can you hear me?"

Nothing. She tried twice more. Where the hell was Sara?

*   *   *

Travis sensed something wasn't right the minute he walked into Bidwell Textiles with Dan Thompson at his side. Everybody seemed to be staring at him. He nodded at several supervisors, but they looked away. They'd probably heard about Hodges and were blaming him. That's the trouble with being in charge, he thought. Anything bad happened, and it was always your fault.

"Let's go to my office," he told Dan. "We'll grab a cup of coffee and discuss the inspection."

They made their way through the plant. Travis opened the door to his office—and came to an abrupt standstill at the sight. J.T. Bidwell sat at his desk, and a sheriff's deputy stood on either side of the door. Several well-dressed men were going through his files. Jim Frank, the OSHA inspector he'd dealt with in the past, stood next to the mayor. The mayor? Even the guy from the newspaper was present. And that snake handler, Purvis Dill, for Pete's sake! What the hell was he doing there? Why were any of them there, for that matter?

"What's going on?" he asked, his stomach knotting with anxiety.

"Come in, Travis," J.T. motioned him in. "I have some bad news, I'm afraid. Mr. Hodges died last night. There was severe and irreparable damage to his nasal cavity, his larynx, and his lungs. These gentlemen have been running tests on our dyes. They tell me the anthracene levels were twenty times higher than what's acceptable."

"I already know about Hodges," Travis said, "but what's this got to do with me?"

"Your friend here, Jim Frank, tells us you've been buying supplies dirt cheap from the black market and turning in invoices for the regular price. I can only assume you're skimming. You've obviously made a lot of money while risking my employees' health, and I aim to see you pay for that. You also endangered lives by locking the doors on the workers. Have you forgotten what happened at that chicken processing place?"

"I was trying to stop people from sneaking out for a smoke," Travis said.

J.T. went on as though he hadn't heard. "And then there's the matter of bribing OSHA officials. You're going to prison for a very long time, Travis."

Travis was so stunned he was only vaguely aware of the handcuffs going around his wrists. "You can't prove anything," he said. "Ask Dan Thompson about me. He'll tell you I'm on the up-and-up."

Dan looked at him. "You're shit, man."

"You bastard!" Travis looked around the room. "I've got pictures of this man drunk on his ass, screwing somebody."

"You don't get it, do you, Travis?" J.T. said.

Travis shook his head as if to clear it, but nothing was clear at the moment. "Get what?"

J.T. stood and rounded the desk. "It was all a setup. Jim Frank blew the whistle some time ago and put everything in motion. All of it was perfectly orchestrated." He stepped closer, so close that Travis could feel his breath on his cheek when he next spoke. "It's my way of getting back at you for my son's death."

"I don't know what the hell you're talking about," Travis snapped.

Jim Frank stepped forward. "You've got a big mouth when you drink, Travis, you know that? You told me all about it. That's when I decided to come forward."

"You'll never be able to pin that one on me, old man," Travis told J.T.

J.T. Bidwell smiled. "And you'll never be vice president, my friend."

Etheridge snapped several pictures before they took Travis away.

The men shook hands. J.T. thanked Purvis and handed him an envelope. "This is a little something for going to all that trouble. You obviously care a great deal about your coworkers. I want you to go by Personnel next week and update your application. You'd make a good supervisor, son.''

The mayor regarded Etheridge. "Did you get everything?"

He held up his tape recorder. "Every last word. I'd like to get a few pictures."

"Yes, definitely. I'd like for you to get photos of me standing next to Mr. Bidwell with the OSHA people behind us." Etheridge snapped a dozen pictures. After a few minutes, the office thinned out.

"Have you had breakfast?" Mayor Bradley asked. Etheridge shook his head. "Great, why don't you join me? That way we can talk about my plans for better working conditions."

Fifty-one

SARA FINISHED drying the tile around the tub in the guest bathroom and saw that it was clean as new. She removed the earphones of the portable cassette player tucked in the pocket of her skirt, as the last notes of a Pointer Sisters song faded. Her pa would roll over in his refrigeration unit at the ME's office if he knew she was listening to something other than gospel music.

What a terrible thing to think, she told herself. But the man had it coming, after what he'd put her through. She had missed out on so much in her life, just because her pa felt people had to sacrifice all their pleasures to be a good Christian. Sara'd decided a long time ago she didn't want to worship a God that viewed illness and poverty as the road to everlasting life.

She wondered what it would be like to live with Purvis in a house such as Clay's, wondered if she and Purvis even had a future together, for that matter. She'd seen the horrified look on his face as she'd been led away in handcuffs the day before. Could he possibly suspect she was capable of murdering her own father?

Sara took one last look at the bathroom, satisfied that everything was as it should be, then went toward the kitchen for a soda, her reward for scouring all three bathrooms. At home they never drank anything but coffee, tea, or water. Once she got her own place, she was going to have all the colas and root beer she wanted. She would buy a television set, a radio, and as many books as she could afford. Her coffee table would be stacked high with magazines, and she'd have the newspaper delivered right to her door.

She opened the refrigerator and selected a ginger ale. As she was about to flip the top open on the can, the doorbell rang. The drink slipped from her fingers and landed on the floor with a thud that seemed especially loud in the tense silence. Sara glanced around for the shotgun and remembered she'd left it in the hall, just outside the bathroom she'd been cleaning.

Dang, what was wrong with her?

The bell pealed out again. Sara picked up a can, set it on a counter and tried not to panic. Clay had told her salesmen sometimes came by, but most of them didn't care to drive out so far, especially when the houses were spaced such a distance apart. That's probably all it was, a salesman. After all, nobody knew where she was.

The bell rang again, and Sara decided she'd better go for the gun just in case. She wished now that she hadn't opened the windows, but the tile cleaner had been so strong, and she hoped to air the house while she'd cleaned. She moved to the doorway. The curtains billowed away from the window. Anybody standing outside would be able to see in.

Dropping to her knees, Sara crawled, fast as she could, across the living room. Her knees ached by the time she reached the hall and found the gun. She could feel her heart beating frantically as she sat there for what seemed a very long time. Finally, she thought she heard the sound of an engine. Whoever it was had obviously decided nobody was home. She waited a few minutes more. Nothing, only the sound of her own breathing.

Deciding she was safe, Sara stood and crossed the living room to the kitchen. She leaned the shotgun against the counter and reached for her drink with trembling hands. She took a sip and listened. Something didn't feel right. It was an eerie thought, one that made her shiver.

Like having a piece of ice dropped down the back of your dress.

She wasn't alone.

She reached for the shotgun. She'd barely had time to cock it before something flew through one of the glass panes over the back door, shattering glass all over Clay's beautiful wooden floors. Fear rose up in the back of her throat, and Sara aimed the gun as a hand slipped through the broken window and unlocked the door.

Her hand on the trigger, she held her breath. The knob turned, and the door was pushed open. The person stepped inside and did a double take at the gun.

Sara sighed a breath of relief and lowered the gun. "Oh, it's you. You just about scared me to death."

Meg started to reach for the phone in Fred's car, but it rang before she could pick it up. She hesitated only a second before answering. "Oh, Purvis, hi. How'd you know where to reach me?"

"I called your office," he said. "I'd like for you to try and pass a message to Maybelline if you could. Tell her not to pick me up at work till the end of the day."

Meg was curious as hell about what was going on at the textile mill, but she was caught up in her own dramas at the moment. "I certainly don't mind telling her, Purvis. Is Maybelline coming by my office?"

"No. I just figured you could call Sara and have her pass it on when Maybelline drops her clothes off."

"That's highly unlikely. Nobody knows where Sara is."

Silence at first. "Oh. Well, then, I'm sorry I bothered you," Purvis said. "I must've misunderstood. Thanks, anyway."

"Wait! Don't hang up! Just hold on." She saw Fred talking to one of the deputies and waved him over.

"I need to borrow your car," she told him the minute he was in hearing distance.

"My *car*?" he said, his expression suggesting he'd rather cut off a body part first. "But I just got it."

"I wouldn't ask if it weren't an emergency," she told him.

He hesitated. "You won't smoke in it?"

"I wouldn't think of it."

"And no eating in it either. Oh, and I don't want you to drive on any dirt roads if you can help it, and I'm going to be very angry if you hit a mud hole."

Meg felt her eyes glaze over. "I could become a nun with less trouble, Fred. Now, are you going to give me your damn keys, or do you want me to tell the whole damn town your girlfriend doesn't know your name?"

"That was mean." He offered her the keys.

"I'm talking life and death here, pal," she said, starting the engine.

"Then let me come with you."

"No, that'll just lessen my odds." She winked. "Just kidding." Reaching for the stick, she put the gears into drive and shot off like a rocket. In the rearview mirror, she could see Fred standing in the road with his hand over his heart. Meg yanked up the phone. "Purvis, you still there?"

"Yes. I distinctly remember Maybelline telling me she visited Sara last night at Clay's house. That's when she agreed to bring Sara's things to her today."

None of what he said made sense. "That's simply not true, Purvis," Meg replied. "I was with Sara all evening. I even shared the same bedroom with her."

He was quiet. "Maybe she lied to me because I was upset with her for keeping my truck so late. But she definitely knew where Sara was hiding out. If you and Clay didn't tell her, who did?"

"The only other person who knew was Nate Overton, and he's dead."

"The sheriff is dead?" Purvis said, in disbelief. "Was it his heart?"

"Cause of death hasn't been established yet; they only

discovered the body a couple of hours ago. I think every-one pretty much figured it was his heart until they found a timber rattler in the bedroom with him.''

"Oh, my God," Purvis whispered. "He had a terrible fear of snakes."

"Who knew that?"

"I don't think the general public was aware, but it was obvious to us at the church. I think that's one of the reasons he agreed to take payoffs. Just so he didn't have to come around."

"Does Maybelline handle snakes?"

"Not if she can help it. Why? You don't think May-belline—"

"I don't know what to think. Look, I can't talk—"

"If she hurts Sara, I'll kill her her," he blurted.

"Why would Maybelline hurt her sister?"

"Jealousy," he said. "She's got to know how I feel about Sara. And she knows I'm leaving. She's probably figured out that we're going together."

"Why would that upset her?" When he didn't answer, she became insistent. "If you know something, Purvis, you have to tell me."

"Maybelline and I have been lovers for some time now," he said. "I broke it off a month ago. She didn't take it well. I recently found out—" He sighed heavily. "I recently found out she's my half sister."

"Have you told her?"

"She knows. She's known all along. Unfortunately, she didn't bother to share that information with me."

"Where are you, Purvis?" she asked.

"A pay phone in the break room. At the mill," he reminded her.

"Give me the number." Using one hand to steer, Meg reached into her purse for a notebook and pencil. She jotted down the number. The car swerved to one side of the road. "Sit tight till I call you back."

"Where are you going?"

"To check out a hunch," she said, being deliberately

vague. She started to hang up, but Purvis stopped her.

"Listen, I'm not saying Maybelline is behind this, but there's a loaded .38 Smith and Wesson under the seat of my truck," he said. "She knows about it. Thought I should warn you in case—well, you know."

"Thanks, Purvis. You just made my day."

Fifty-two

MEG KNEW Clay's house was empty the minute she entered it, but she checked all the rooms just in case. From the looks of it, Sara had been scrubbing tile all morning. The broken glass at the kitchen door sent her into a state of panic. She should never have left Sara alone. If anything happened, it would be all her fault.

She started from the room, then spied the shotgun leaning against the wall. God, she hated guns. Then she thought of Sara again, helpless and scared in the hands of a killer. She muttered a string of curses and grabbed it.

Meg peeled out of the driveway a moment later, cigarette in one hand, cell phone in the other. Surely, Fred could forgive her for smoking in his car under these circumstances. She dialed the number Purvis had given her, and he picked up on the first ring.

"Sara's missing," she said, shifting gears and building speed.

"Do you think Maybelline has her?"

"I don't know." Meg paused for a stop sign, then went on. "I think the person who has Sara is the same one who left that snake in the sheriff's bedroom. But you said Maybelline wasn't a snake handler, so that pretty much rules her out."

"Unless the snakes didn't present a danger," Purvis said. "Temple Beechum didn't die from snake bites either. He had bites on him, but venom wasn't injected."

Meg, in the process of lighting another cigarette, was forced to slam on her brake when a car pulled in front of her. She let several colorful expletives fly, then realized she had a minister on the other end. "Oh, my, did you hear that? We must be on a party line. You said venom wasn't injected in Temple Beechum's bites. How does something like that happen?"

"It's called a dry bite. It still hurts like the dickens, though."

"Why would a snake not inject venom into its victim?" Meg asked, trying to make sense of what he was saying.

"One reason could be because the snake made a recent kill and hadn't had time to build up its venom supply. Another reason, of course, is that the snake was milked beforehand. And that wouldn't surprise me in this case." He told her about the coffee can he'd found in Temple Beechum's desk.

"Does Maybelline know how to milk a snake?"

"We used to do it as kids. She was always careful to use special gloves, though. Like the ones doctor's offices and hospitals use nowadays to prevent needle pricks. Laboratories pay good money for the antivenin.

"Snakes are easy to come by, especially in the spring or fall. You find them sunbathing on rocks. Temple would pay us twenty-five cents for every snake we brought him."

Meg shuddered at the thought of a parent telling children to hunt poisonous snakes. "That's not much money," she said.

"Which is why we supplemented our income by selling the milk."

"Do you think Maybelline is capable of murder?" Meg said.

He was thoughtful for a moment. "I don't know. I don't think I even know who she is anymore."

"Okay, listen. I'm five minutes from where you are. I want you to be waiting in the parking lot when I get there. We don't have any time to waste. Oh, and one more thing.

While you're waiting for me, try to think of where May-belline might take Sara. If she didn't want her to be found"—she paused—"for a while," she added on a softer note. Meg hung up and pushed the accelerator to the floor.

The cell phone rang, and Meg snatched it up, hoping it would be somebody telling her Sara had been found safe. Clay almost barked at her from the other end. "Where the hell are you? Fred said you took off in his car, mumbling something about life and death."

"Sara's gone, Clay. I'm picking up Purvis, and we're going to look for her."

"Not unless you have a dozen deputies with you," he said tersely. "Do you want to end up like Nate? Go straight to the sheriff's office and tell them what you have."

"That's just it, Clay. I don't have anything yet. Once Purvis and I sift through what we know, then I'll call. Trust me on this."

"Goddammit, Meg! I just picked out your engagement ring. There's no point in sizing it if you're going to wind up dead!"

"Clay, honey, you call him and tell him to make the ring a size seven, and the karat a size two."

"Does this mean you'll marry me?"

"You promise to get off my back about finding Sara?"

"You swear to call the sheriff's office before you do anything?"

"Yes, Clay, I promise. I have to go now."

Meg hung up. She was getting engaged! And she wasn't even petrified. In fact, she was thrilled. She promised God she would be a good wife to Clay. And she vowed to stop searching for a paid killer to take Roy out.

Meg turned into the parking lot of the textile mill. Several patrol cars sat at the entrance. Who said nothing ever happened in Blalock? She suddenly spotted Purvis hurrying in her direction. "What's going on?" she said as the phone began to ring again. Clay, no doubt.

"Our operations manager was just arrested."

Meg felt her jaw drop. "Travis Lytle?"

"Yes. You know him?"

"He's my brother-in-law."

"I'm sorry."

"I'm ecstatic. My sister will be, too, when she hears."

"Aren't you going to answer the phone?"

"I'm sure it's a wrong number. I've been getting them all morning." Probably Clay calling back with more stipulations on their engagement agreement. She wasn't about to make a lot of promises she couldn't keep. "Why was Travis arrested?"

Purvis gave her a brief rundown of what had occurred as she sped out of the entrance and left the mill behind. She headed for the mountains.

"Sounds serious," she said. "Think he'll get the death penalty?"

Purvis looked shocked at first. Finally, he smiled. "We can always hope. Where are we going?"

Meg glanced at him. "I was hoping *you* could tell me."

"I'm not sure about anything right now," he said. "If Maybelline really did take Sara, there's a chance they could be at their grandparents' old place. But it's falling apart, and there are neighbors nearby. If Maybelline was planning to . . . you know, *hurt* Sara, she'd want to go some place completely private."

A lightbulb flashed in Meg's brain. "The shack!" Purvis shot her a questioning look. "You know, the place you played in as kids. You used to hold mock church services. You were the minister."

Purvis colored. "Sara told you about that?"

"Yes. She said she sometimes goes there to be alone even now."

This time the color seemed to drain from his face completely. "Oh, God."

"What is it?"

"I hope she hasn't . . . seen anything."

Meg was getting angry. "Purvis, what the hell are you talking about!"

He looked away, shamefaced. "That's where Maybelline and I have been secretly meeting for months now. Until recently," he added.

Meg rolled her eyes. "Purvis, get a grip! God is not going to hunt you down like a dog just because you've had sex a few times without benefit of marriage." A blush climbed up his neck and spread to his cheeks. "Now, stop wallowing in all that guilt and give me directions to this bordello of yours."

"Just keep going straight for a while. Has anybody ever told you that you drive too fast?" he said, both hands pressed against the dashboard.

"Nobody's ever ridden with me and lived," she said. "Okay, back to business. Can you think of any reason Maybelline would want to see her father dead?"

"Reverend Beechum found out about us." Purvis glanced out the window and was quiet for a minute. "The last conversation I had with him, he planned to banish me and Maybelline from the church for what we'd done. The best I can figure is my father had an affair with the reverend's wife."

Meg thought of the skeleton. Death by strangulation. "Temple Beechum knew about the affair?"

Purvis nodded. "I assume he told Maybelline."

"Okay, Purvis, I asked you earlier if you thought Maybelline was capable of murder. Do you?"

He shifted in his seat. "I have my suspicions."

"Let's hear them."

"You know that reporter from your paper who was found with a gunshot wound to his head?"

Meg looked at him. "You mean Al Murphy? What about him?"

"Well, this Murphy caught wind of some of the problems we were having at the mill. Like I said, Travis violated a lot of safety regulations, which is why we've had several injuries, and now a death. He was buying inferior products from the black market and skimming profits. On top of that, he was forcing women to perform sexual acts in order to keep their job.''

"Sounds like someone killed the wrong man," she said. She realized now where all Travis's money had come from.

"I even heard J.T. Bidwell accuse him of killing his son last year, but I don't know anything about that. Anyway, I'd been keeping a journal for months. It listed all the offenses I was aware of. I even interviewed some of the women. I'd planned to wait until I had enough to hang Travis.

"Anyway, this reporter from the *Gazette* starts snooping around on the pretense of doing stories on various employees in celebration of Bidwell Textiles' eighty years of service, and he's following Travis around like a puppy. Finally, it hits me what the guy's up to. Travis would have figured it out, too, if he hadn't been so anxious to get his picture in the paper. I knew this reporter didn't really give a hoot about the mill workers; he was just trying to make a name for himself. And I wouldn't have cared except he was drunk so much of the time, I was afraid he was going to blow it.''

"What does any of this have to do with Maybelline?''

"I made the mistake of telling her. She was furious because she hoped I'd be this great hero once I went to J.T. Bidwell with what I had. She figured I'd get a big promotion and make good money. You have to remember, those girls were never allowed to have anything nice. All they knew was strife, hard work, and prayer. Could be Maybelline was hoping we'd get married and she'd have a better life.

"Next thing I knew, this reporter's dead. I naturally assumed Travis found out what he was really up to and put a bullet in his head. I never thought Mr. Murphy committed suicide; he was too full of himself. Then I discover one of my father's guns is missing, the same make and caliber Mr. Murphy was clutching when they found him.

Not only that, Maybelline borrowed my truck the night of his death.''

''Why didn't you tell somebody?''

Purvis sighed and shook his head. ''I didn't have proof, and I didn't want to believe it. Besides, I was afraid of what she might do. Not to me, but her sister. As much as I hate to admit it, I've sometimes felt Maybelline was very close to the edge.''

''You're probably right,'' Meg told him. It was beginning to sound as if the woman was capable of anything. Even murder.

Fifty-three

MAYBELLINE PARKED Purvis's truck behind a strand of tall pines to keep it from being visible from the road. "C'mon, Sara," she said, climbing out of the pickup and grabbing her purse as well as the gun. "Don't dawdle."

They crossed the road and started through the woods at a fast pace. "Do you know who's after me?" Sara asked her older sister.

Maybelline stopped dead in her tracks. She looked torn. Finally, she sighed. "It's Purvis," she said. "I didn't want to have to tell you, knowin' how you feel 'bout him, but that's who it is. I'm sorry."

Sara was so stunned she couldn't speak for a moment. "I don't believe you."

"It's true, little sister. And that's not all. Purvis has been usin' me for sex. Now he wants you, because you're pure. I was pure, too, before he convinced me to lay with him."

Sara's eyes glistened with tears. "Why didn't you tell me?"

"You wouldn'ta believed me. You're doubtin' me even now. Why do you think I tried so hard to get you away from these here mountains? I knew what he was up to. I would rather see you dead than watch Purvis do to you the same he's done to me."

Sara felt as though her heart were breaking. "I never even suspected."

"You've always been such a big baby, Sara. Pa was too protective." She sighed. "I regret the day I promised Mama to look after you."

"What?"

"It's a long story, and we don't have time."

Sara grabbed her sleeve. "Tell me."

"She'd been unhappy with Pa for a long time. Just like you, he never let her out of her sight. She was just waitin' for the opportunity to leave. I didn't know it at the time, but she planned to run away with another man. That man just happened to be my real father. Mama and I were close. She promised to come back for us, but she asked me to look out for you until then."

"Pa wasn't your real father?" Sara asked, shocked.

"No. Amos Dill was my daddy. And Pa discovered her climbin' out the window in our bedroom before she could get away."

"Did he beat her?"

"No, he didn't beat her," Maybelline said. "Start walkin', Sara. We don't have all day."

Sara tried to hurry, but she was more interested in what her sister had to say. "So if Mama didn't run off, where'd she go?"

"Pa killed her."

"What!" Sara almost shrieked the word.

Maybelline immediately covered the girl's mouth. "Shhh! Not so loud. We don't want anyone to hear us." She removed her hand. "It's true, Sara. I saw it with my own two eyes. Pa caught her trying to leave one night, and he grabbed her around the neck and didn't let go until—until there was no life left in her."

Sara shook her head. "No! You're making that up, just like you're making up all this stuff about Purvis."

Maybelline slapped her hard in the face. Sara cried out. "You stupid little bitch. You don't know nothin' 'bout nothin'. I'm amazed sometimes just how dumb you are."

She made a sound of disgust. "But I guess I'd be stupid, too, if my pa kept me locked up like his pet."

A steady stream of tears ran down Sara's cheek. "Why are you so mad at me, Maybelline?"

"Because all I've ever tried to do is help you, and how do you repay me? You steal the man I love. And then when I try to tell you the truth about things, you refuse to listen. Well, you can deny it all you want, but I saw Pa choke our mama to death."

Maybelline reached into her purse and pulled out a newspaper clipping. "Just look. This buildin' crew recently dug up these bones. Some lady doctor was able to rebuild the face, and this is what they ended up with. That's our mama, Sara. That's her, plain as day."

Sara looked at the picture, which resembled the head of a mannequin. "How come you didn't report it?"

"Pa's dead, stupid! What're they going to do to him *now*?"

"No, I mean before. When it happened."

"'Cause Pa said he'd do the same thing to me if I told," Maybelline said. "So I kept quiet all these years, and for what?" She glared at Sara. "He was goin' to tell Purvis the truth about me bein' his half sister. What do you think Purvis would have done about that?"

"But you just said Purvis is bad."

"Bad for you because of the way you are. You wouldn't understand some of the things that go on between men and women, but I do." She suddenly looked smug. "Besides, I'm carrying Purvis's child, and I aim to see him marry me. Anybody tries to stop it"—she held the gun up—"pow."

Startled, Sara jumped. She suddenly found herself trembling all over. "Did you kill Pa?"

"I'm tired of answering your questions. I can see the shack up ahead. Let's go."

"You did, didn't you?"

"Why should you care one way or the other, after how he treated you? You should be thankin' me."

Sara wondered how Maybelline had managed to keep this side of her personality hidden for so long. Or maybe something had happened to bring it to the surface. Her love for Purvis? Perhaps the fear of losing him had pushed her over the edge. "You're going to kill me, too, aren't you?" Sara asked. "That's why you brought me way out here."

Maybelline jabbed her with the gun. "Move."

Sara started walking. Walking and thinking out loud. "You were the one shooting at me in that woods that day." She skidded to a stop and clamped her hand over her mouth as though to keep herself from crying out. "You blew up Meg's camper," she said, tears streaming down her cheeks. "Oh, my God, that poor ranger."

"The park ranger was in the wrong place at the wrong time," Maybelline said. "As for Meg, I figured she'd catch on sooner or later, so I decided to get rid of her before she started askin' too many questions. How was I to know the two of you weren't even in that camper at the time?"

Maybelline shoved the gun hard against Sara's spine, causing her to cry out. "This is the last time I'm goin' to tell you. Keep walkin', or I'll kill you right here and let the animals have you."

Sara stumbled across the thick forest floor. She was not afraid to die. Life as she'd known it had always been hard. Heaven was supposed to be a place of beauty and peace. Streets of gold, she thought. "In my Father's house, there are many mansions," she said, her voice little more than a whisper.

"That's right, Sara," Maybelline said, almost gently. "I'm really doin' you a favor, if you stop and think about it. You don't belong in this world."

They'd arrived at the cabin. "Open the door," Maybelline said.

Sara did as she was told. She realized suddenly that she *was* scared of dying. Not because she feared meeting her maker, but because she hadn't even had a chance to live.

She thought of her dreams of having a radio and TV, of being able to bring books and magazines and soft drinks into her home. That probably wouldn't mean much to most folks, but to her it sounded very close to heaven. Maybelline nudged her forward, and she stumbled into the cabin. Sara noted the disarray, the blankets stuffed into one corner.

"Just think, Sara," Maybelline said, following her in and closing the door behind her. "You'll go to sleep and wake up in heaven. There won't even be any pain. One clean shot through the temple is all. Trust me, I know what I'm doin'."

Sara knew there was no escaping, and even though she feared her sister and the bullet that was meant to kill her, she wanted Maybelline to hear her out. "I have something to say," she told her sister. "I don't understand all this business with you and Purvis, but I forgive you both and harbor no bad feelings."

"That's mighty big of you, little sister."

"As for who you may have killed, you can be forgiven for that as well. But Nate Overton is going to find out you're behind all this and—"

"Nate's dead. His heart just gave out on him. I think he may have suffered a bad scare."

Sara suspected her sister had something to do with whatever had stopped the sheriff's heart from beating. She felt like crying, but she knew this wasn't the time to show weakness. "I would like to thank you for showing me so much love and kindness, Maybelline," she said, trying to appeal to whatever goodness was left in her sister.

"You are so stupid, Sara. You have no idea how much I've hated and resented you. All my life," she said. "Mama was already pregnant with me by Amos Dill when she and Pa married. Amos wanted to marry her, but he already had a wife and son. Pa promised to love me and raise me like his own. What a joke. He acted like he didn't even know I was alive. But when Mama gave birth to you, well, you would have thought you'd come from royalty.

"Pa worshiped you. If I even so much as came up to get a look at my new baby sister, he'd backhand me, and I'd get a beatin' for the littlest thing. Pa wasn't very nice to Mama either. Started knockin' her around, accusin' her of all sorts of things. I reckon that's when she and Amos Dill got to talkin' again, and he agreed to leave his wife. I would hear them plannin' it when they ran into one another at the store or when Mama slipped out to meet him those times Pa was invited to preach at somebody's church. I kept waitin' for Mama to tell me her secret, but she never did. Then, I realized she wasn't takin' me with her." Maybelline's eyes became red. I was so angry that—" She suddenly looked away.

Sara had a feeling she knew what Maybelline had been about to say. "You were so angry that you told Pa what they were planning," Sara finished for her.

Maybelline nodded. "Ma had already handed Amos her suitcase and had one leg out the window when Pa walked into the room. I saw her put something in his coffee cup to make him sleep, but he poured it down the sink when she wasn't lookin'." She took a deep breath. "Pa started treatin' me better after that."

"What about Amos? It didn't seem to hurt their friendship."

"They just went on like before. I reckon Amos wasn't going to tell what he saw, and Pa wasn't going to tell what he knew." Maybelline sighed. "I've wasted too much time talking, Sara. I want you to go get one of those blankets out of the corner."

She did as she was told.

"Spread it out on the floor, and lie down. This'll all be over before you know it. And then—"

Maybelline didn't get to finish her statement. The door was kicked open, and Purvis walked in with a shotgun aimed at her. "Drop it, Maybelline," he ordered.

Fifty-four

"PURVIS!" MAYBELLINE looked thoroughly shaken. "What are you doing here? How did you know where to find us?"

"We just followed the trail of bodies. They eventually led us here."

Sara spoke up. "She killed Pa and the sheriff. And she killed that park ranger 'cause she was trying to get us and—"

Maybelline jammed the gun's muzzle against her cheek. "Shut up!" Purvis started toward them, but Maybelline pulled the hammer back. "Don't try to be a hero," she told him.

"Drop the gun, Maybelline," he repeated.

"No. She'll just come between us."

"Haven't you done enough killing, for God's sake?"

Suddenly, there were tears in her eyes. "You think I'm doin' this because I like it? I'm doin' it for you, Purvis. For us. So we can be together." She frowned at Meg, who was standing behind him. "What's *she* doing here?"

"I've come for Sara," Meg said. "To get her out of your way." She stepped closer. "I've decided to take her back to Atlanta with me so she can go to school like she's always wanted. You and Purvis can finally be together."

Maybelline seemed to ponder it. Finally, she shook her head. Tears slid down her cheeks. "As long as she's alive, Purvis will love her. As long as her heart's beating, it'll belong to him, and his heart will be hers.'' She faced him. ''You can't love a dead woman,'' she said, almost victoriously. ''You can't love rotted flesh.'' She moved the muzzle to Sara's temple.

''Is that how you killed Al Murphy?'' he said, hoping to stall her.

Maybelline looked at him. ''I did that for you. Everythin' that's happened I've done for you. And our baby,'' she added softly.

Purvis couldn't hide his surprise or his repugnance. Did she honestly think he wanted to bring an incest child into the world? He raised the shotgun and took aim. ''Maybelline, if you shoot Sara, I'll kill you.'' He saw her smile. It was a smile that told him she didn't believe he'd kill the woman carrying his child. Maybe she was right. But he could disarm her. She took aim; he no longer had a choice.

Purvis fired a shot, aiming low so he didn't hit her heart. It sounded like an explosion in the small shack, the acrid smell of gunpowder followed.

Maybelline staggered slightly, then righted herself. At first she just looked at him, obviously stunned that he would do such a thing. Then, as if she was seeking proof, she touched her stomach and raised her hand to examine the blood.

Suddenly, she screamed.

Sara closed her eyes and prepared to die.

''You bastard!'' Maybelline cried. ''You killed our baby.''

Purvis was so shaken by her screams, he wasn't prepared for what came next. In one fluid move, she swung the gun around and began firing. It took a couple of seconds, but dumbly, he realized she was shooting at him. As if watching the action unfold from outside his body, he heard her screeching cry, saw her knees fold beneath her. He was vaguely aware he'd been hit. Suddenly he couldn't stand or hold his head up. A look of horror crossed Sara's face. Her mouth moved but no words came out. He felt a great searing pain in his chest. He hit the ground, tasted dirt. He strugged, gave up the fight.

Silence. Sara couldn't look at him. ''Is he dead?''

Meg didn't have a chance to answer before one final shot rang out. Instinctively she grabbed Sara and pulled her to the ground. There was a dull thud as Maybelline's body fell beside them. One clean shot through the temple.

Fifty-five

THREE DAYS later, Clay entered the guest room with a breakfast tray. He found Meg sitting up in bed staring at the wall. "Okay, you've been depressed long enough," he said, setting the tray in her lap. He leaned forward and kissed her lightly on the lips. "Do you realize you've gone seventy-two hours without a cigarette? That has to be a record for you."

She'd been too tired to walk to the garage for one. "Are you complaining?"

"Not at all. But you're going to have to start taking phone calls, Meg. People will think I've got you locked in the basement."

She took a sip of coffee. "Have I missed anything important?"

"Well, they found enough evidence to hold Travis over for trial. Beryl says hurry up and get better, 'cause the two of you are celebrating as soon as you're up and about."

"Any other earth-shattering news while I was in my self-induced coma?"

"Your mother wants you to go shopping with her, but I told her you'd have to get back to her on it. She and your father have decided to take a cruise. It's a second honeymoon thing."

"Yeah, right."

"I'm serious."

She just looked at him. "Has Sara called?"

"Yes. She's staying with a friend of mine. The two of you probably need to talk things out as soon as you're up to it."

"They wouldn't even let us in the same room when we arrived at the sheriff's office," she said. "You'd have thought we were the killers. They probably would've locked us up if you hadn't been there."

"They were just in a bad mood 'cause I'd spent the previous hour ranting and raving about you being in danger and nobody even knowing where the hell you were. If you hadn't called when you did, I think they would have gagged me and handcuffed me to a fire hydrant."

She was thoughful. "Did you give Etheridge that message about Al Murphy?"

"Yes. He sounded relieved to hear it. I think it's been weighing on him heavily."

Meg nodded and sipped her coffee in silence. She sensed his restlessness. "What?"

"Nothing. Just drink your coffee and relax. Oh, I brought you a powdered donut."

She picked up the donut and took a bite. White stuff flew everywhere, so she reached for the cloth napkin. Something fell out. Her engagement ring. Meg shook her head. "Clay, you're going to have to stop doing corny stuff like this if you want me to marry you."

"Does that mean I should take the new car back?"

"What new car?"

"The one I'm giving you as a wedding present. To replace your other set of wheels."

"You bought me a car?" she said, her voice ringing in disbelief.

"Just like Fred's, except it's red. Does the ring fit?"

"Yeah, yeah, yeah. You bought me a new Miata?"

He looked amused. "Yes, but you can't drive it till after the wedding."

"Then, we'll have to get married right away. *Despite*

what folks will say, since I'm supposed to be newly widowed and all.''

"But you've been traumatized.''

"Oh, hell, I've been traumatized plenty of times. Try walking in on your husband while he's wearing a garter belt. I always bounce right back from trauma. Besides, I want to get married before Sara leaves for Atlanta.'' She held her hand out and examined the ring with pleasure. "Damned if that's not the biggest diamond I've ever seen. I'm almost embarrassed to accept it. Now, when are we getting married?''

He pondered it. "I suppose we can move the date up a bit. How about June?''

"June! Jesus, Clay, that's more than six months away.''

"Are you worried about your biological clock?''

"No, I'm thinking my car could get dry rot just sitting there. How about we get married at Christmas? Think about it and get back to me, okay?'' She set the breakfast tray aside and scrambled out of bed. "I want to look at my car. I can practice driving it when we go down to apply for our marriage license.''

He laughed softly and reached for her. He caught her look of surprise before he pulled her down on the bed and kissed her deeply. They could go for the marriage license later. Right now, he had other things on his mind.

"Does this mean you're really, finally, going to marry me after all these years?''

Meg blinked back sudden tears. "Yes, Clay, I'll marry you. I should warn you, though—I haven't had much luck with men.''

He stroked her cheek tenderly. "I'd say your luck is about to change.''

Fall Victim to Pulse-Pounding Thrillers
by *The New York Times*
Bestselling Author

JOY FIELDING

SEE JANE RUN
71152-4/$6.50 US

Her world suddenly shrouded by amnesia, Jane Whittaker wanders dazedly through Boston, her clothes blood-soaked and her pocket stuffed with $10,000. Where did she get it? And can she trust the charming man claiming to be her husband to help her untangle this murderous mystery?

TELL ME NO SECRETS
72122-8/$5.99 US

Following the puzzling disappearance of a brutalized rape victim, prosecutor Jess Koster is lined up as the next target of an unknown stalker with murder on his mind.

DON'T CRY NOW
71153-2/$6.99 US

Happily married Bonnie Wheeler is living the ideal life—until her husband's ex-wife turns up horribly murdered. And it looks to Bonnie as if she—and her innocent, beautiful daughter—may be next on the killer's list.

Nationally Bestselling Author
of the Peter Decker and Rina Lazarus Novels

Faye Kellerman

"Faye Kellerman is a master of mystery."
Cleveland Plain Dealer

JUSTICE
72498-7/$6.99 US/$8.99 Can

L.A.P.D. Homicide Detective Peter Decker and his wife and confidante Rina Lazarus have a daughter of their own. So the savage murder of a popular high school girl on prom night strikes home . . . very hard.

SANCTUARY
72497-9/$6.99 US/$8.99 Can

A diamond dealer and his family have disappeared, but their sprawling L.A. estate is undisturbed and their valuables untouched. When a second dealer is found murdered, Detective Peter Decker and his wife Rina are catapulted into a heartstopping maze of murder and intrigue.

PRAYERS FOR THE DEAD
72624-6/$6.99 US/$8.99 Can
"First-rate. . . fascinating. . .
an unusually well-written detective story."
Los Angeles Times Book Review